THE WONDROUS WONDERS

CAMILLE JOURDY

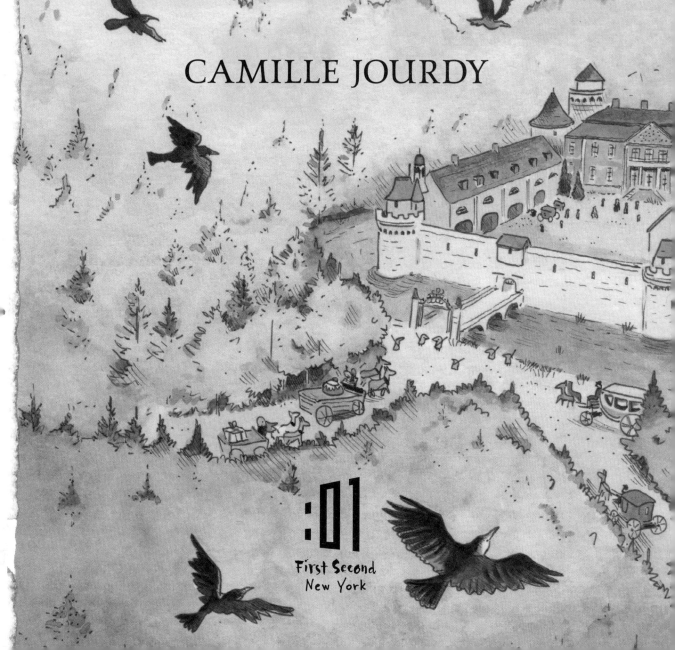

:01

First Second
New York

:01

First Second

Published by First Second
First Second is an imprint of Roaring Brook Press,
a division of Holtzbrinck Publishing Holdings Limited Partnership
120 Broadway, New York, NY 10271
firstsecondbooks.com
mackids.com

Library of Congress Control Number: 2022901856

Our books may be purchased in bulk for promotional, educational, or business use.
Please contact your local bookseller or the Macmillan Corporate and Premium Sales Department
at (800) 221-7945 ext. 5442 or by email at MacmillanSpecialMarkets@macmillan.com.

FIRST

EDITION

First American edition, 2022
Translated by Montana Kane
American edition edited by Mark Siegel and Hazel Newlevant
Editorial assistance from Robyn Chapman and Tess Banta
Cover design by Kirk Benshoff
Interior book design by Sunny Lee and Yan L. Moy
Lettering and word balloons by Alison Acton
Production editing by Kat Kopit

First published in France under the title *Les Vermeilles* © Actes Sud, Paris, 2019

Printed in China by RR Donnelley Asia Printing Solutions Ltd., Dongguan City, Guangdong Province

ISBN 978-1-250-79911-1
1 3 5 7 9 10 8 6 4 2

Don't miss your next favorite book from First Second!
For the latest updates go to firstsecondnewsletter.com and sign up for our enewsletter.

BY ART
WE LIVE

For my children

And for Quentin,
in memory of our walks
in the woods...

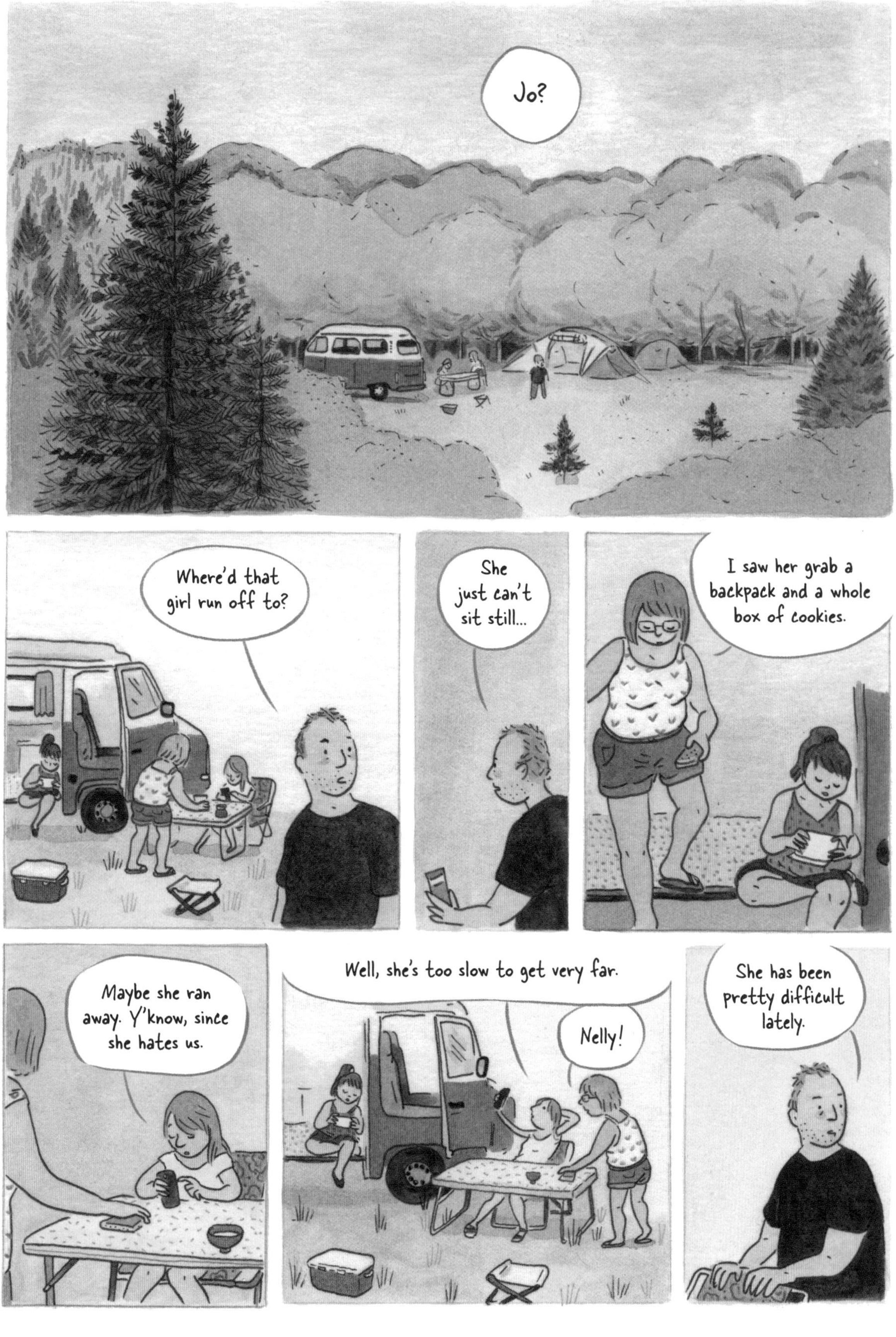
Jo?
Where'd that girl run off to?
She just can't sit still...
I saw her grab a backpack and a whole box of cookies.
Maybe she ran away. Y'know, since she hates us.
Well, she's too slow to get very far.
Nelly!
She has been pretty difficult lately.

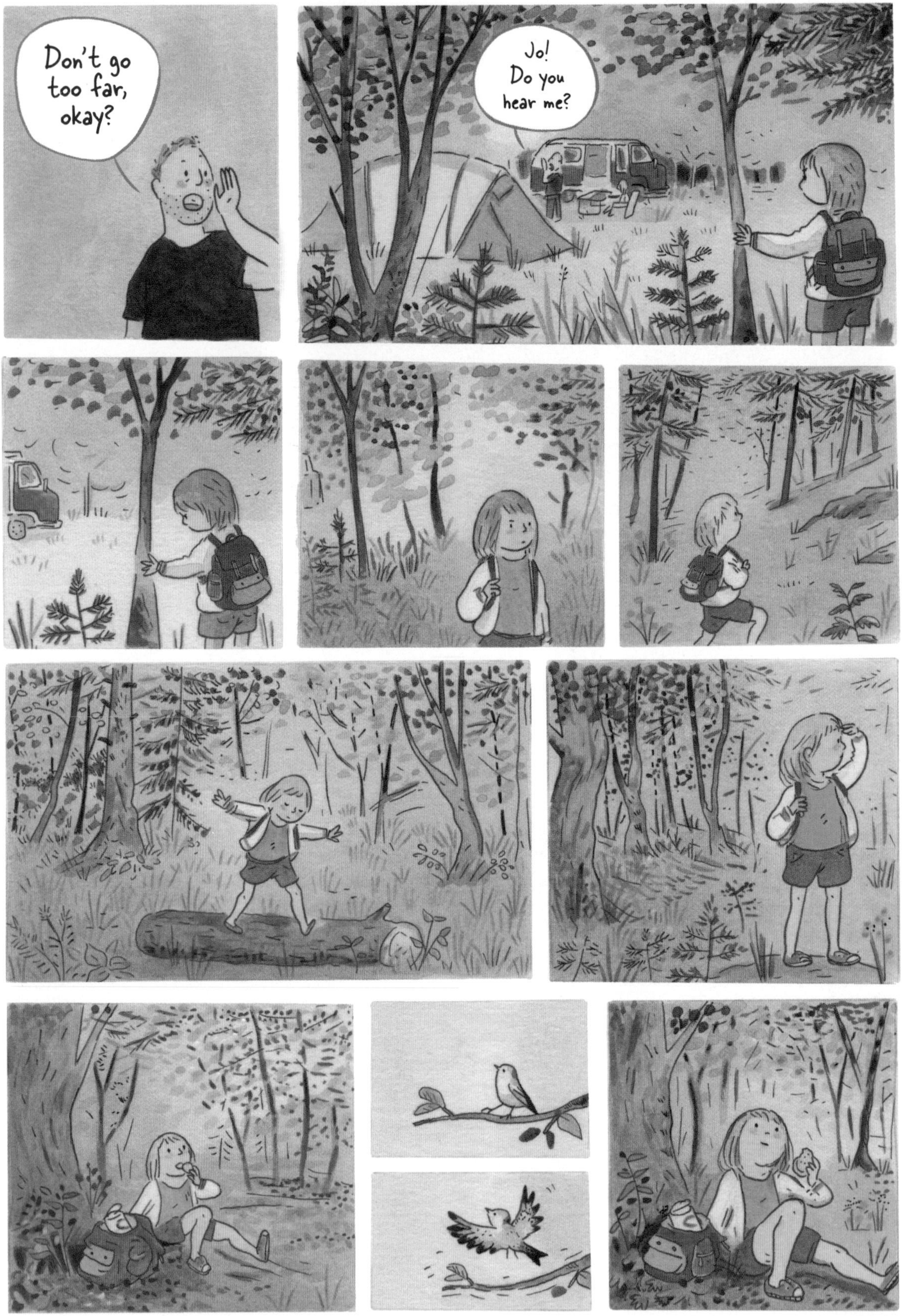
Don't go too far, okay?
Jo! Do you hear me?

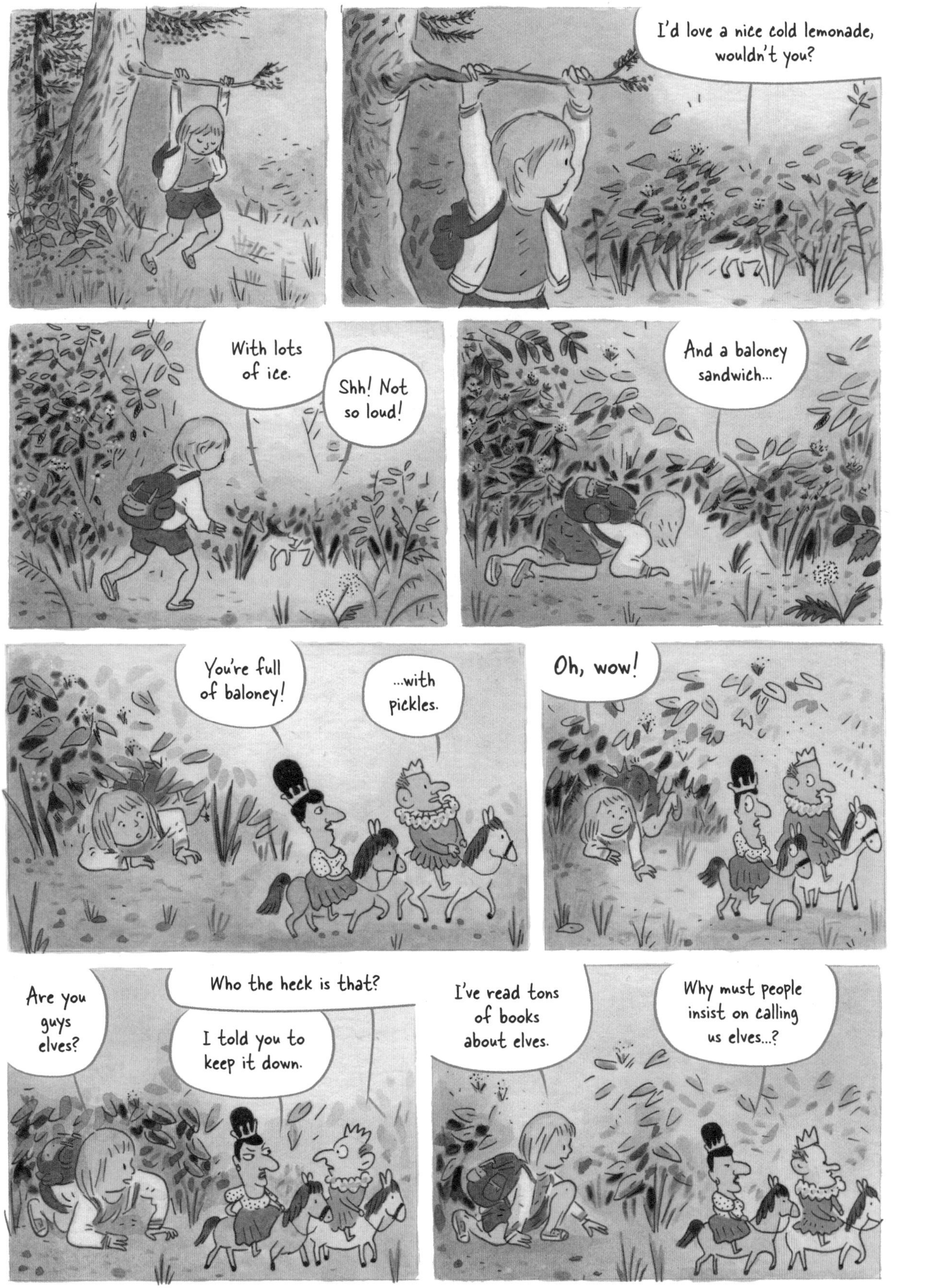
I'd love a nice cold lemonade, wouldn't you?
With lots of ice.
Shh! Not so loud!
And a baloney sandwich...
You're full of baloney!
...with pickles.
Oh, wow!
Are you guys elves?
Who the heck is that?
I told you to keep it down.
I've read tons of books about elves.
Why must people insist on calling us elves...?

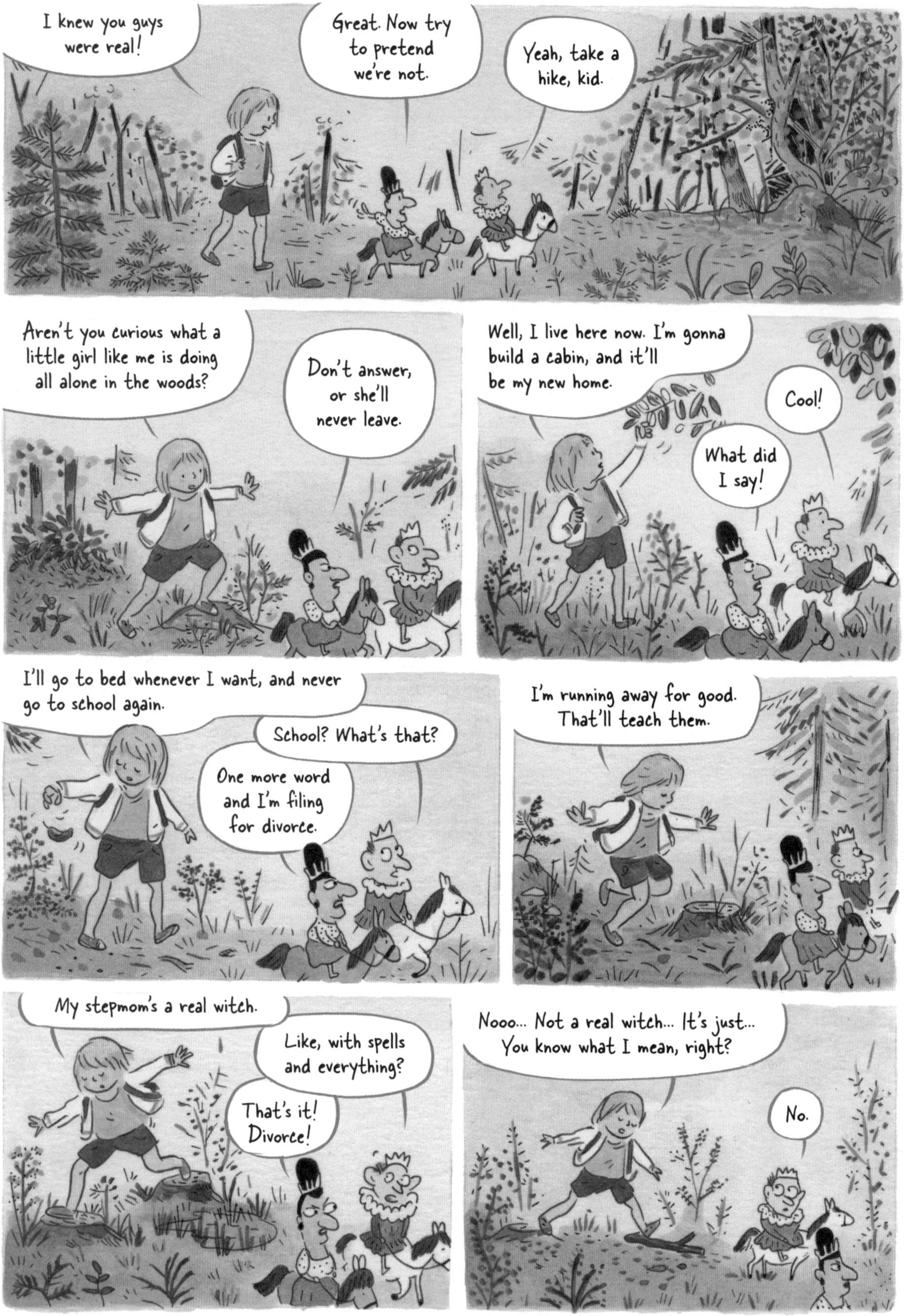
I knew you guys were real!
Great. Now try to pretend we're not.
Yeah, take a hike, kid.
Aren't you curious what a little girl like me is doing all alone in the woods?
Don't answer, or she'll never leave.
Well, I live here now. I'm gonna build a cabin, and it'll be my new home.
Cool!
What did I say!
I'll go to bed whenever I want, and never go to school again.
School? What's that?
One more word and I'm filing for divorce.
I'm running away for good. That'll teach them.
My stepmom's a real witch.
Like, with spells and everything?
That's it! Divorce!
Nooo... Not a real witch... It's just... You know what I mean, right?
No.

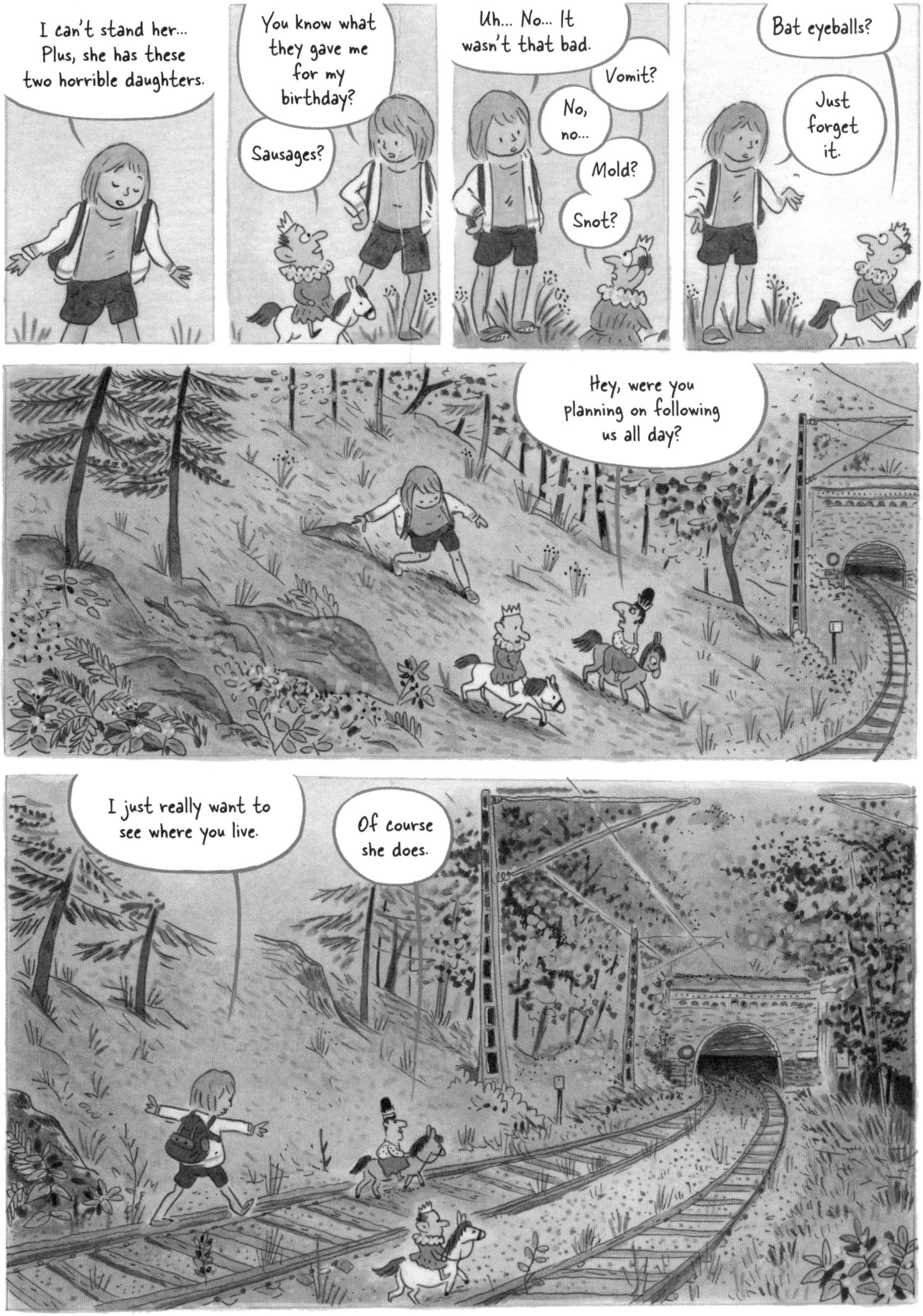
I can't stand her... Plus, she has these two horrible daughters.
You know what they gave me for my birthday?
Sausages?
Uh... No... It wasn't that bad.
Vomit?
No, no...
Mold?
Snot?
Bat eyeballs?
Just forget it.
Hey, were you planning on following us all day?
I just really want to see where you live.
Of course she does.

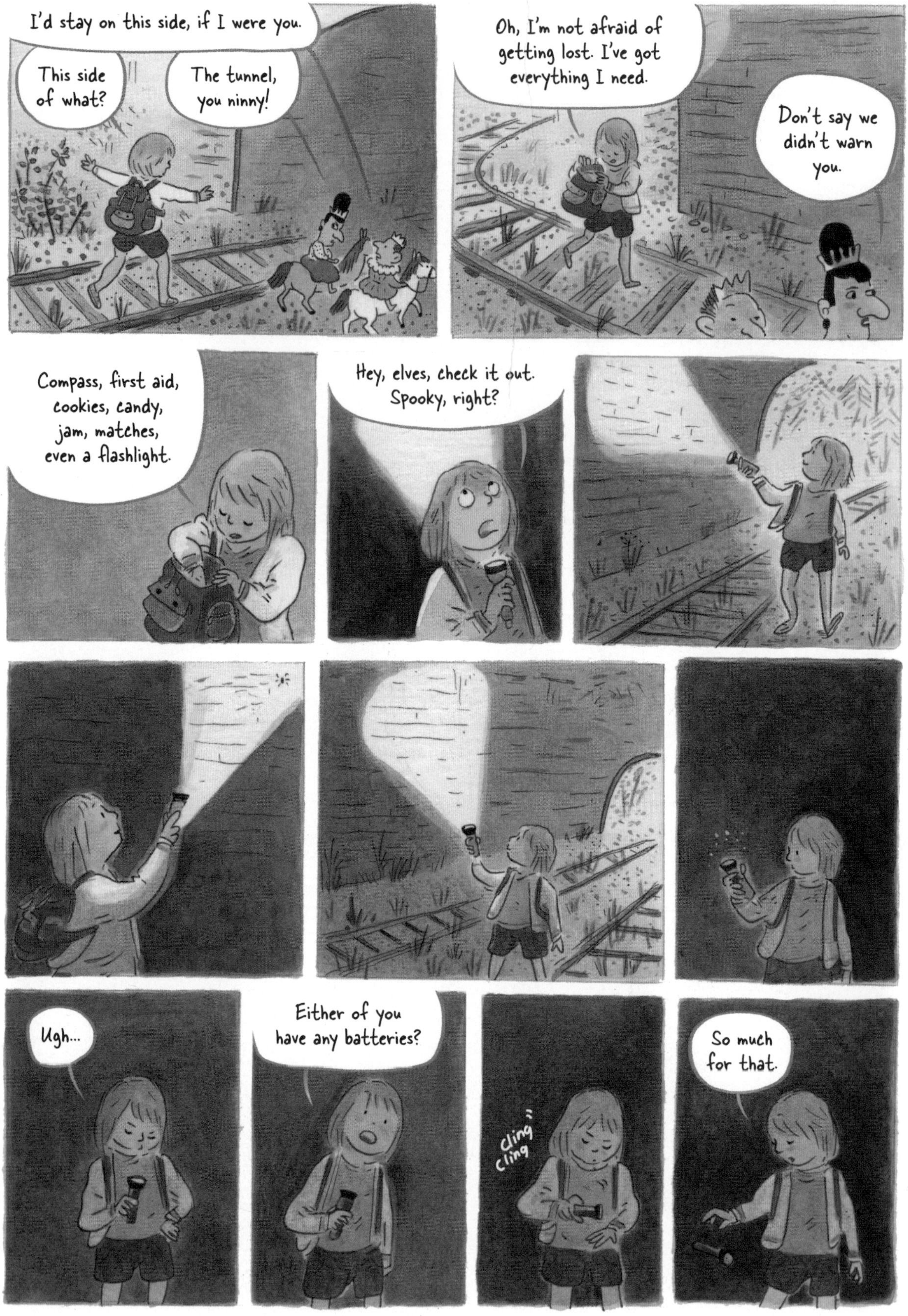
I'd stay on this side, if I were you.
This side of what?
The tunnel, you ninny!
Oh, I'm not afraid of getting lost. I've got everything I need.
Don't say we didn't warn you.
Compass, first aid, cookies, candy, jam, matches, even a flashlight.
Hey, elves, check it out. Spooky, right?
Ugh...
Either of you have any batteries?
Cling Cling
So much for that.

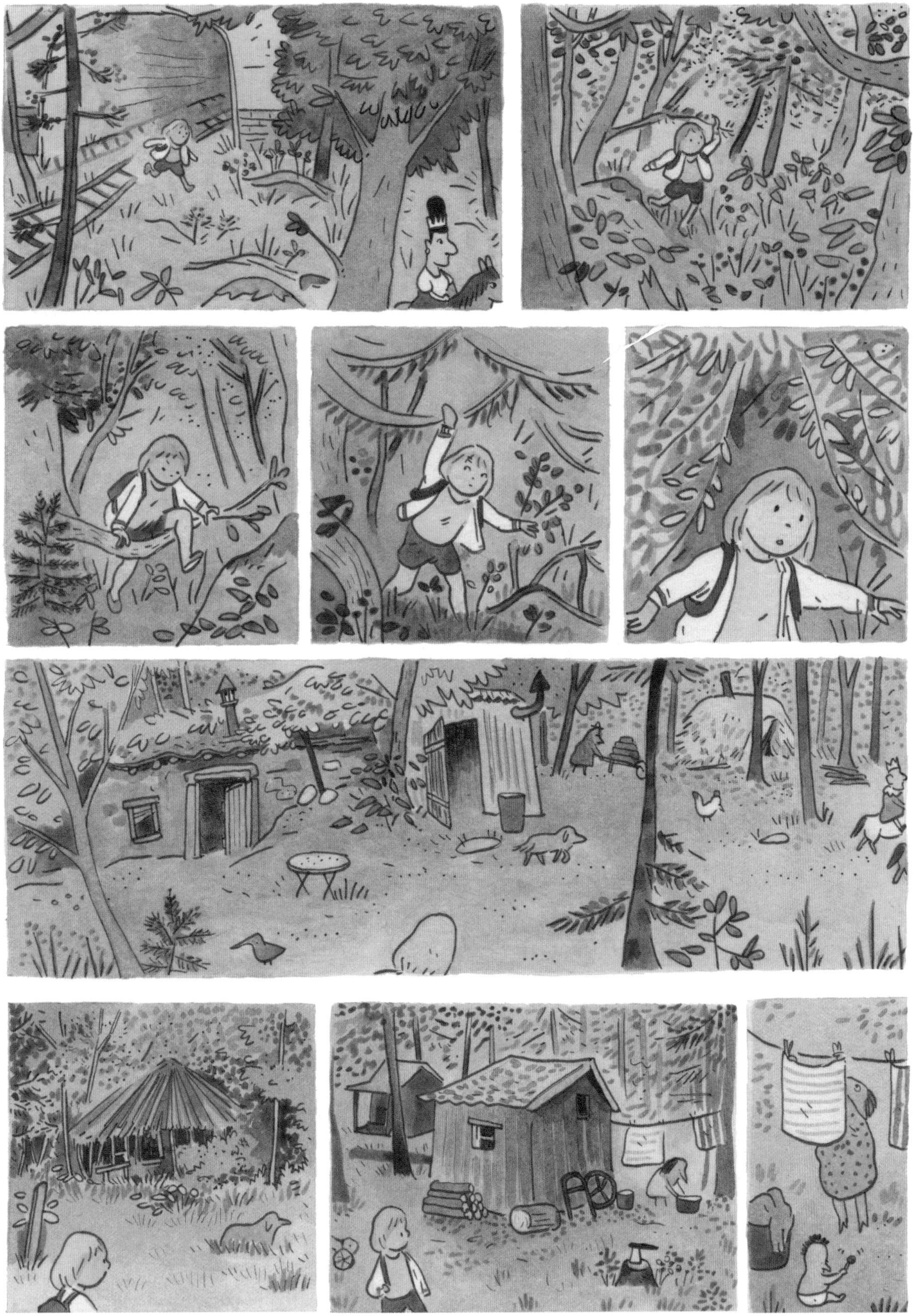

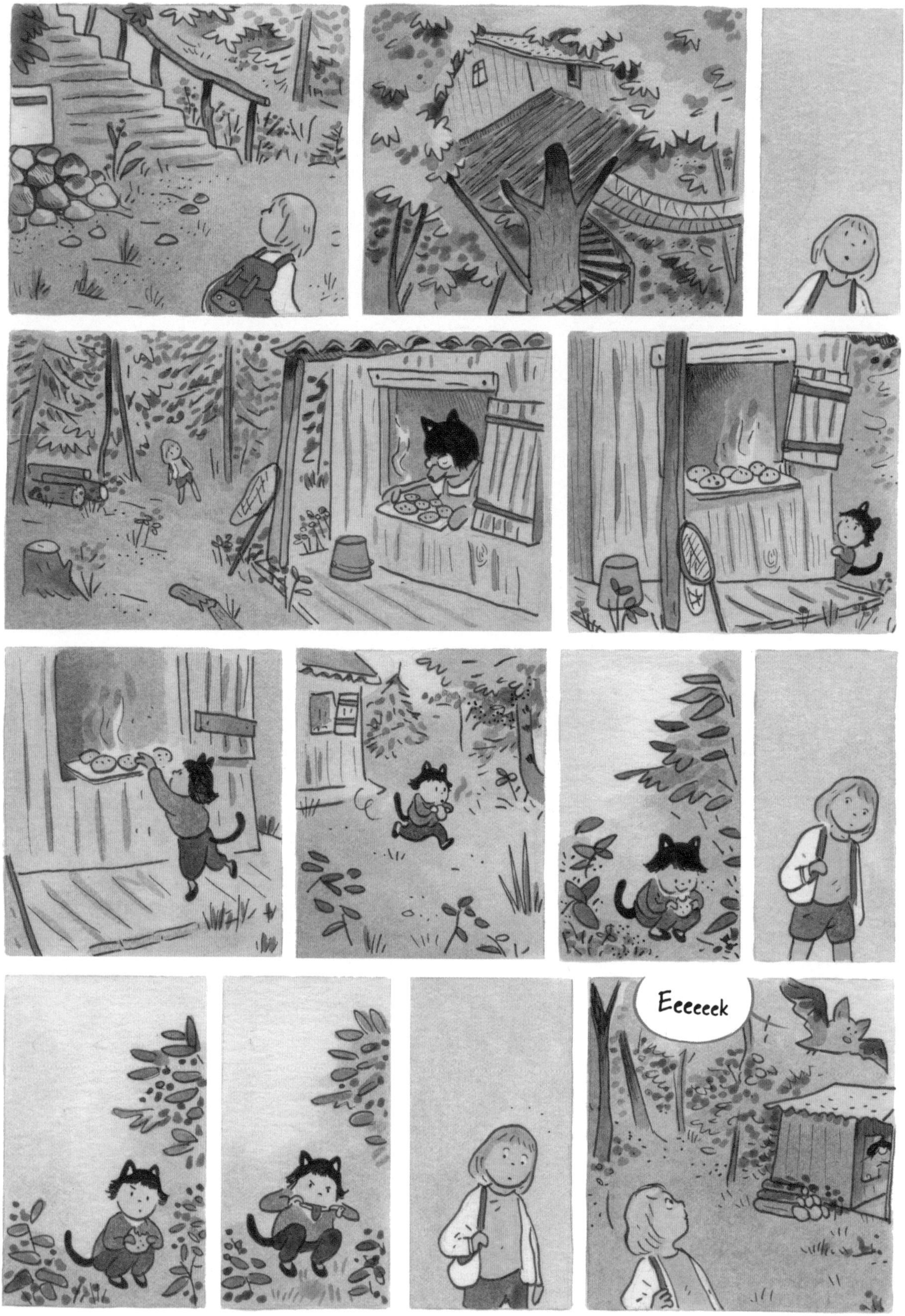
Eeeeeek

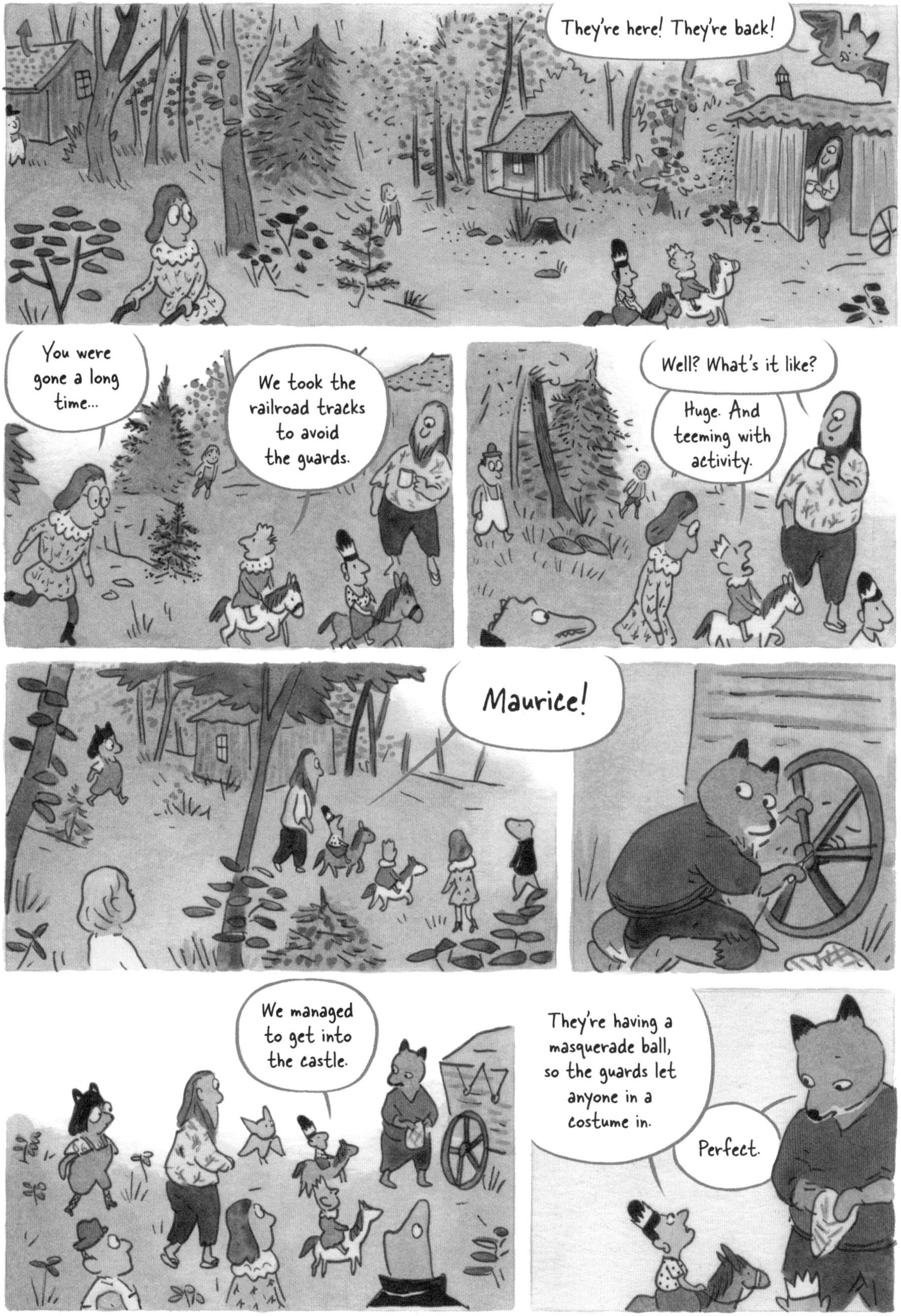
They're here! They're back!
You were gone a long time...
We took the railroad tracks to avoid the guards.
Well? What's it like?
Huge. And teeming with activity.
Maurice!
We managed to get into the castle.
They're having a masquerade ball, so the guards let anyone in a costume in.
Perfect.

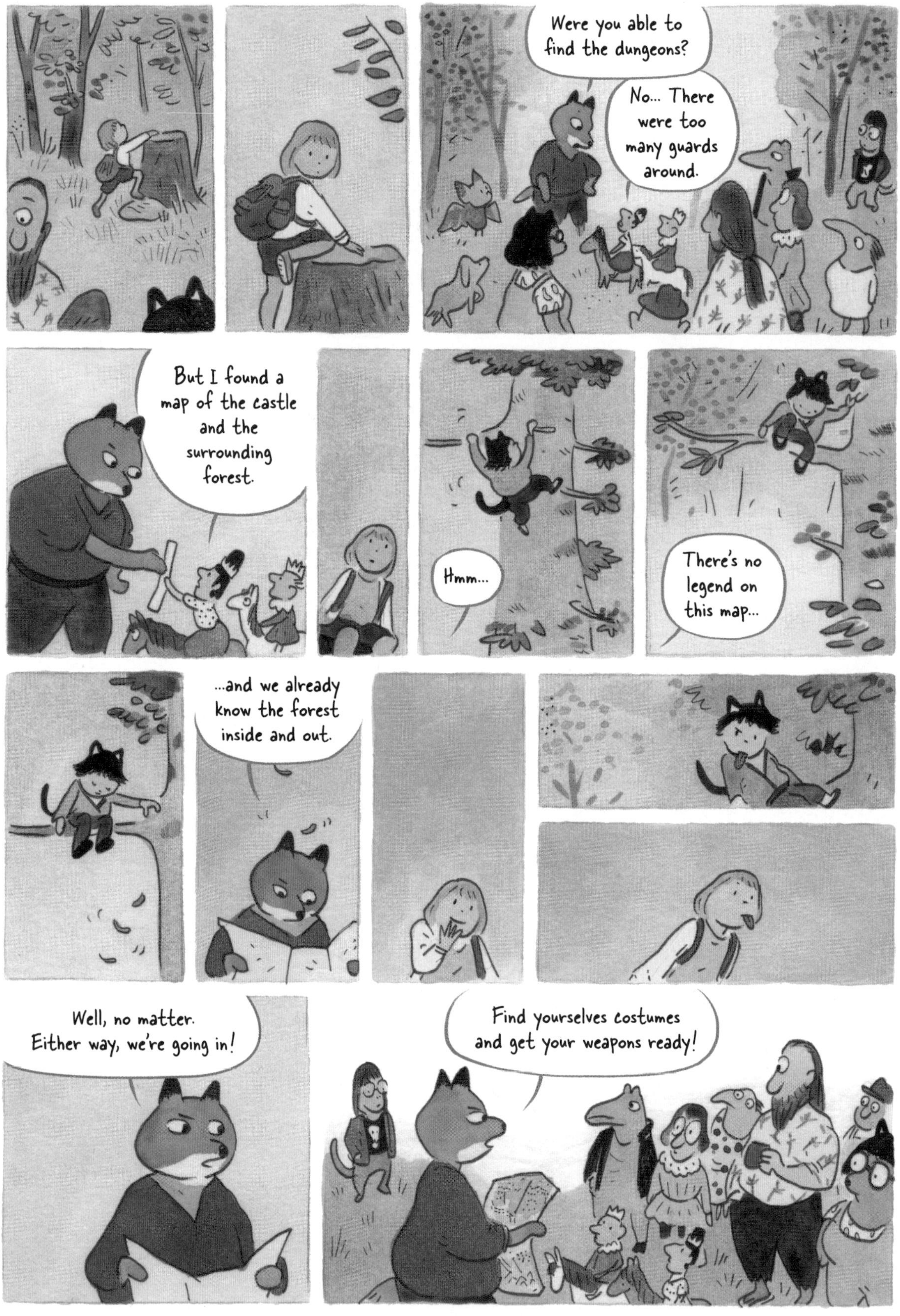
Were you able to find the dungeons?
No... There were too many guards around.
But I found a map of the castle and the surrounding forest.
Hmm...
There's no legend on this map...
...and we already know the forest inside and out.
Well, no matter. Either way, we're going in!
Find yourselves costumes and get your weapons ready!

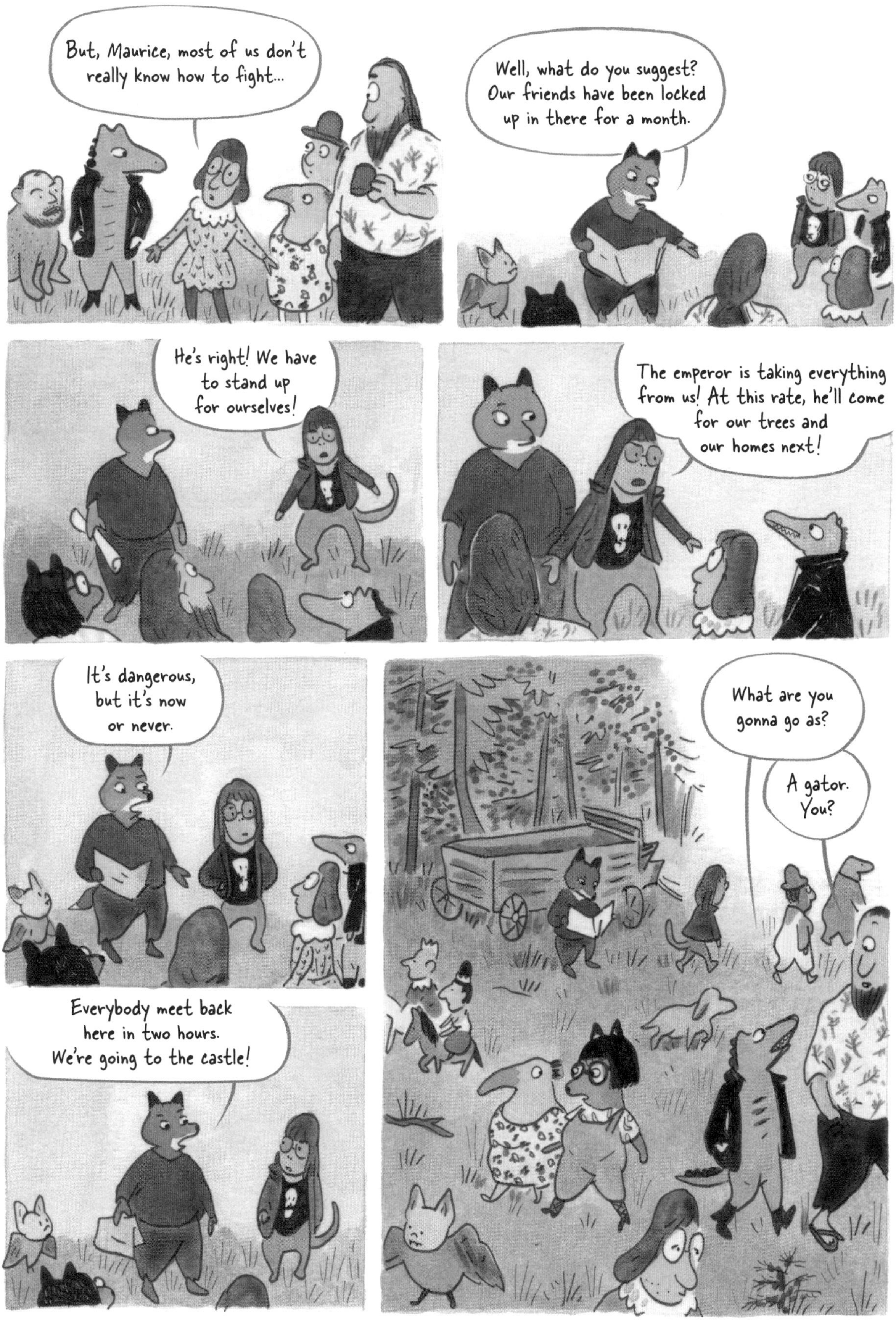

But, Maurice, most of us don't really know how to fight...
Well, what do you suggest? Our friends have been locked up in there for a month.
He's right! We have to stand up for ourselves!
The emperor is taking everything from us! At this rate, he'll come for our trees and our homes next!
It's dangerous, but it's now or never.
Everybody meet back here in two hours. We're going to the castle!
What are you gonna go as?
A gator. You?

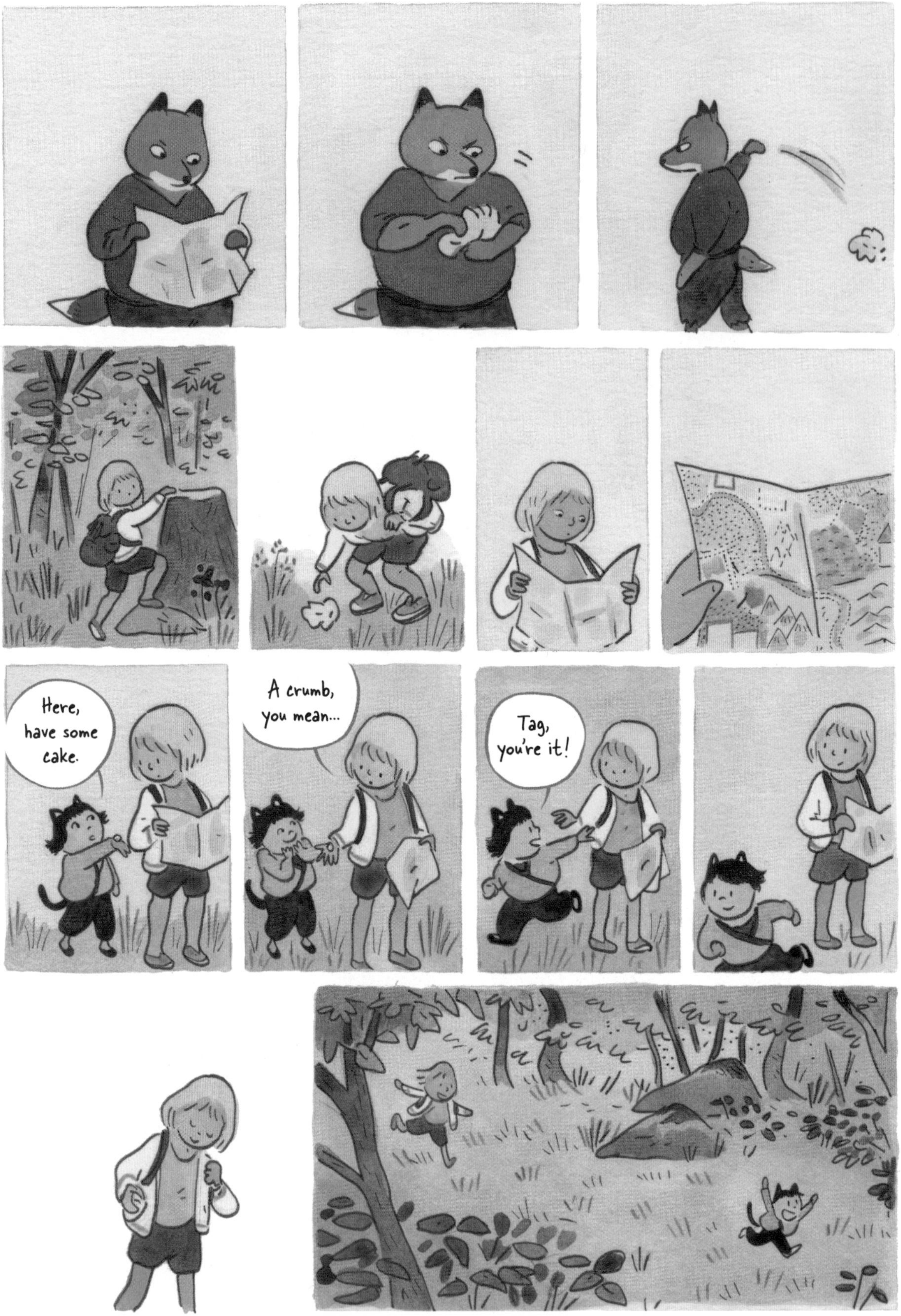
Here, have some cake.
A crumb, you mean...
Tag, you're it!

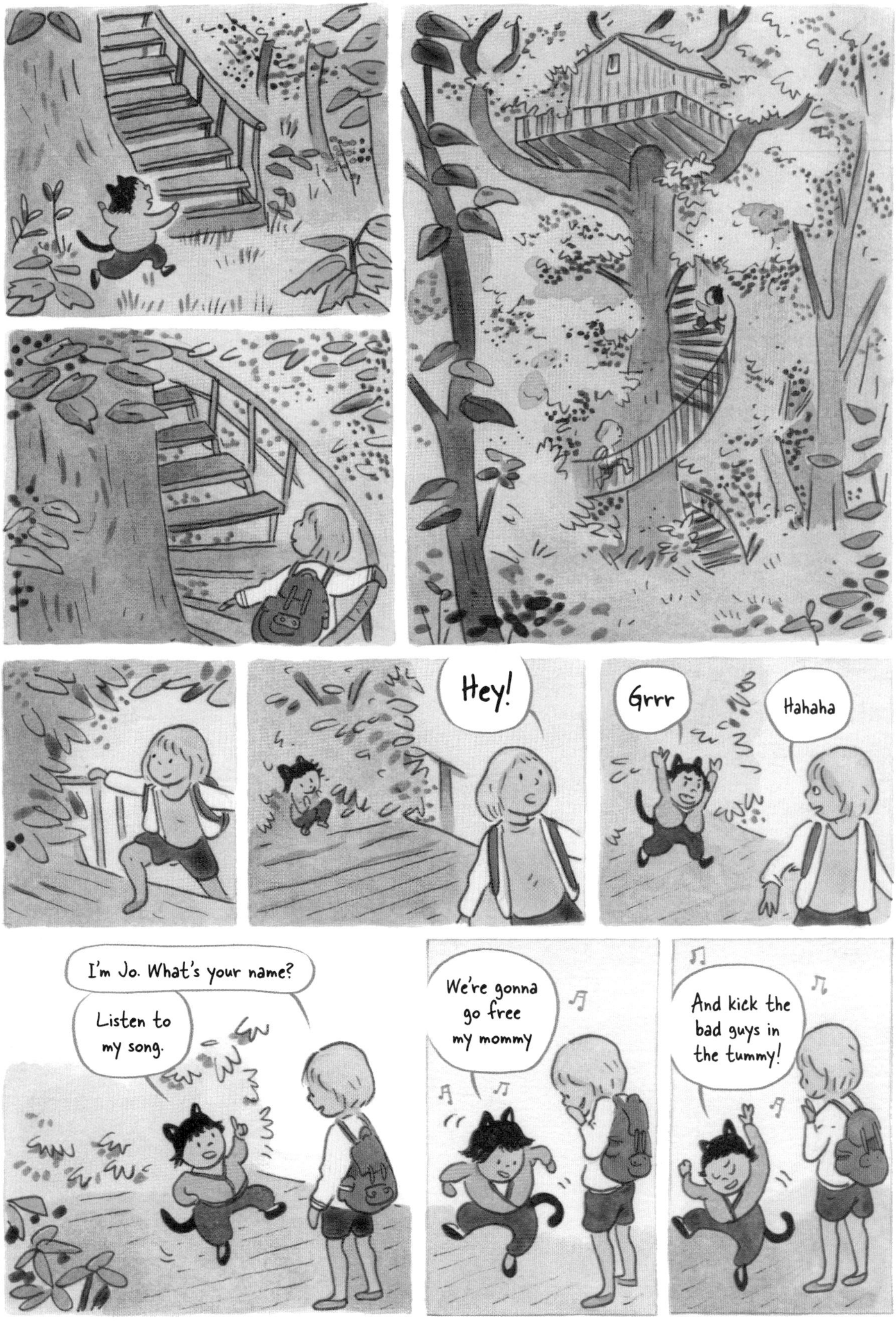
Hey!
Grrr
Hahaha
I'm Jo. What's your name?
Listen to my song.
We're gonna go free my mommy
And kick the bad guys in the tummy!

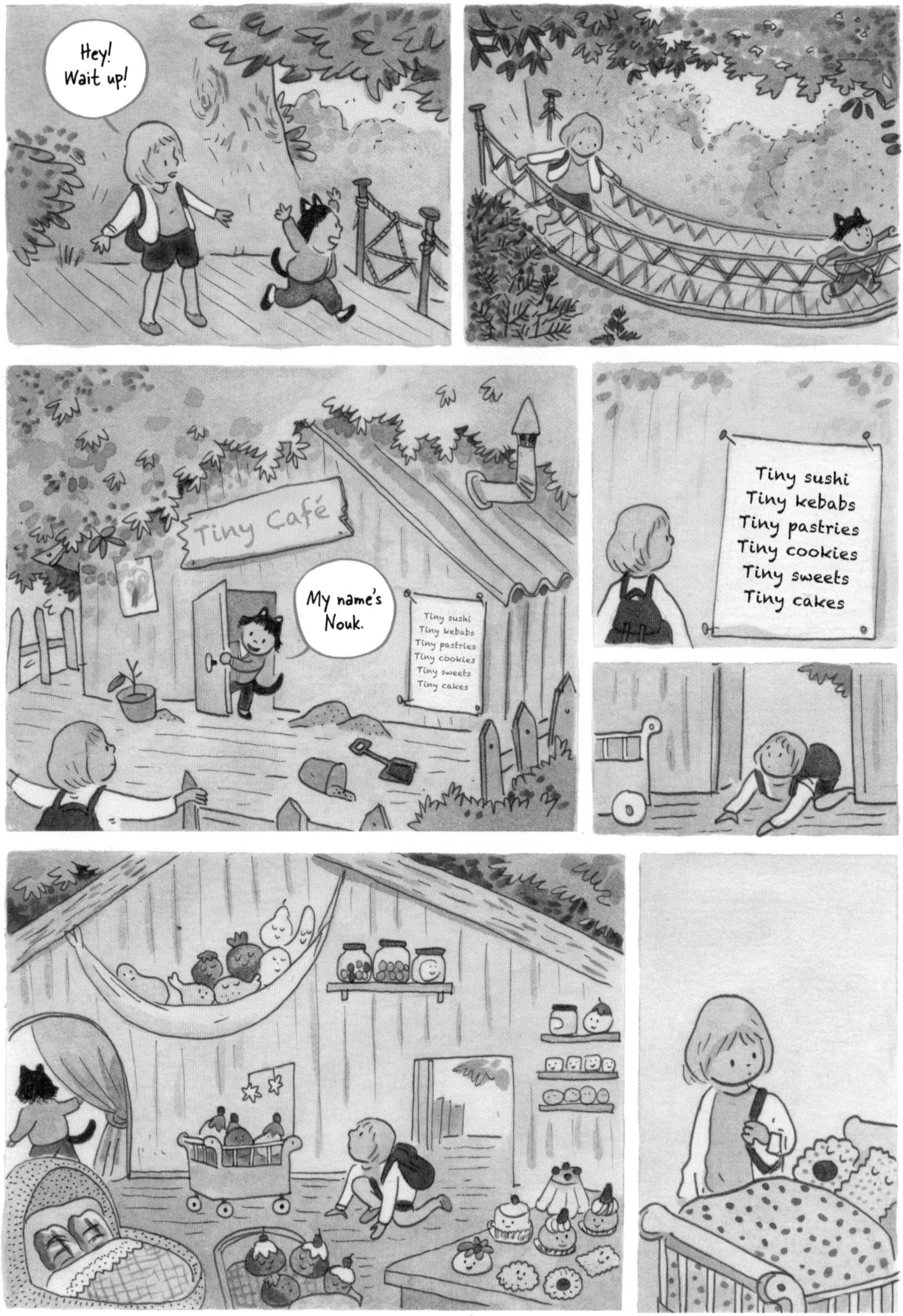
Hey! Wait up!
Tiny Café
My name's Nouk.
Tiny sushi
Tiny kebabs
Tiny pastries
Tiny cookies
Tiny sweets
Tiny cakes
Tiny sushi
Tiny kebabs
Tiny pastries
Tiny cookies
Tiny sweets
Tiny cakes

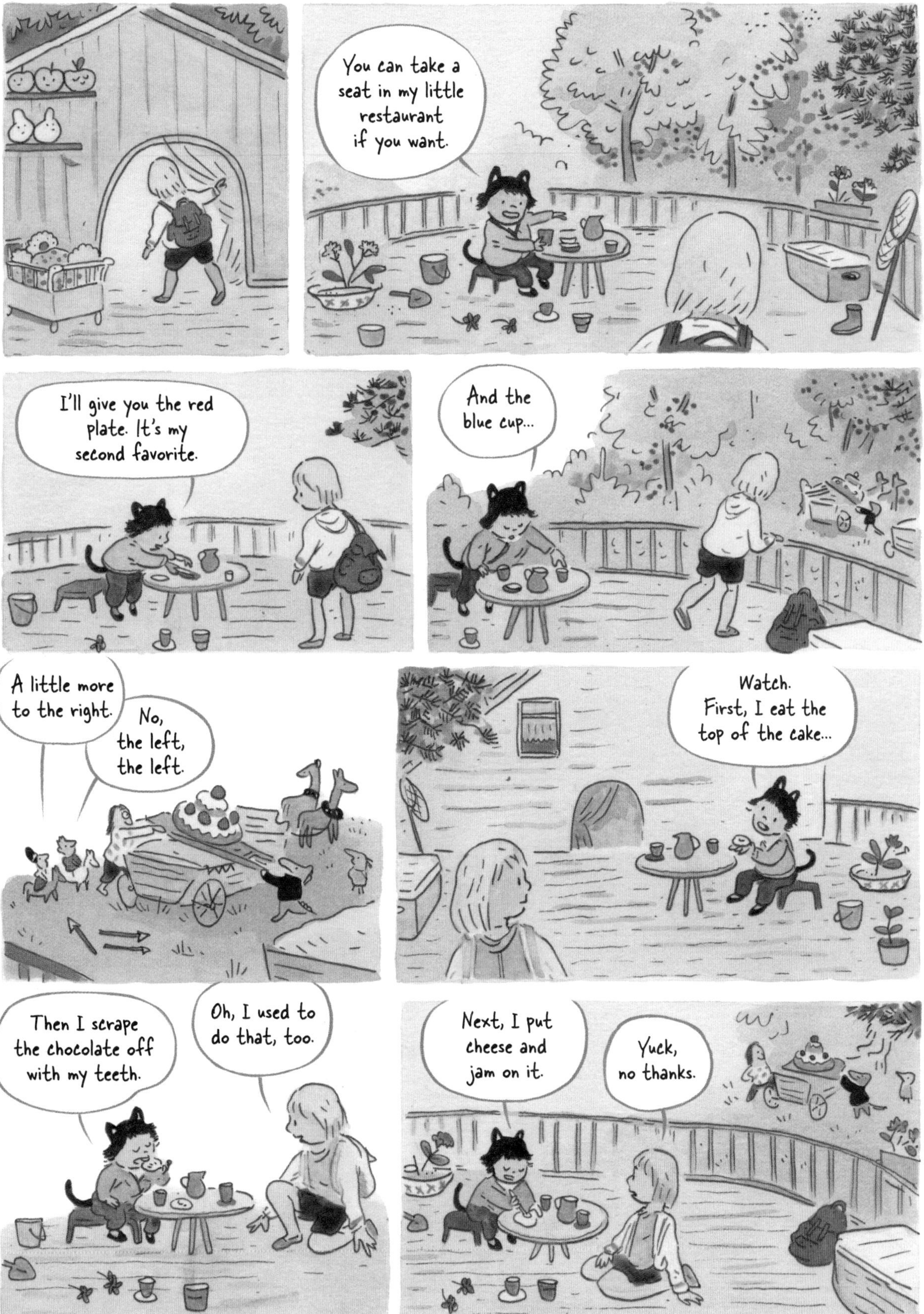
You can take a seat in my little restaurant if you want.
I'll give you the red plate. It's my second favorite.
And the blue cup...
A little more to the right.
No, the left, the left.
Watch. First, I eat the top of the cake...
Then I scrape the chocolate off with my teeth.
Oh, I used to do that, too.
Next, I put cheese and jam on it.
Yuck, no thanks.

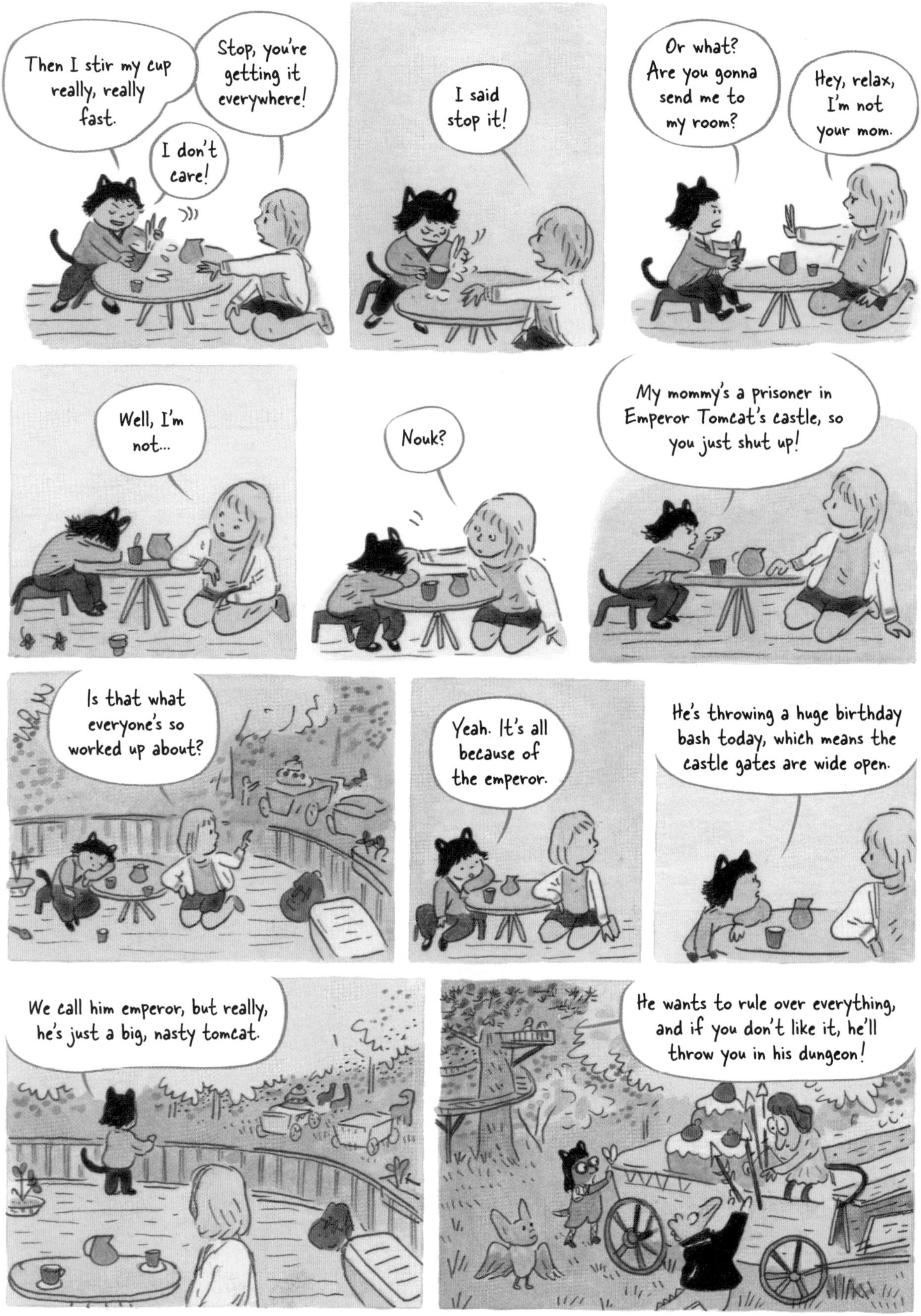
Then I stir my cup really, really fast.
I don't care!
Stop, you're getting it everywhere!
I said stop it!
Or what? Are you gonna send me to my room?
Hey, relax, I'm not your mom.
Well, I'm not...
Nouk?
My mommy's a prisoner in Emperor Tomcat's castle, so you just shut up!
Is that what everyone's so worked up about?
Yeah. It's all because of the emperor.
He's throwing a huge birthday bash today, which means the castle gates are wide open.
We call him emperor, but really, he's just a big, nasty tomcat.
He wants to rule over everything, and if you don't like it, he'll throw you in his dungeon!

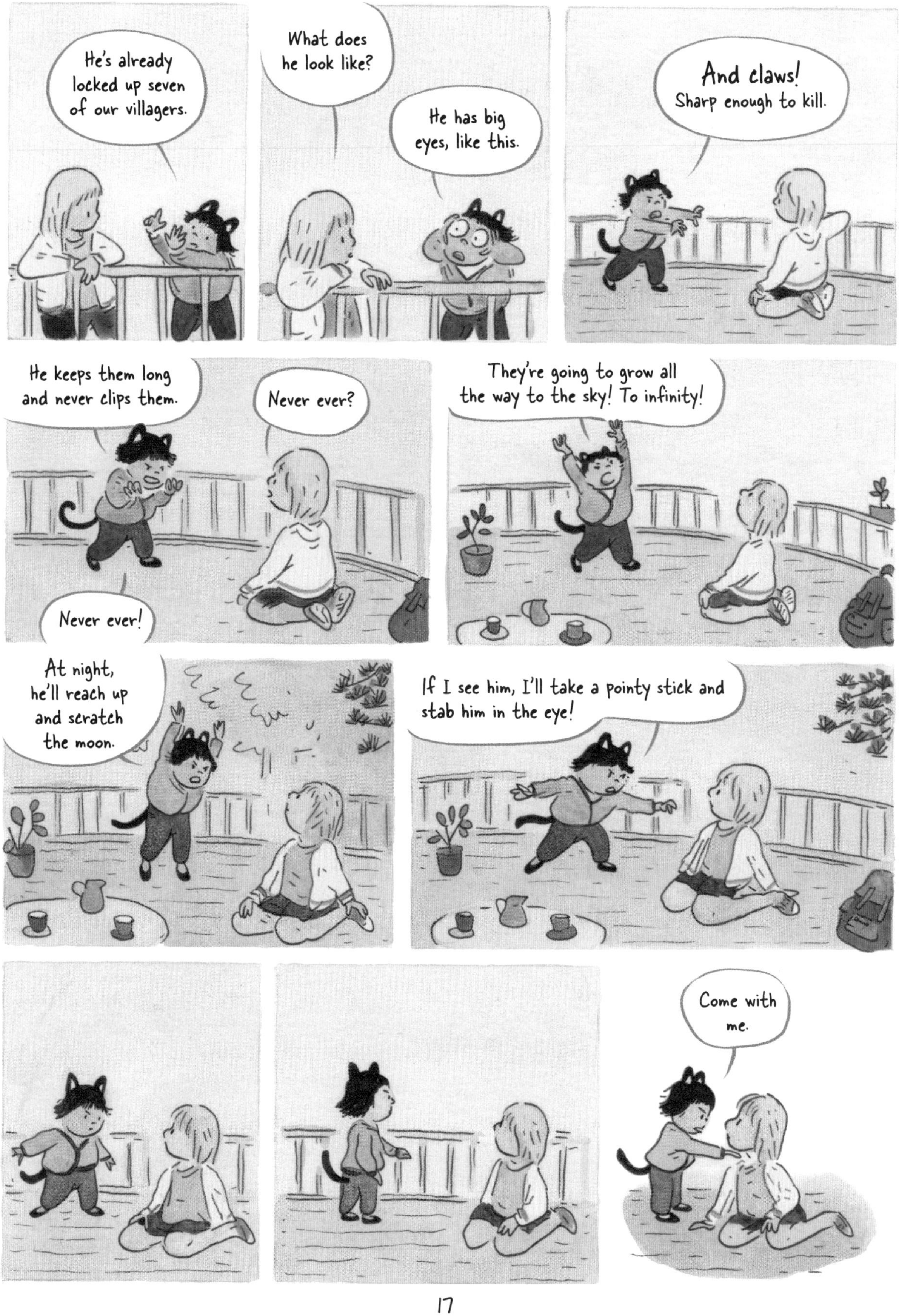
He's already locked up seven of our villagers.
What does he look like?
He has big eyes, like this.
And claws! Sharp enough to kill.
He keeps them long and never clips them.
Never ever?
Never ever!
They're going to grow all the way to the sky! To infinity!
At night, he'll reach up and scratch the moon.
If I see him, I'll take a pointy stick and stab him in the eye!
Come with me.

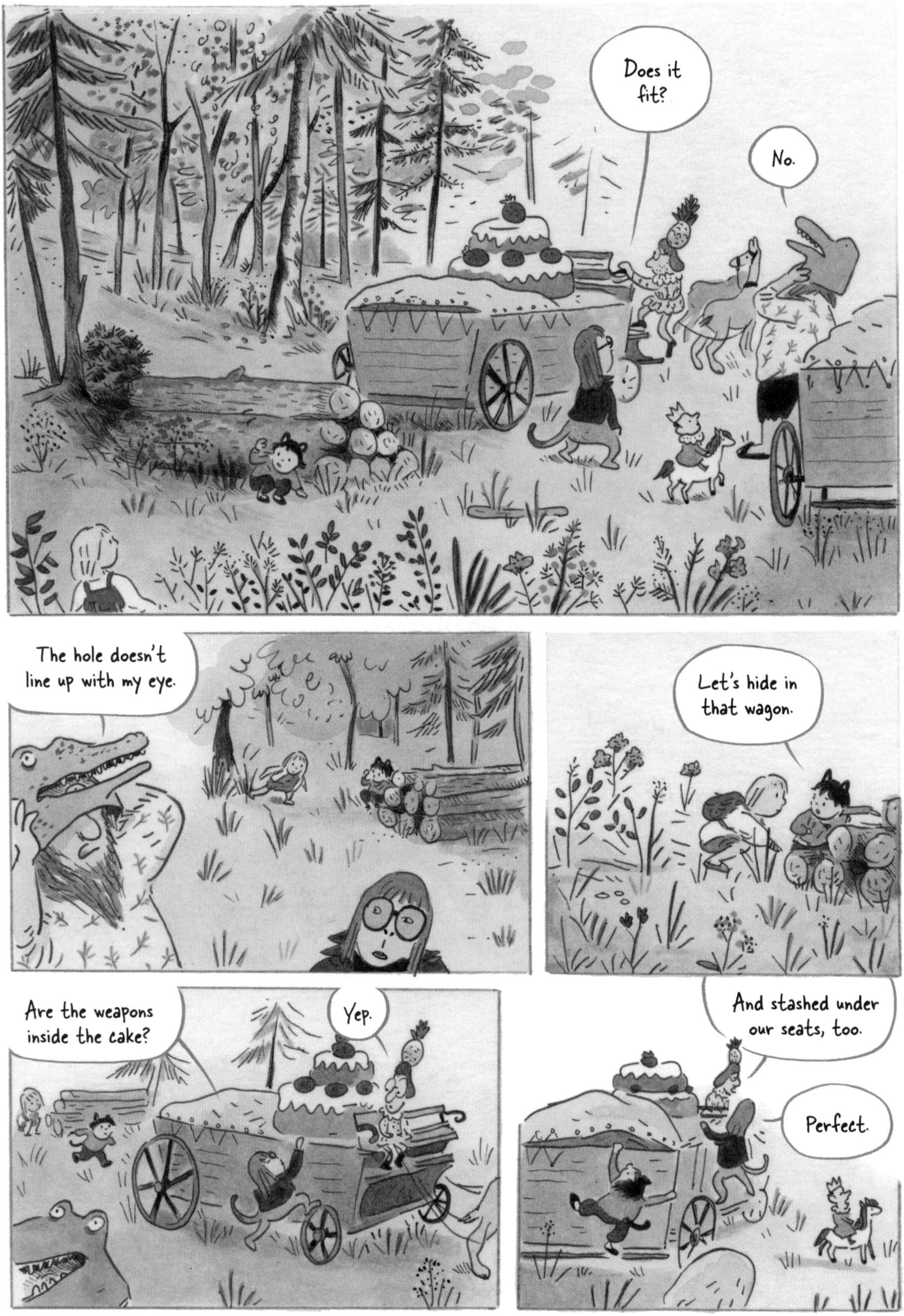
Does it fit?
No.
The hole doesn't line up with my eye.
Let's hide in that wagon.
Are the weapons inside the cake?
Yep.
And stashed under our seats, too.
Perfect.

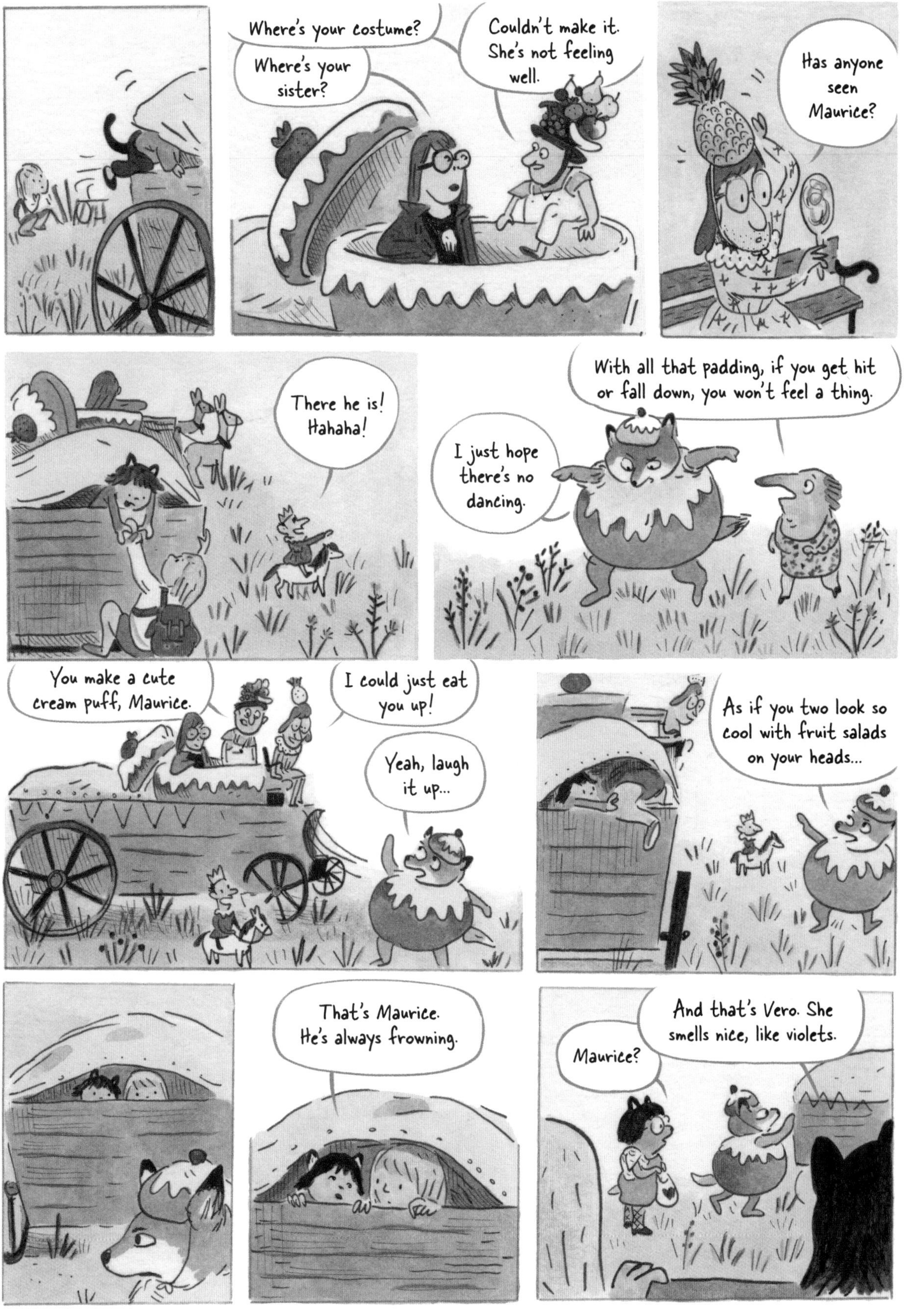
Where's your costume?
Where's your sister?
Couldn't make it. She's not feeling well.
Has anyone seen Maurice?
There he is! Hahaha!
With all that padding, if you get hit or fall down, you won't feel a thing.
I just hope there's no dancing.
You make a cute cream puff, Maurice.
I could just eat you up!
Yeah, laugh it up...
As if you two look so cool with fruit salads on your heads...
That's Maurice. He's always frowning.
And that's Vero. She smells nice, like violets.
Maurice?

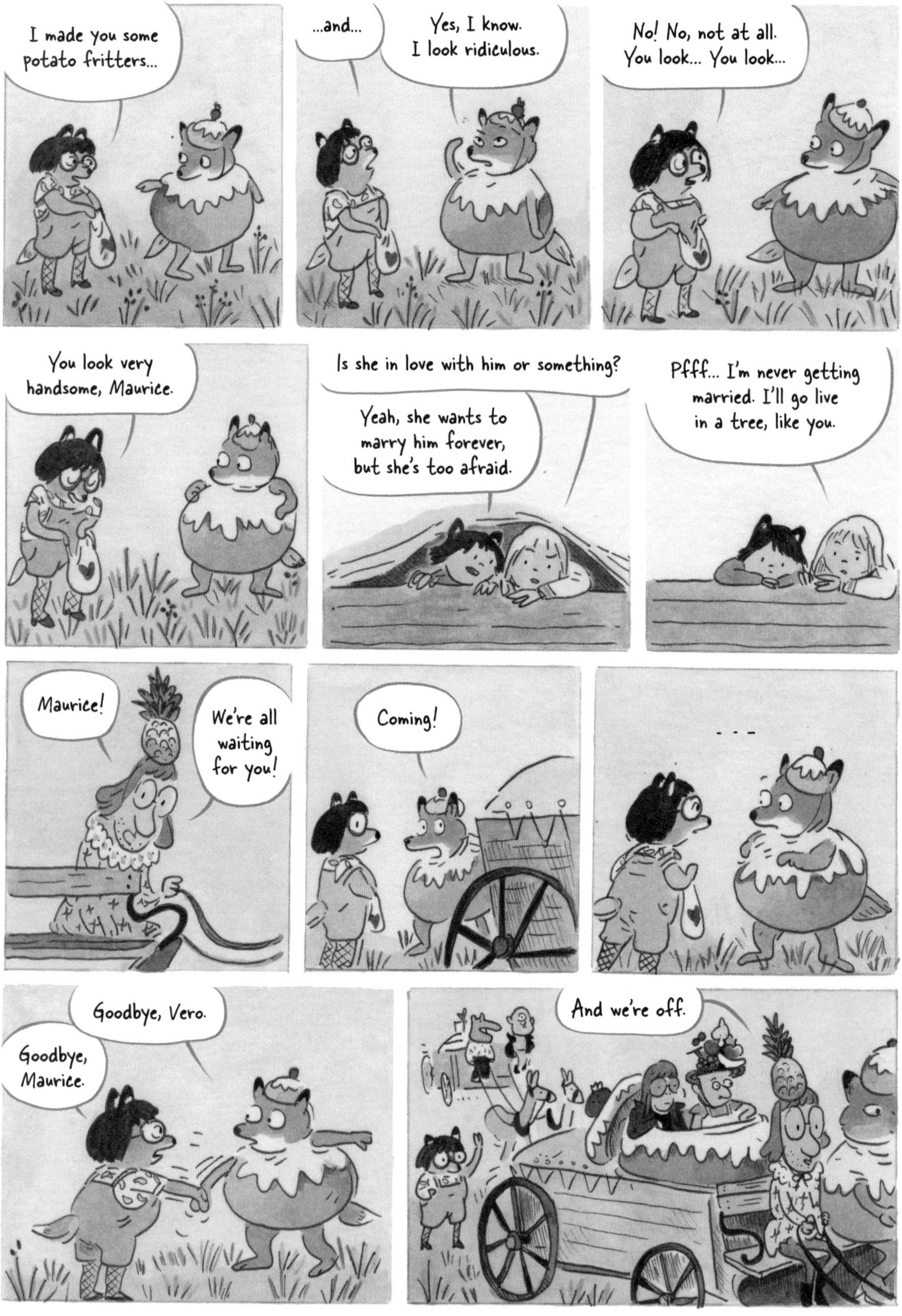
I made you some potato fritters...
...and...
Yes, I know. I look ridiculous.
No! No, not at all. You look... You look...
You look very handsome, Maurice.
Is she in love with him or something?
Yeah, she wants to marry him forever, but she's too afraid.
Pfff... I'm never getting married. I'll go live in a tree, like you.
Maurice!
We're all waiting for you!
Coming!
...
Goodbye, Vero.
Goodbye, Maurice.
And we're off.

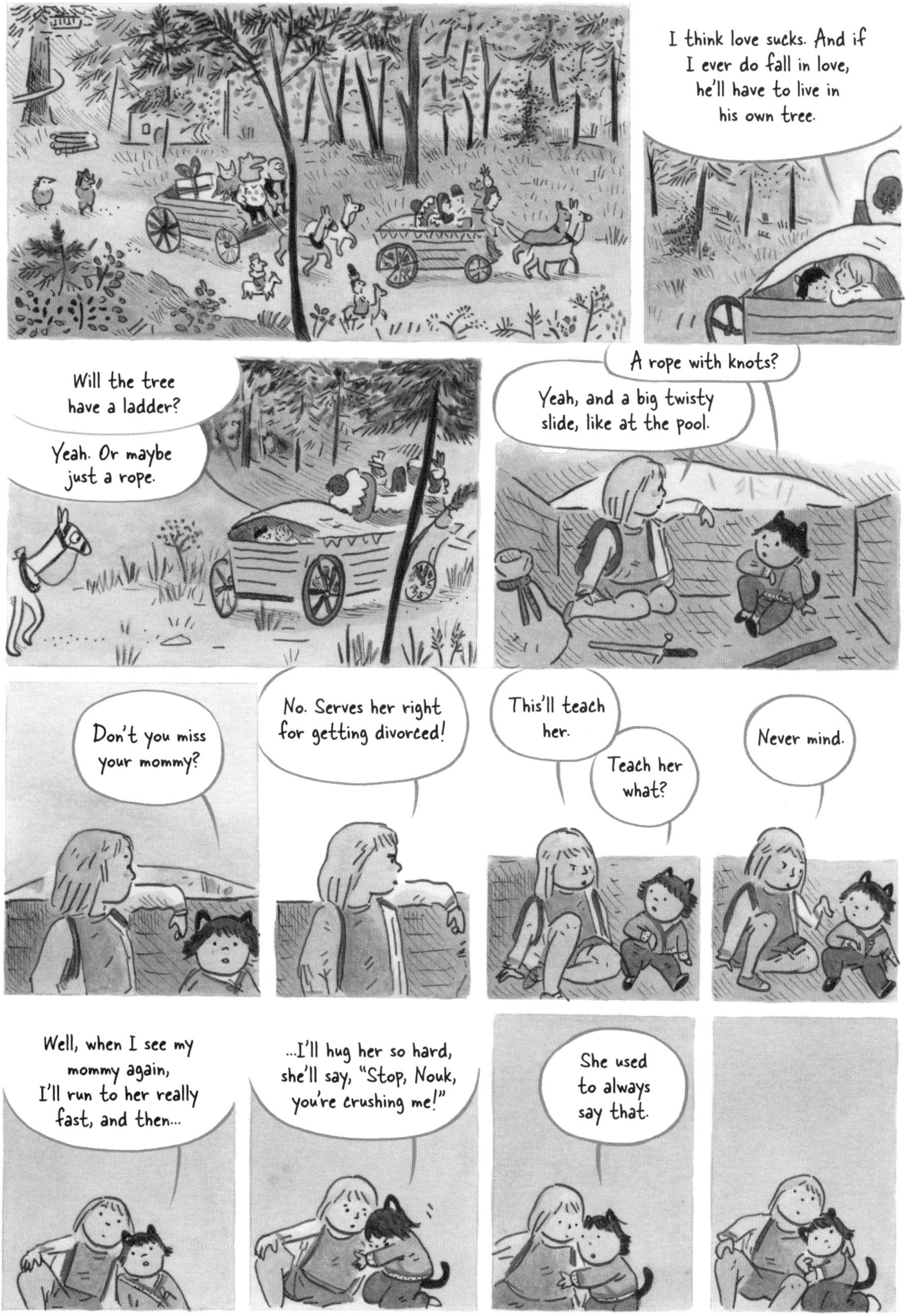
I think love sucks. And if I ever do fall in love, he'll have to live in his own tree.
Will the tree have a ladder?
Yeah. Or maybe just a rope.
A rope with knots?
Yeah, and a big twisty slide, like at the pool.
Don't you miss your mommy?
No. Serves her right for getting divorced!
This'll teach her.
Teach her what?
Never mind.
Well, when I see my mommy again, I'll run to her really fast, and then...
...I'll hug her so hard, she'll say, "Stop, Nouk, you're crushing me!"
She used to always say that.

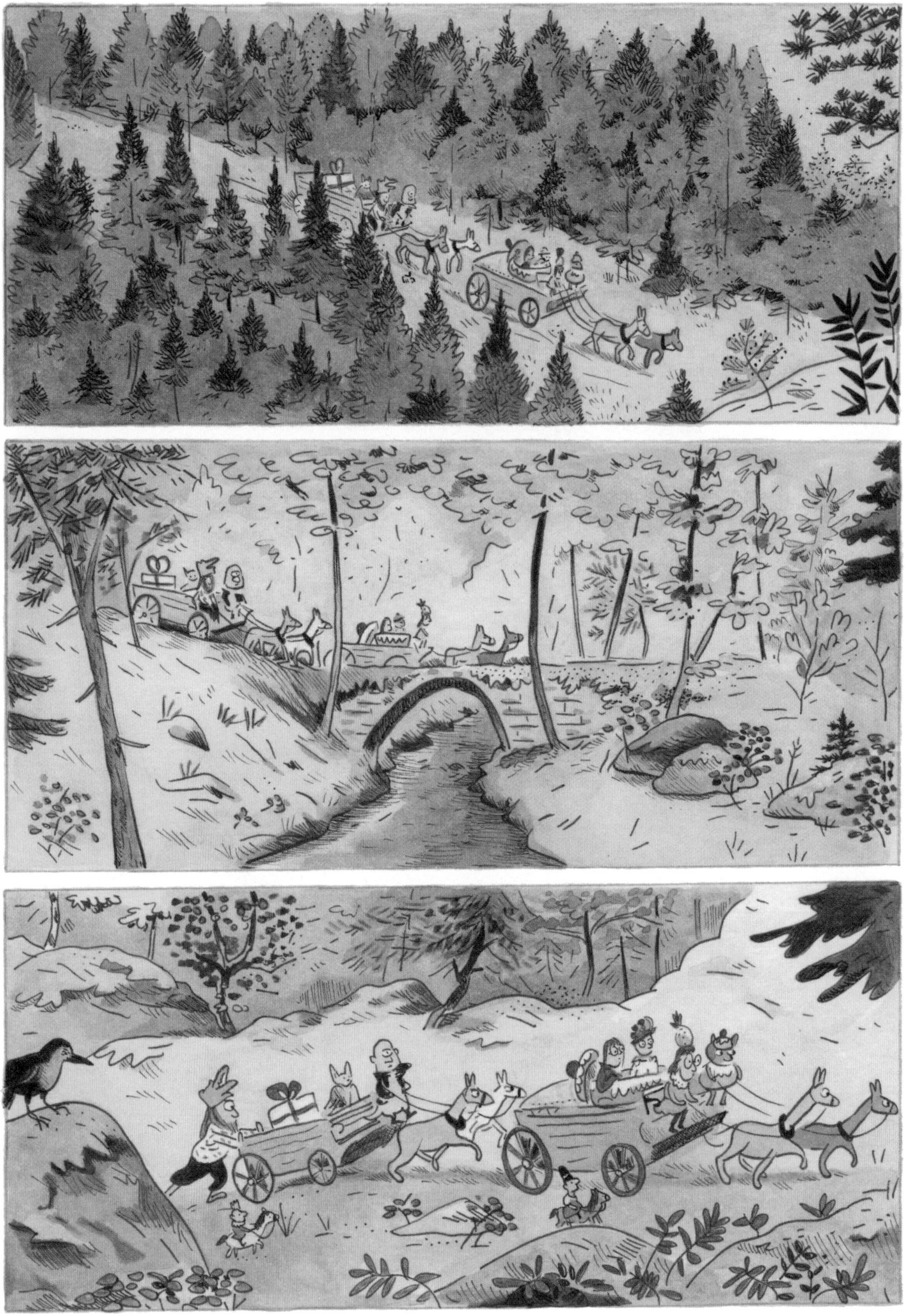

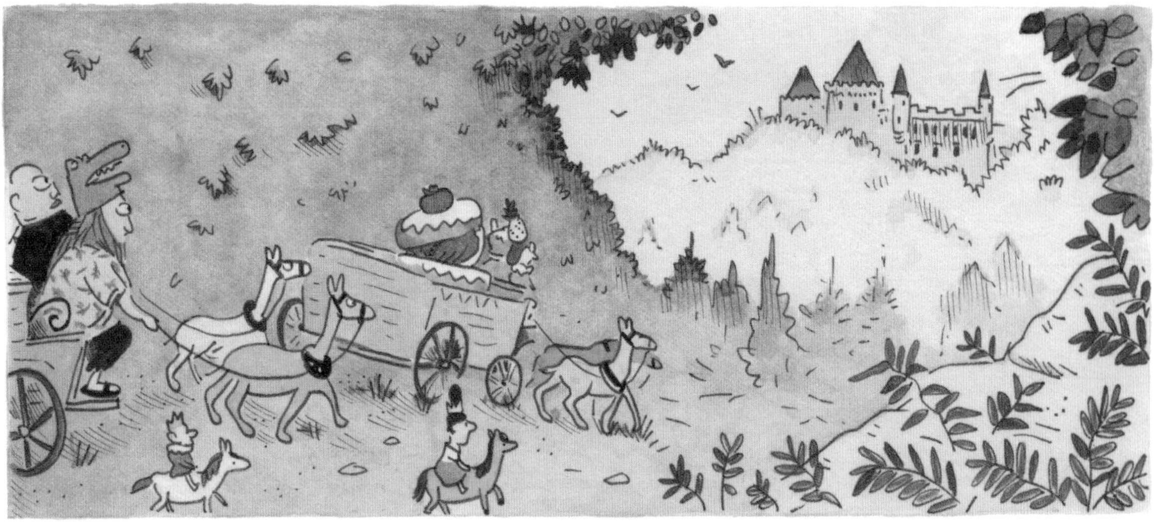

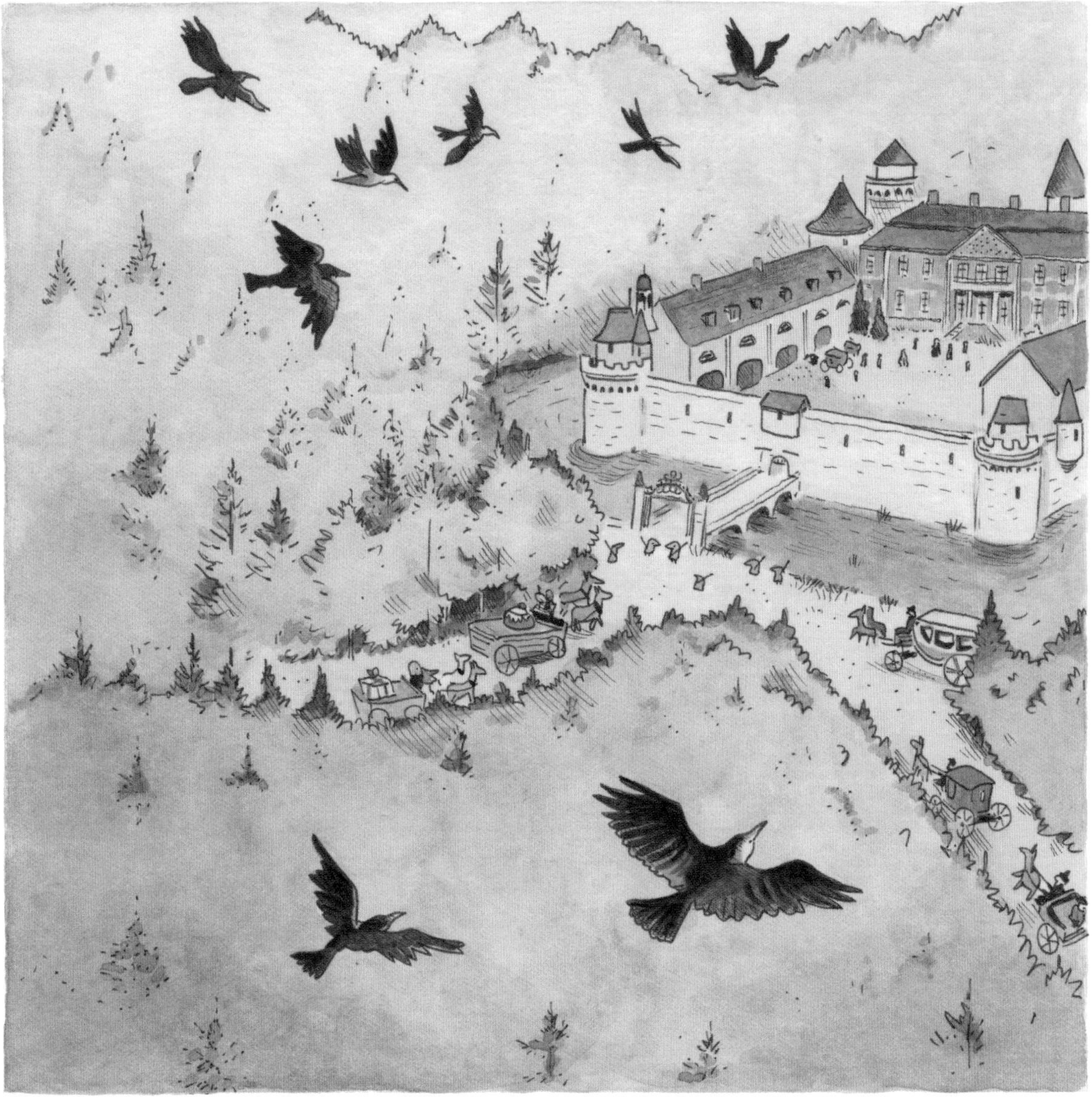

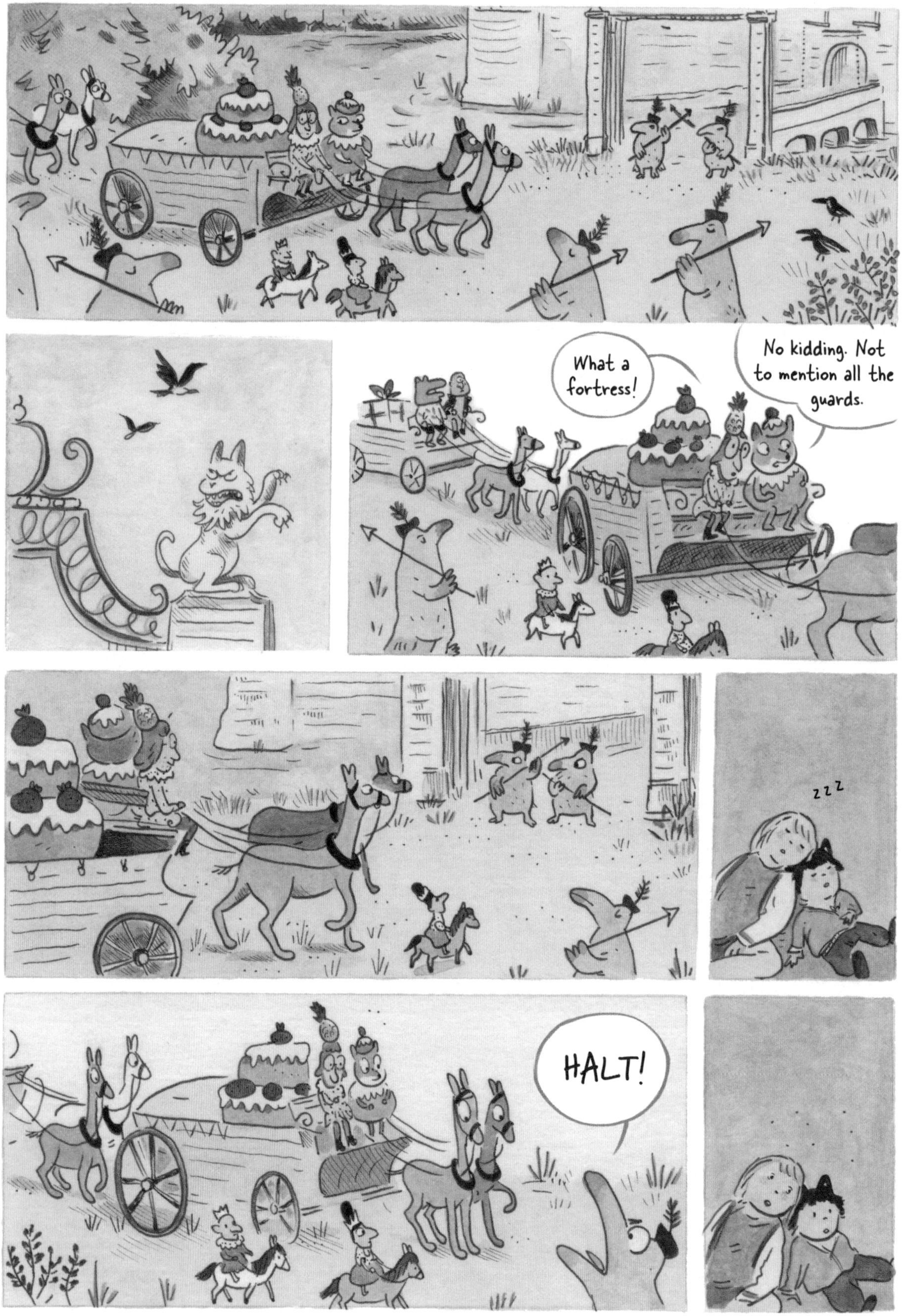
What a fortress!
No kidding. Not to mention all the guards.
Z Z Z
HALT!

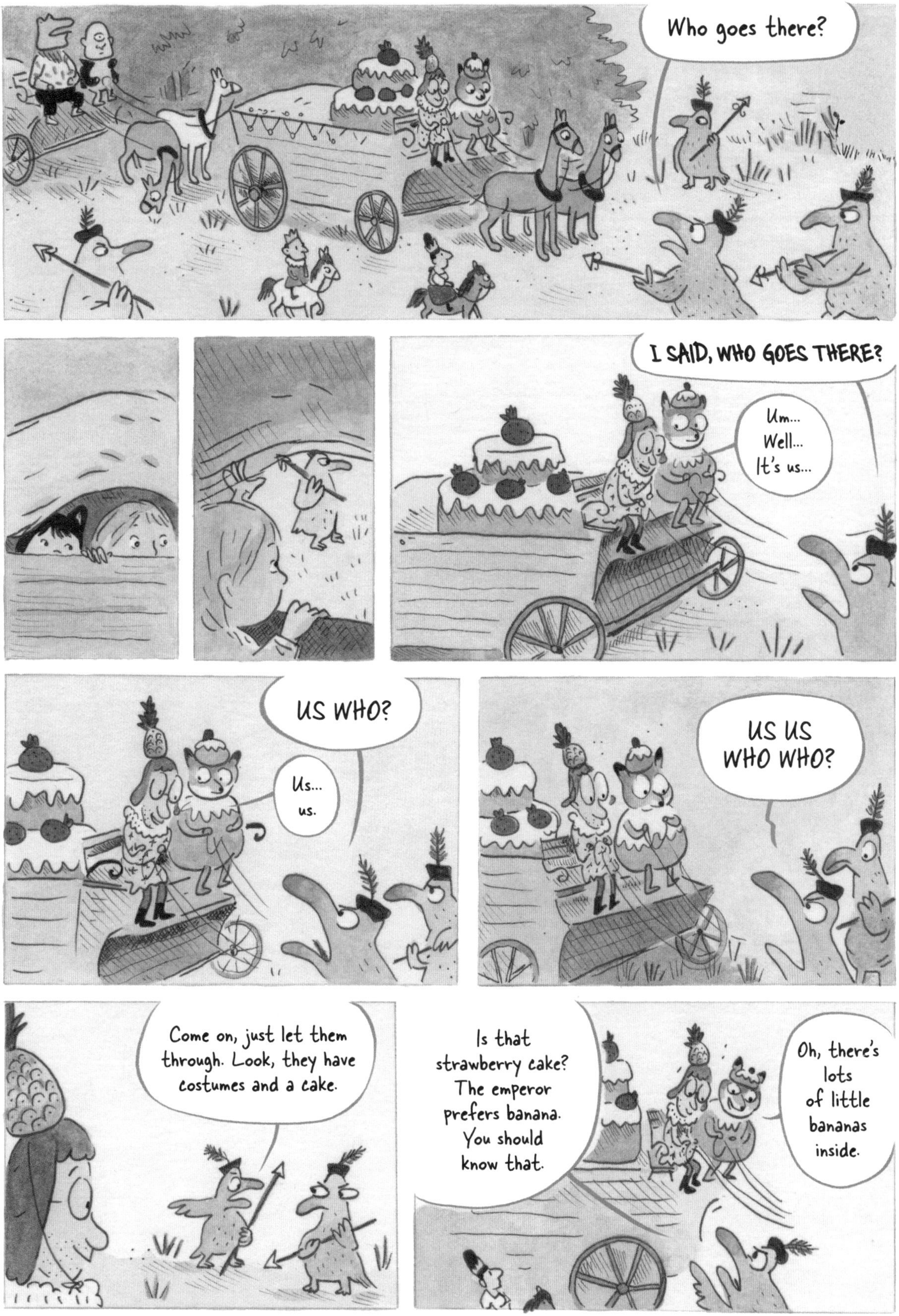
Who goes there?
I SAID, WHO GOES THERE?
Um... Well... It's us...
US WHO?
Us... us.
US US WHO WHO?
Come on, just let them through. Look, they have costumes and a cake.
Is that strawberry cake? The emperor prefers banana. You should know that.
Oh, there's lots of little bananas inside.

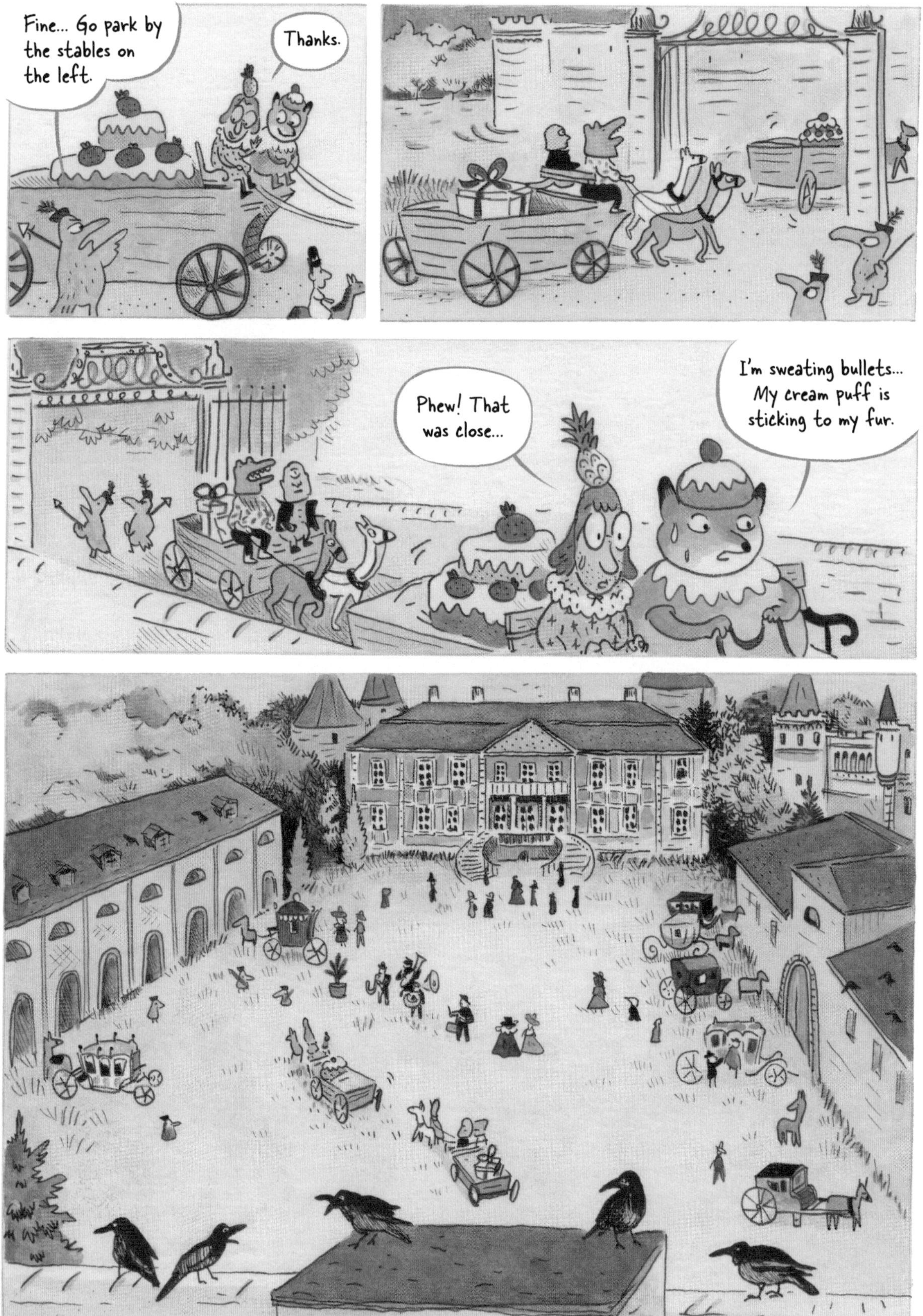
Fine... Go park by the stables on the left.
Thanks.
Phew! That was close...
I'm sweating bullets... My cream puff is sticking to my fur.

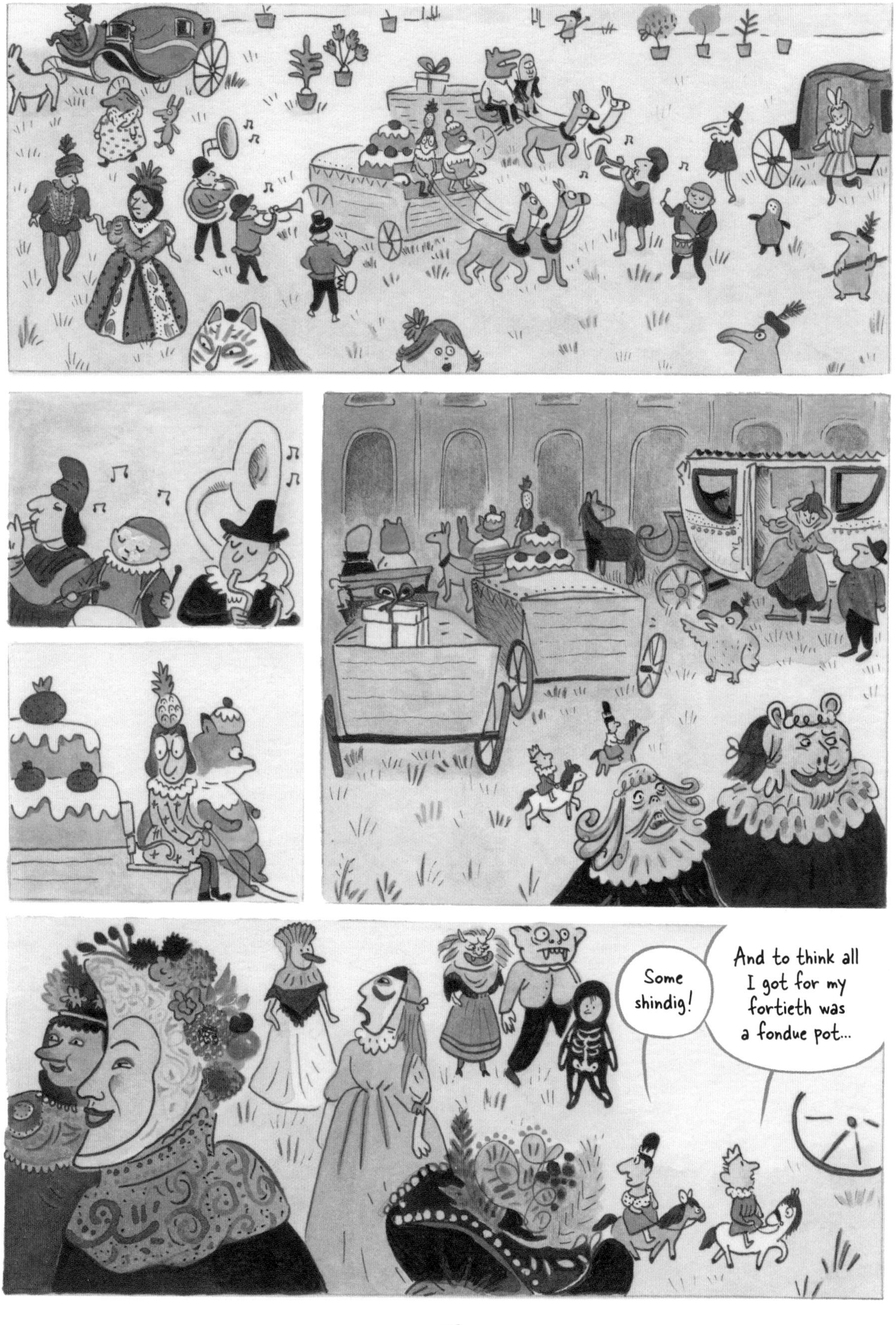
Some shindig!
And to think all I got for my fortieth was a fondue pot...

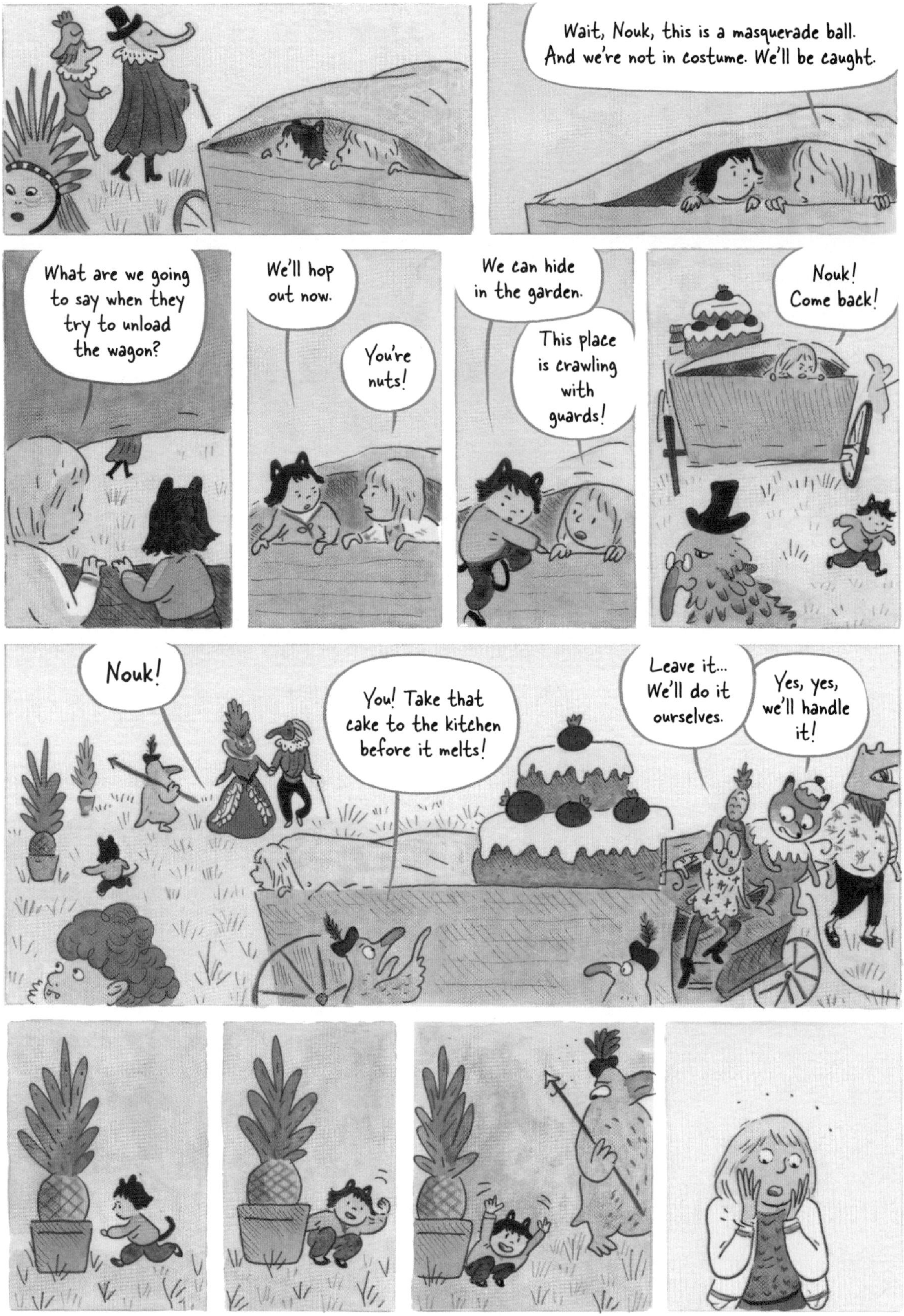
Wait, Nouk, this is a masquerade ball. And we're not in costume. We'll be caught.
What are we going to say when they try to unload the wagon?
We'll hop out now.
You're nuts!
We can hide in the garden.
This place is crawling with guards!
Nouk! Come back!
Nouk!
You! Take that cake to the kitchen before it melts!
Leave it... We'll do it ourselves.
Yes, yes, we'll handle it!

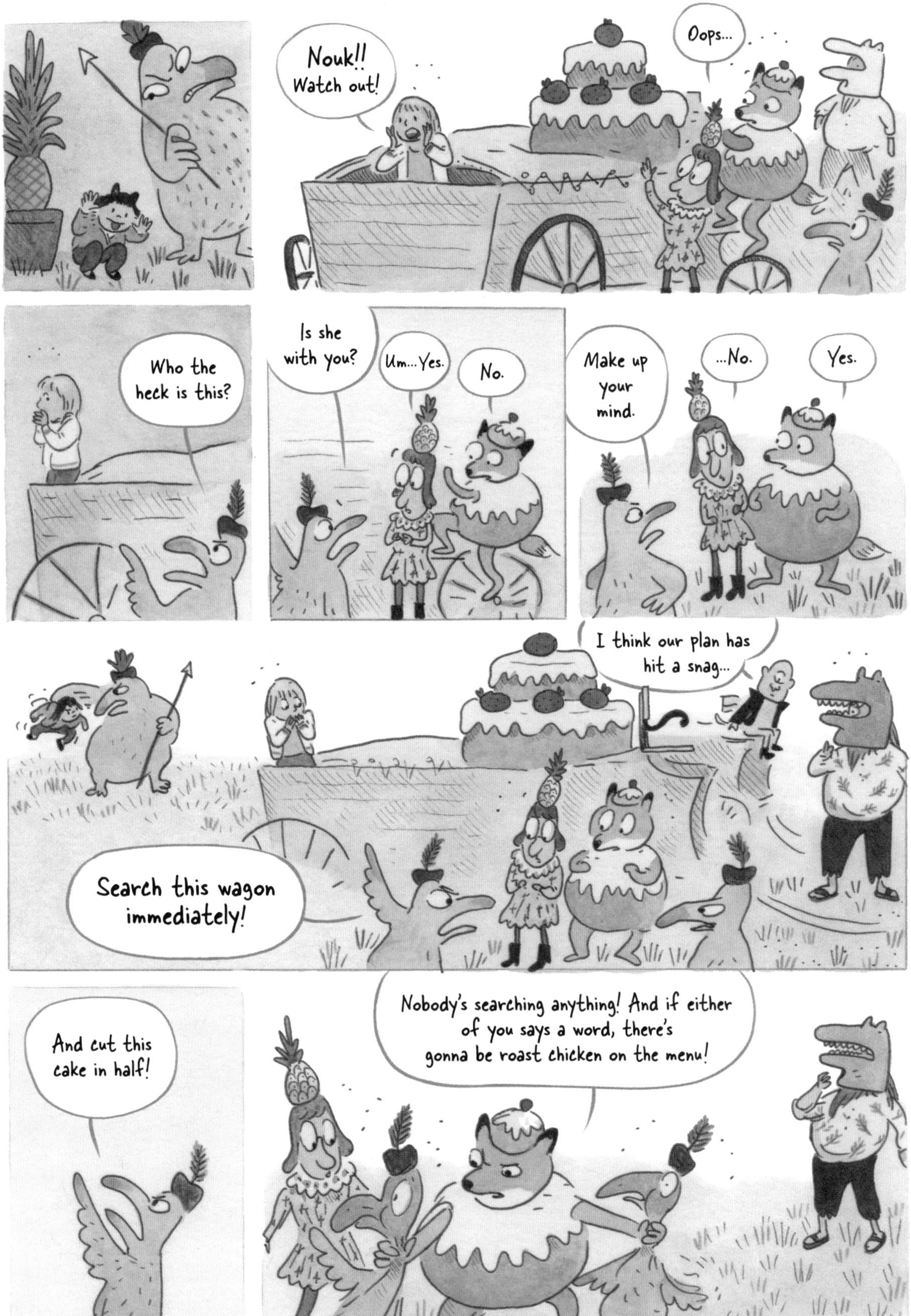
Nouk!! Watch out!
Oops...
Who the heck is this?
Is she with you?
Um... Yes.
No.
Make up your mind.
...No.
Yes.
I think our plan has hit a snag...
Search this wagon immediately!
And cut this cake in half!
Nobody's searching anything! And if either of you says a word, there's gonna be roast chicken on the menu!

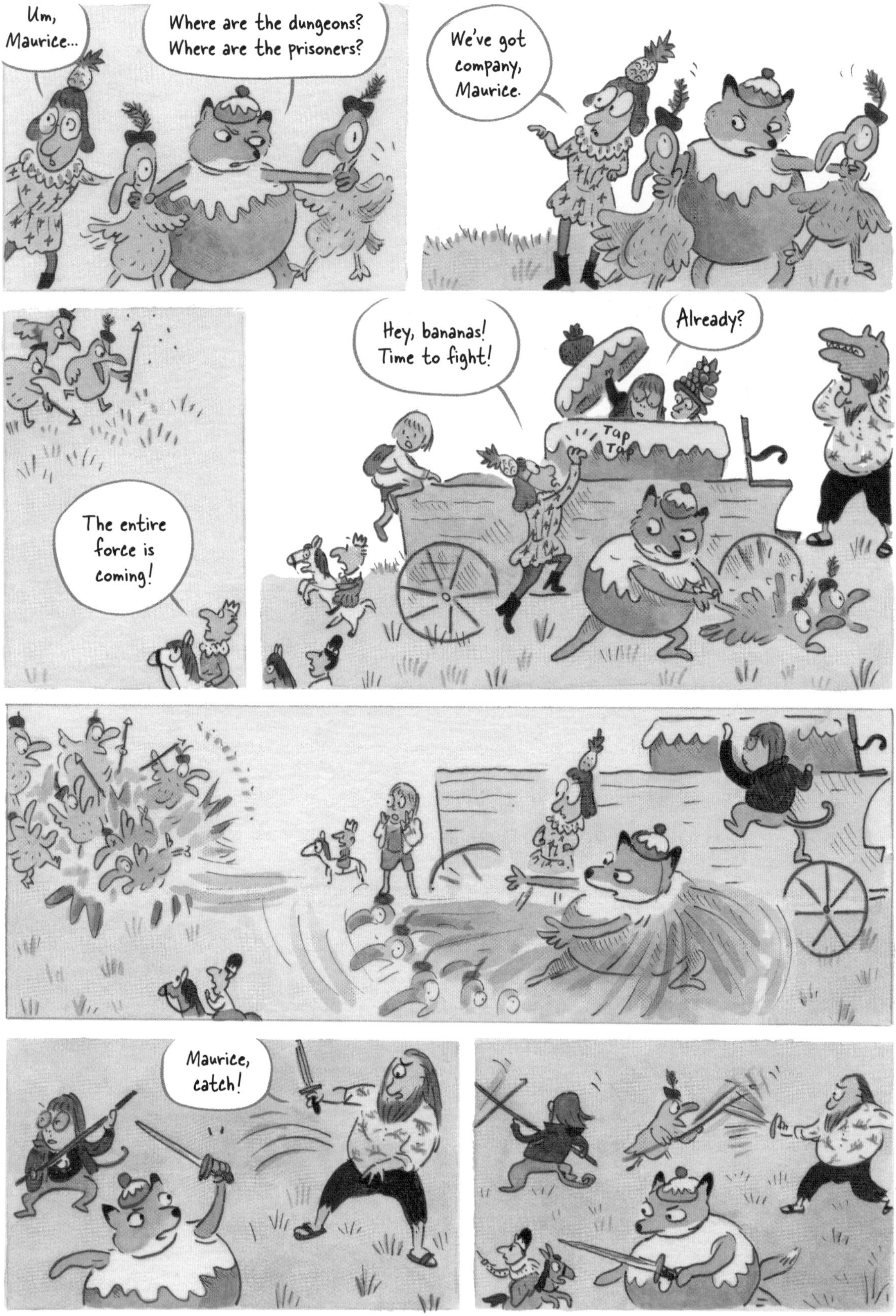
Um, Maurice...
Where are the dungeons? Where are the prisoners?
We've got company, Maurice.
The entire force is coming!
Hey, bananas! Time to fight!
Already?
Tap Tap
Maurice, catch!

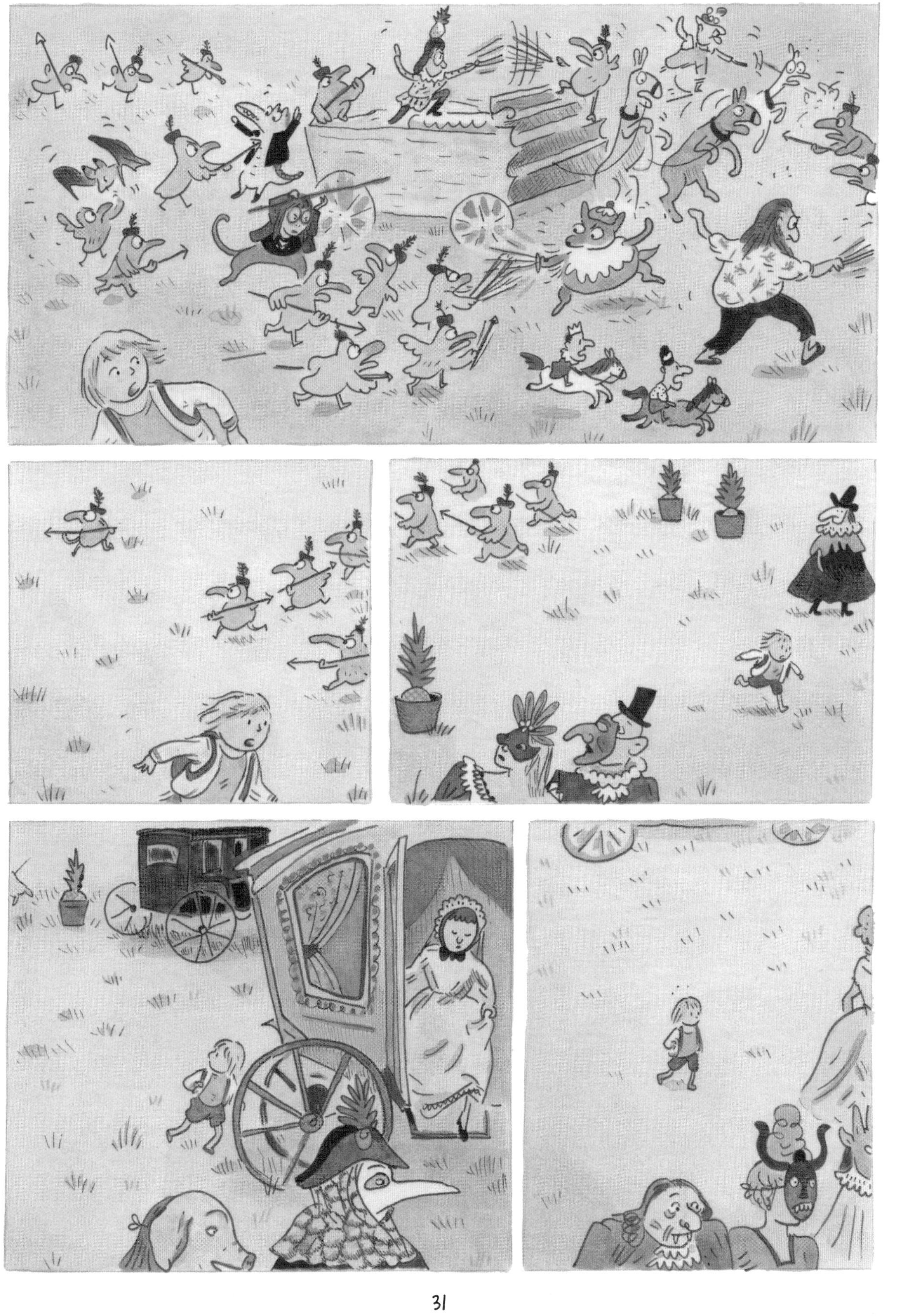

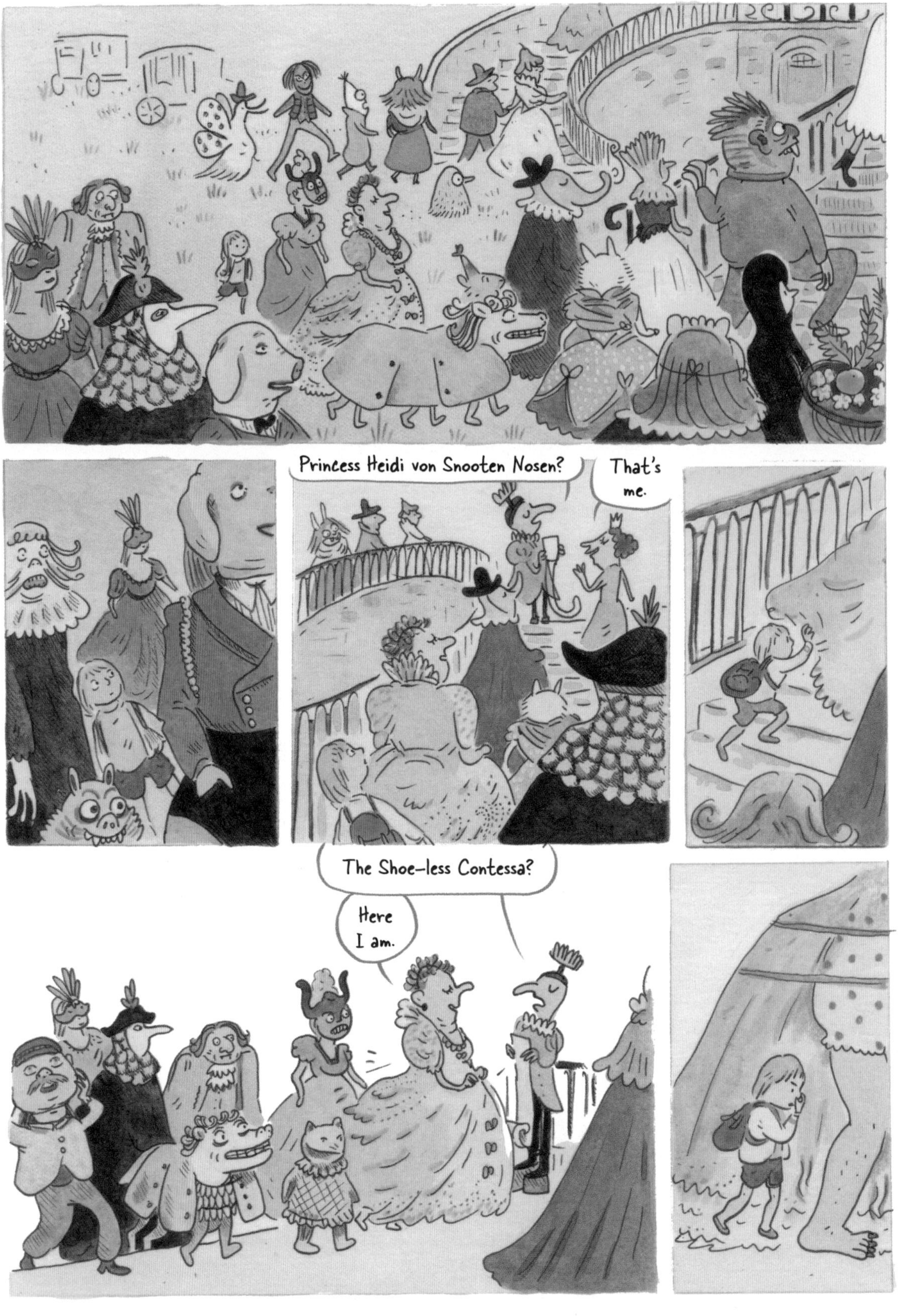
Princess Heidi von Snooten Nosen?
That's me.
The Shoe-less Contessa?
Here I am.

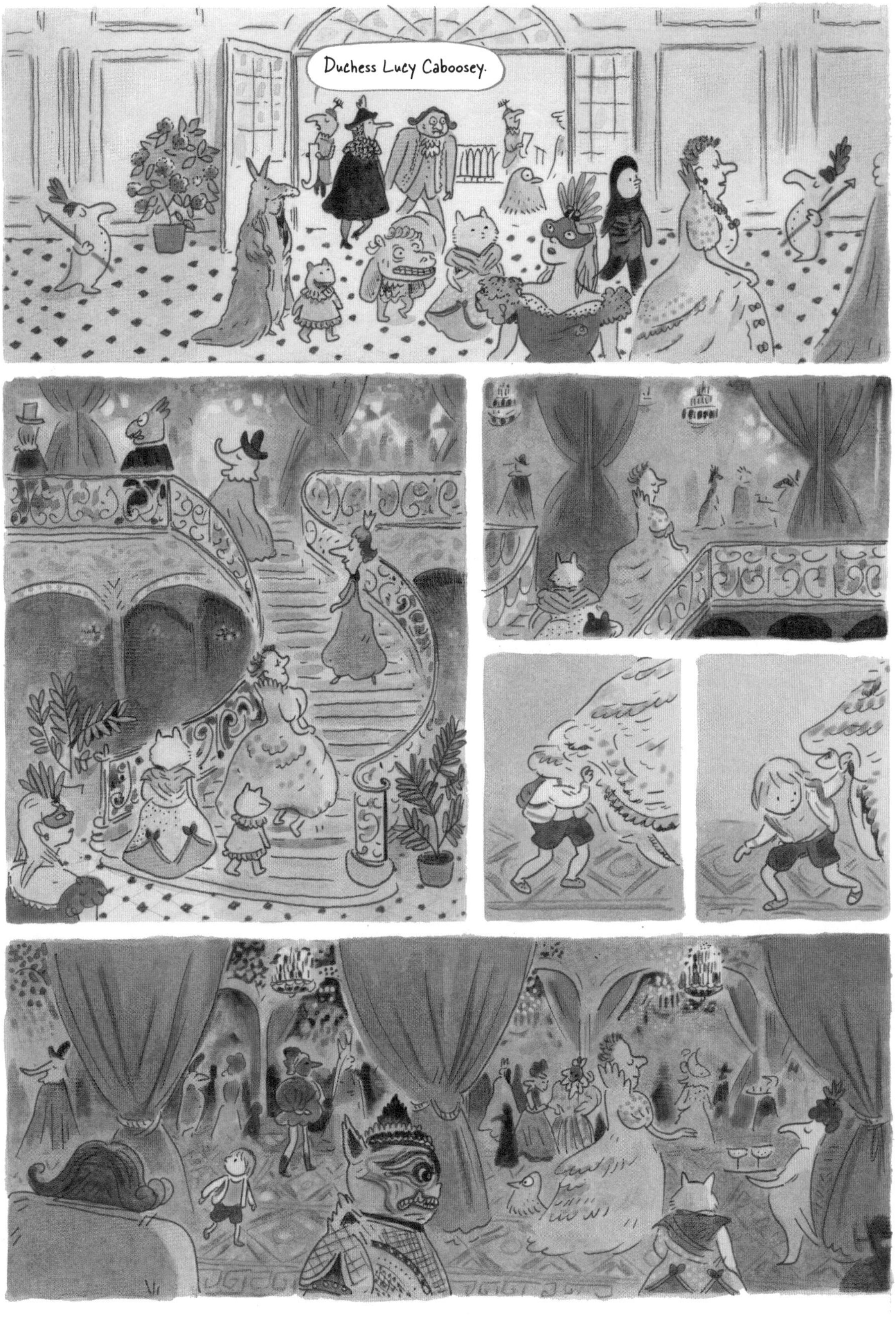
Duchess Lucy Caboosey.

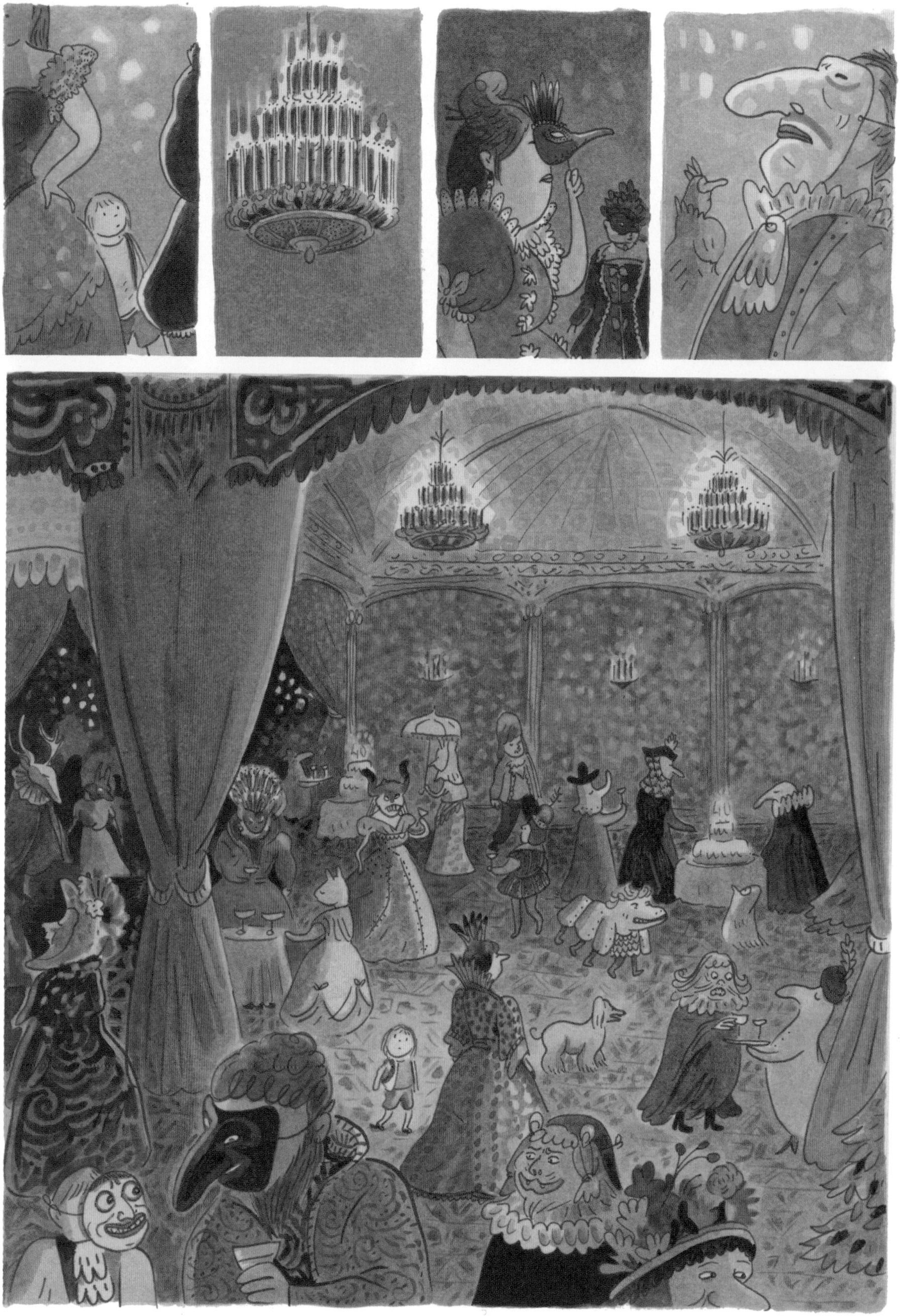

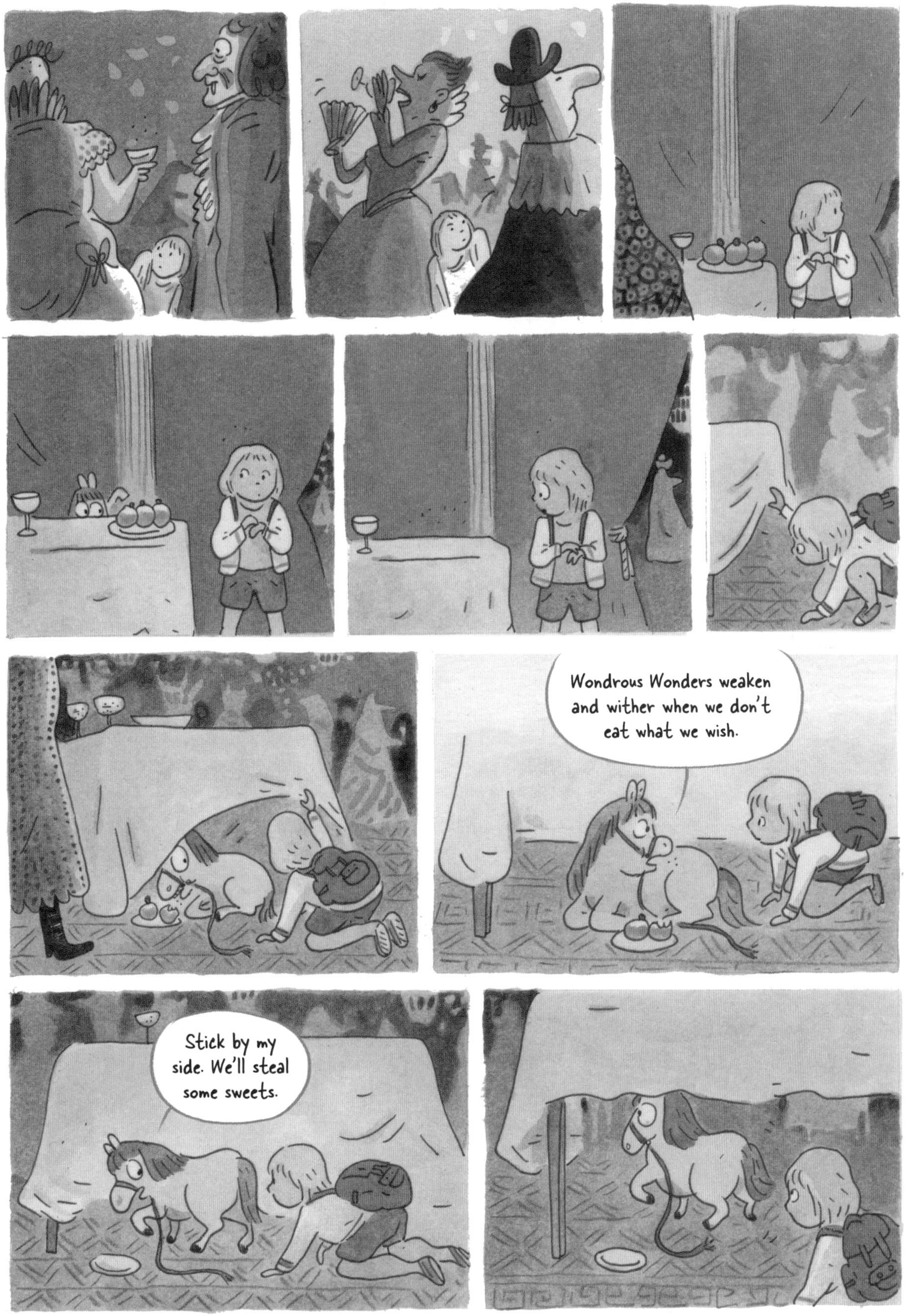
Wondrous Wonders weaken and wither when we don't eat what we wish.
Stick by my side. We'll steal some sweets.

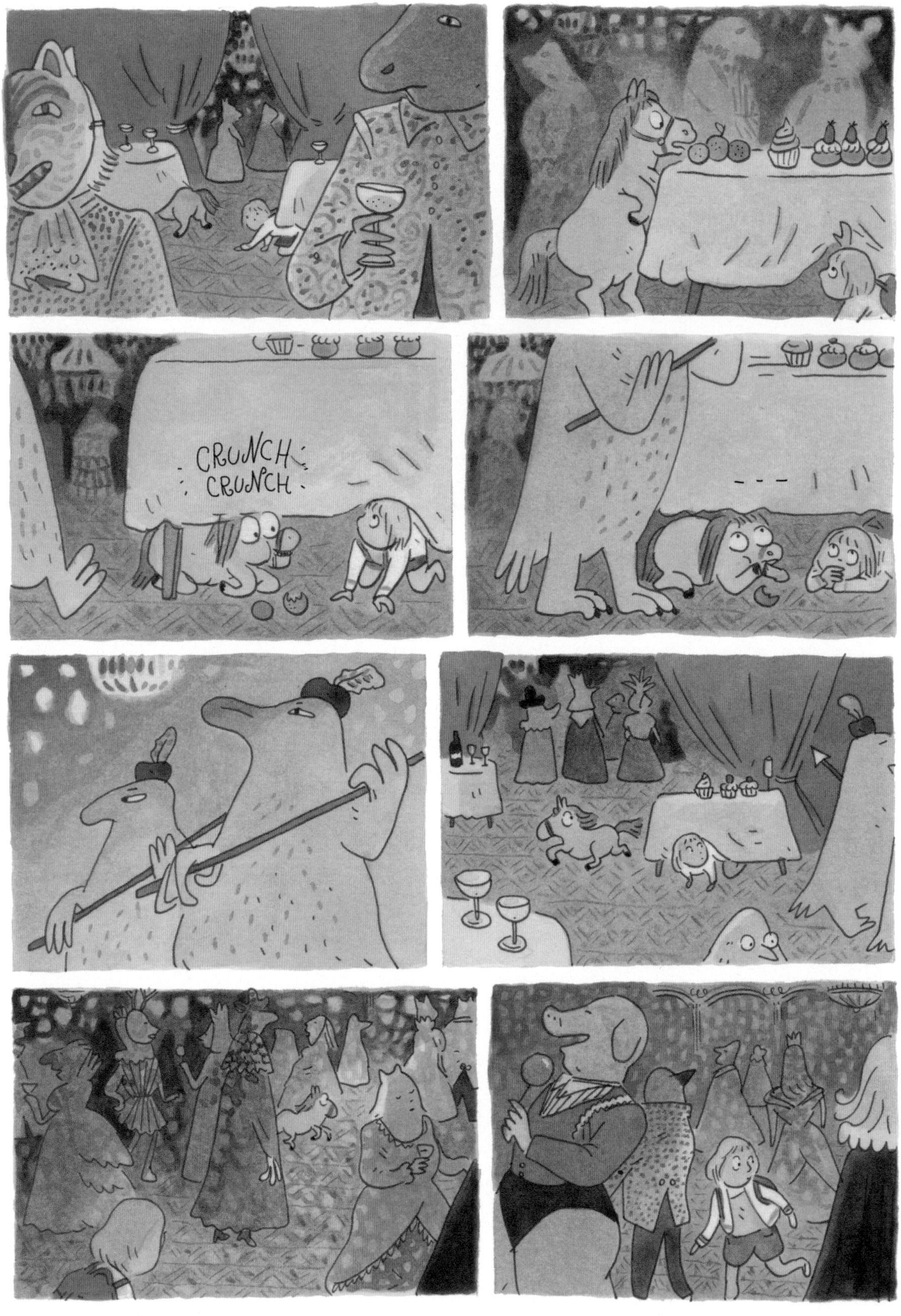
CRUNCH
CRUNCH
- - -

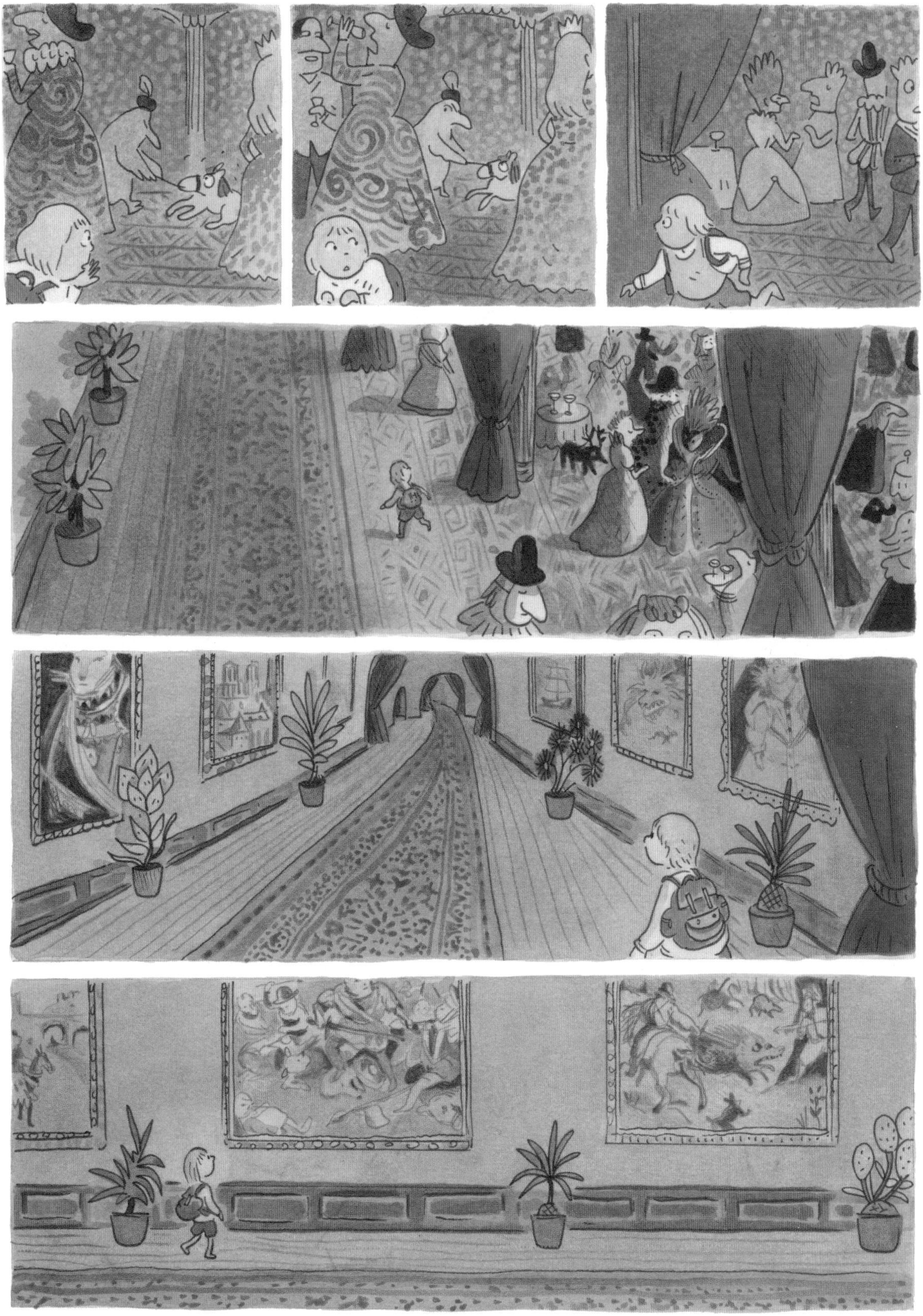

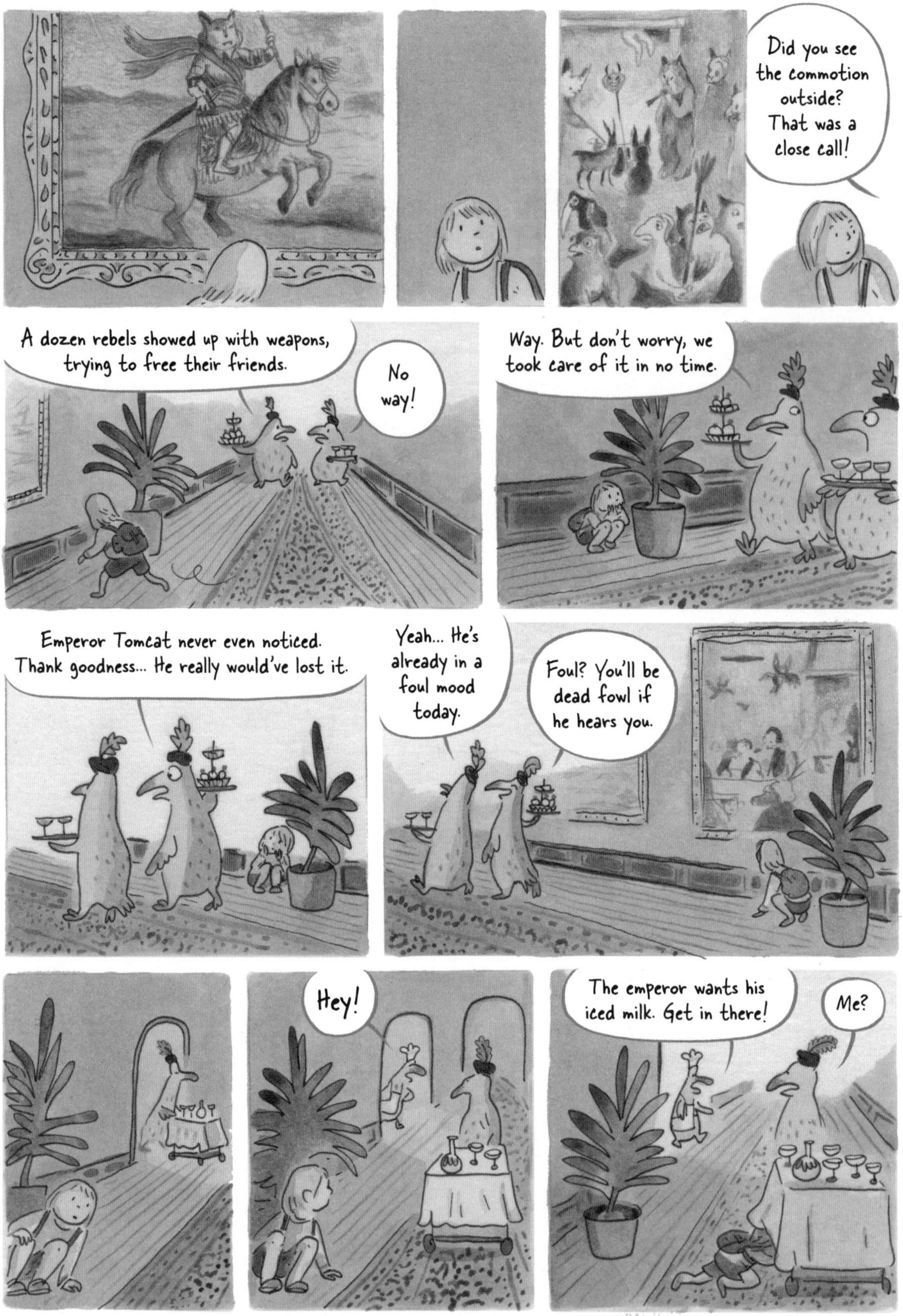
Did you see the commotion outside? That was a close call!
A dozen rebels showed up with weapons, trying to free their friends.
No way!
Way. But don't worry, we took care of it in no time.
Emperor Tomcat never even noticed. Thank goodness... He really would've lost it.
Yeah... He's already in a foul mood today.
Foul? You'll be dead fowl if he hears you.
Hey!
The emperor wants his iced milk. Get in there!
Me?

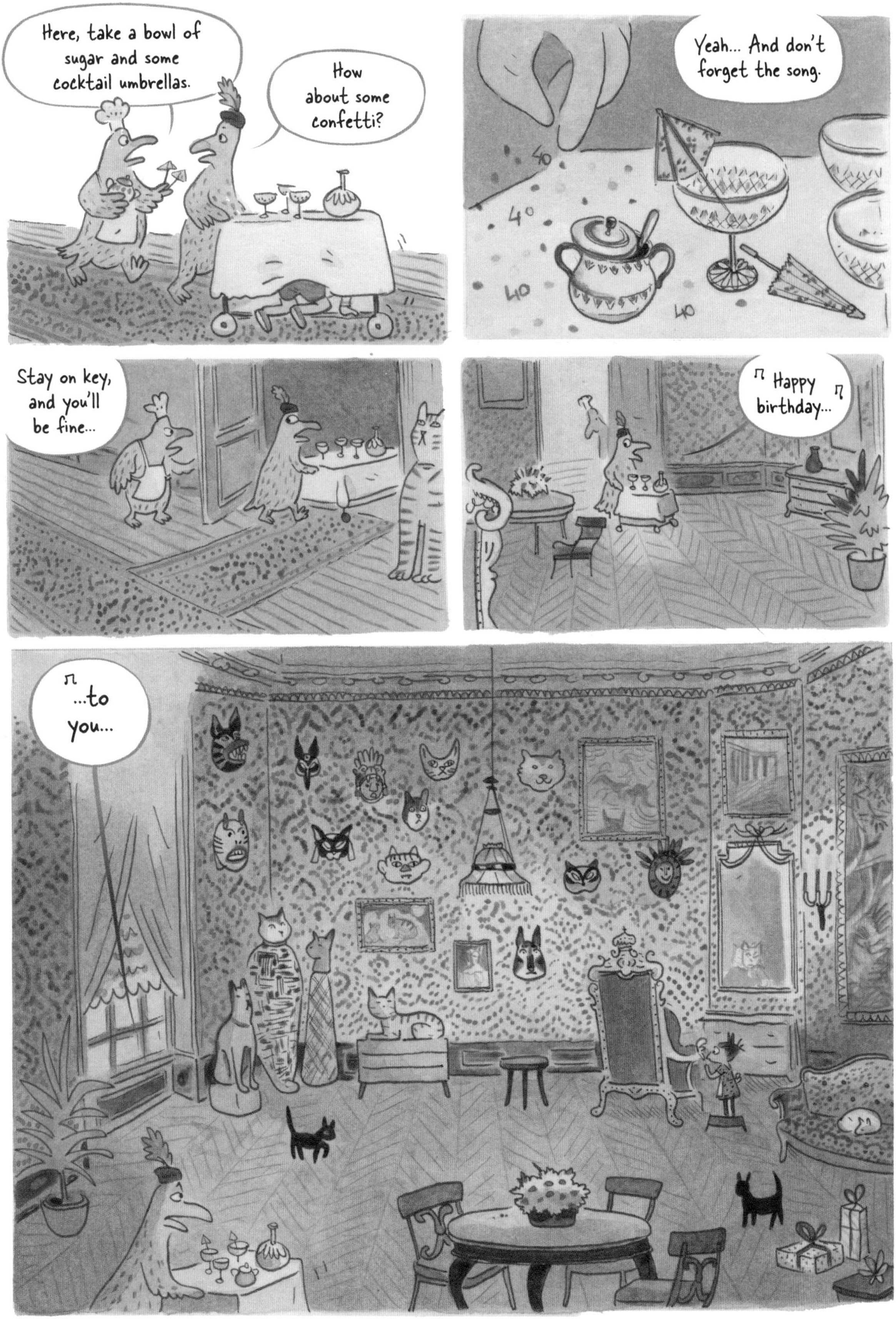

Here, take a bowl of sugar and some cocktail umbrellas.
How about some confetti?
Yeah... And don't forget the song.
Stay on key, and you'll be fine...
♫ Happy birthday... ♫
♫ ...to you...

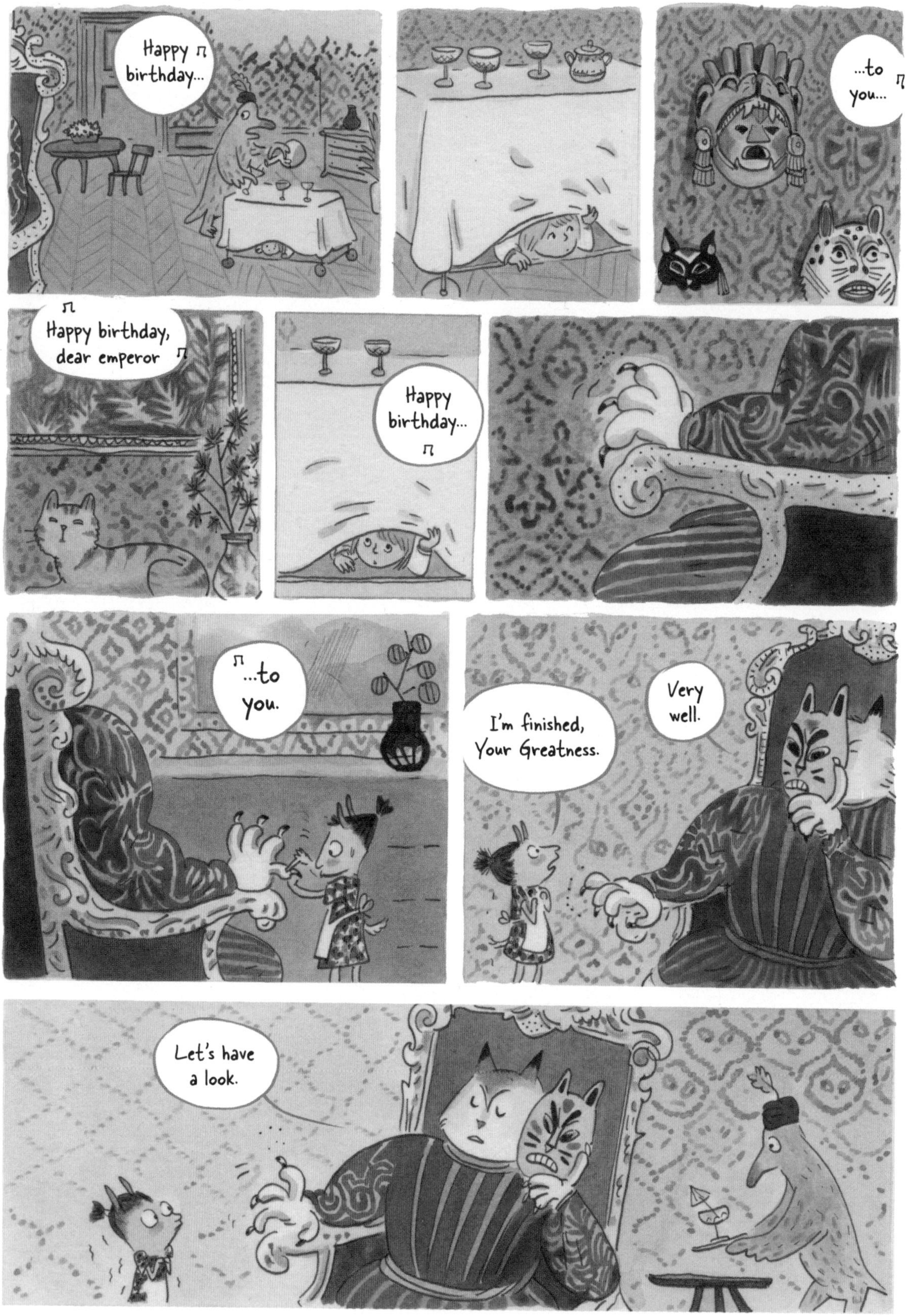
Happy birthday...
...to you...
Happy birthday, dear emperor
Happy birthday...
...to you.
I'm finished, Your Greatness.
Very well.
Let's have a look.

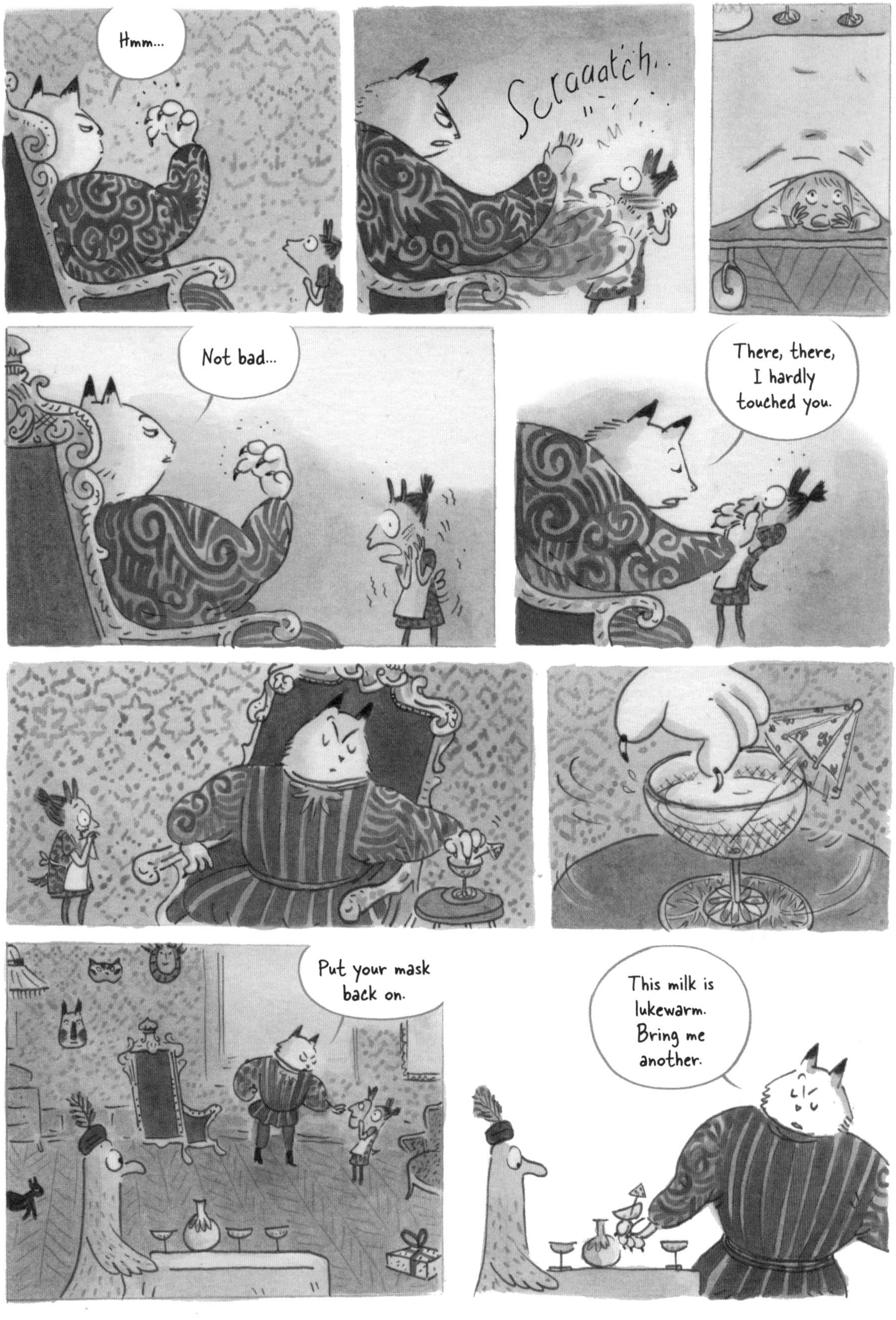
Hmm...
Scraaatch..
Not bad...
There, there, I hardly touched you.
Put your mask back on.
This milk is lukewarm. Bring me another.

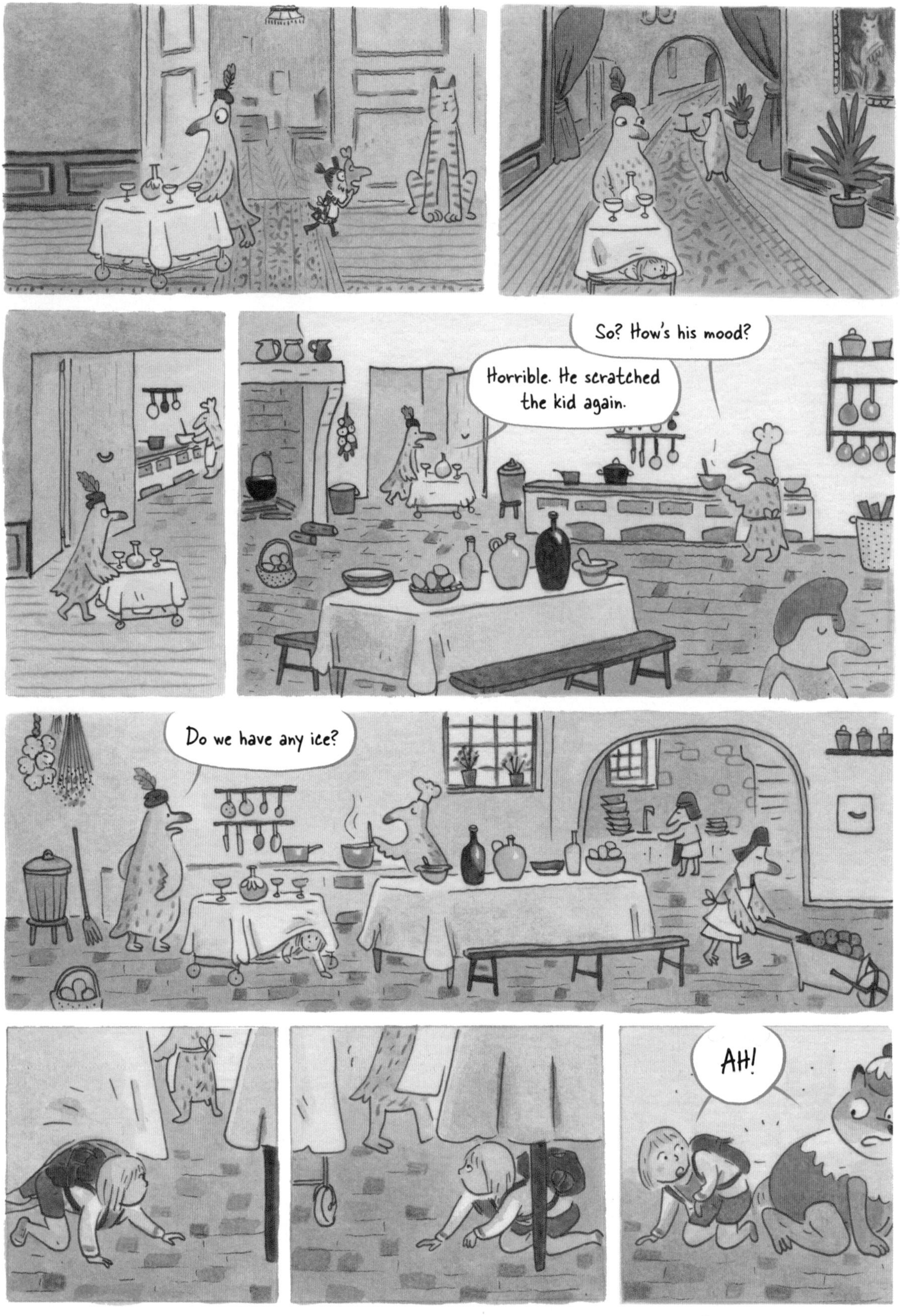
So? How's his mood?
Horrible. He scratched the kid again.
Do we have any ice?
AH!

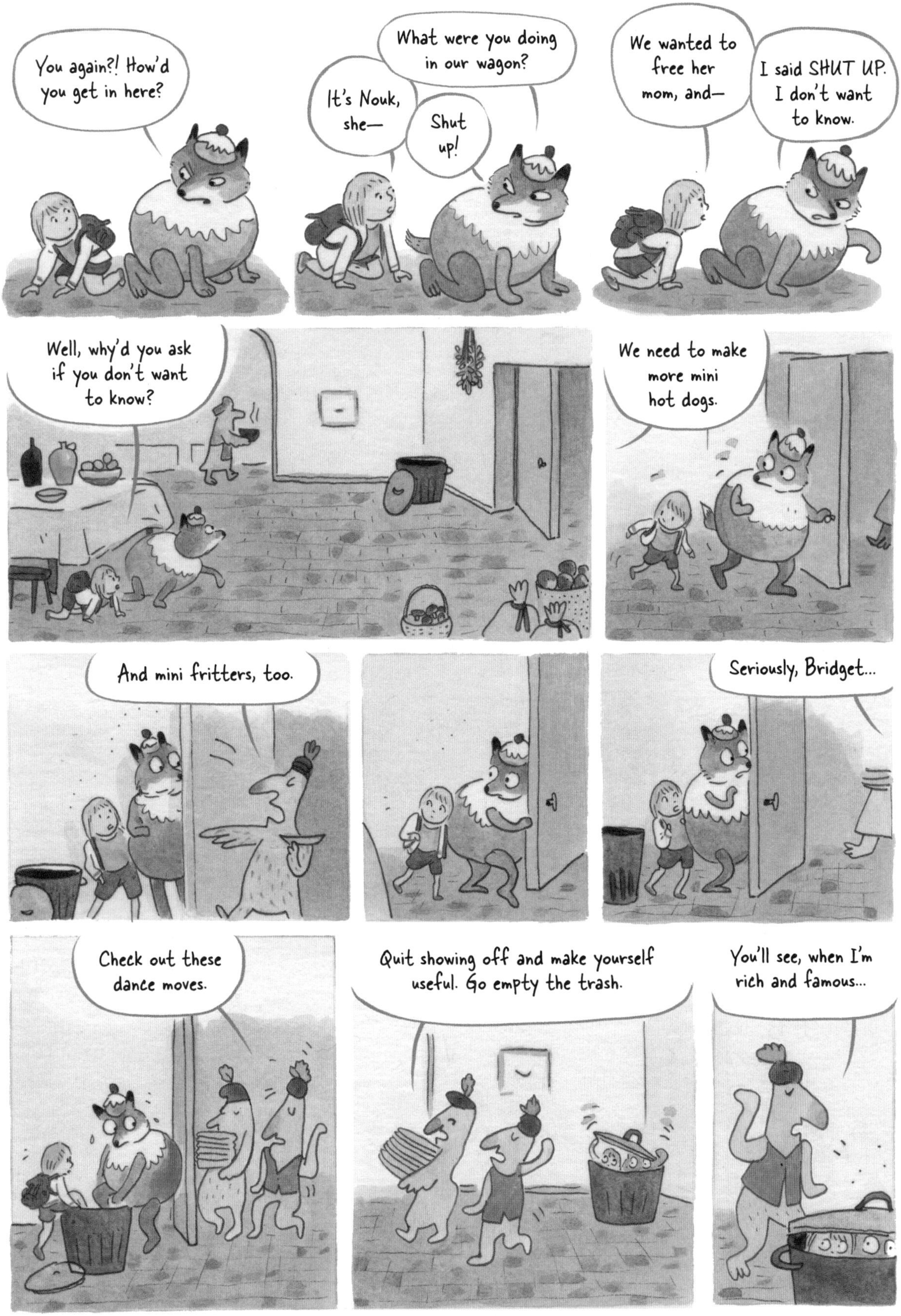
You again?! How'd you get in here?
What were you doing in our wagon?
It's Nouk, she—
Shut up!
We wanted to free her mom, and—
I said SHUT UP. I don't want to know.
Well, why'd you ask if you don't want to know?
We need to make more mini hot dogs.
And mini fritters, too.
Seriously, Bridget...
Check out these dance moves.
Quit showing off and make yourself useful. Go empty the trash.
You'll see, when I'm rich and famous...

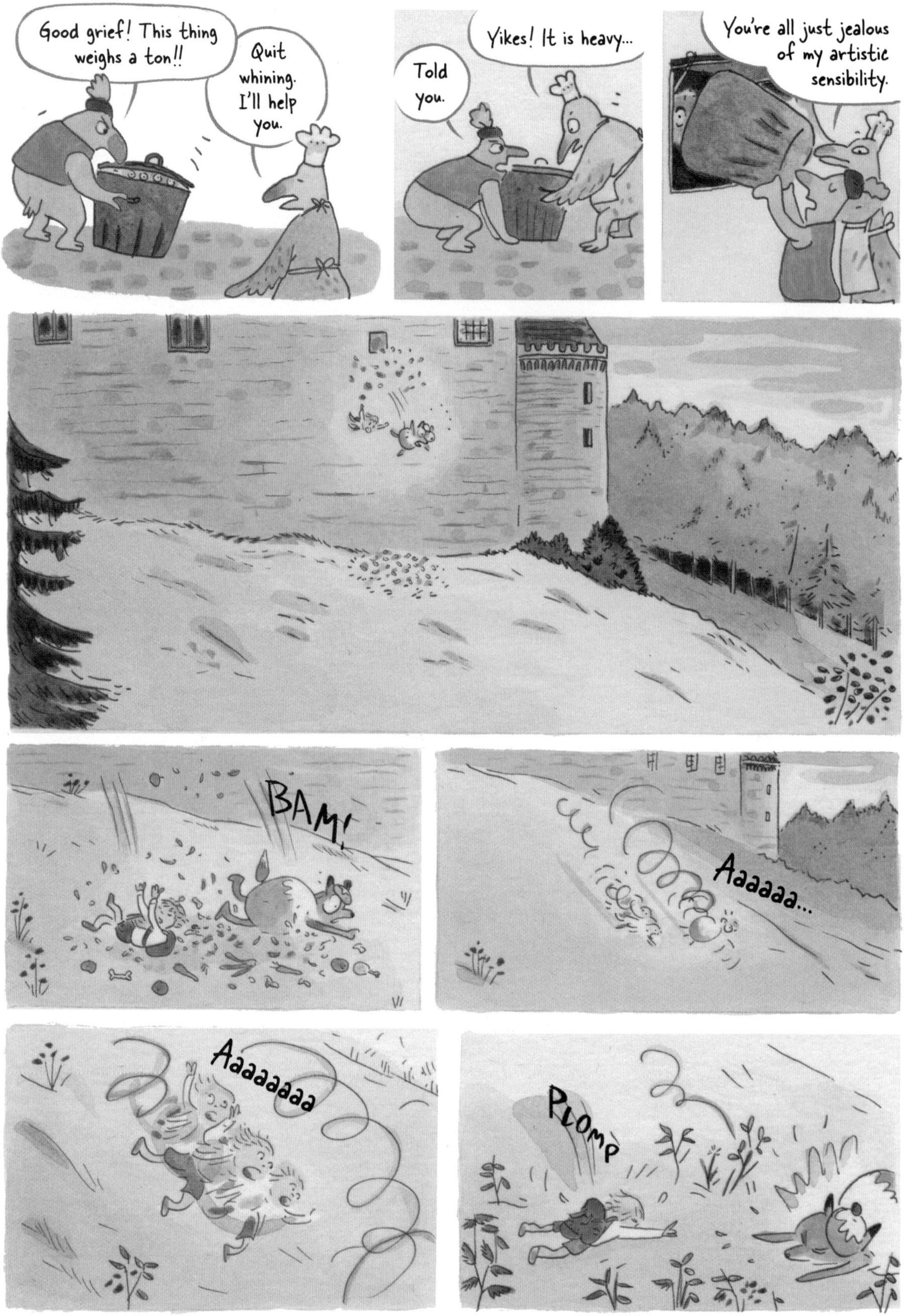
Good grief! This thing weighs a ton!!
Quit whining. I'll help you.
Yikes! It is heavy...
Told you.
You're all just jealous of my artistic sensibility.
BAM!
Aaaaaa...
Aaaaaaaa
PLOMP

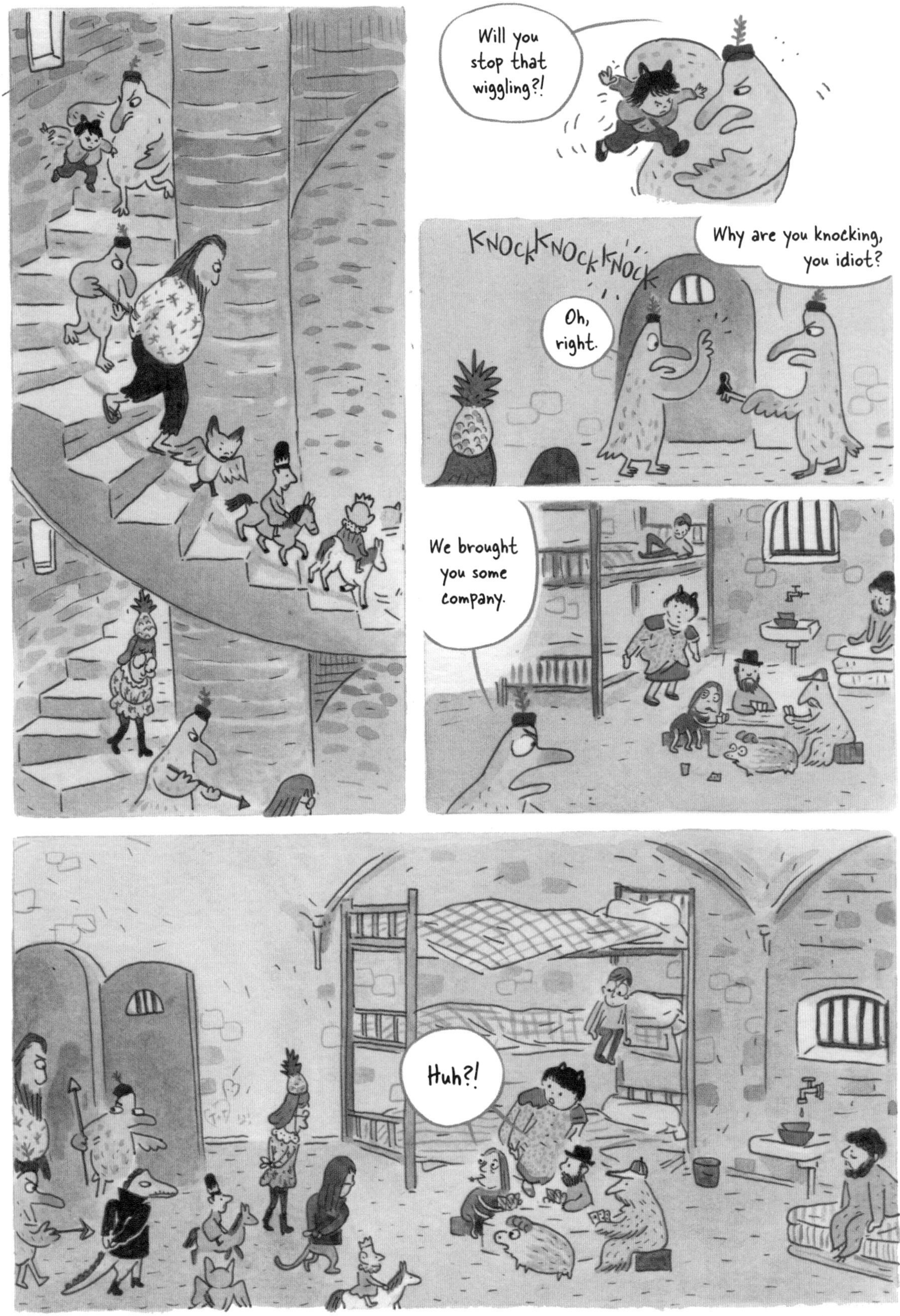
Will you stop that wiggling?!
KNOCK KNOCK KNOCK
Why are you knocking, you idiot?
Oh, right.
We brought you some company.
Huh?!

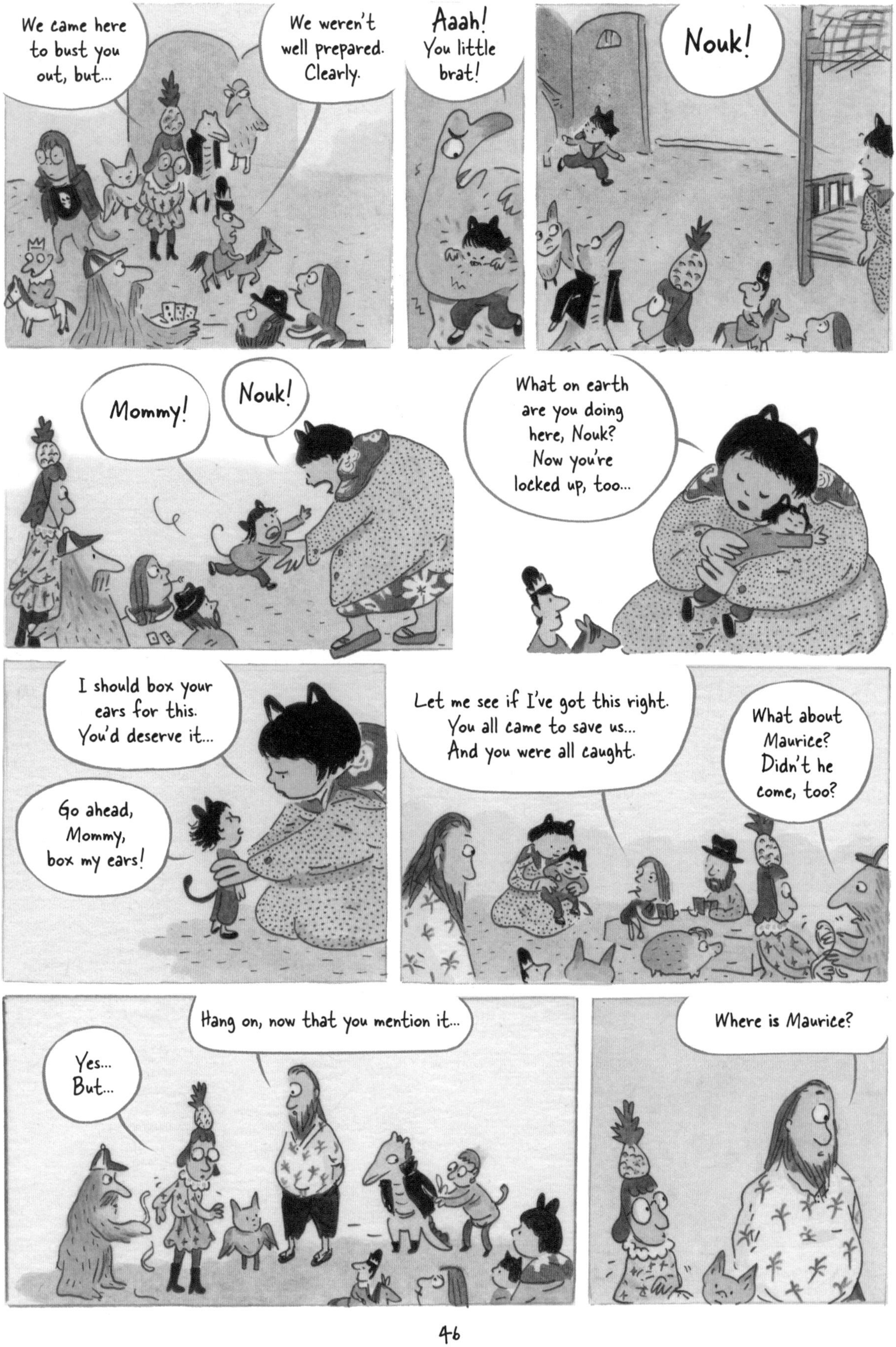

We came here to bust you out, but...
We weren't well prepared. Clearly.
Aaah! You little brat!
Nouk!
Mommy!
Nouk!
What on earth are you doing here, Nouk? Now you're locked up, too...
I should box your ears for this. You'd deserve it...
Go ahead, Mommy, box my ears!
Let me see if I've got this right. You all came to save us... And you were all caught.
What about Maurice? Didn't he come, too?
Yes... But...
Hang on, now that you mention it...
Where is Maurice?

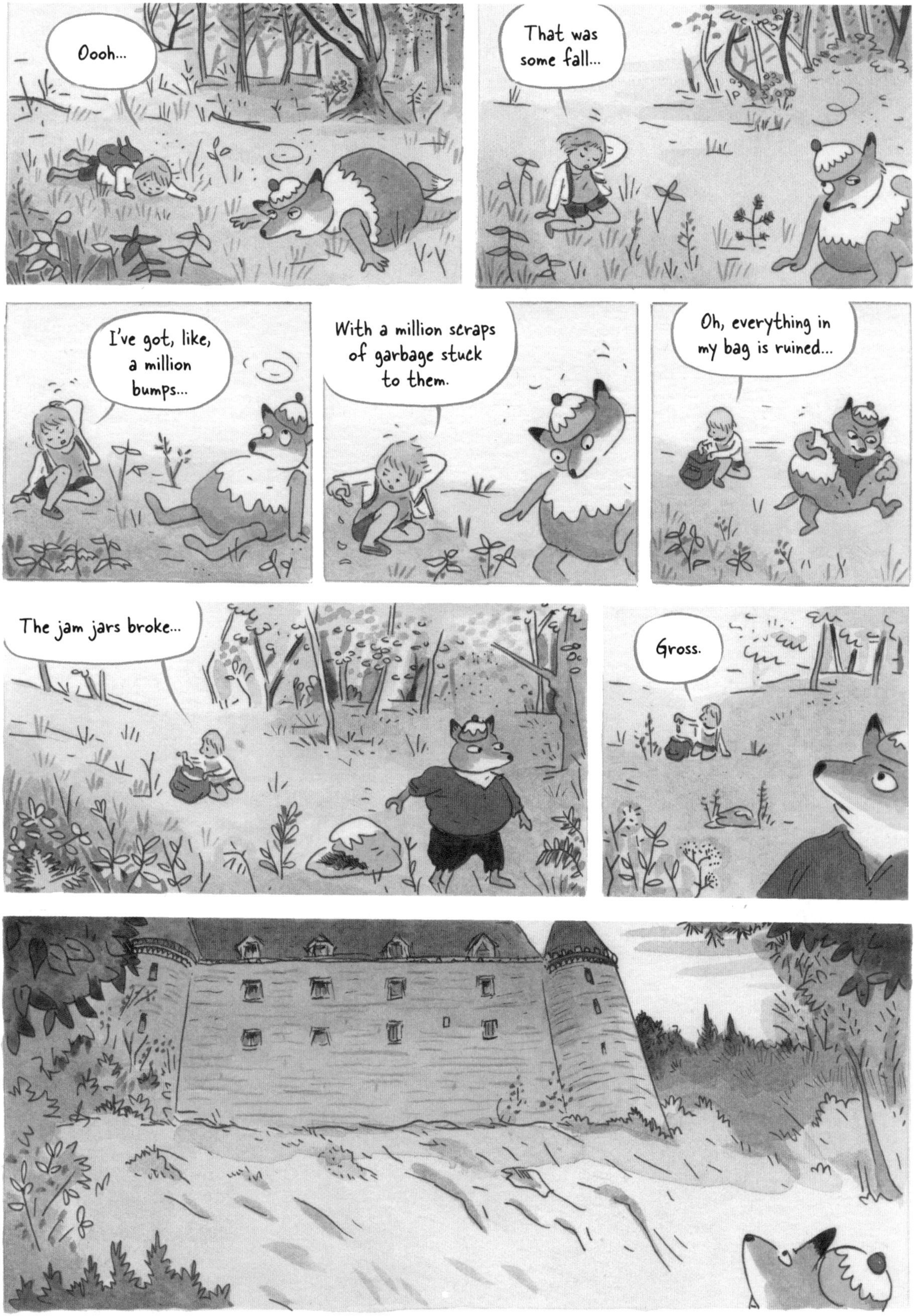
Oooh...
That was some fall...
I've got, like, a million bumps...
With a million scraps of garbage stuck to them.
Oh, everything in my bag is ruined...
The jam jars broke...
Gross.

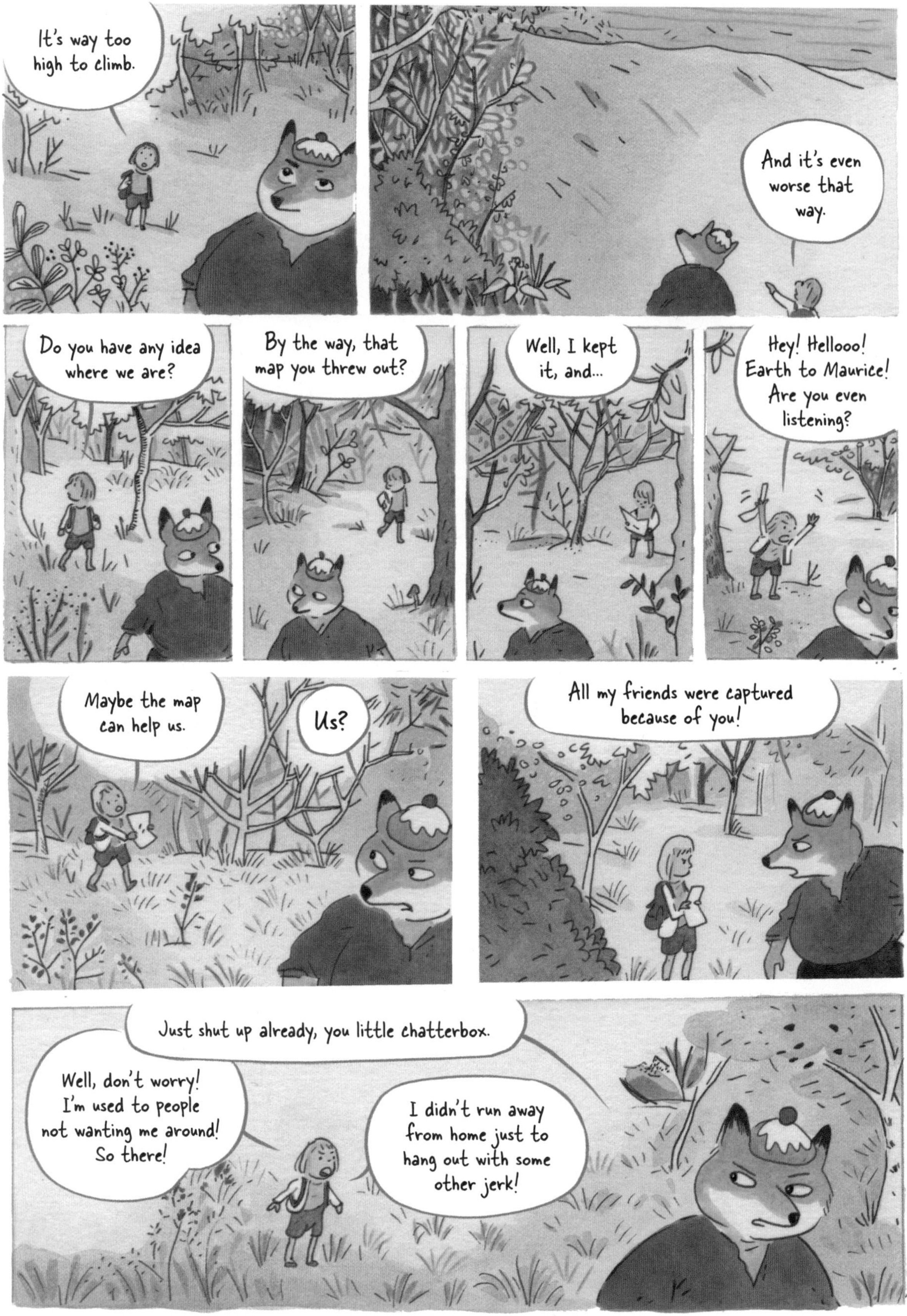

It's way too high to climb.
And it's even worse that way.
Do you have any idea where we are?
By the way, that map you threw out?
Well, I kept it, and...
Hey! Hellooo! Earth to Maurice! Are you even listening?
Maybe the map can help us.
Us?
All my friends were captured because of you!
Just shut up already, you little chatterbox.
Well, don't worry! I'm used to people not wanting me around! So there!
I didn't run away from home just to hang out with some other jerk!

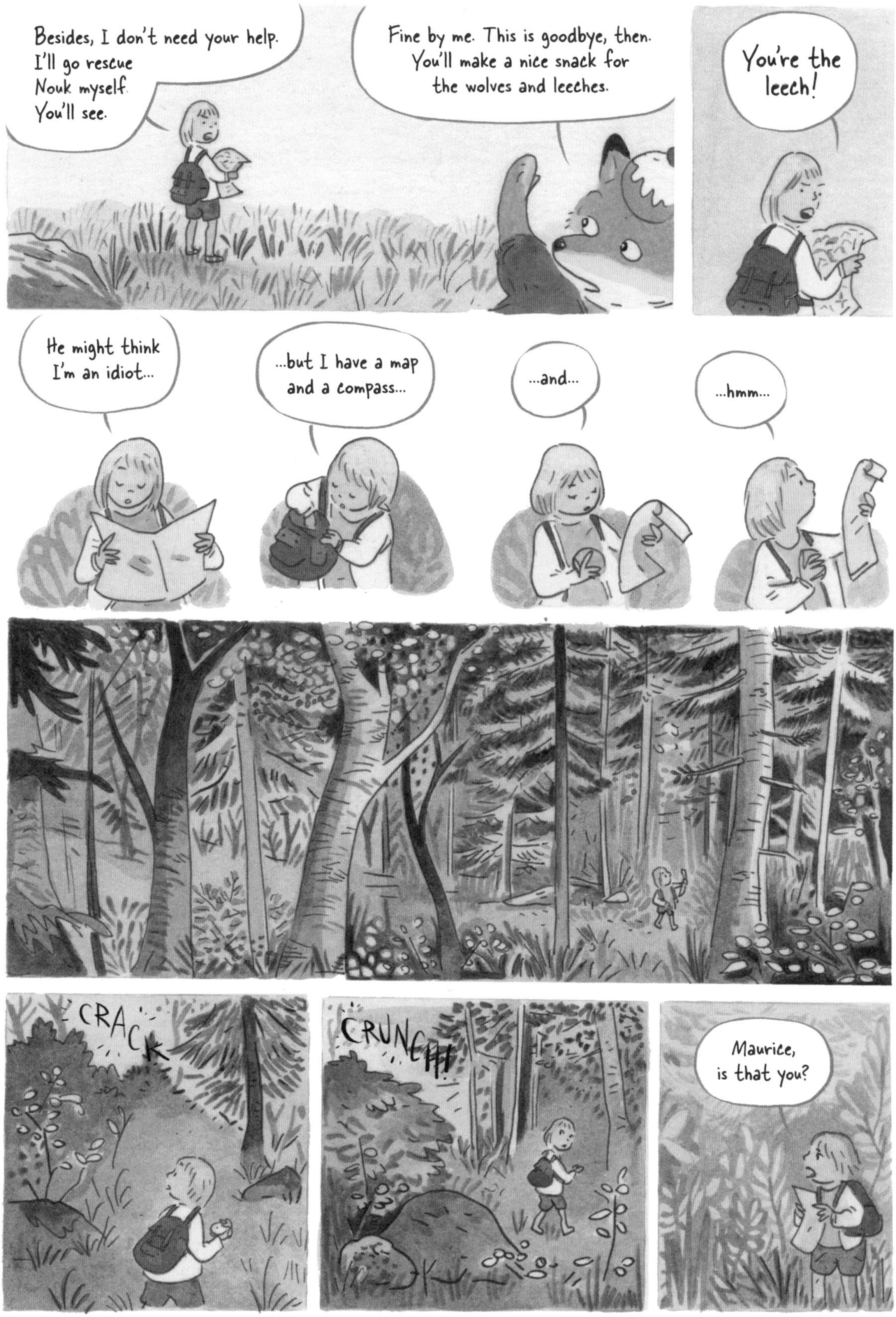
Besides, I don't need your help. I'll go rescue Nouk myself. You'll see.
Fine by me. This is goodbye, then. You'll make a nice snack for the wolves and leeches.
You're the leech!
He might think I'm an idiot...
...but I have a map and a compass...
...and...
...hmm...
CRACK
CRUNCH!
Maurice, is that you?

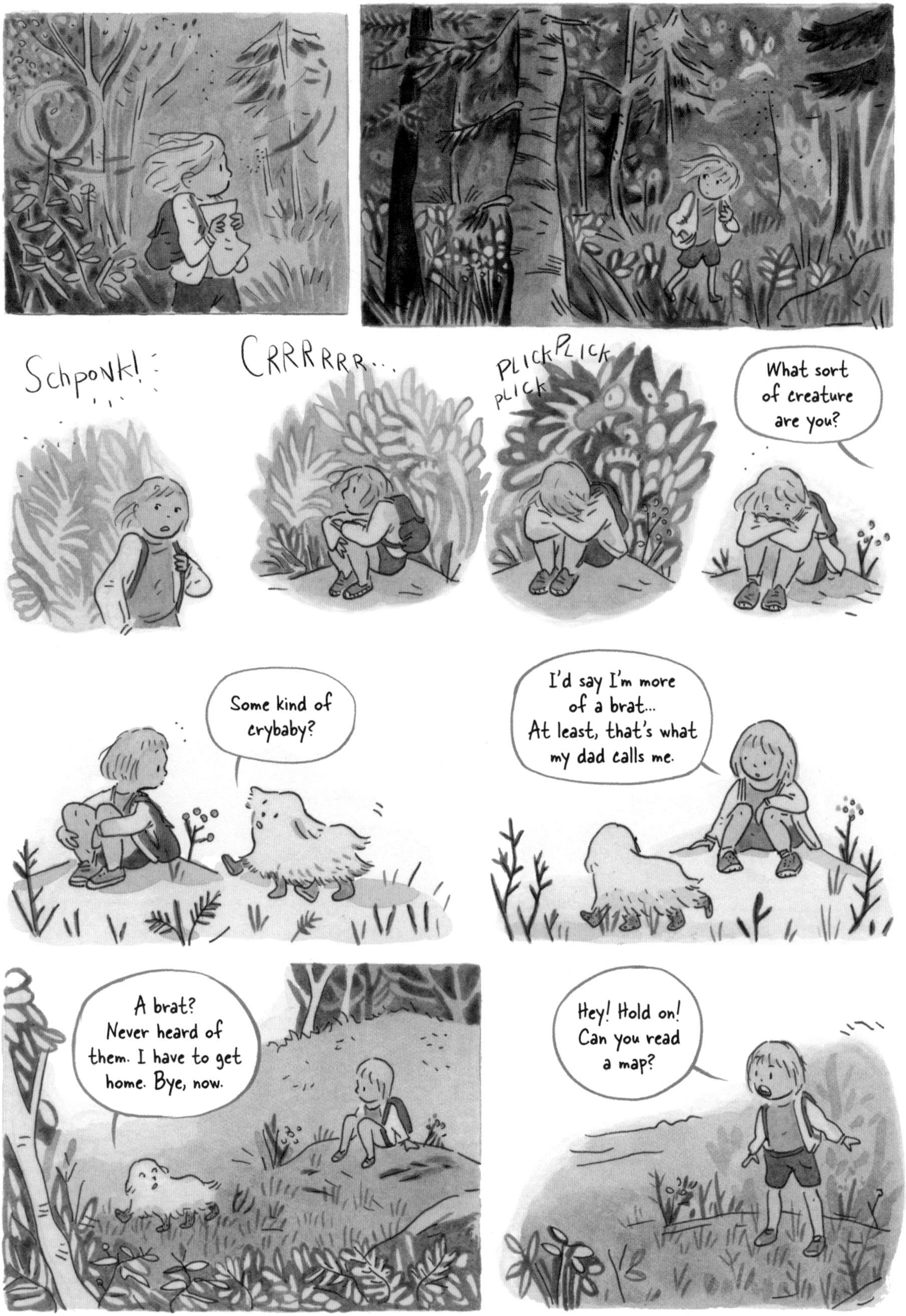
SCHPONK!
CRRRRRR...
PLICK PLICK PLICK
What sort of creature are you?
Some kind of crybaby?
I'd say I'm more of a brat... At least, that's what my dad calls me.
A brat? Never heard of them. I have to get home. Bye, now.
Hey! Hold on! Can you read a map?

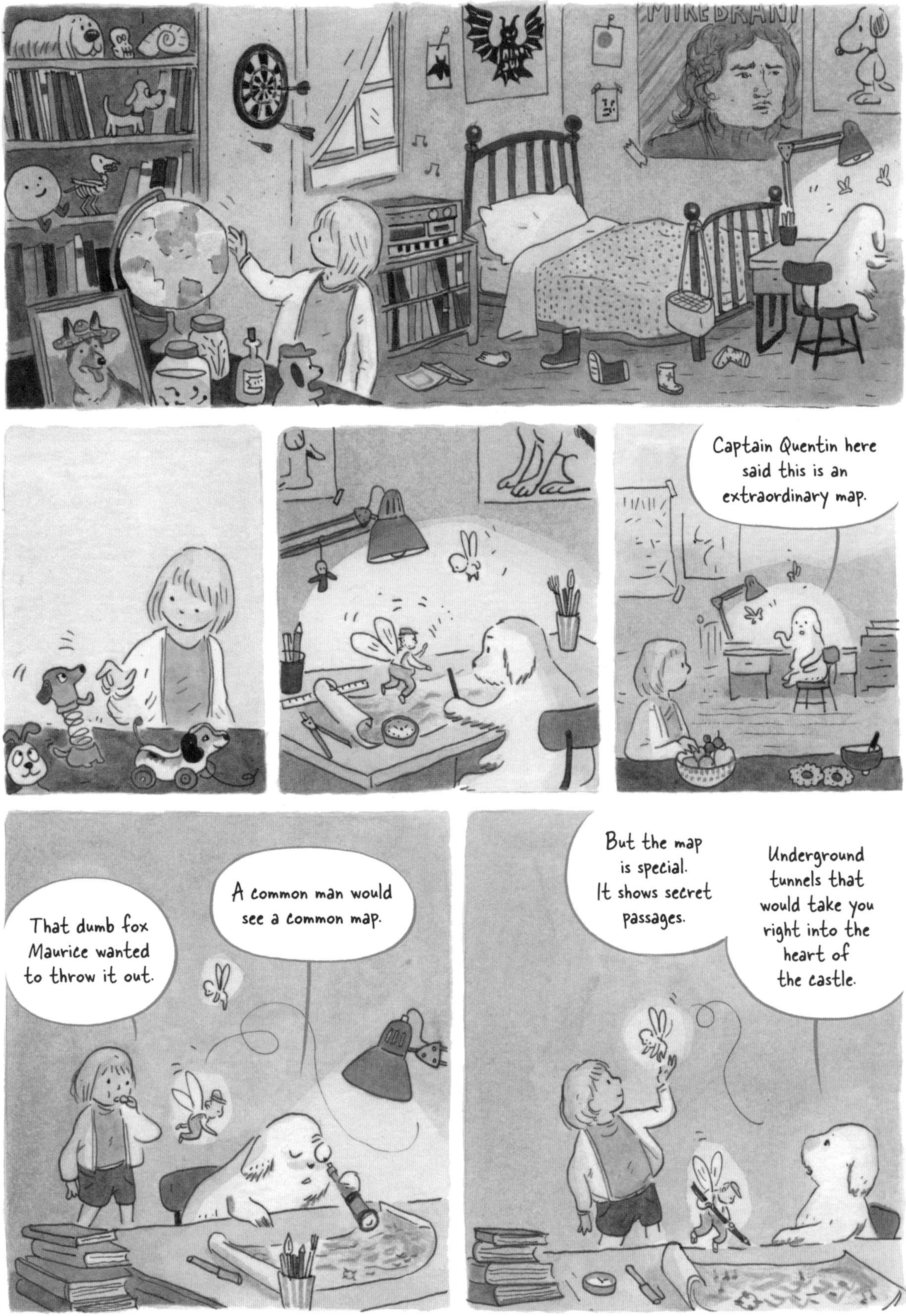
MIKE BRANT
Captain Quentin here said this is an extraordinary map.
That dumb fox Maurice wanted to throw it out.
A common man would see a common map.
But the map is special. It shows secret passages.
Underground tunnels that would take you right into the heart of the castle.

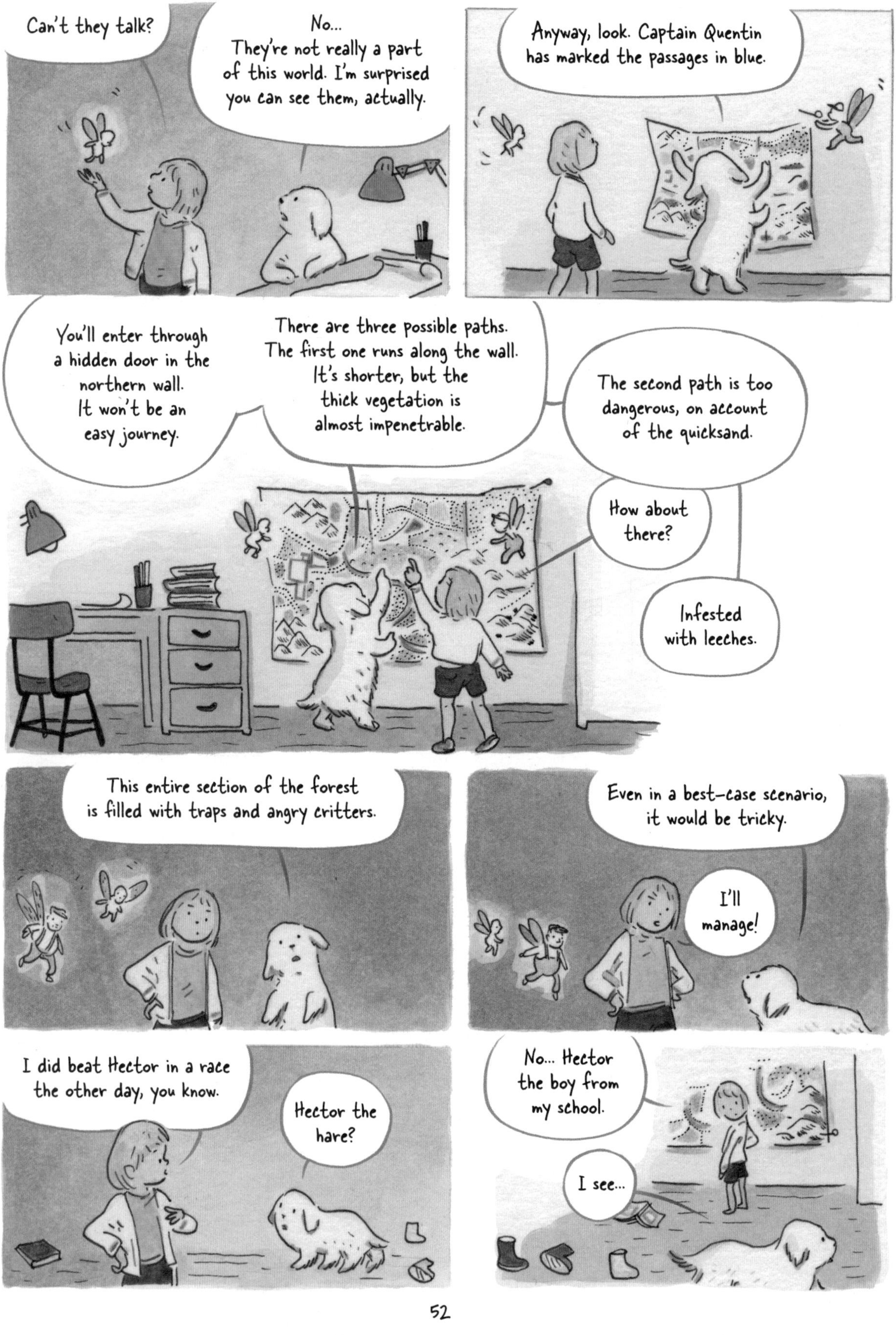
Can't they talk?
No... They're not really a part of this world. I'm surprised you can see them, actually.
Anyway, look. Captain Quentin has marked the passages in blue.
You'll enter through a hidden door in the northern wall. It won't be an easy journey.
There are three possible paths. The first one runs along the wall. It's shorter, but the thick vegetation is almost impenetrable.
The second path is too dangerous, on account of the quicksand.
How about there?
Infested with leeches.
This entire section of the forest is filled with traps and angry critters.
Even in a best-case scenario, it would be tricky.
I'll manage!
I did beat Hector in a race the other day, you know.
Hector the hare?
No... Hector the boy from my school.
I see...

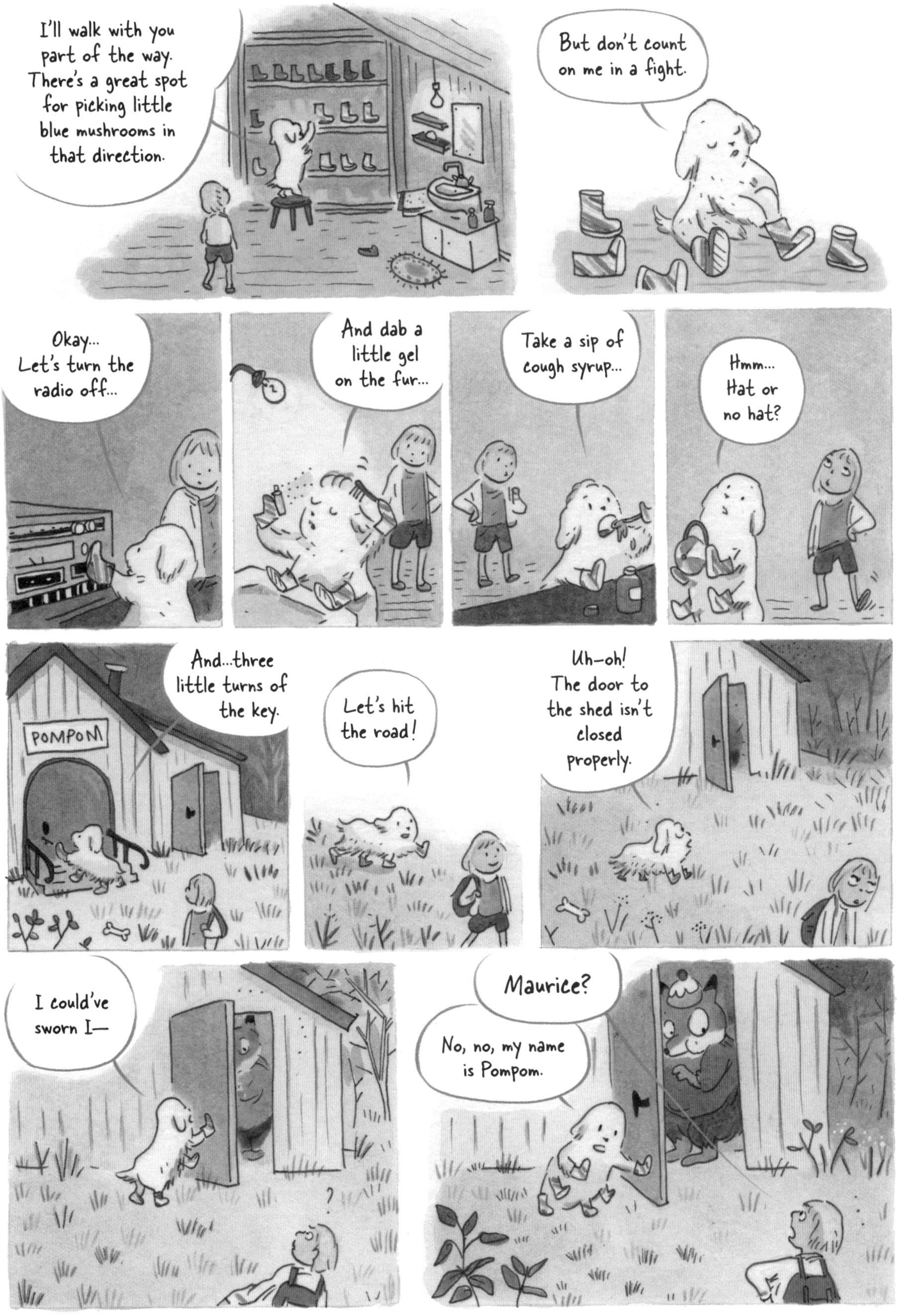
I'll walk with you part of the way. There's a great spot for picking little blue mushrooms in that direction.
But don't count on me in a fight.
Okay... Let's turn the radio off...
And dab a little gel on the fur...
Take a sip of cough syrup...
Hmm... Hat or no hat?
POMPOM
And...three little turns of the key.
Let's hit the road!
Uh-oh! The door to the shed isn't closed properly.
I could've sworn I—
?
Maurice?
No, no, my name is Pompom.

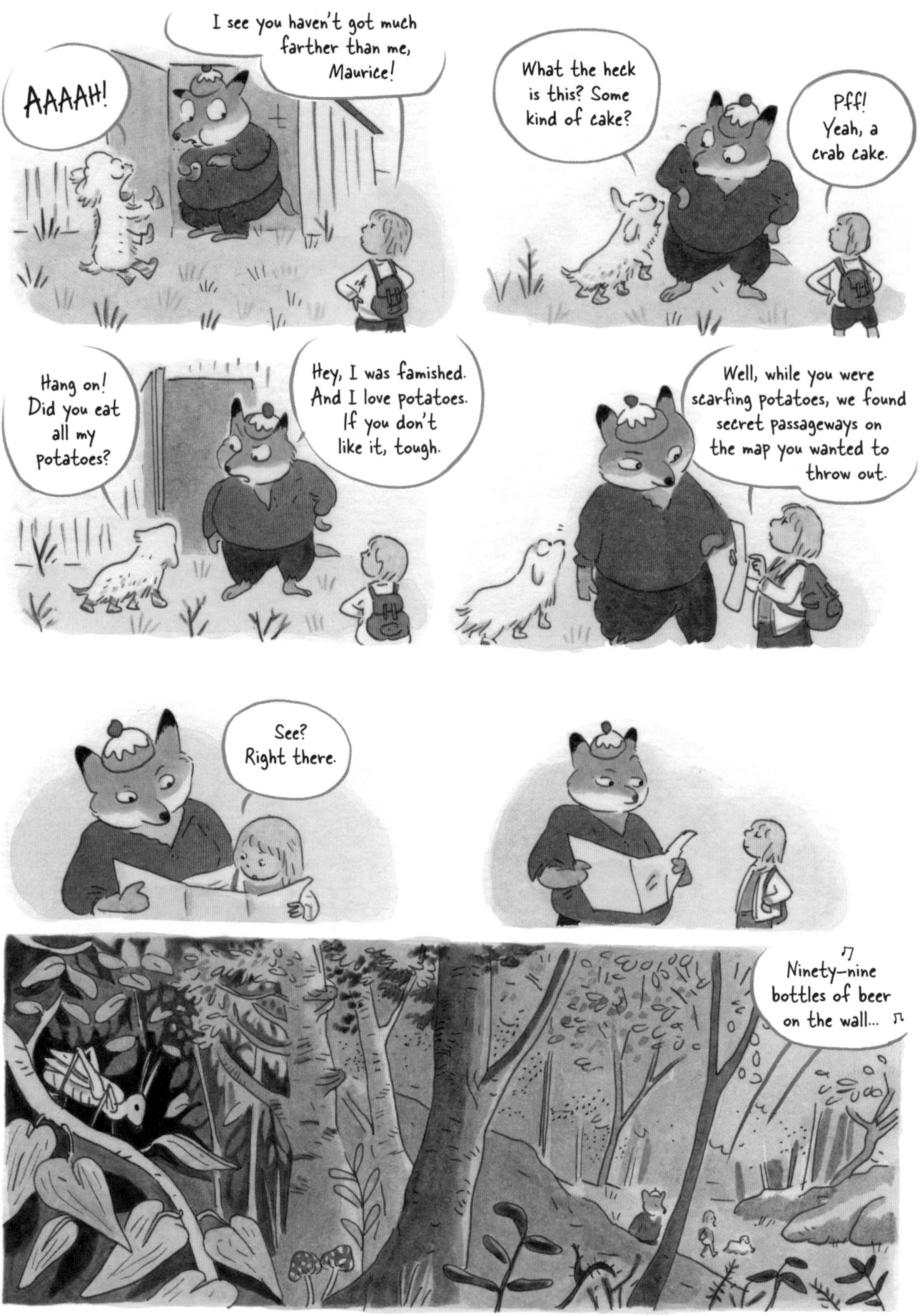

AAAAH!
I see you haven't got much farther than me, Maurice!
What the heck is this? Some kind of cake?
Pff! Yeah, a crab cake.
Hang on! Did you eat all my potatoes?
Hey, I was famished. And I love potatoes. If you don't like it, tough.
Well, while you were scarfing potatoes, we found secret passageways on the map you wanted to throw out.
See? Right there.
Ninety-nine bottles of beer on the wall...

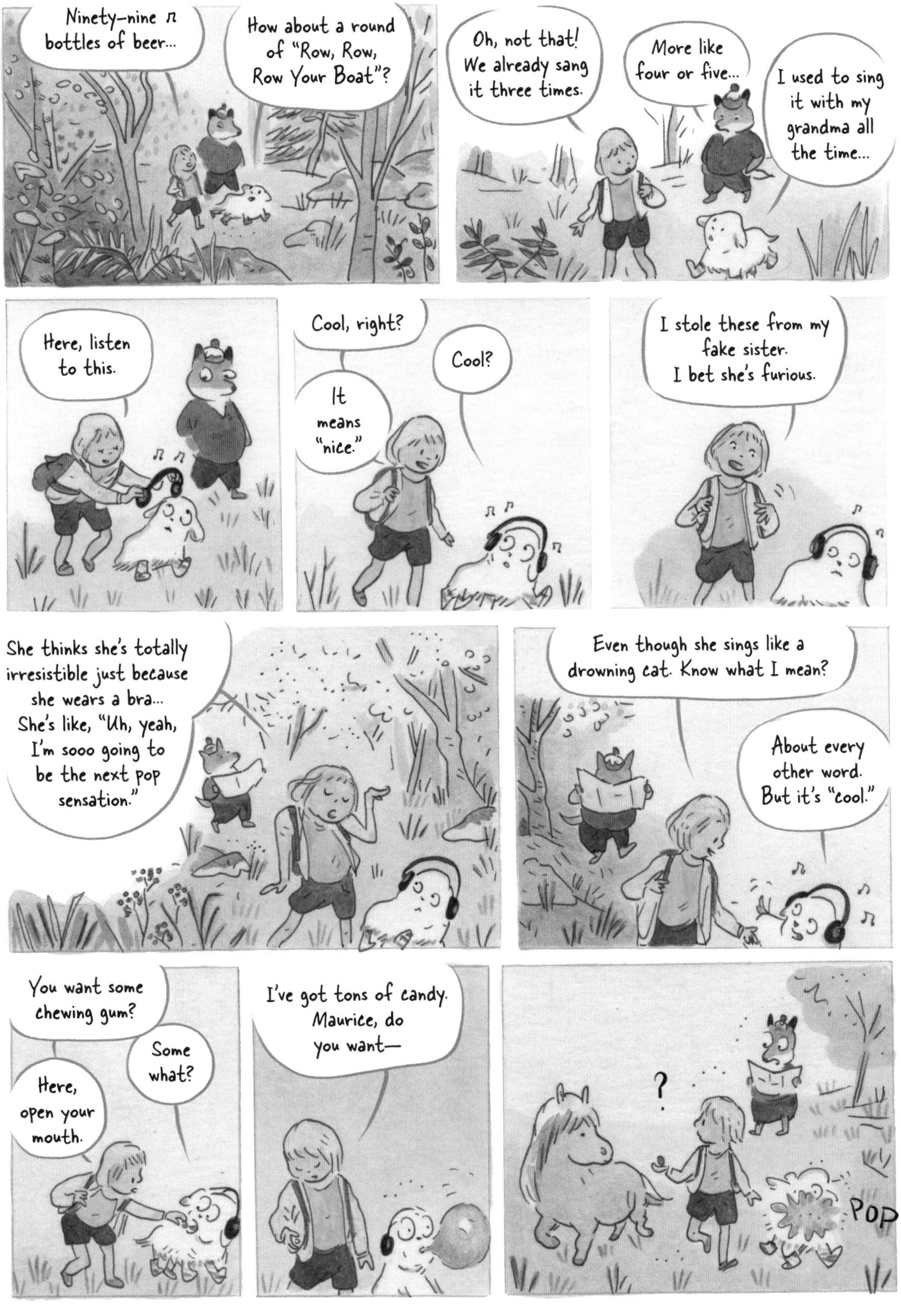
Ninety-nine ♫ bottles of beer...
How about a round of "Row, Row, Row Your Boat"?
Oh, not that! We already sang it three times.
More like four or five...
I used to sing it with my grandma all the time...
Here, listen to this.
Cool, right?
Cool?
It means "nice."
I stole these from my fake sister. I bet she's furious.
She thinks she's totally irresistible just because she wears a bra... She's like, "Uh, yeah, I'm sooo going to be the next pop sensation."
Even though she sings like a drowning cat. Know what I mean?
About every other word. But it's "cool."
You want some chewing gum?
Some what?
Here, open your mouth.
I've got tons of candy. Maurice, do you want—
?
POP

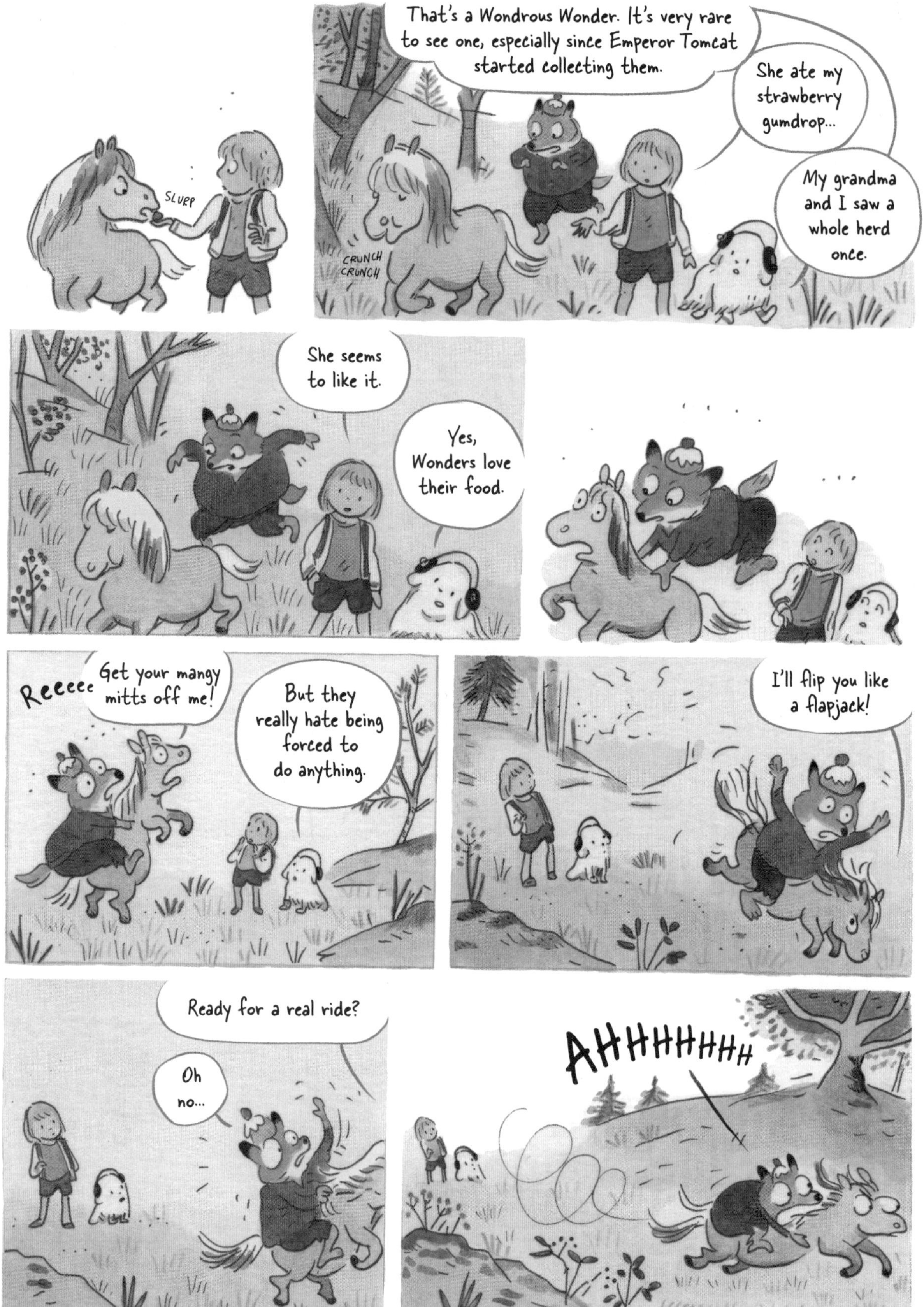
SLURP
CRUNCH CRUNCH
That's a Wondrous Wonder. It's very rare to see one, especially since Emperor Tomcat started collecting them.
She ate my strawberry gumdrop...
My grandma and I saw a whole herd once.
She seems to like it.
Yes, Wonders love their food.
Reeeee
Get your mangy mitts off me!
But they really hate being forced to do anything.
I'll flip you like a flapjack!
Ready for a real ride?
Oh no...
AHHHHHHH

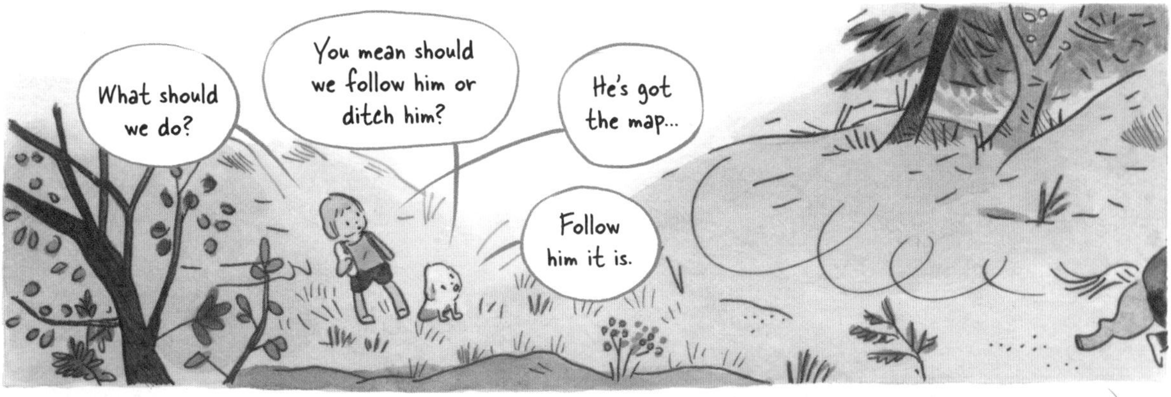
What should we do?
You mean should we follow him or ditch him?
He's got the map...
Follow him it is.

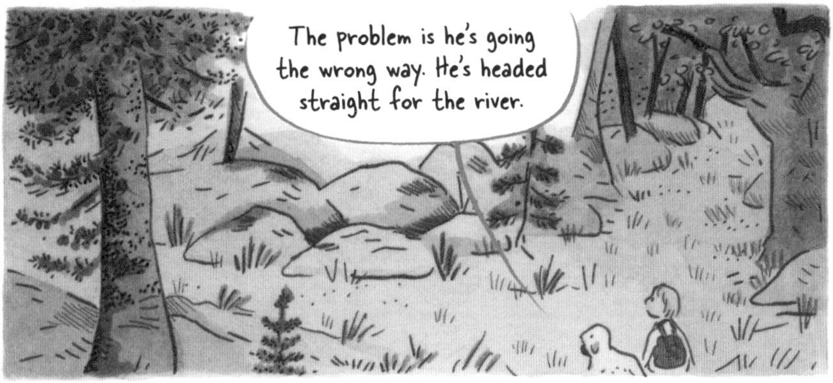
The problem is he's going the wrong way. He's headed straight for the river.

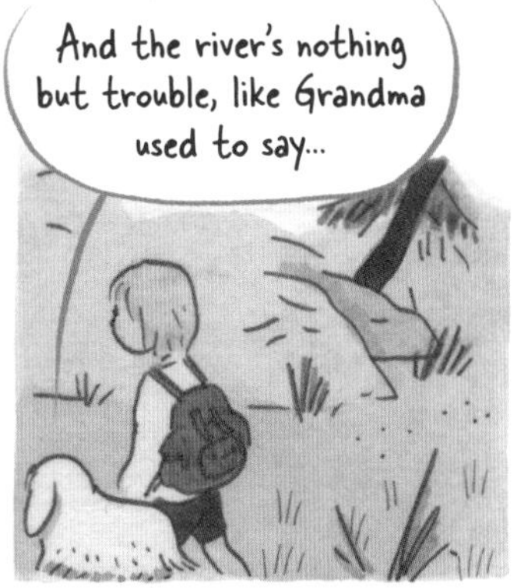
And the river's nothing but trouble, like Grandma used to say...

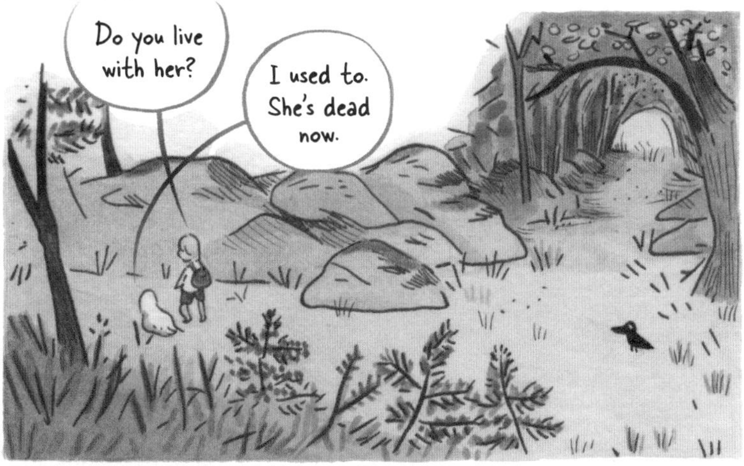
Do you live with her?
I used to. She's dead now.

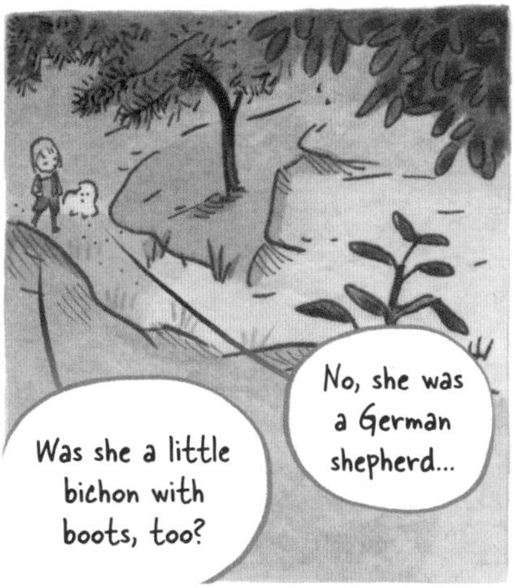
Was she a little bichon with boots, too?
No, she was a German shepherd...

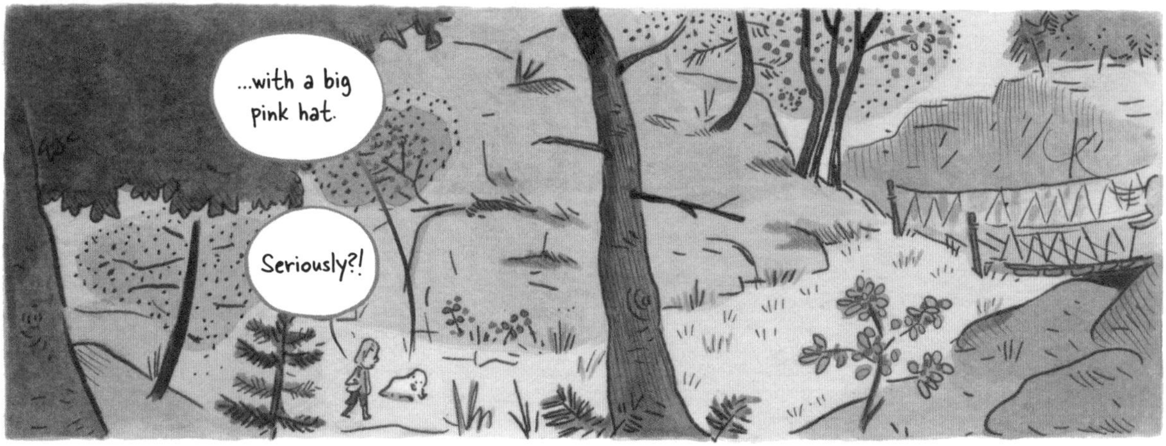
...with a big pink hat.
Seriously?!

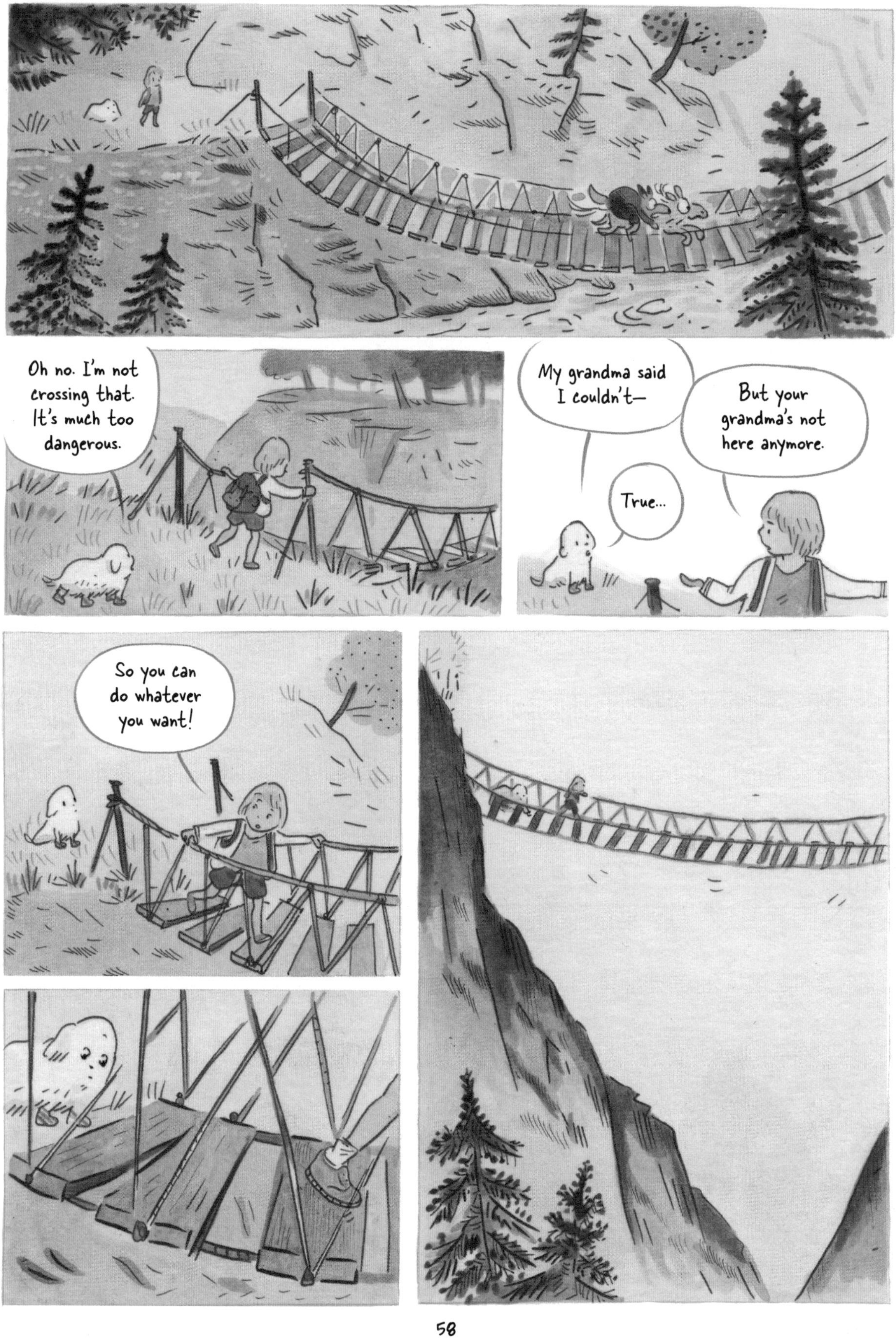
Oh no. I'm not crossing that. It's much too dangerous.
My grandma said I couldn't—
But your grandma's not here anymore.
True...
So you can do whatever you want!

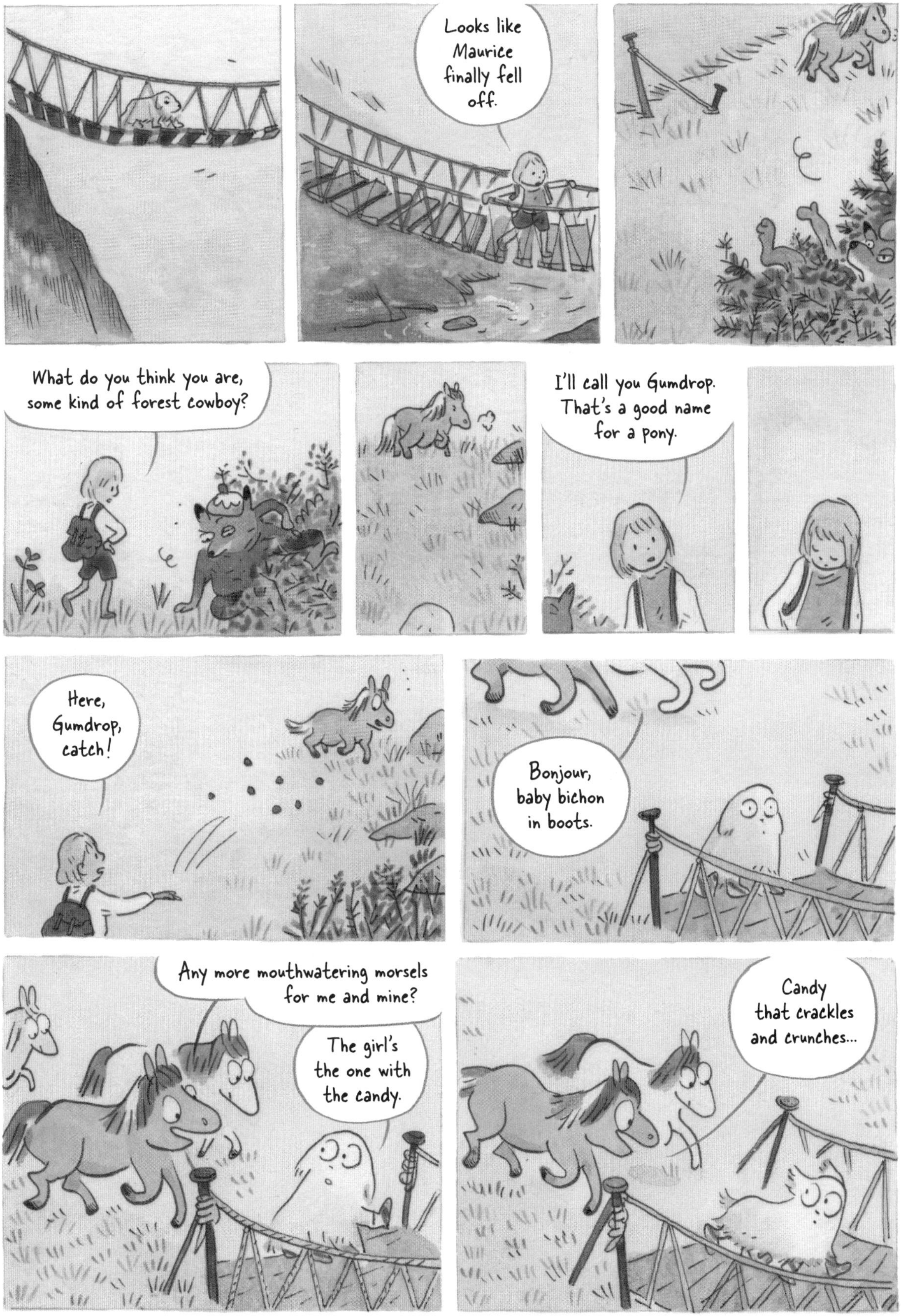

Looks like Maurice finally fell off.
What do you think you are, some kind of forest cowboy?
I'll call you Gumdrop. That's a good name for a pony.
Here, Gumdrop, catch!
Bonjour, baby bichon in boots.
Any more mouthwatering morsels for me and mine?
The girl's the one with the candy.
Candy that crackles and crunches...

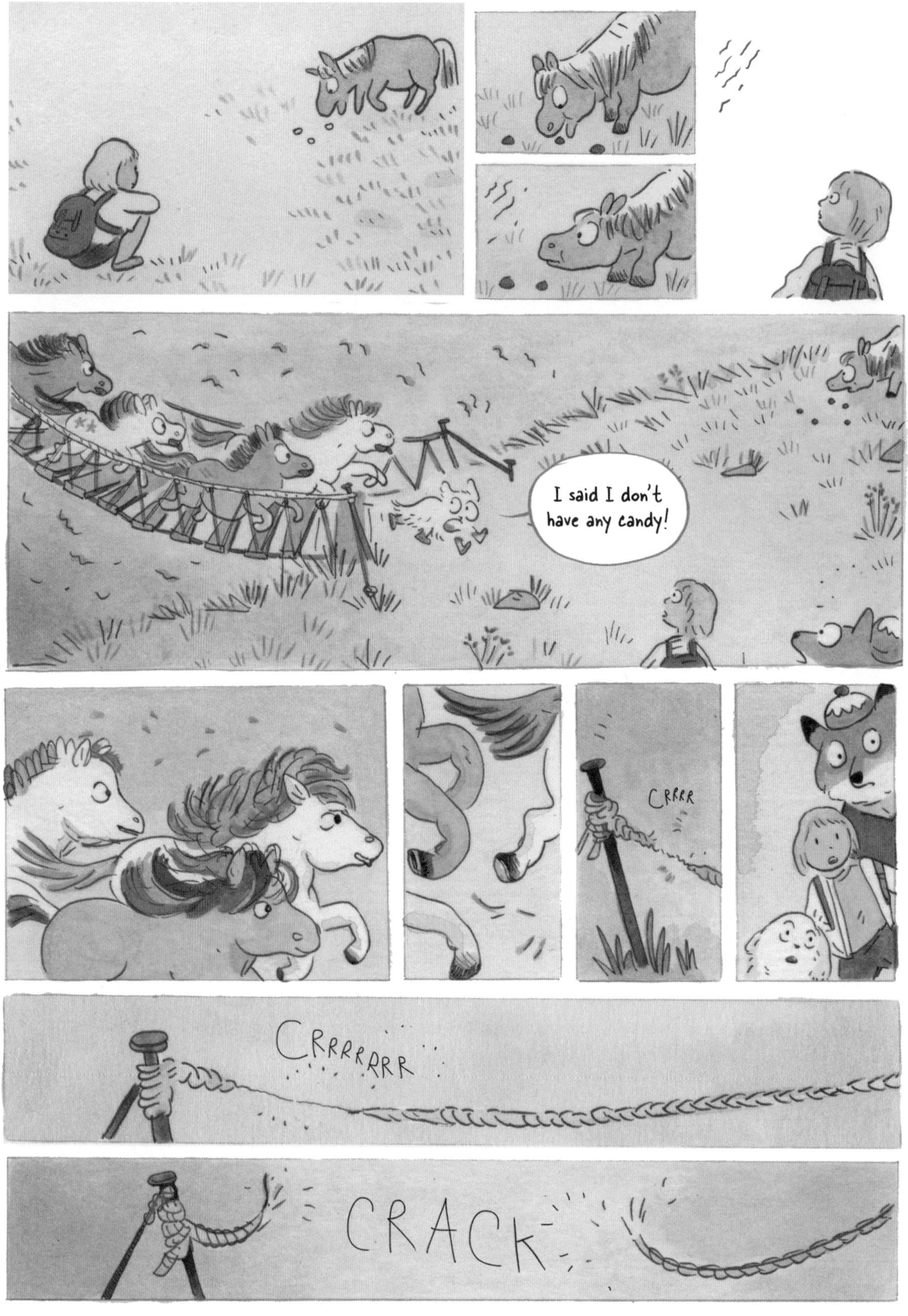
I said I don't have any candy!
CRRRR
CRRRRRRR
CRACK

Noooooo!!

We're stranded...

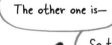

Tell me there's another bridge.

There is no other bridge!

The other one is—

So there is another bridge?

GRRR

It's a day's journey from here! We have to go all the way around the mountain!

You're still wearing your cream puff hat...

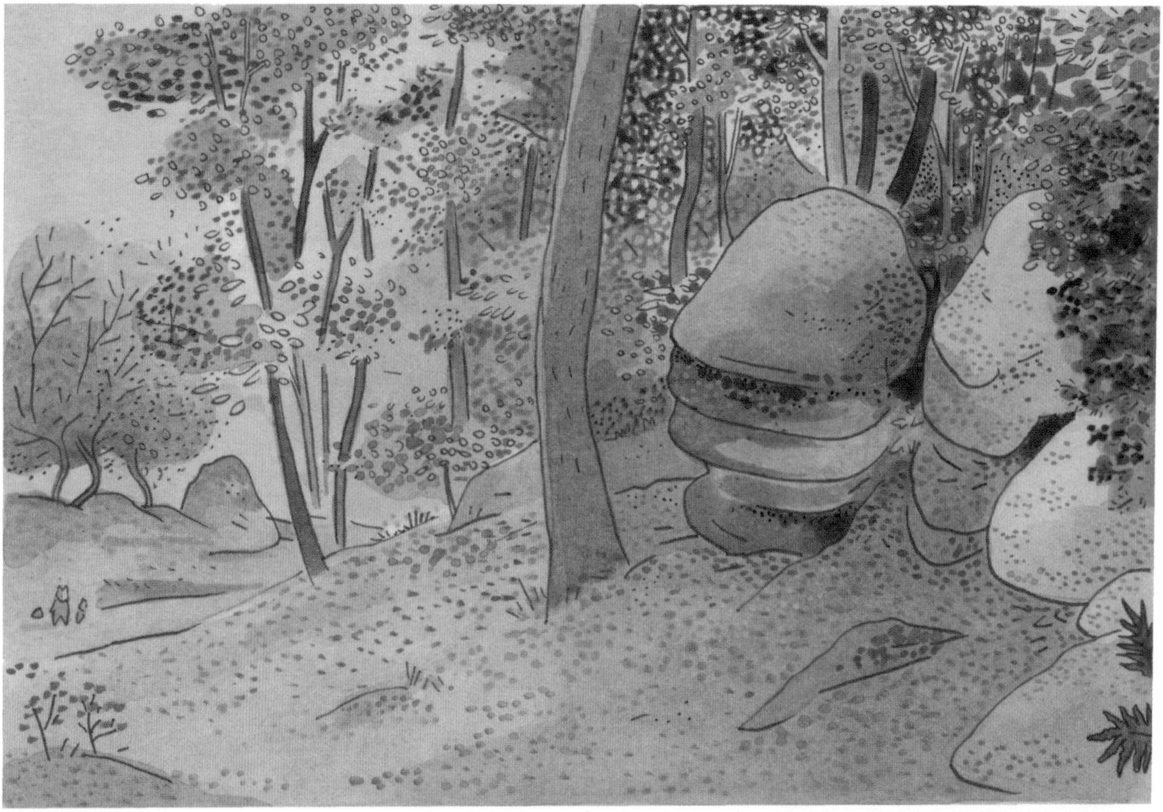

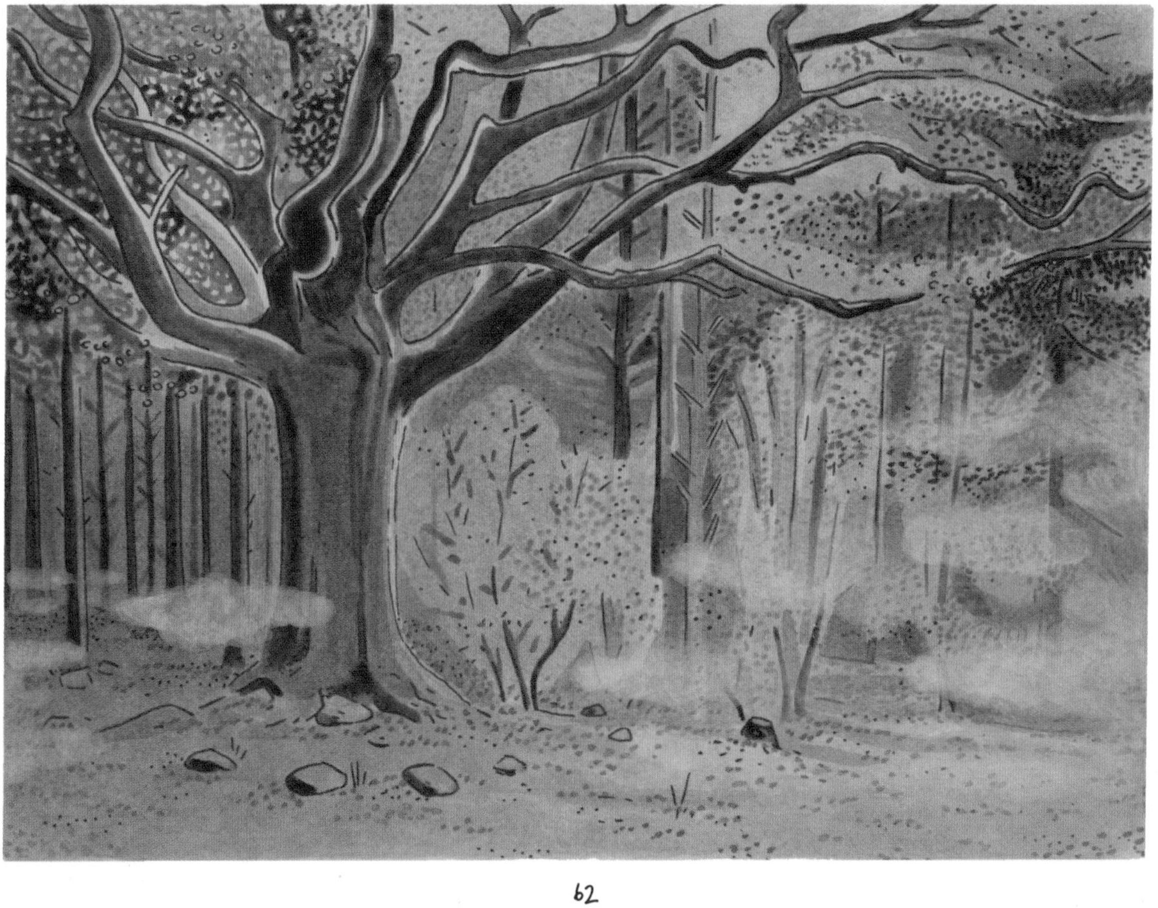

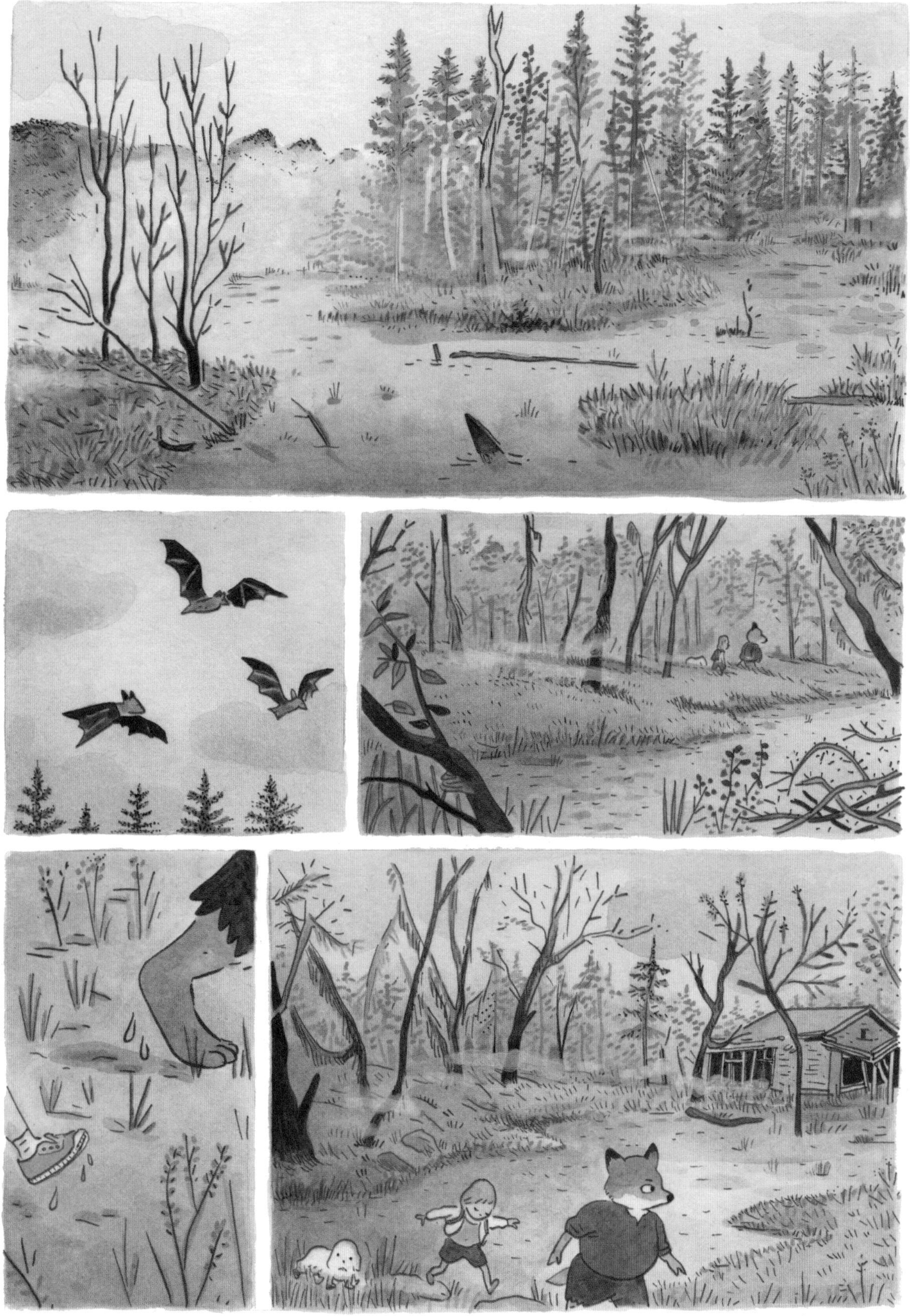

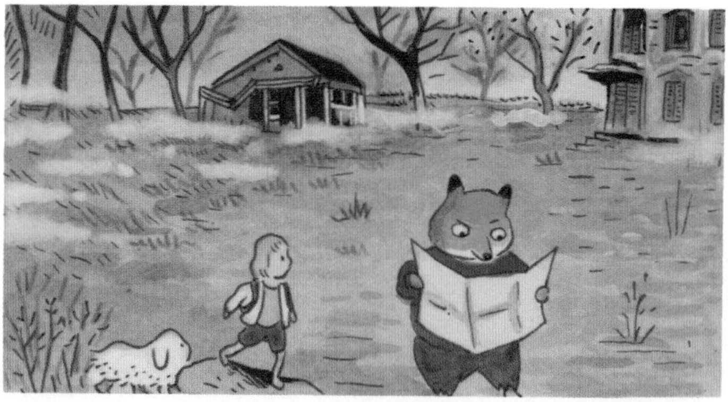

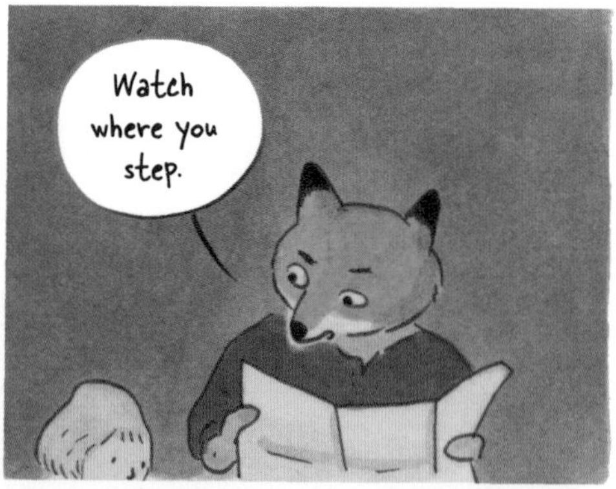
Watch where you step.

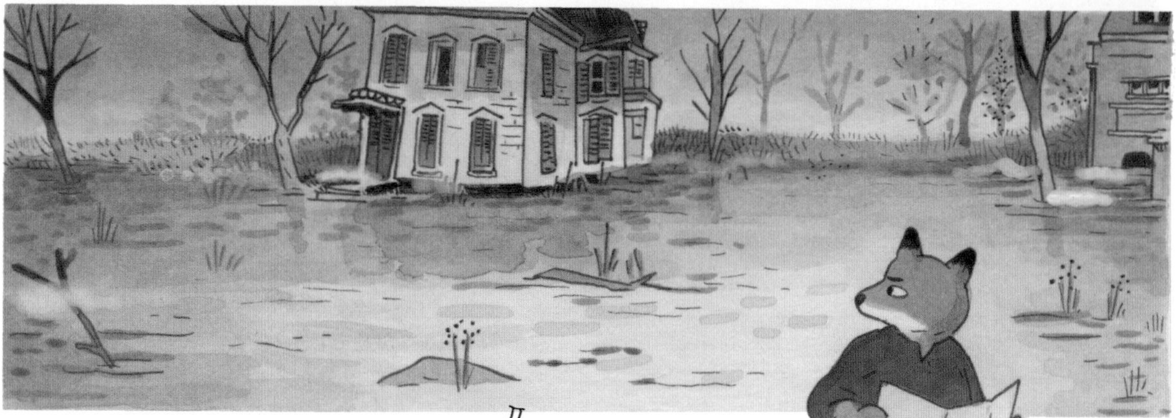

Through the dark woods and the murky bog...

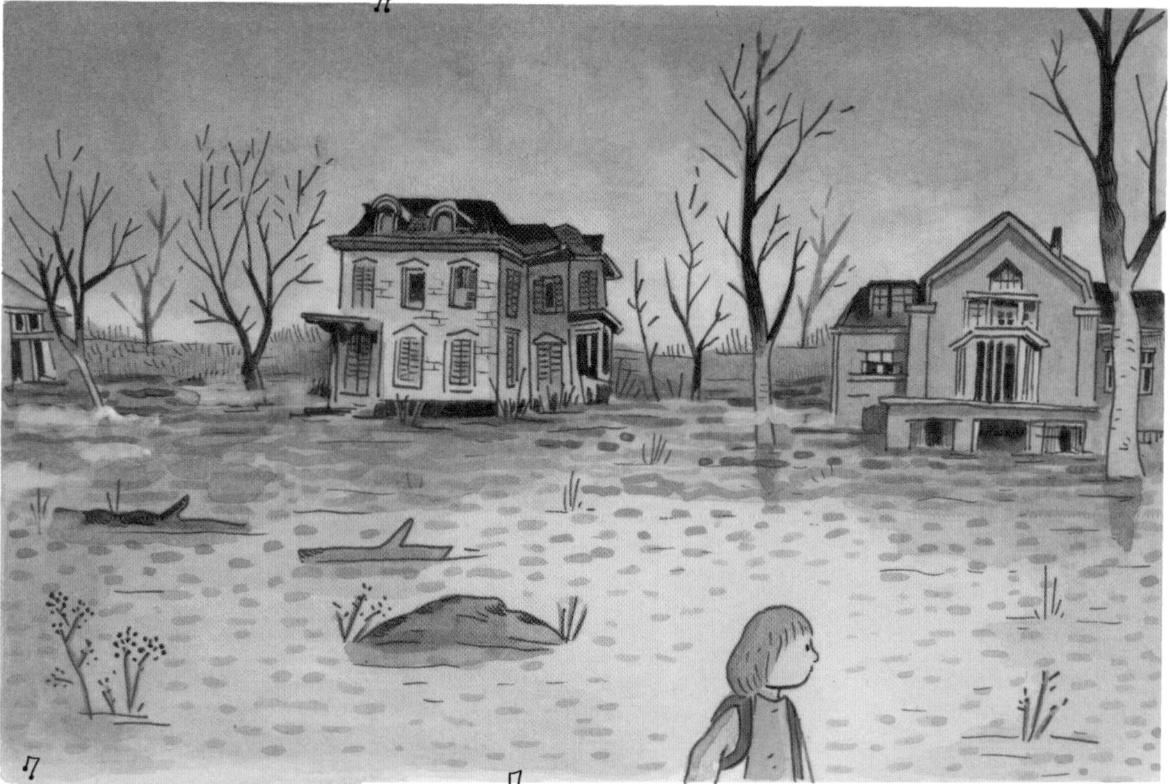

...the wandering children continue to slog...

Deep in the forest, not far from our home, rats crawl from their nests and nightmares roam... ♫

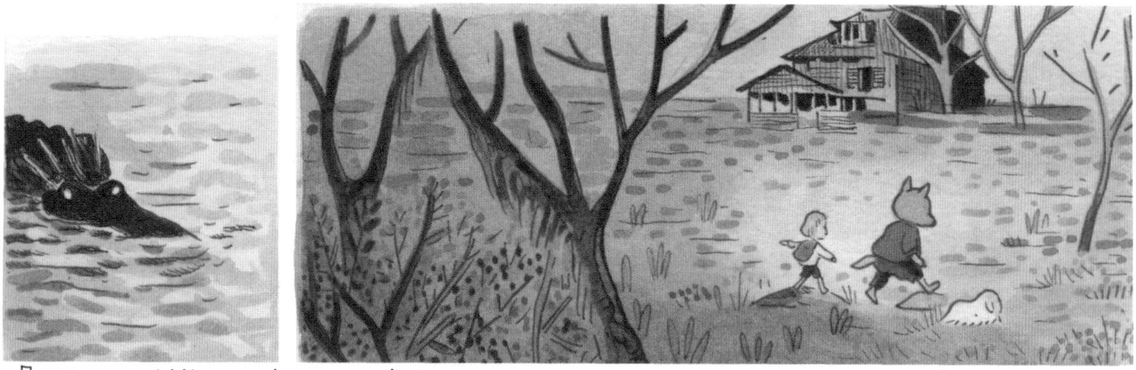

♫ Take care, little one, stay in your bed... ♫

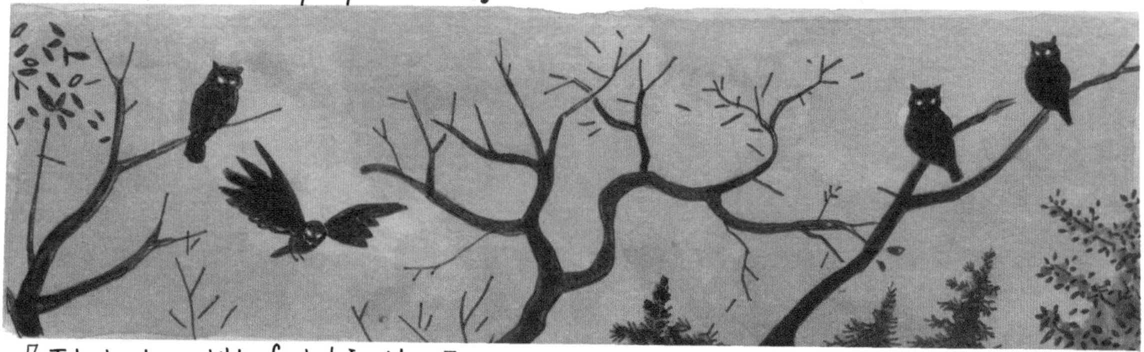

♫ Take heed, my child, of what I said... ♫

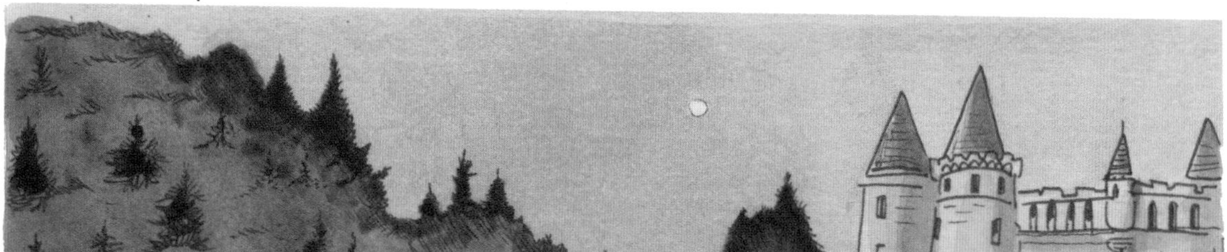

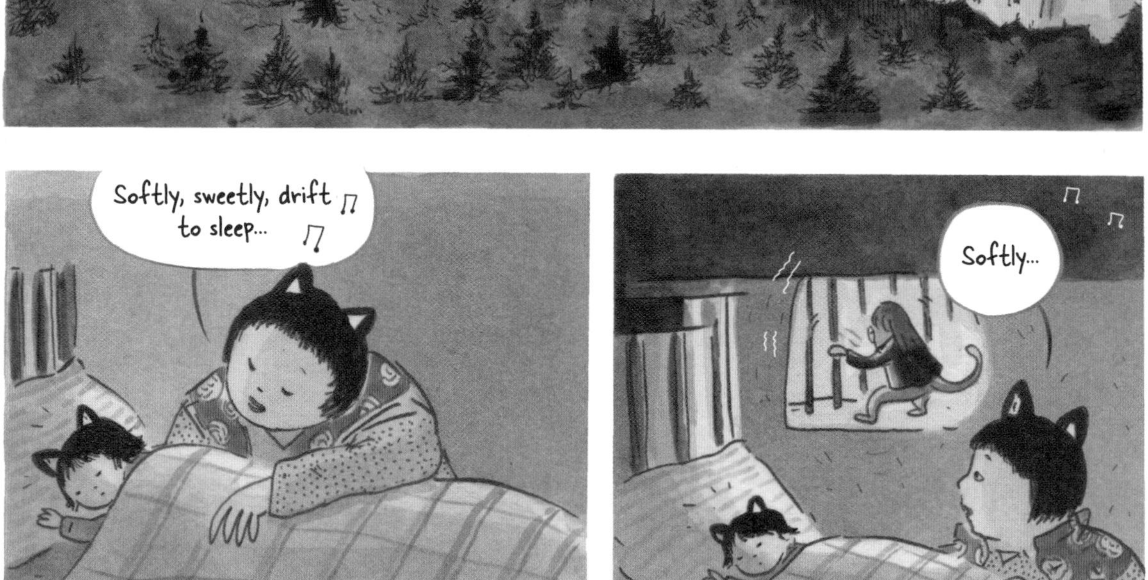
Softly, sweetly, drift to sleep... ♫ ♫
Softly...

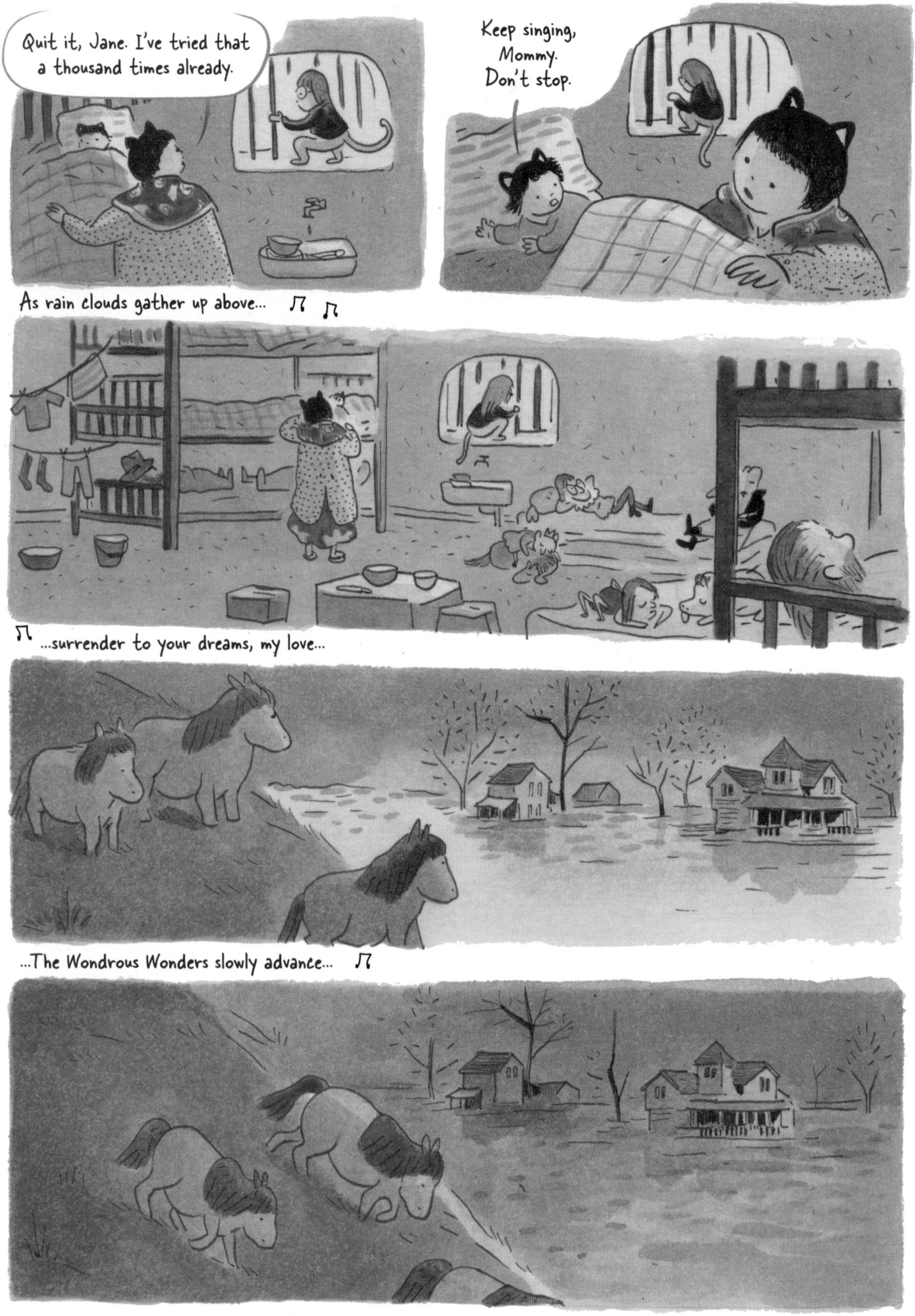
Quit it, Jane. I've tried that a thousand times already.
Keep singing, Mommy. Don't stop.
As rain clouds gather up above...
...surrender to your dreams, my love...
...The Wondrous Wonders slowly advance...

While the costumed guests wildly dance...

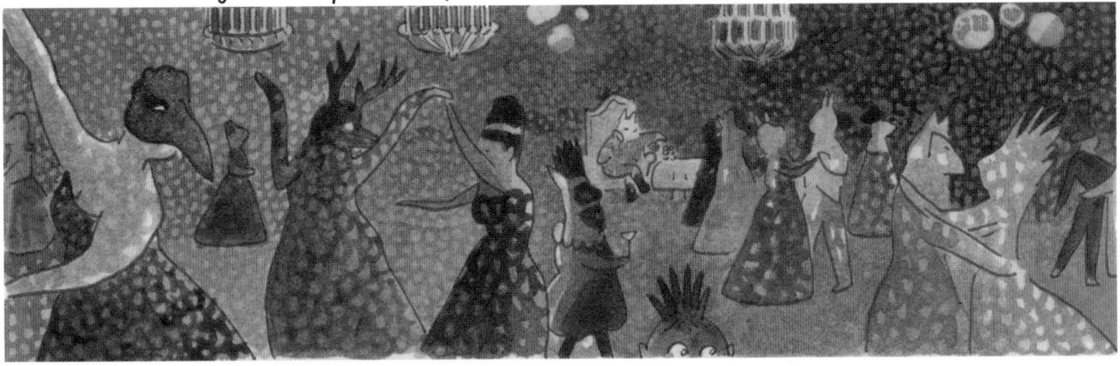

Take care, my sweet, of the lies masks hide...

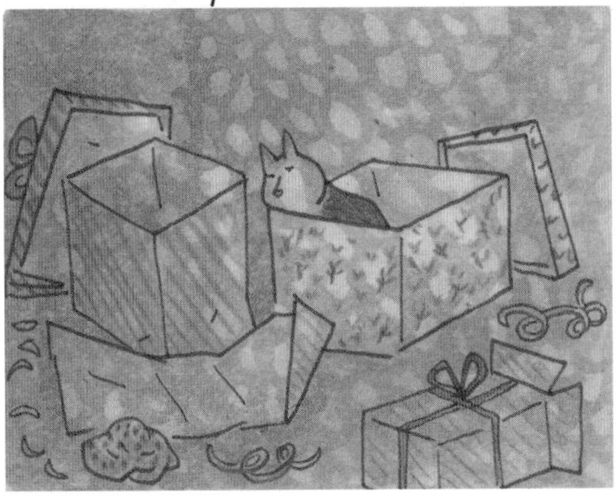

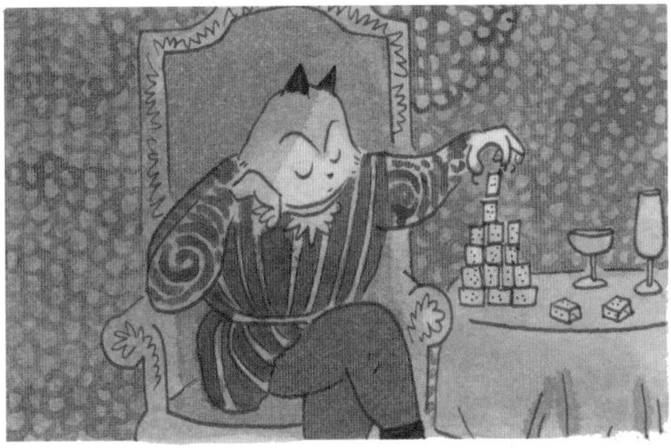

Come home, my dear, for it's safe inside...

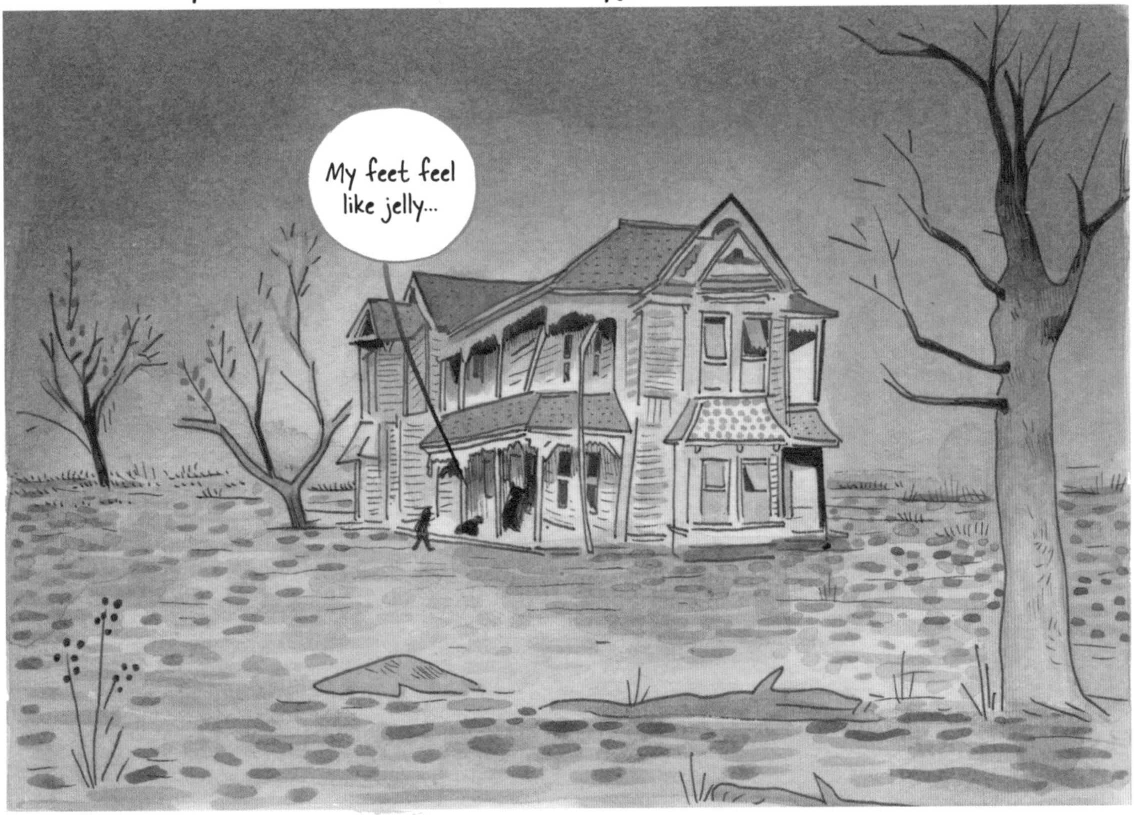
My feet feel like jelly...

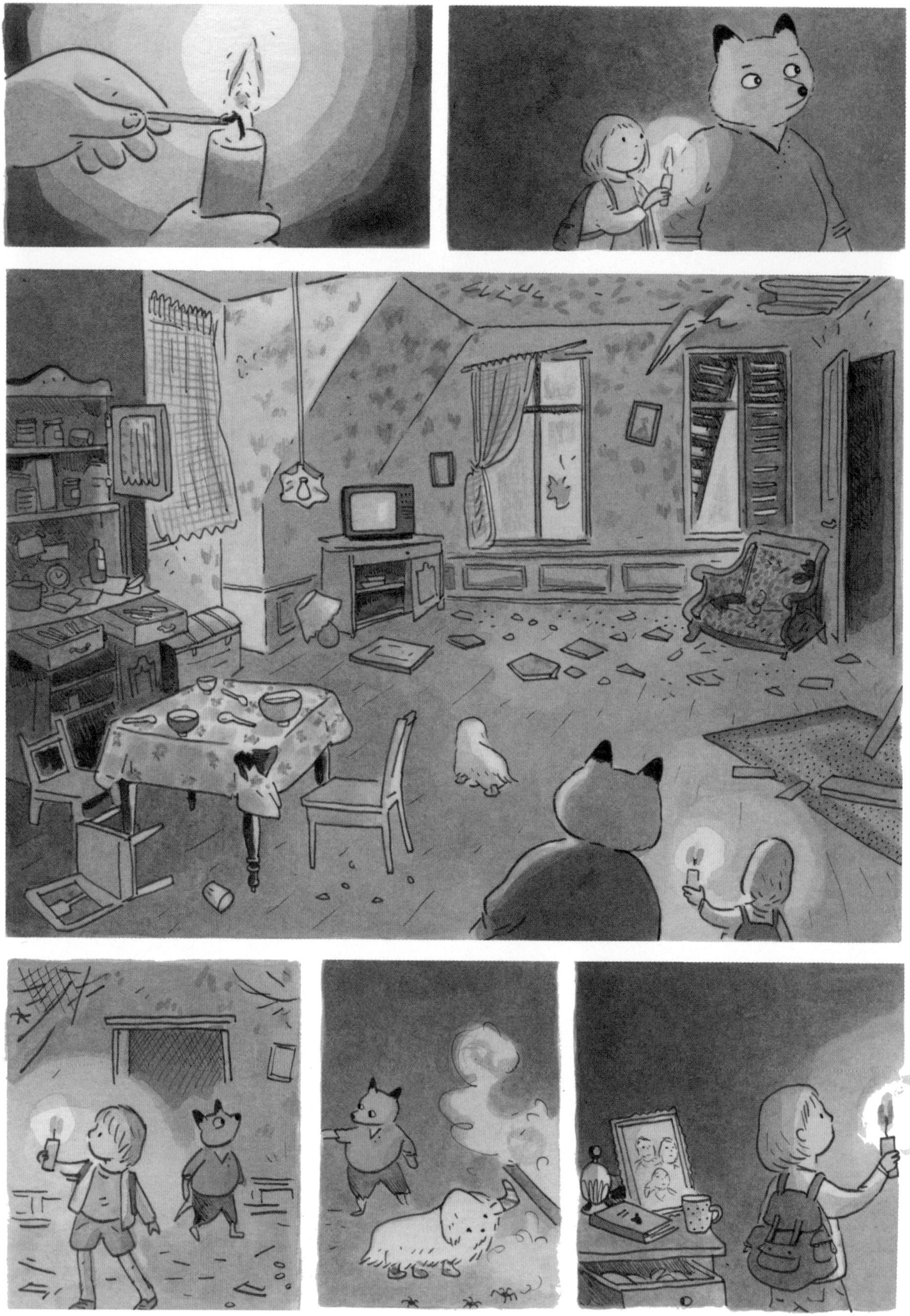

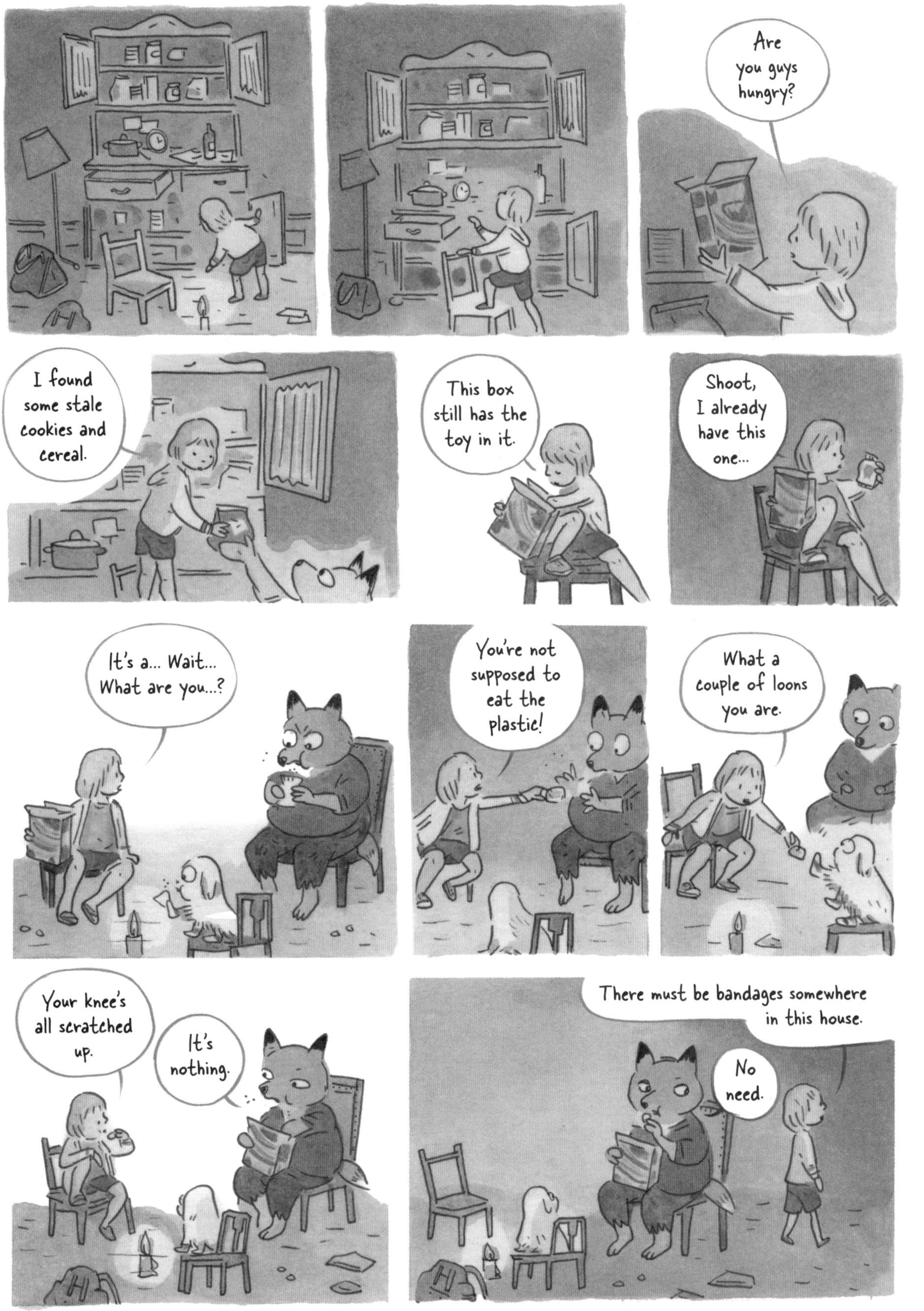
Are you guys hungry?
I found some stale cookies and cereal.
This box still has the toy in it.
Shoot, I already have this one...
It's a... Wait... What are you...?
You're not supposed to eat the plastic!
What a couple of loons you are.
Your knee's all scratched up.
It's nothing.
There must be bandages somewhere in this house.
No need.

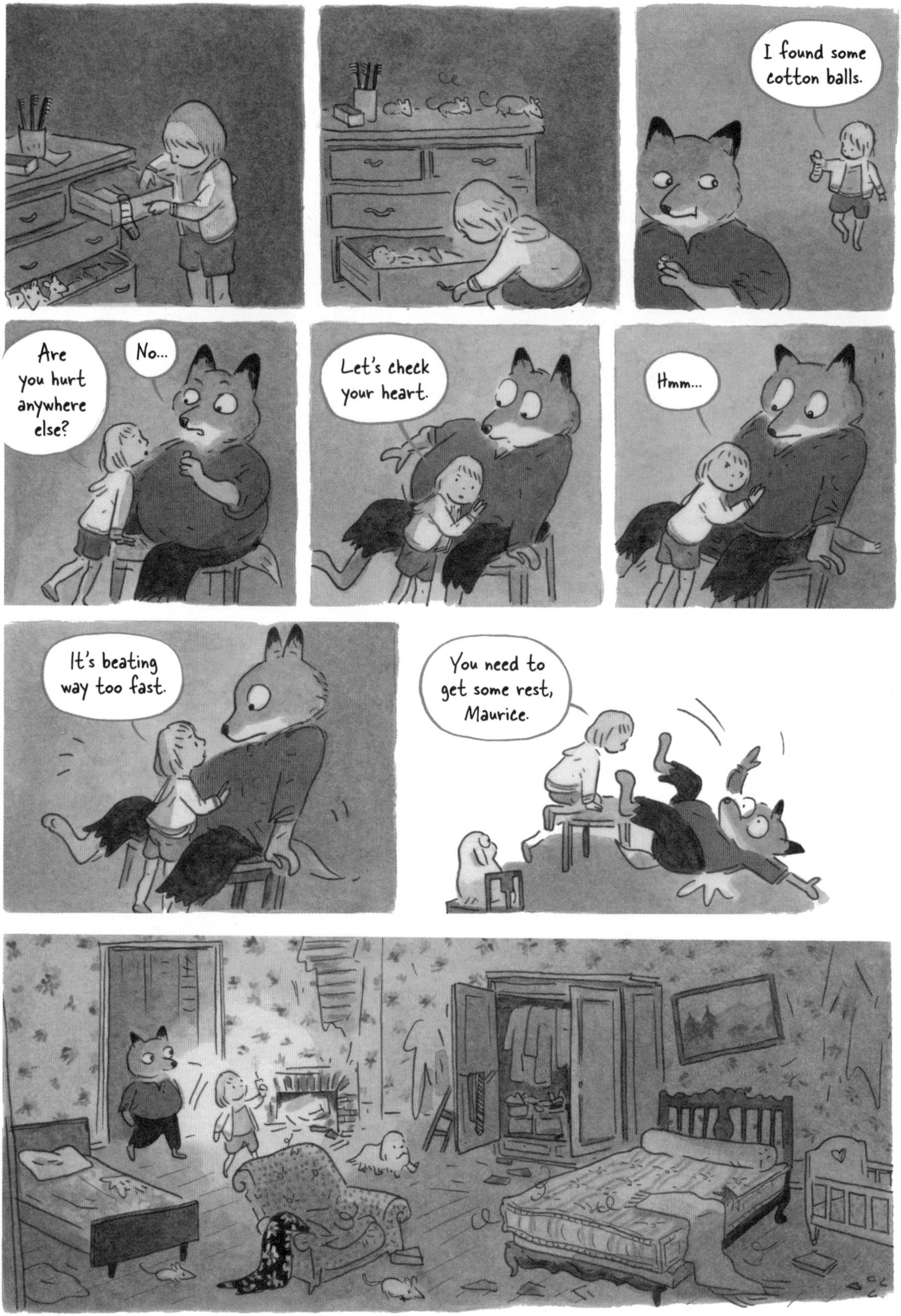
I found some cotton balls.
Are you hurt anywhere else?
No...
Let's check your heart.
Hmm...
It's beating way too fast.
You need to get some rest, Maurice.

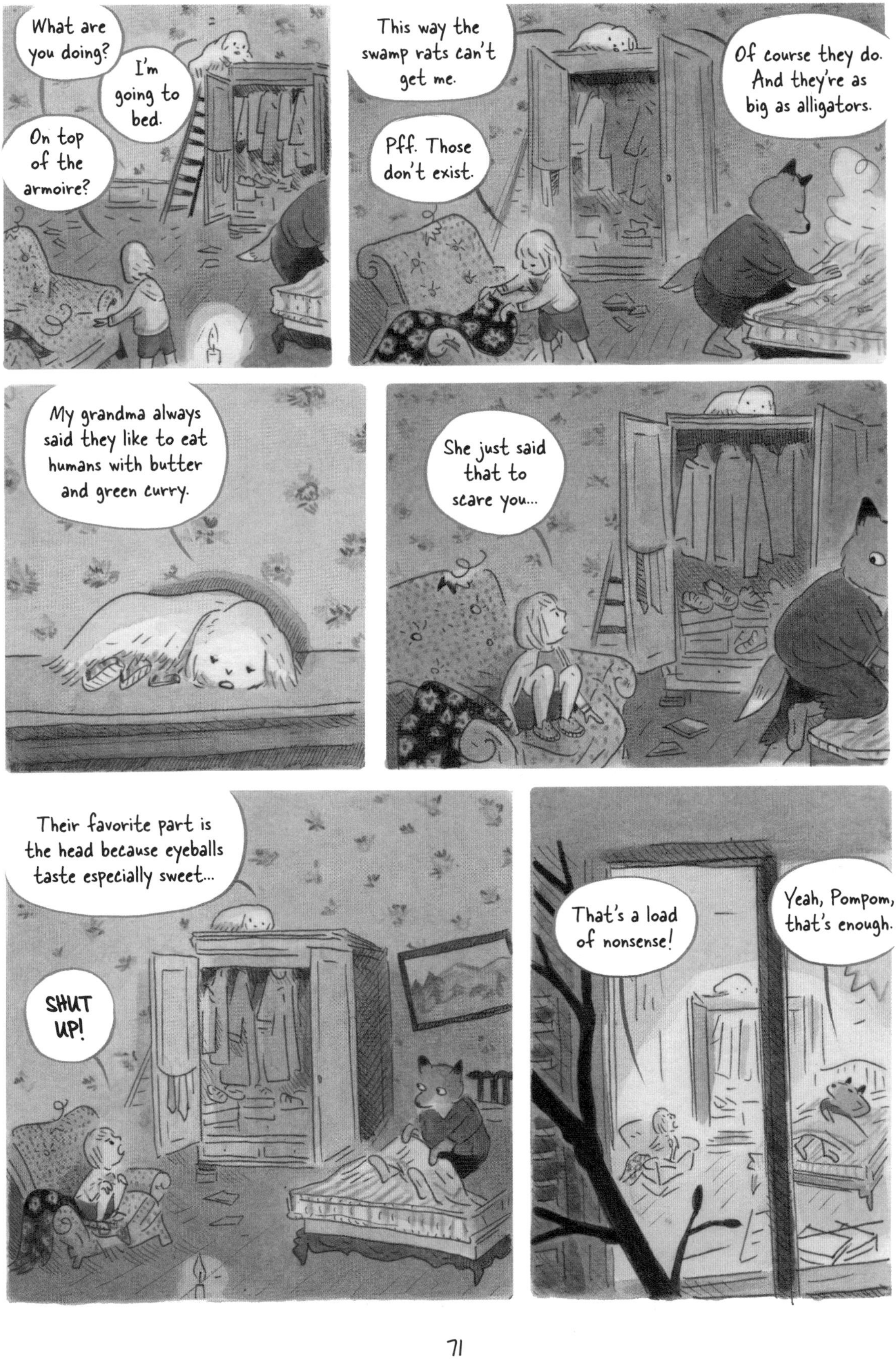
What are you doing?
I'm going to bed.
On top of the armoire?
This way the swamp rats can't get me.
Pff. Those don't exist.
Of course they do. And they're as big as alligators.
My grandma always said they like to eat humans with butter and green curry.
She just said that to scare you...
Their favorite part is the head because eyeballs taste especially sweet...
SHUT UP!
That's a load of nonsense!
Yeah, Pompom, that's enough.

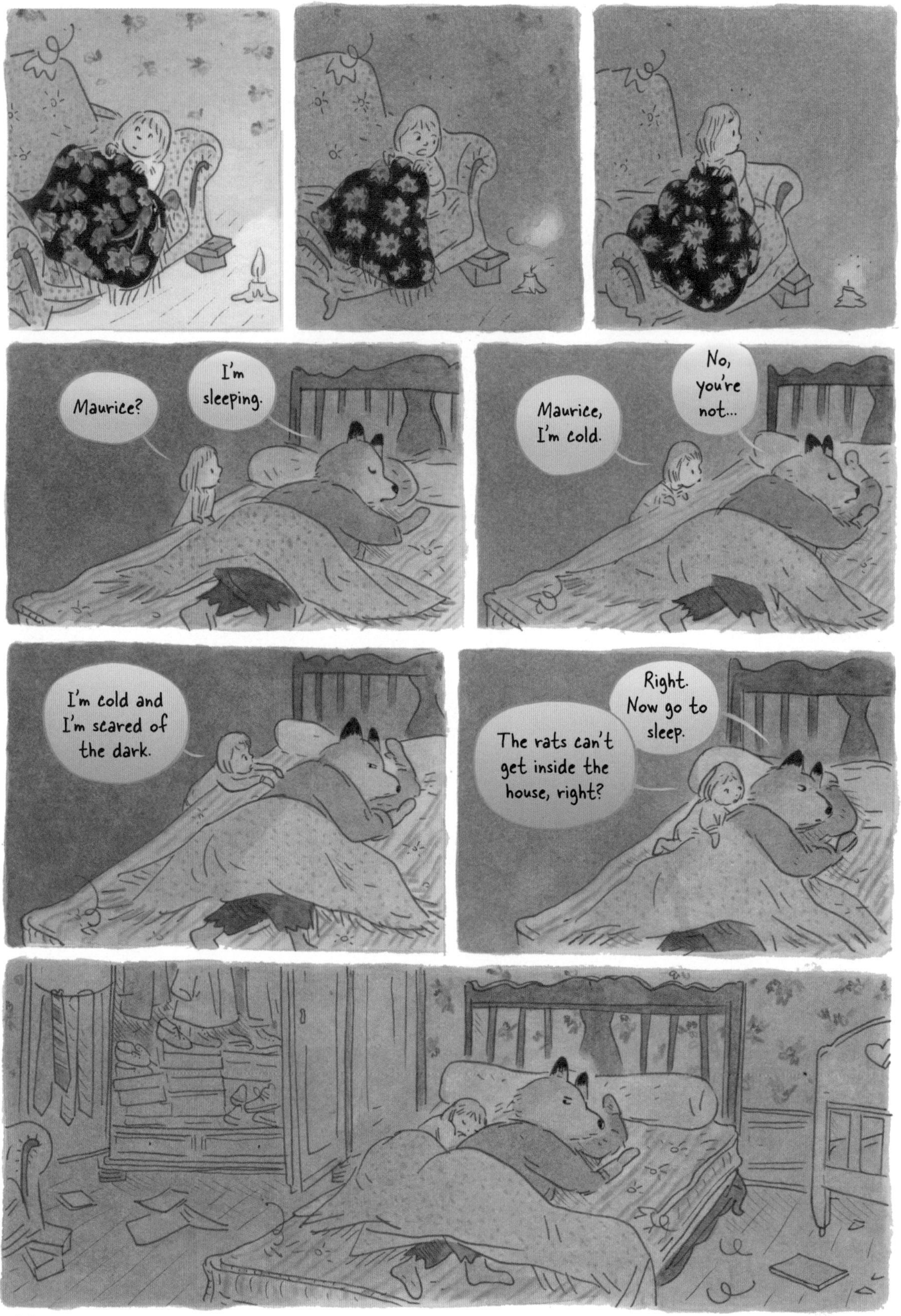
Maurice?
I'm sleeping.
Maurice, I'm cold.
No, you're not...
I'm cold and I'm scared of the dark.
Right. Now go to sleep.
The rats can't get inside the house, right?

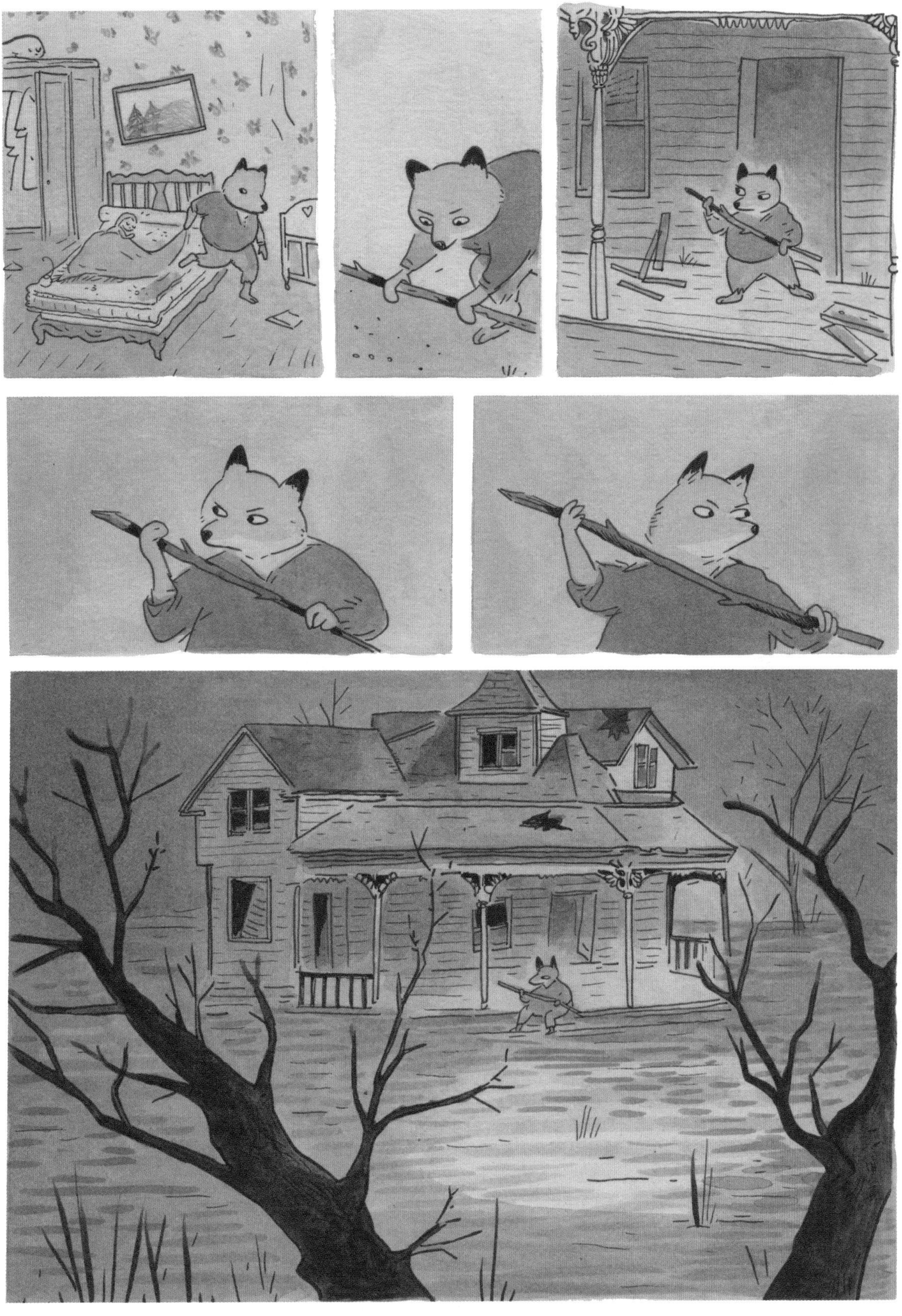

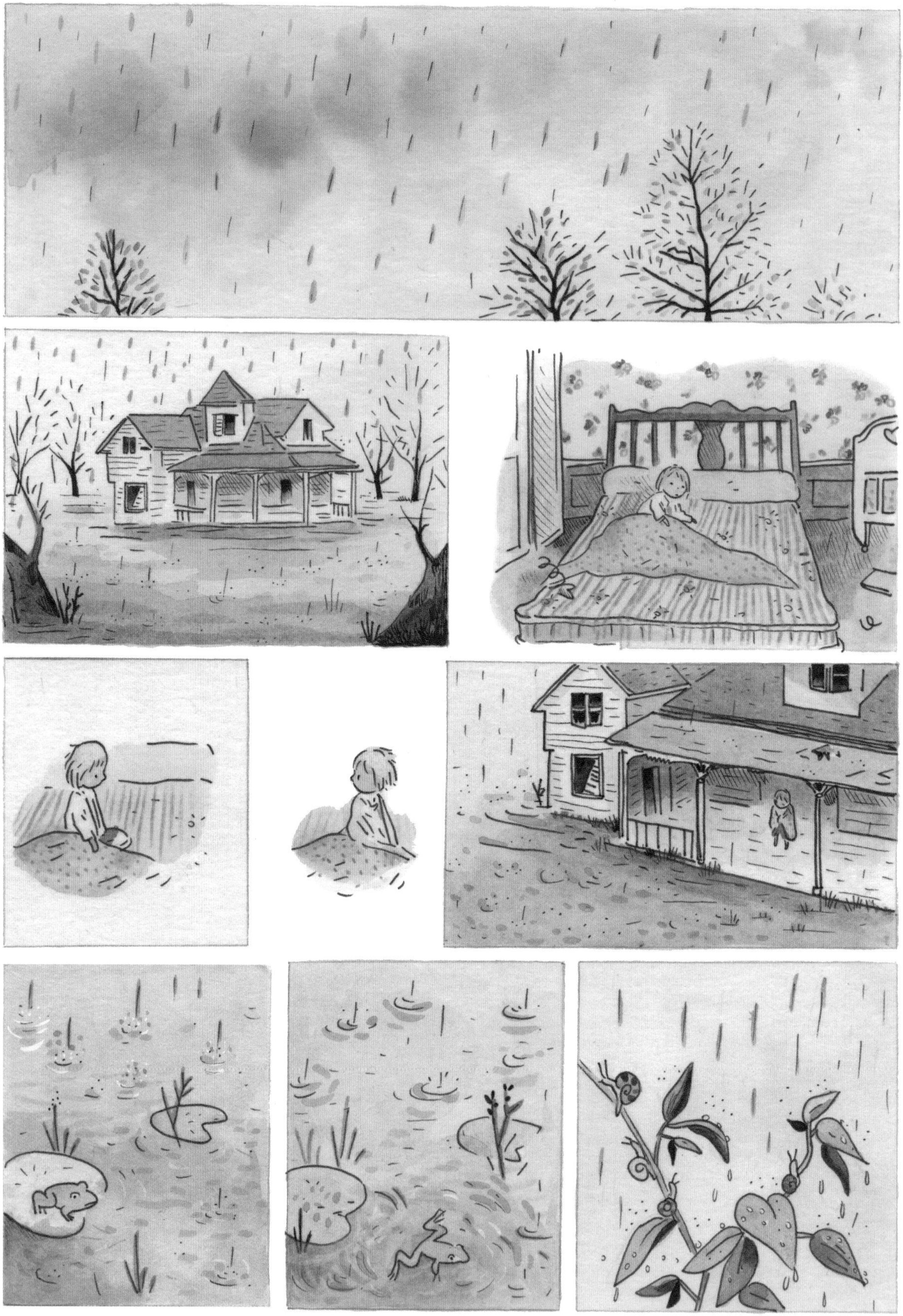

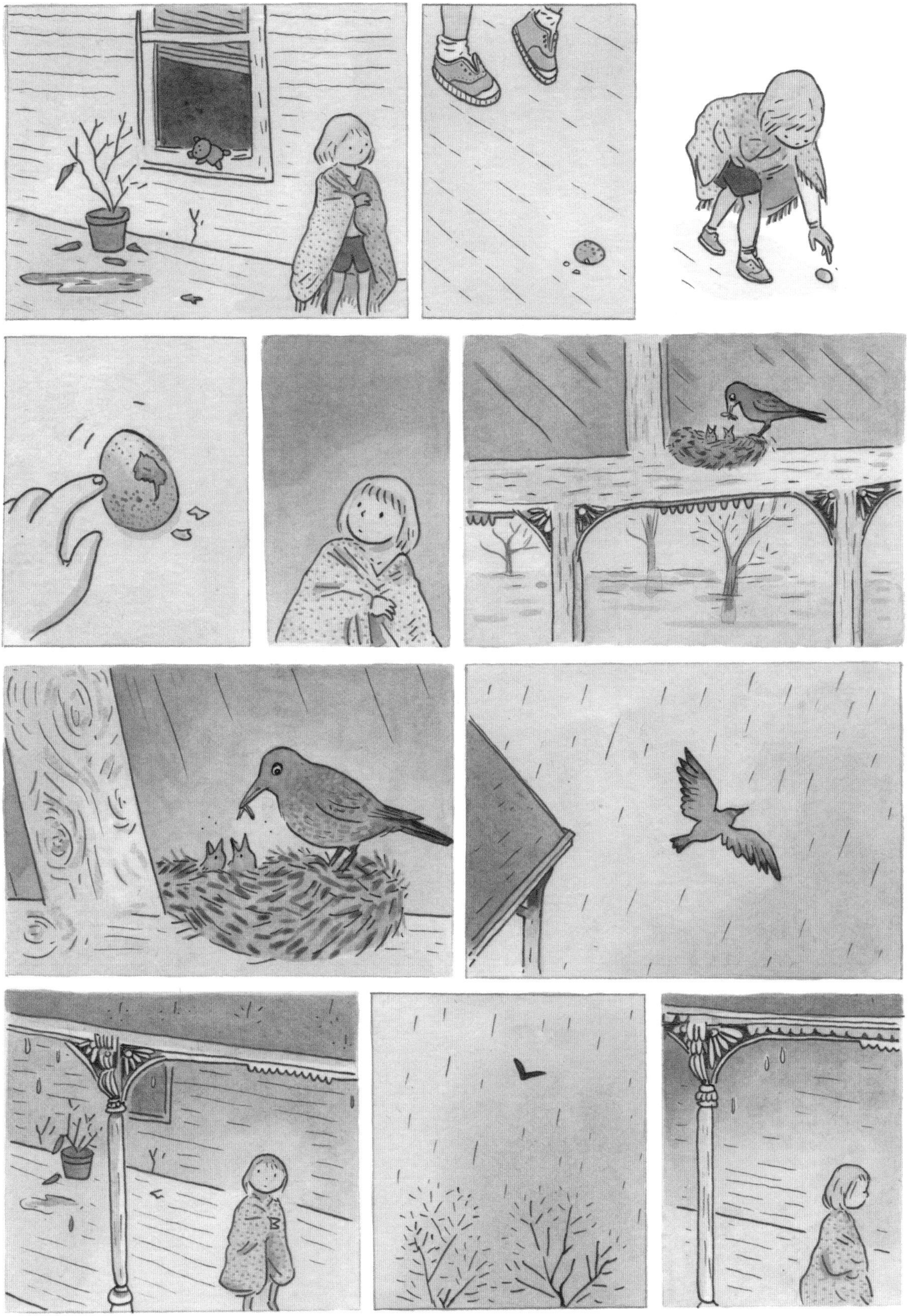

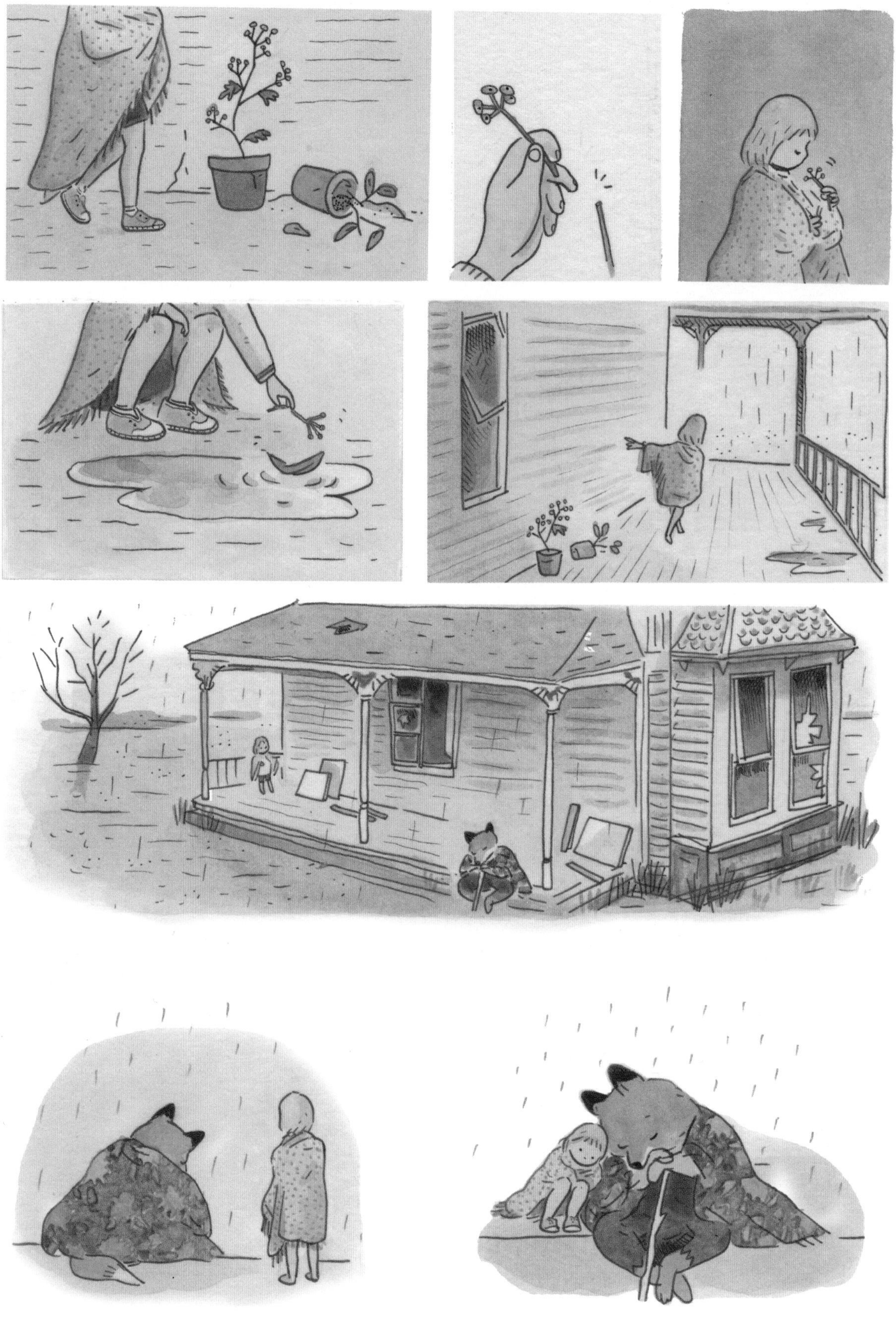

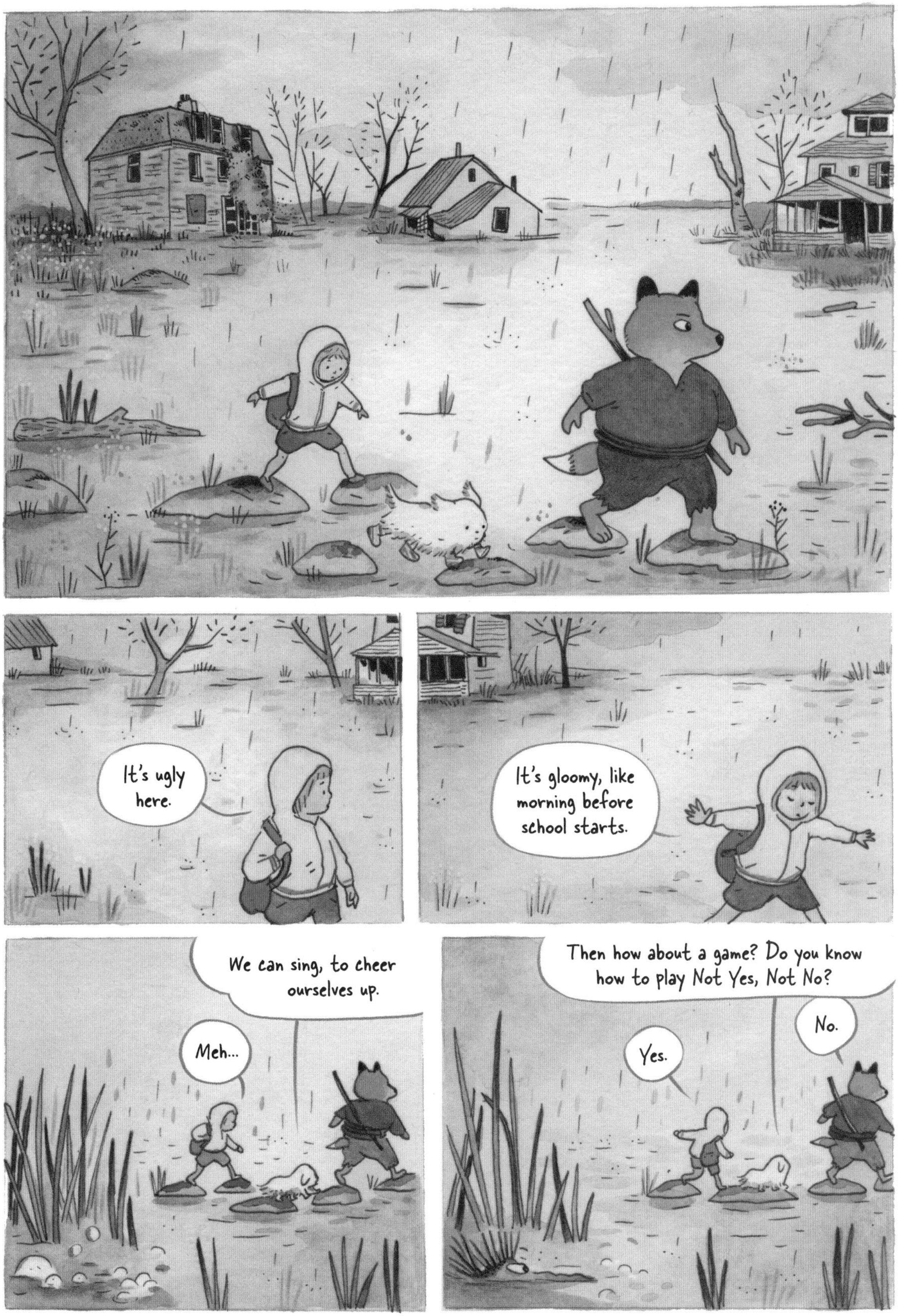
It's ugly here.
It's gloomy, like morning before school starts.
We can sing, to cheer ourselves up.
Meh...
Then how about a game? Do you know how to play Not Yes, Not No?
Yes.
No.

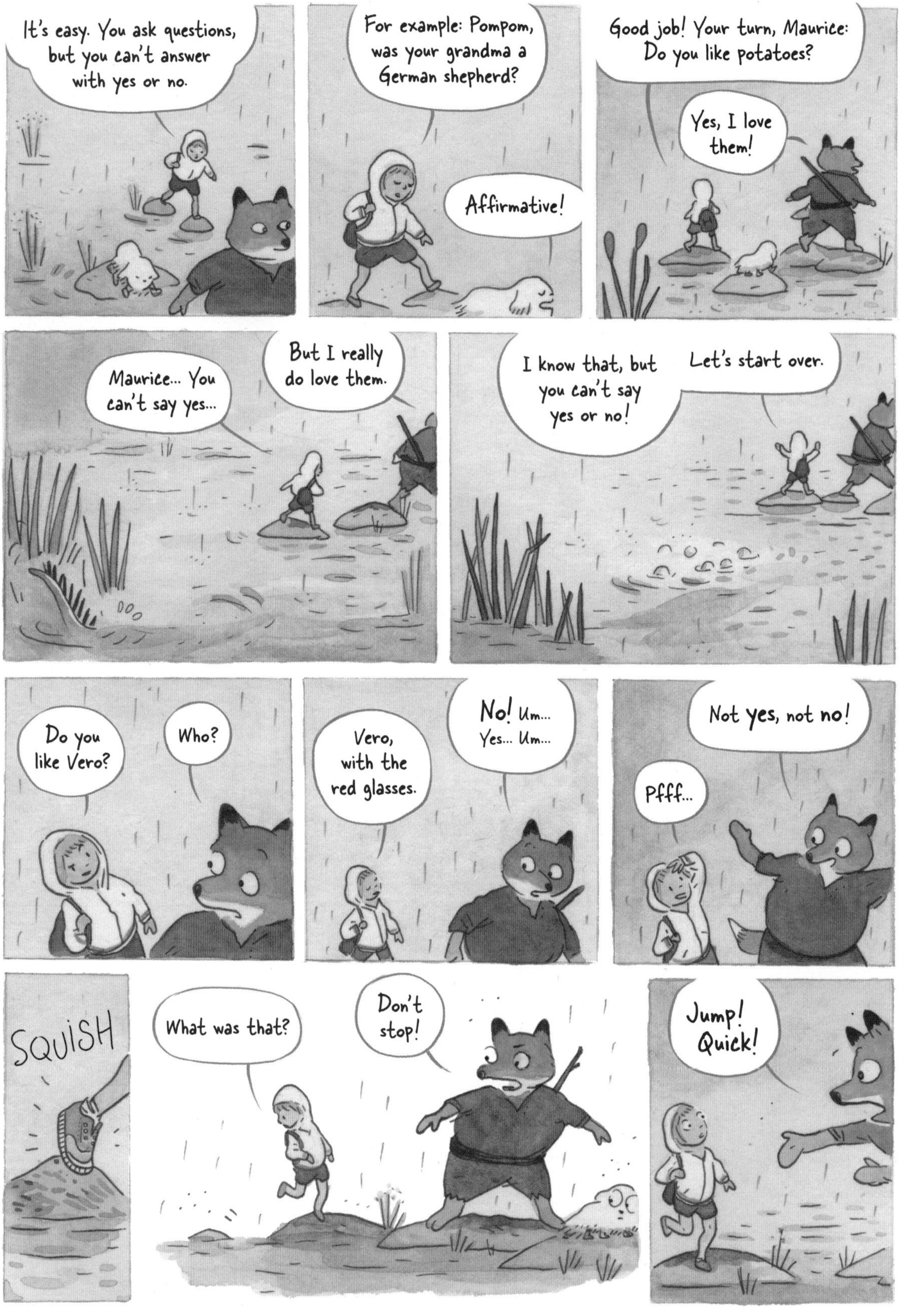

It's easy. You ask questions, but you can't answer with yes or no.
For example: Pompom, was your grandma a German shepherd?
Affirmative!
Good job! Your turn, Maurice: Do you like potatoes?
Yes, I love them!
Maurice... You can't say yes...
But I really do love them.
I know that, but you can't say yes or no!
Let's start over.
Do you like Vero?
Who?
Vero, with the red glasses.
No! Um... Yes... Um...
Not yes, not no!
Pfff...
SQUISH
What was that?
Don't stop!
Jump! Quick!

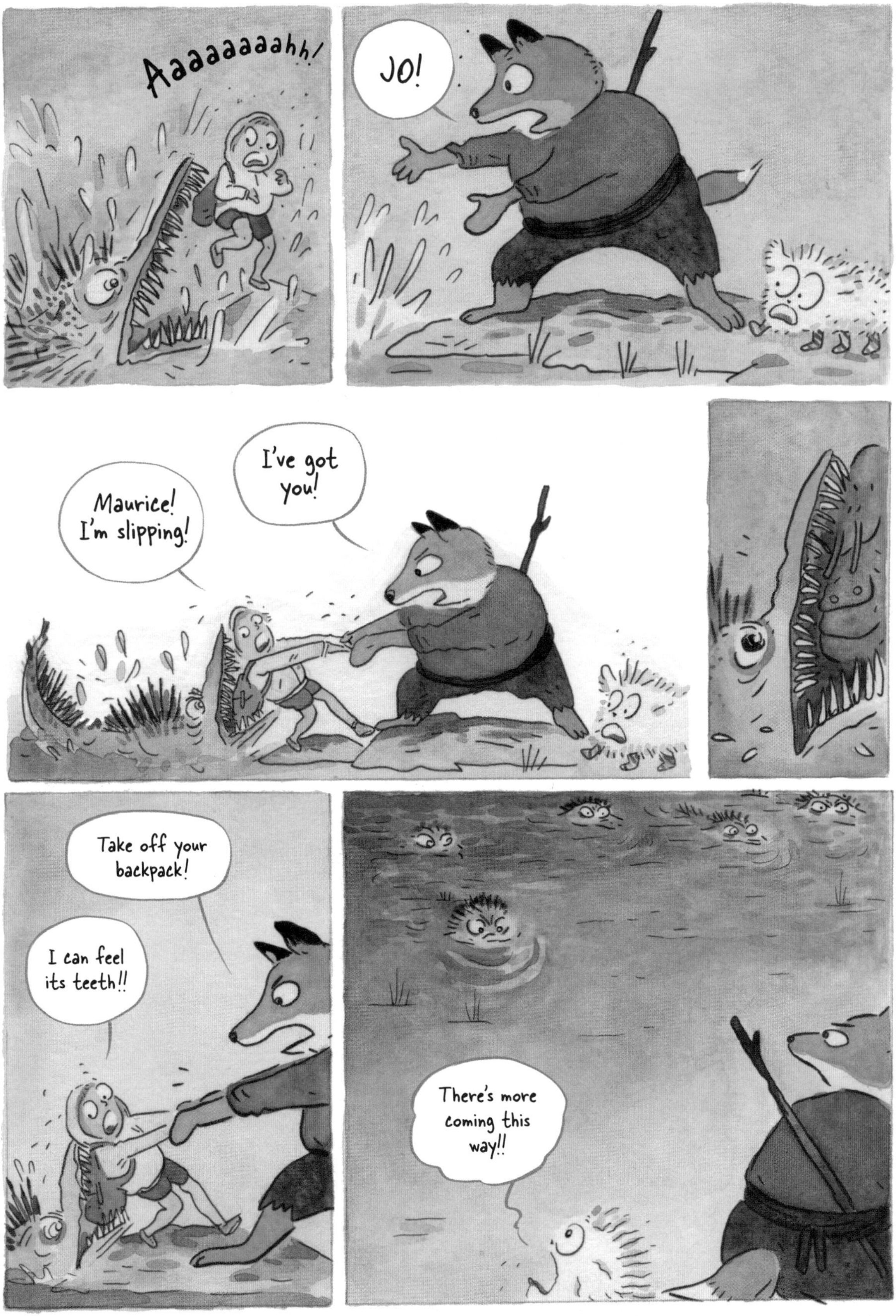

Aaaaaaaahh!
JO!
Maurice! I'm slipping!
I've got you!
Take off your backpack!
I can feel its teeth!!
There's more coming this way!!

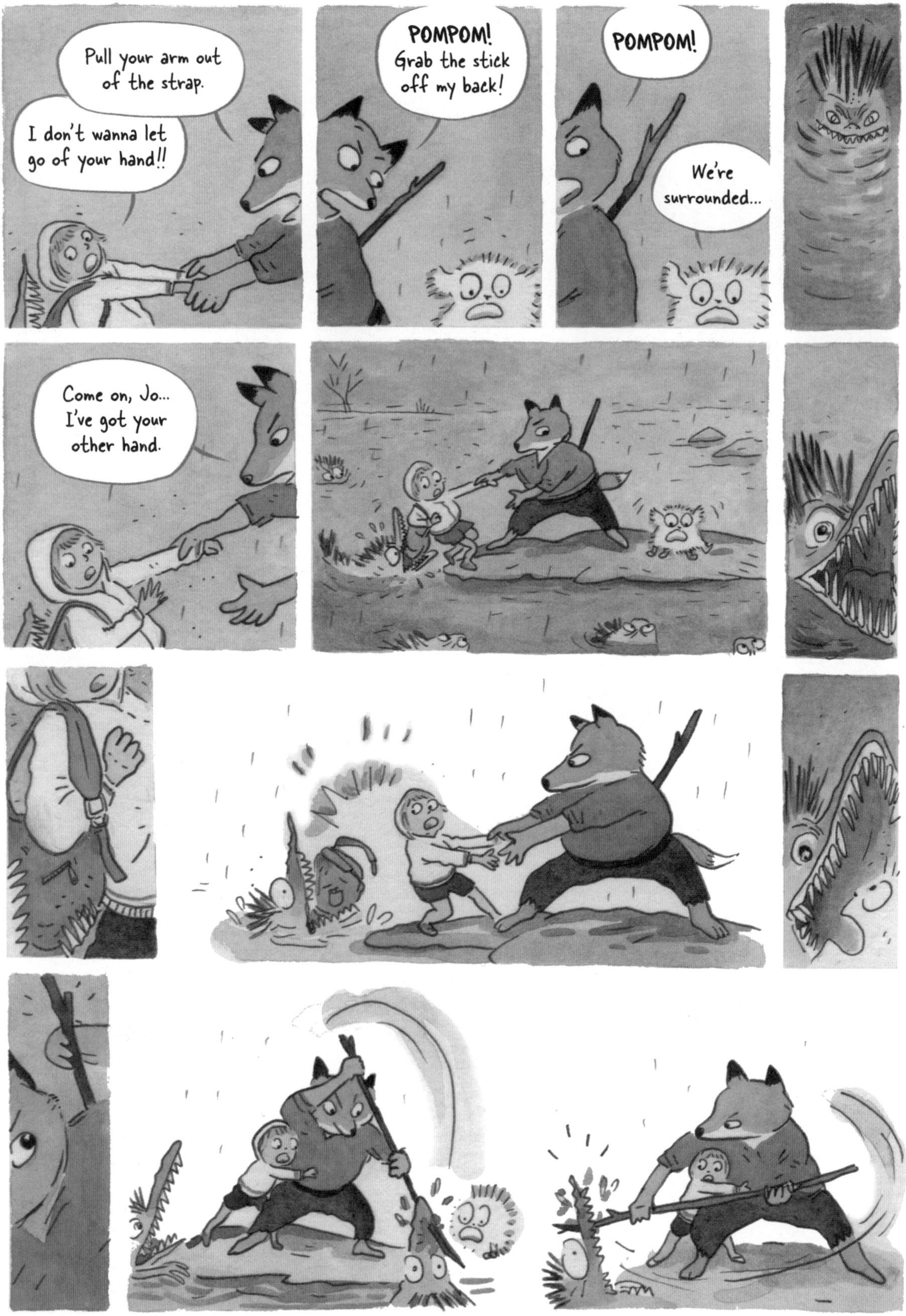
Pull your arm out of the strap.
I don't wanna let go of your hand!!
POMPOM! Grab the stick off my back!
POMPOM!
We're surrounded...
Come on, Jo... I've got your other hand.

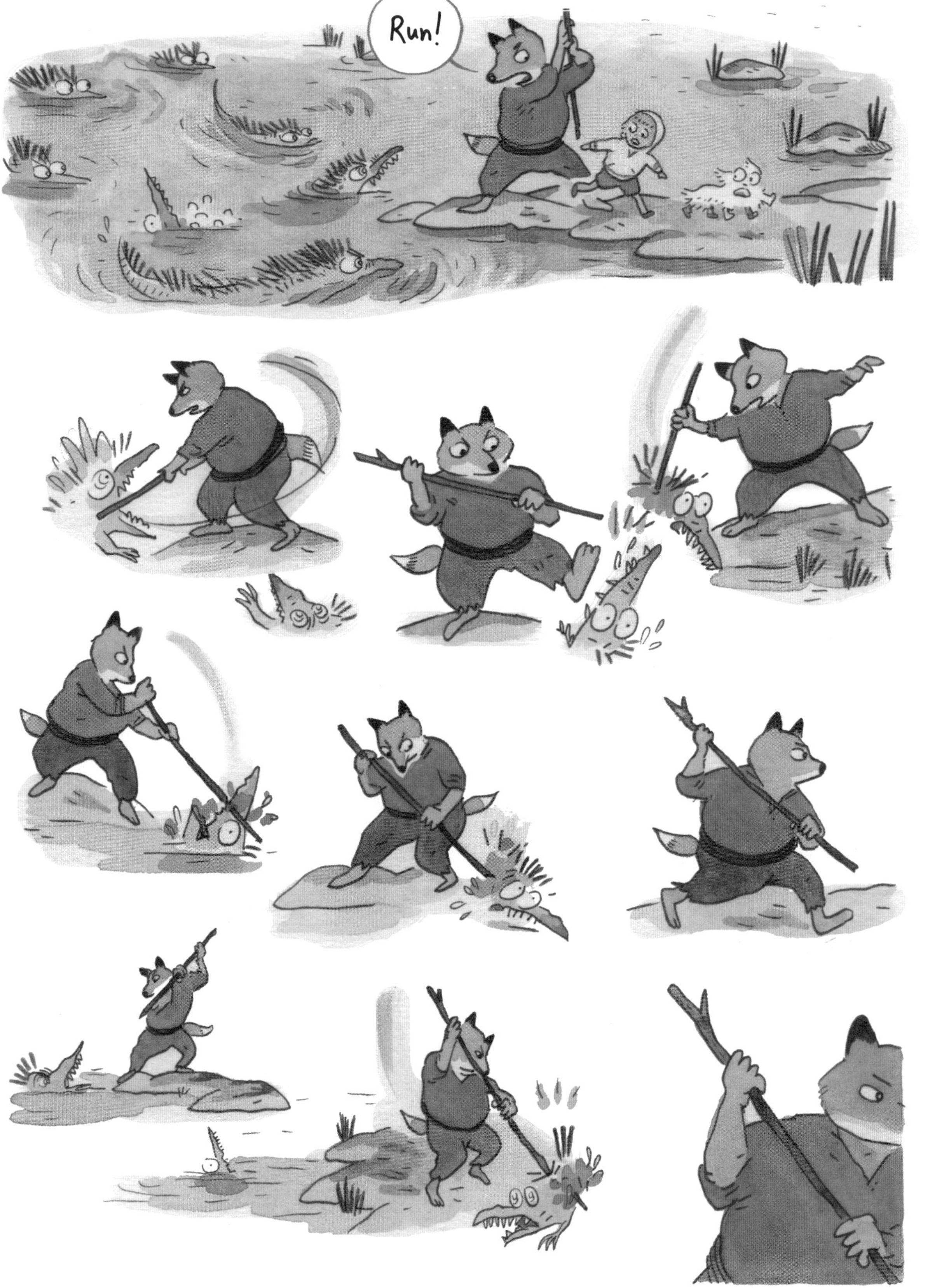
Run!

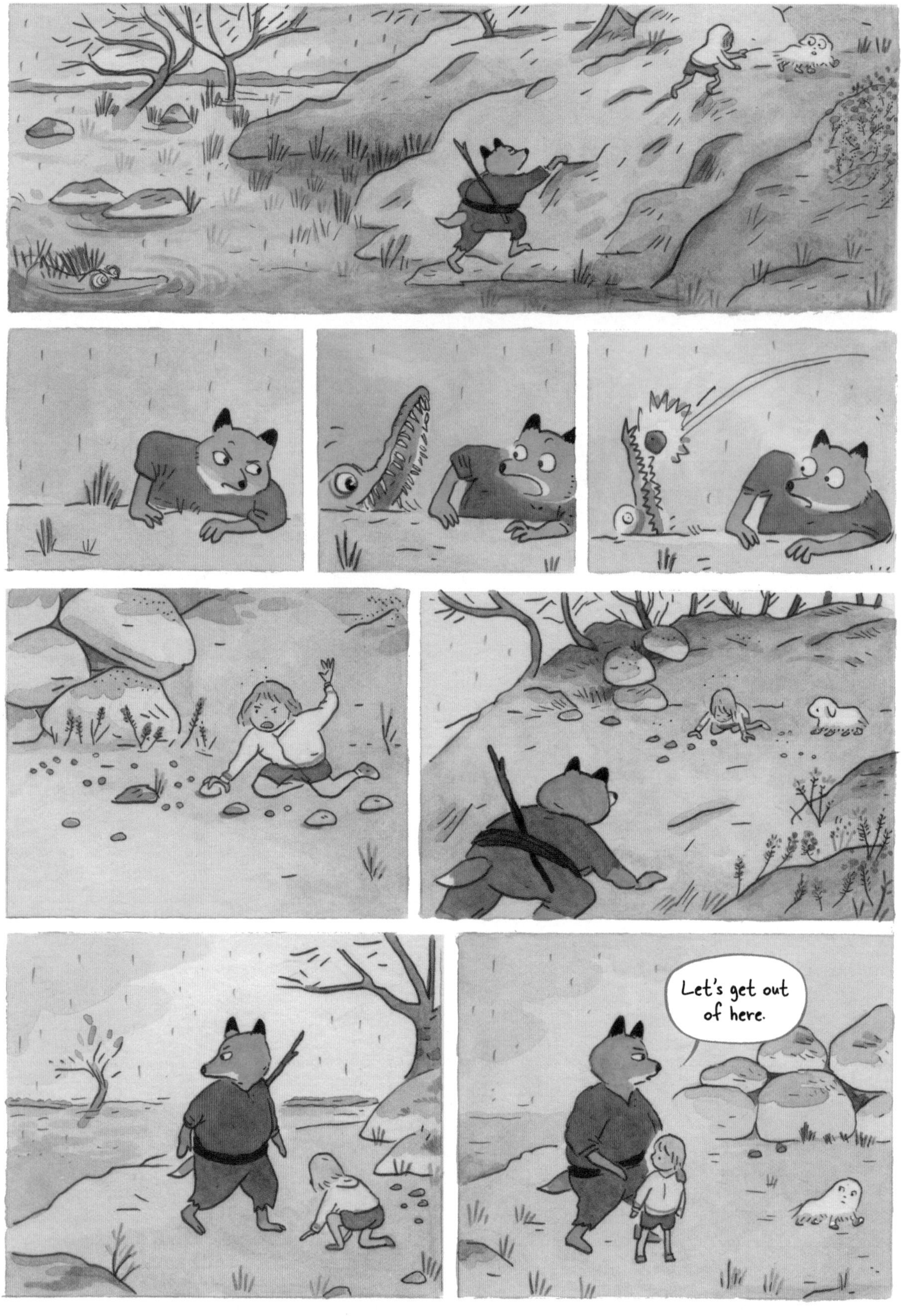
Let's get out of here.

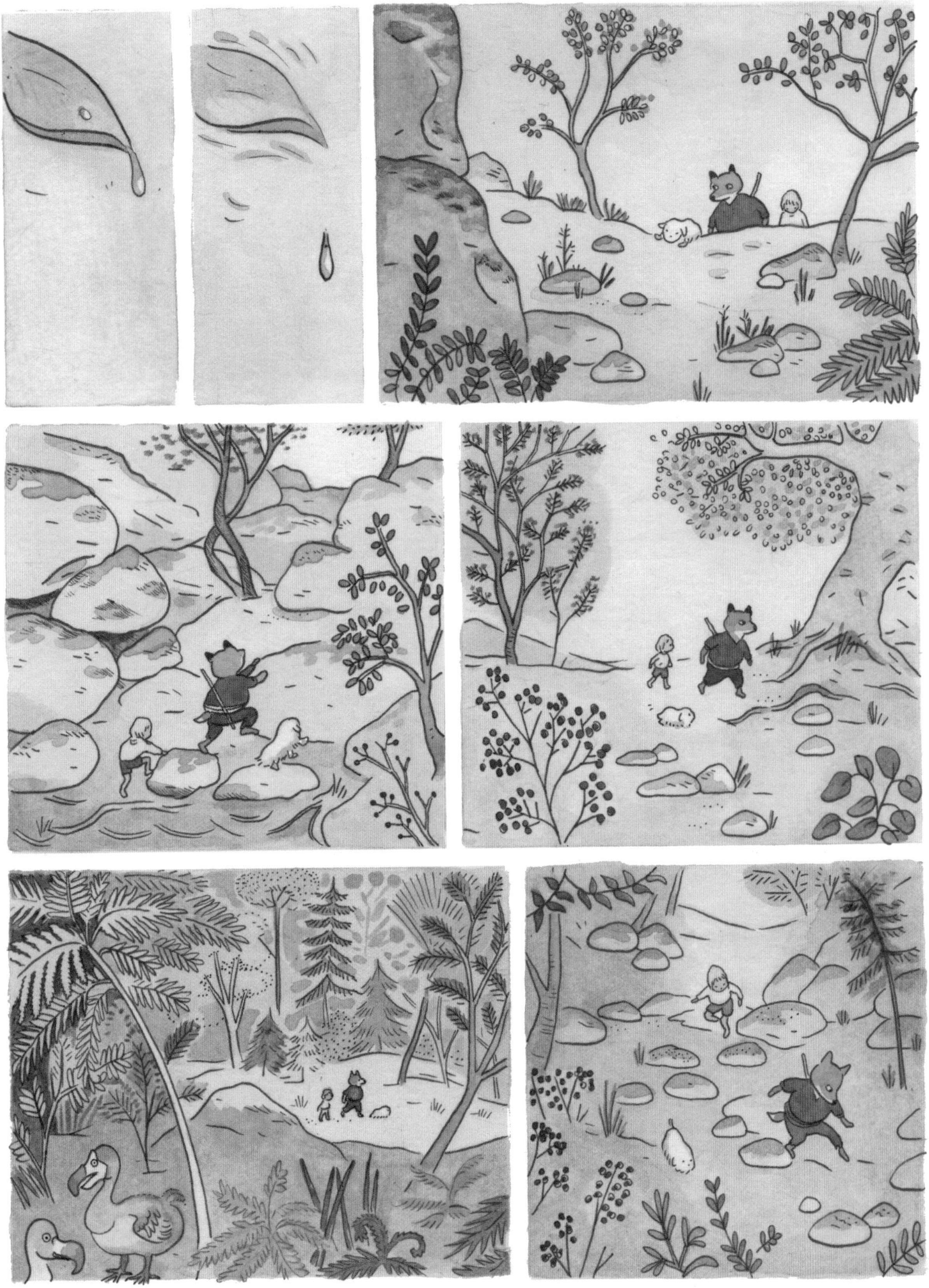

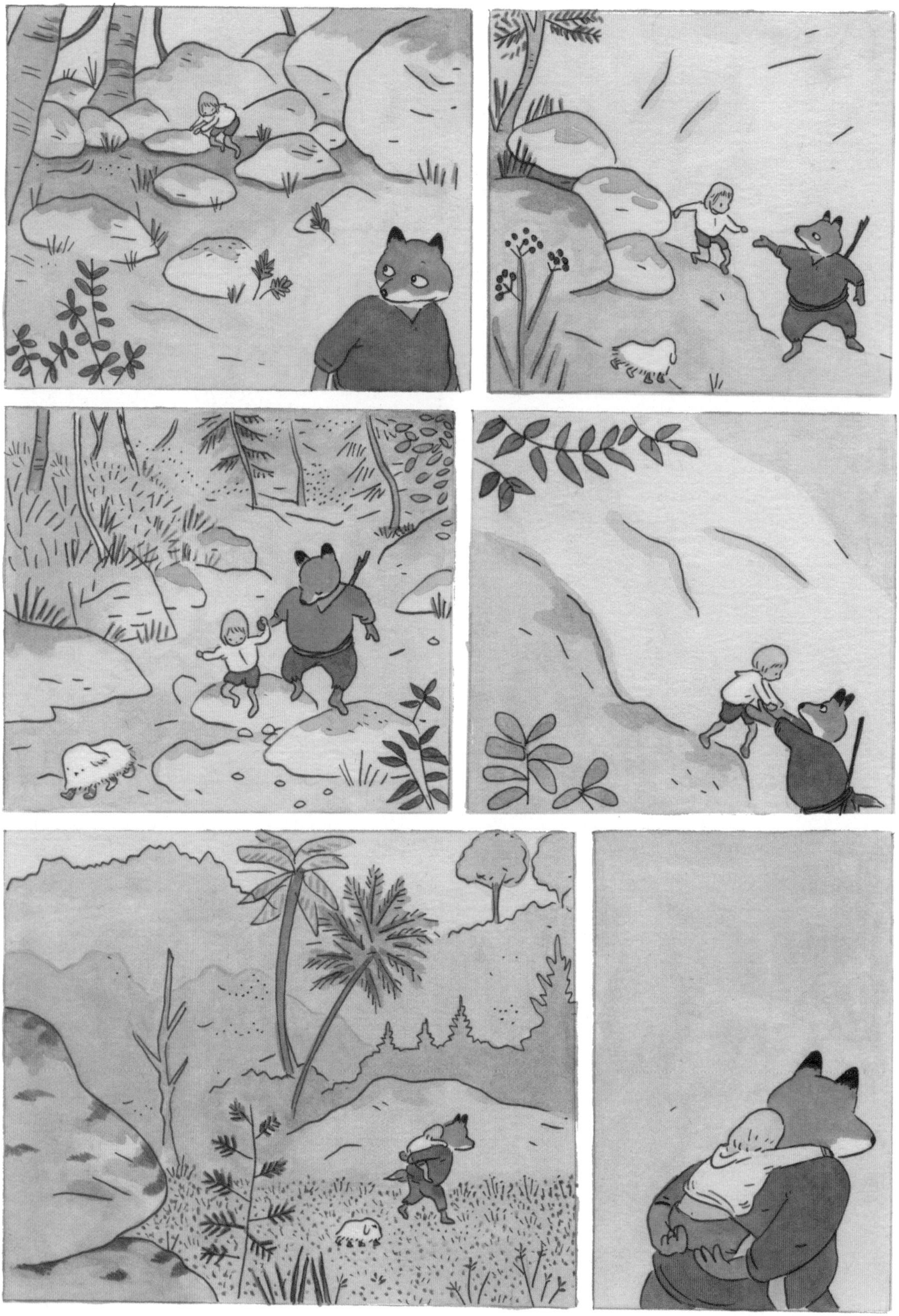

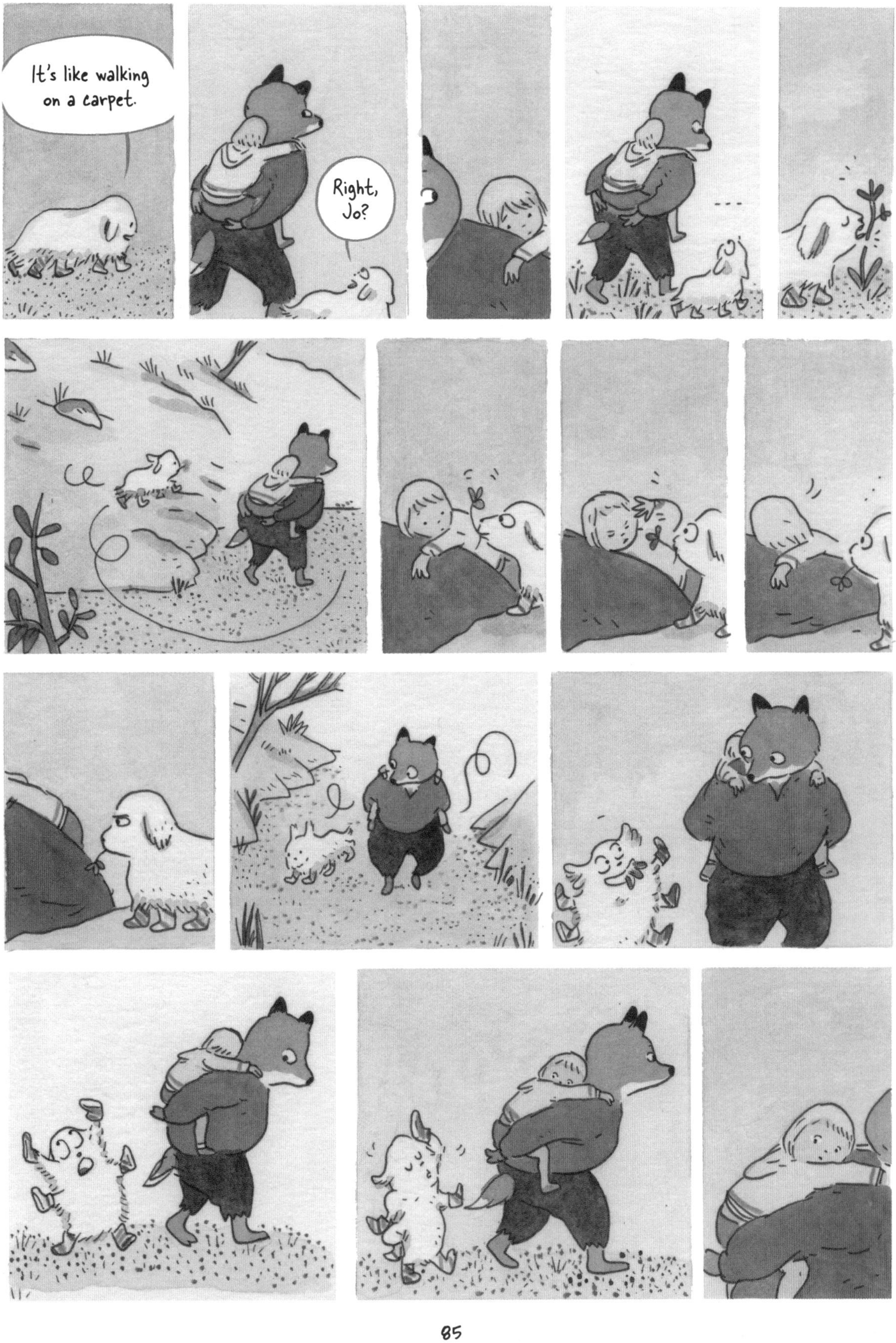
It's like walking on a carpet.
Right, Jo?
...

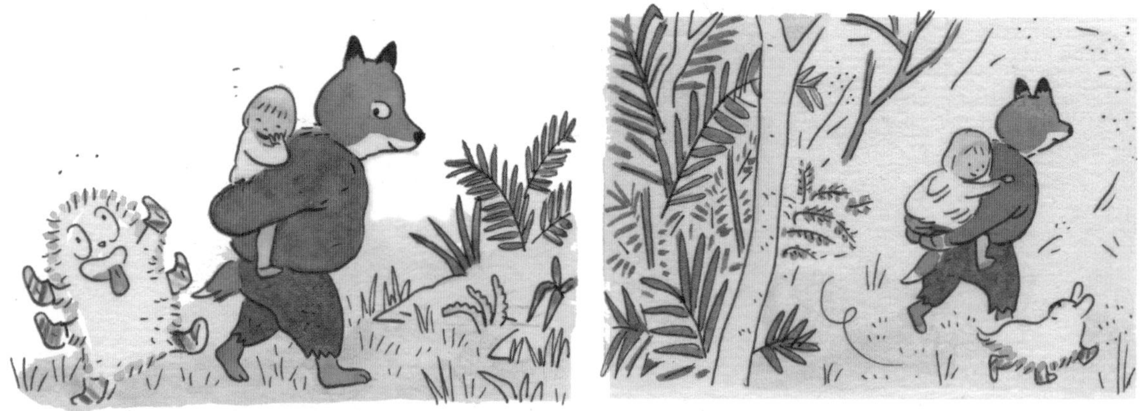

The trees grew so tall and their leaves were so large that you could barely glimpse the sky.

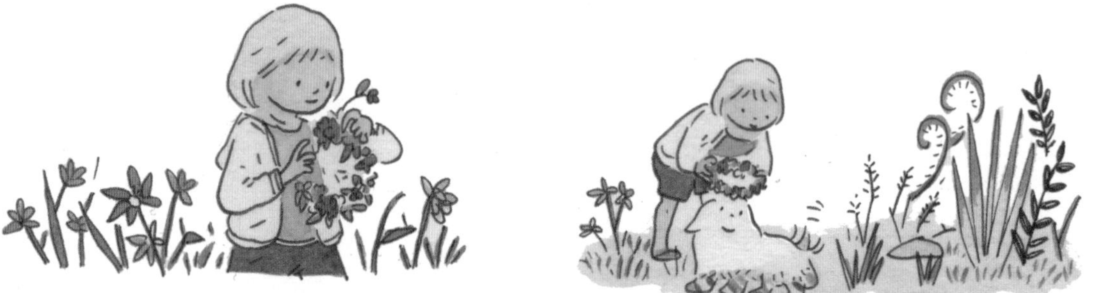

So it was that our travelers passed through this dreamlike realm...

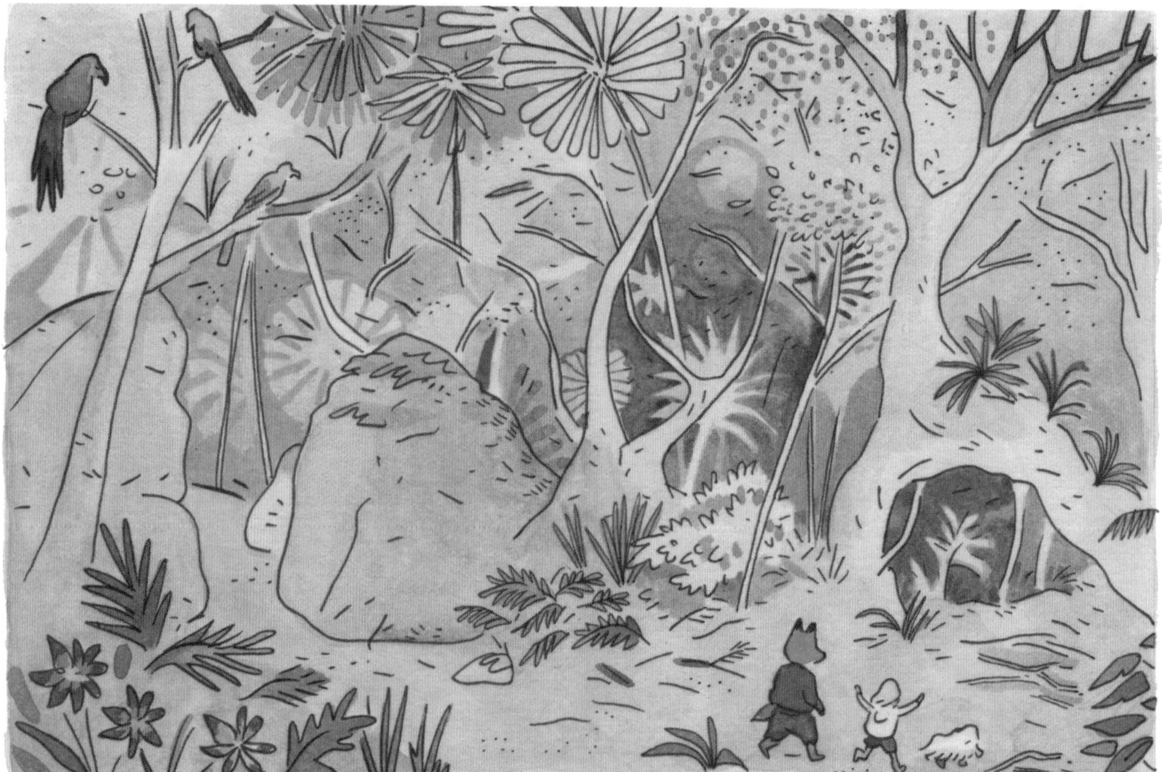

...their cares lifting and their guard slipping...

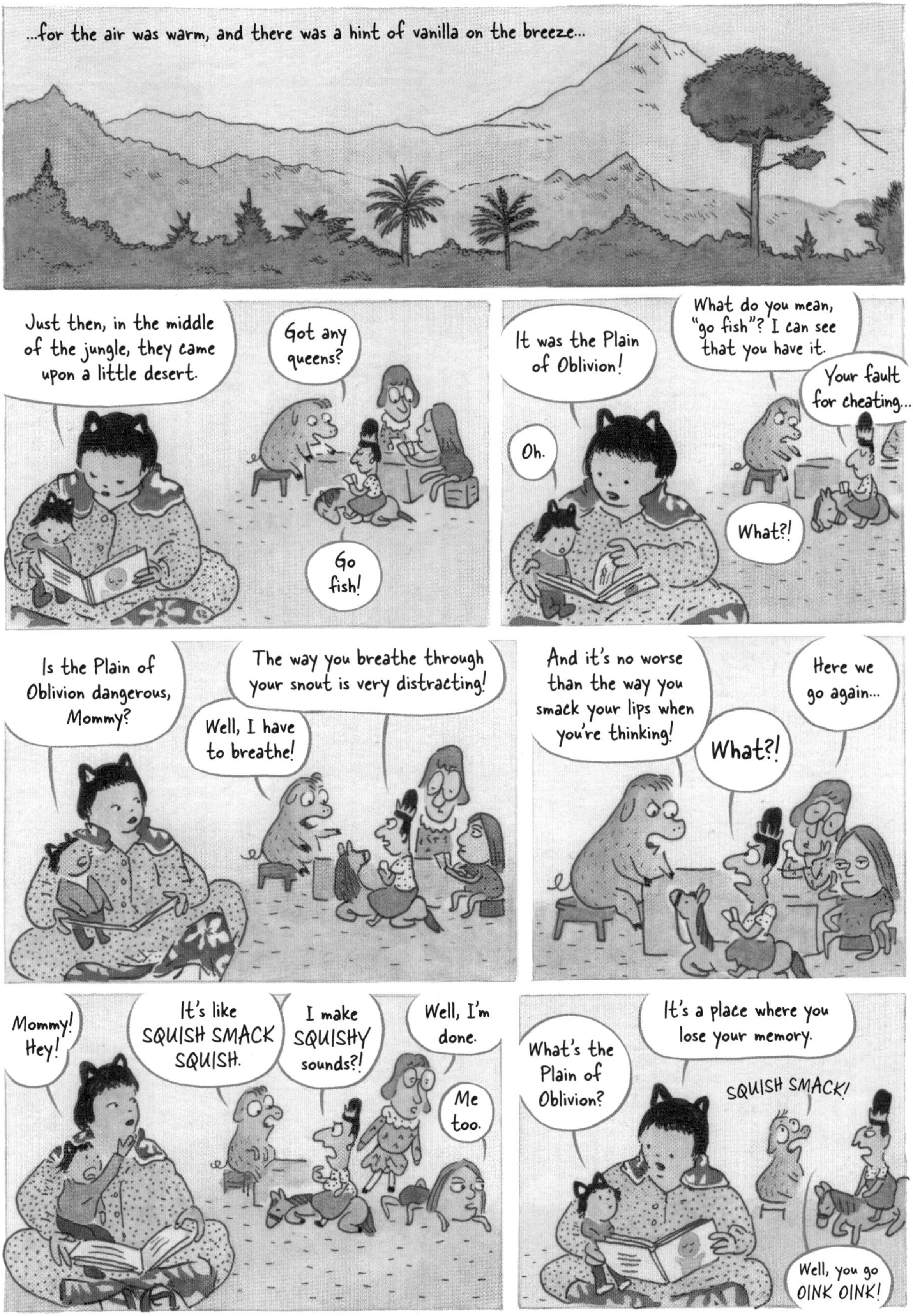
...for the air was warm, and there was a hint of vanilla on the breeze...
Just then, in the middle of the jungle, they came upon a little desert.
Got any queens?
Go fish!
It was the Plain of Oblivion!
What do you mean, "go fish"? I can see that you have it.
Your fault for cheating...
Oh.
What?!
Is the Plain of Oblivion dangerous, Mommy?
The way you breathe through your snout is very distracting!
Well, I have to breathe!
And it's no worse than the way you smack your lips when you're thinking!
What?!
Here we go again...
Mommy! Hey!
It's like SQUISH SMACK SQUISH.
I make SQUISHY sounds?!
Well, I'm done.
Me too.
What's the Plain of Oblivion?
It's a place where you lose your memory.
SQUISH SMACK!
Well, you go OINK OINK!

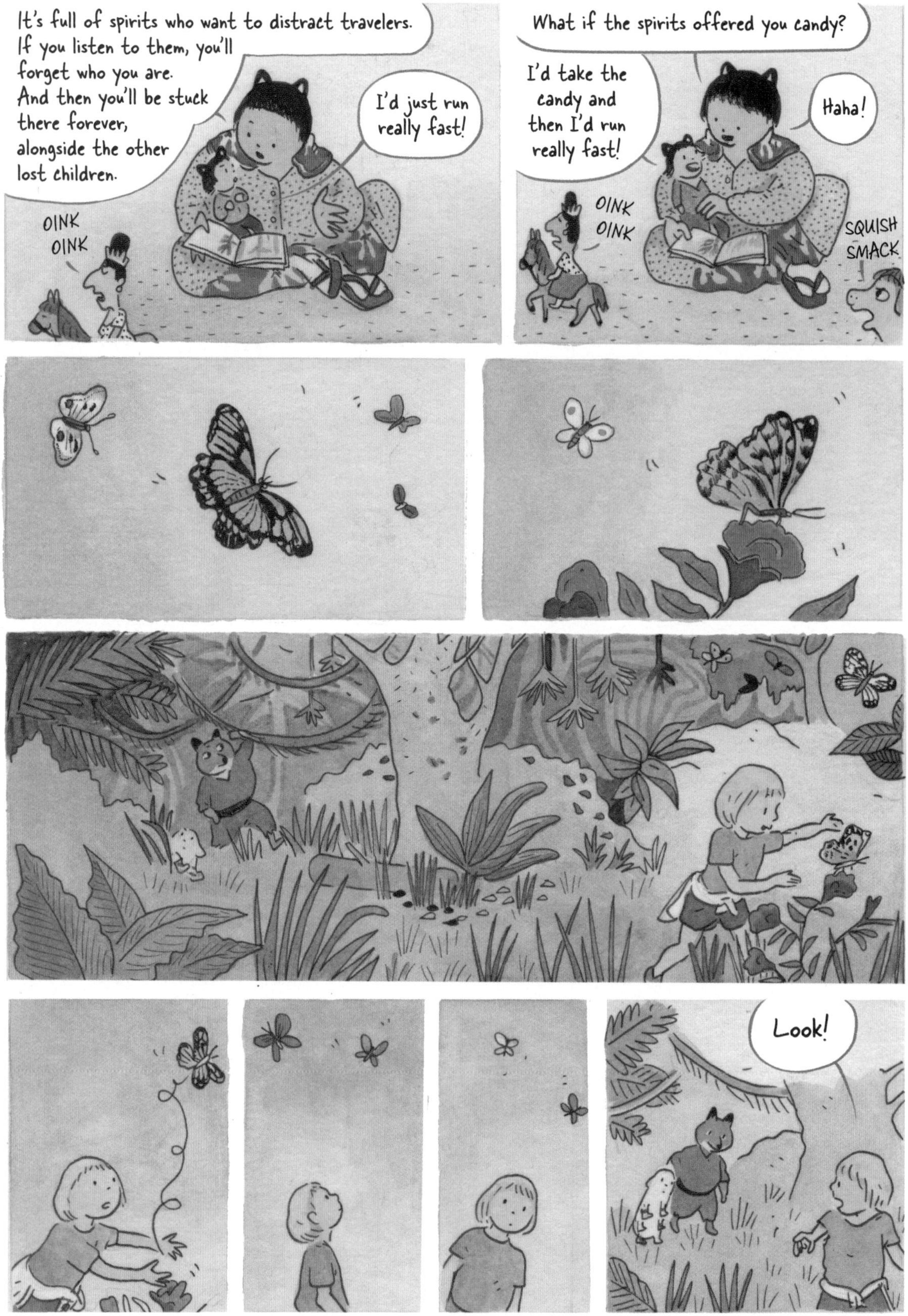
It's full of spirits who want to distract travelers. If you listen to them, you'll forget who you are. And then you'll be stuck there forever, alongside the other lost children.
I'd just run really fast!
OINK OINK
What if the spirits offered you candy?
I'd take the candy and then I'd run really fast!
Haha!
OINK OINK
SQUISH SMACK
Look!

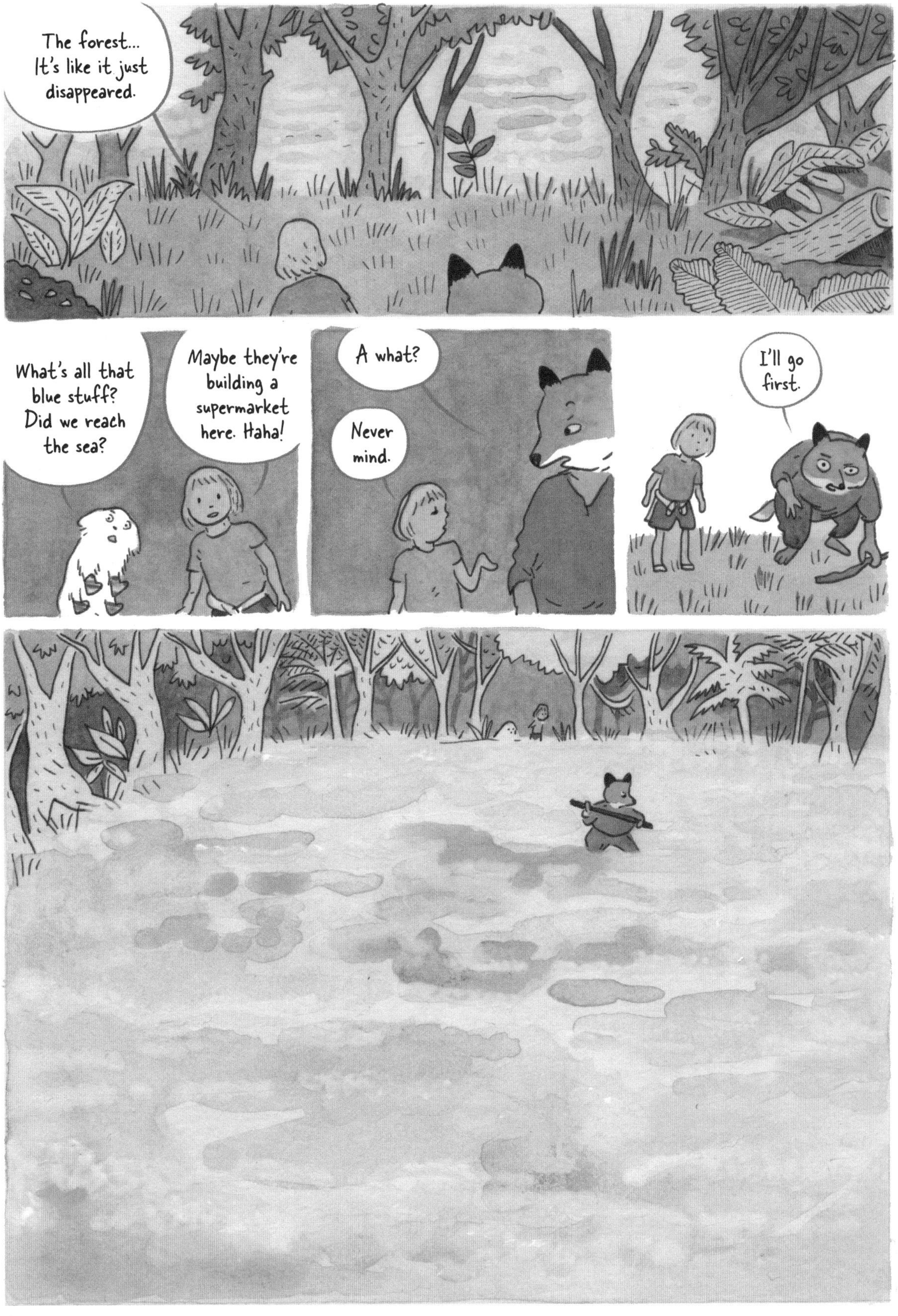
The forest... It's like it just disappeared.
What's all that blue stuff? Did we reach the sea?
Maybe they're building a supermarket here. Haha!
A what?
Never mind.
I'll go first.

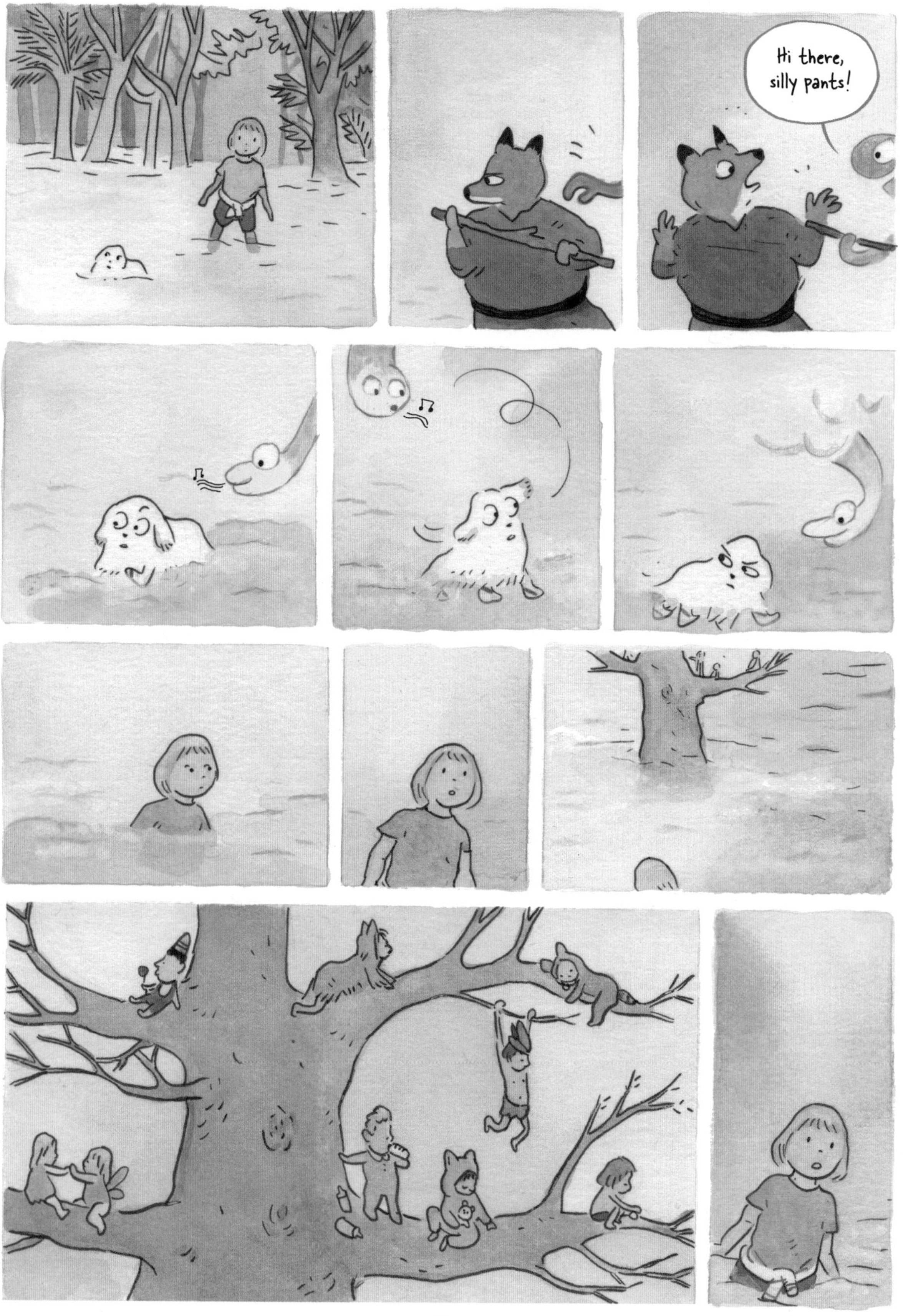
Hi there, silly pants!

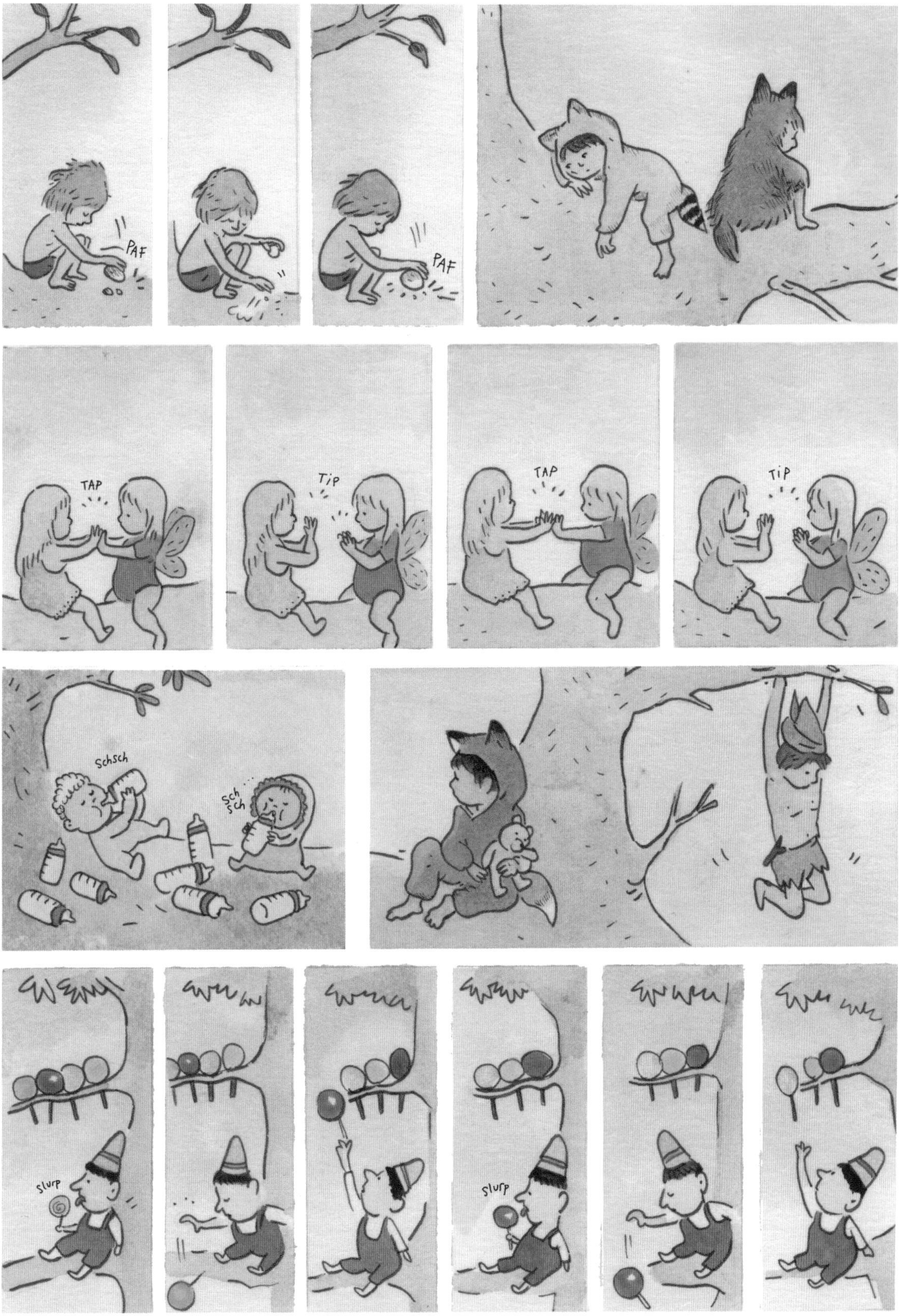
PAF
PAF
TAP
TiP
TAP
TiP
schsch
sch sch
slurp
slurp

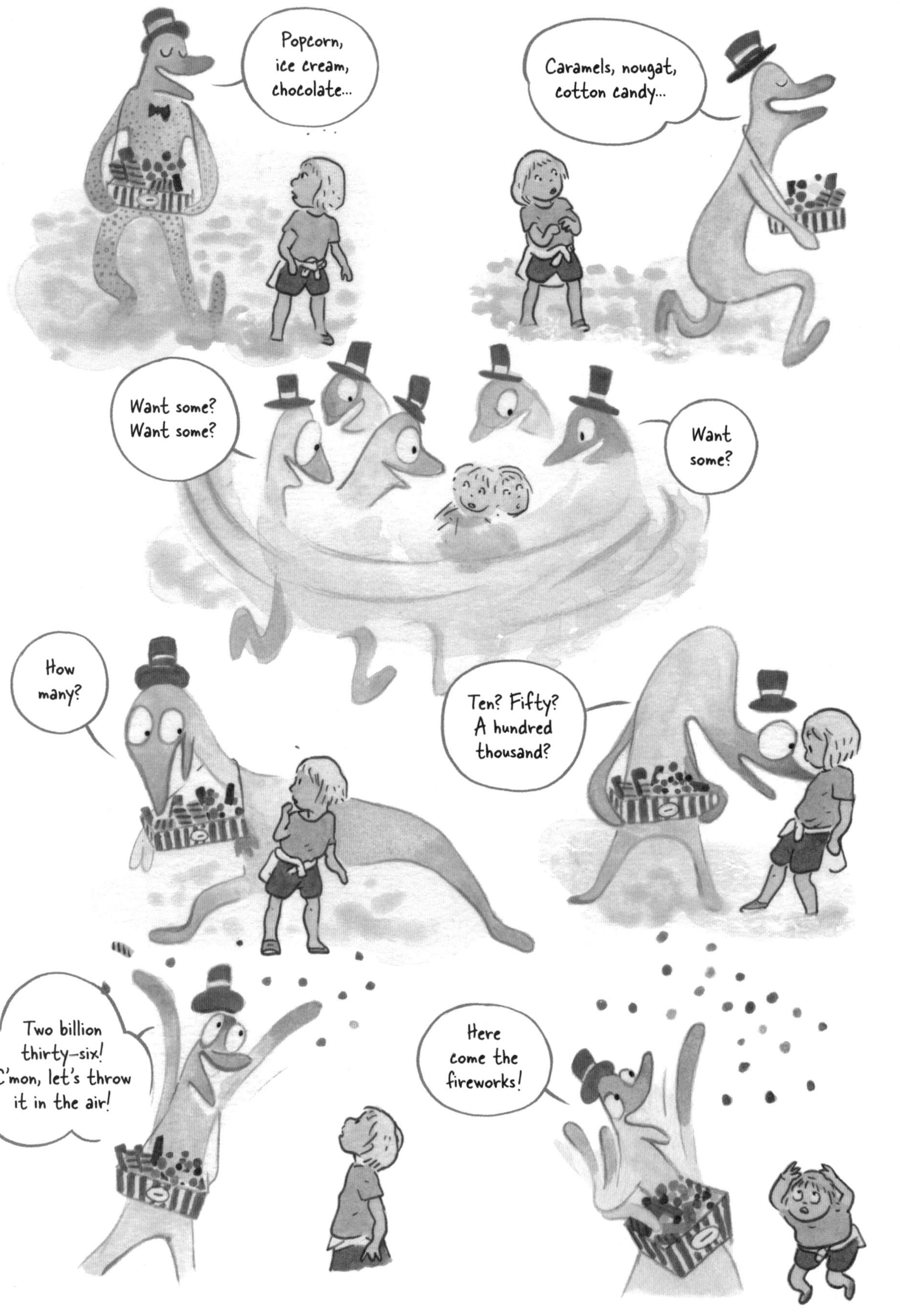
Popcorn, ice cream, chocolate...
Caramels, nougat, cotton candy...
Want some? Want some?
Want some?
How many?
Ten? Fifty? A hundred thousand?
Two billion thirty-six! C'mon, let's throw it in the air!
Here come the fireworks!

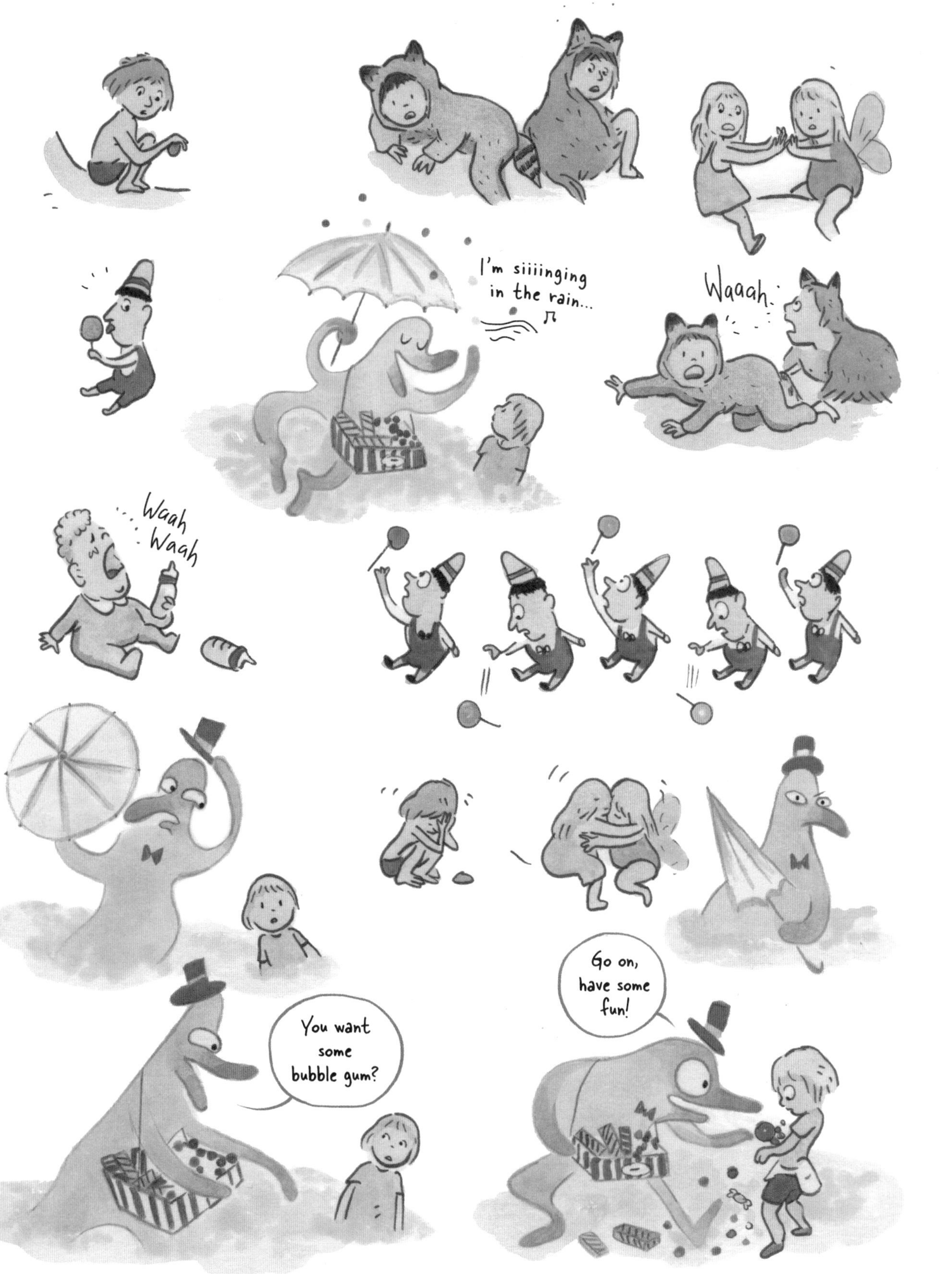
I'm siiiinging in the rain...
Waaah
Waah Waah
You want some bubble gum?
Go on, have some fun!

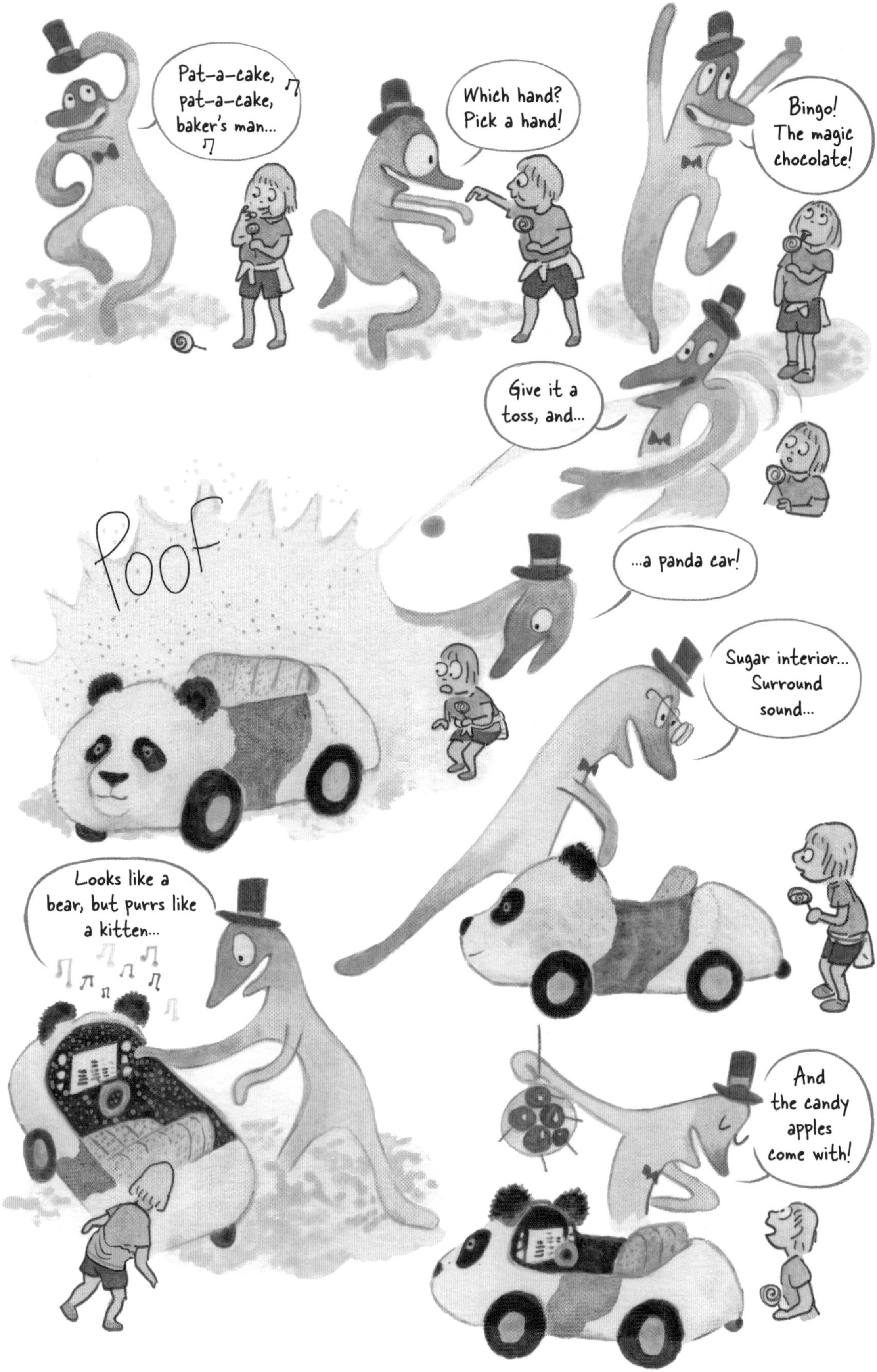
Pat-a-cake, pat-a-cake, baker's man...
Which hand? Pick a hand!
Bingo! The magic chocolate!
Give it a toss, and...
Poof
...a panda car!
Sugar interior... Surround sound...
Looks like a bear, but purrs like a kitten...
And the candy apples come with!

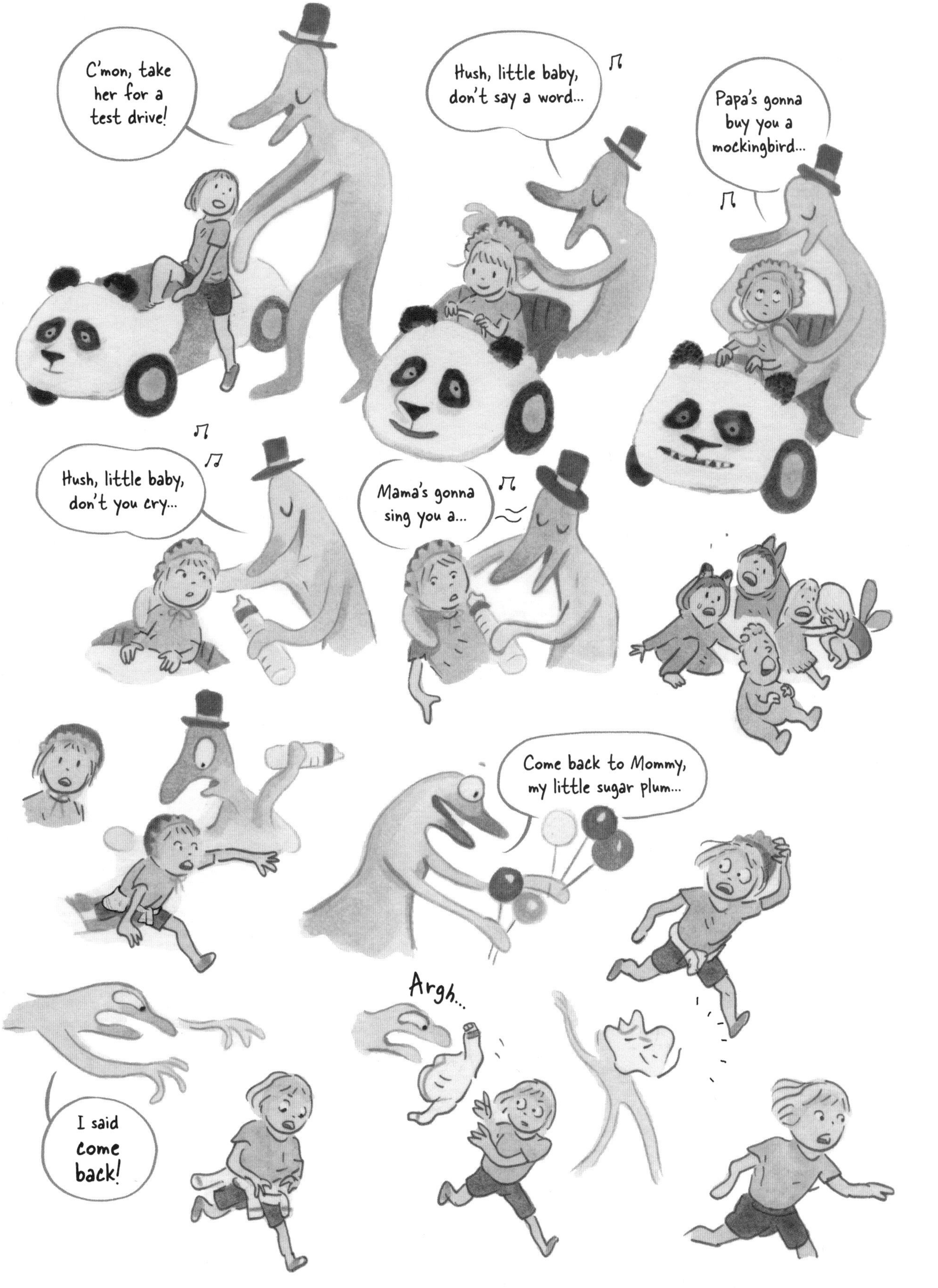

C'mon, take her for a test drive!
Hush, little baby, don't say a word...
Papa's gonna buy you a mockingbird...
Hush, little baby, don't you cry...
Mama's gonna sing you a...
Come back to Mommy, my little sugar plum...
Argh...
I said come back!

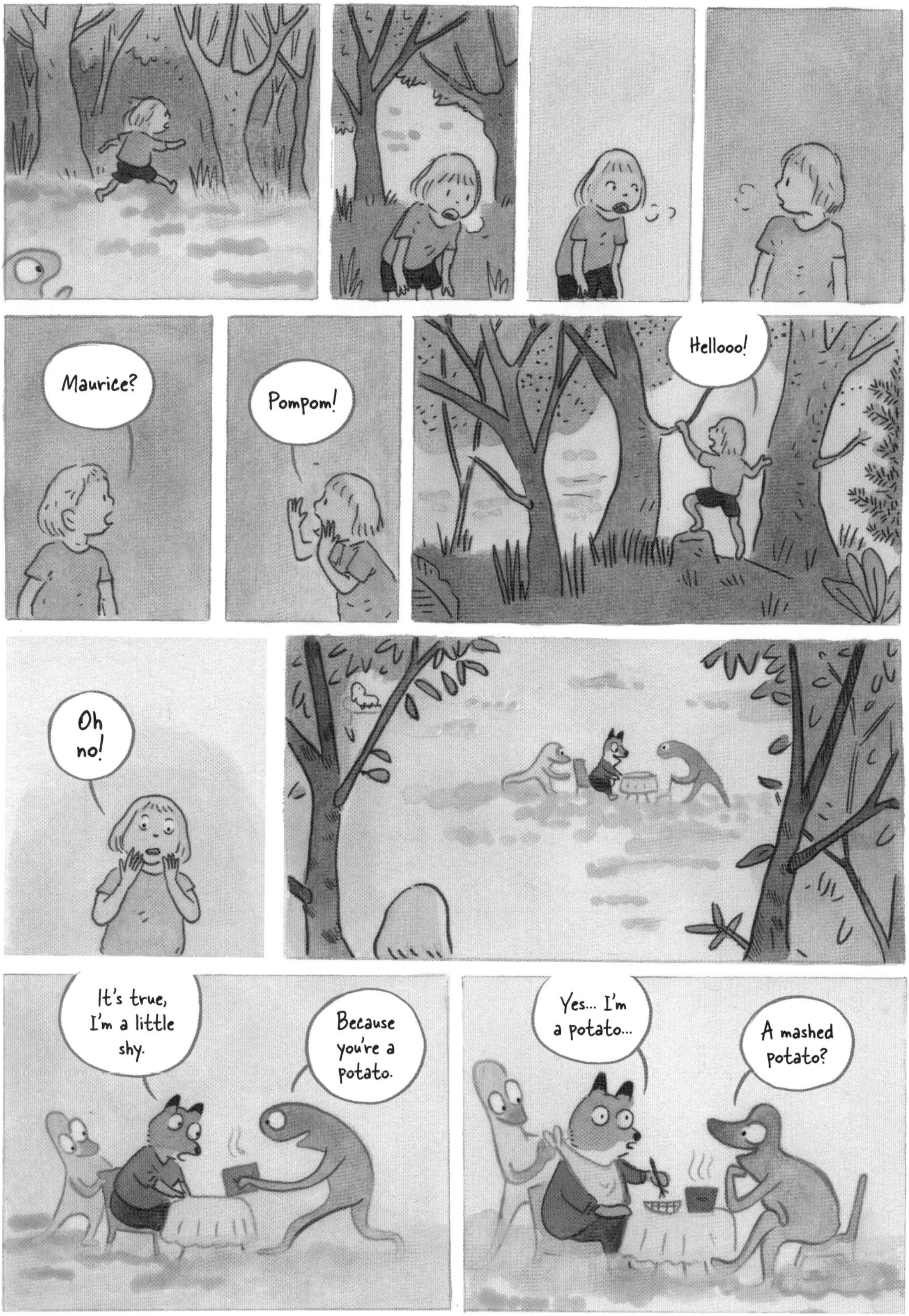

Maurice?
Pompom!
Hellooo!
Oh no!
It's true, I'm a little shy.
Because you're a potato.
Yes... I'm a potato...
A mashed potato?

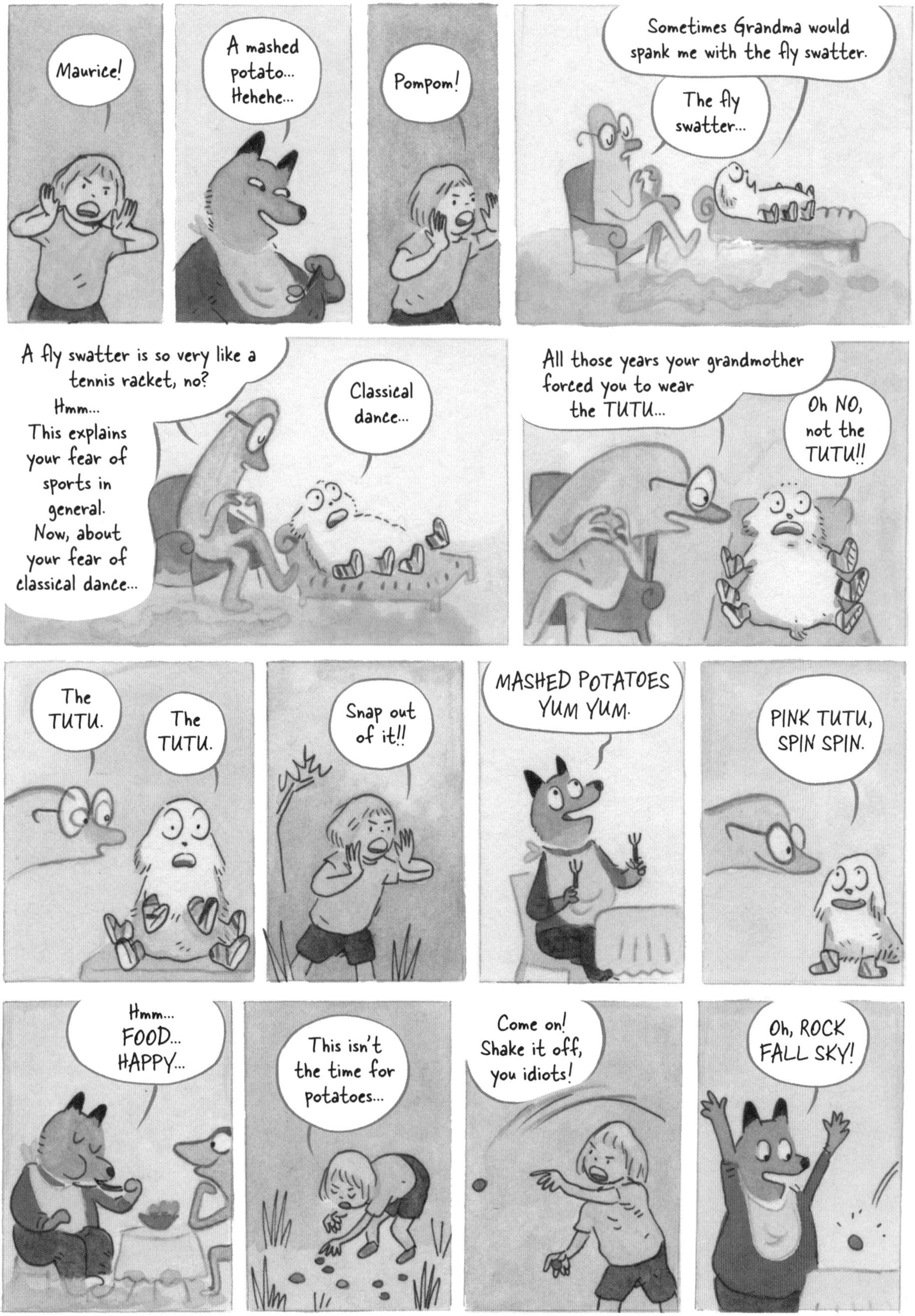
Maurice!
A mashed potato... Hehehe...
Pompom!
Sometimes Grandma would spank me with the fly swatter.
The fly swatter...
A fly swatter is so very like a tennis racket, no? Hmm... This explains your fear of sports in general. Now, about your fear of classical dance...
Classical dance...
All those years your grandmother forced you to wear the TUTU...
Oh NO, not the TUTU!!
The TUTU.
The TUTU.
Snap out of it!!
MASHED POTATOES YUM YUM.
PINK TUTU, SPIN SPIN.
Hmm... FOOD... HAPPY...
This isn't the time for potatoes...
Come on! Shake it off, you idiots!
Oh, ROCK FALL SKY!

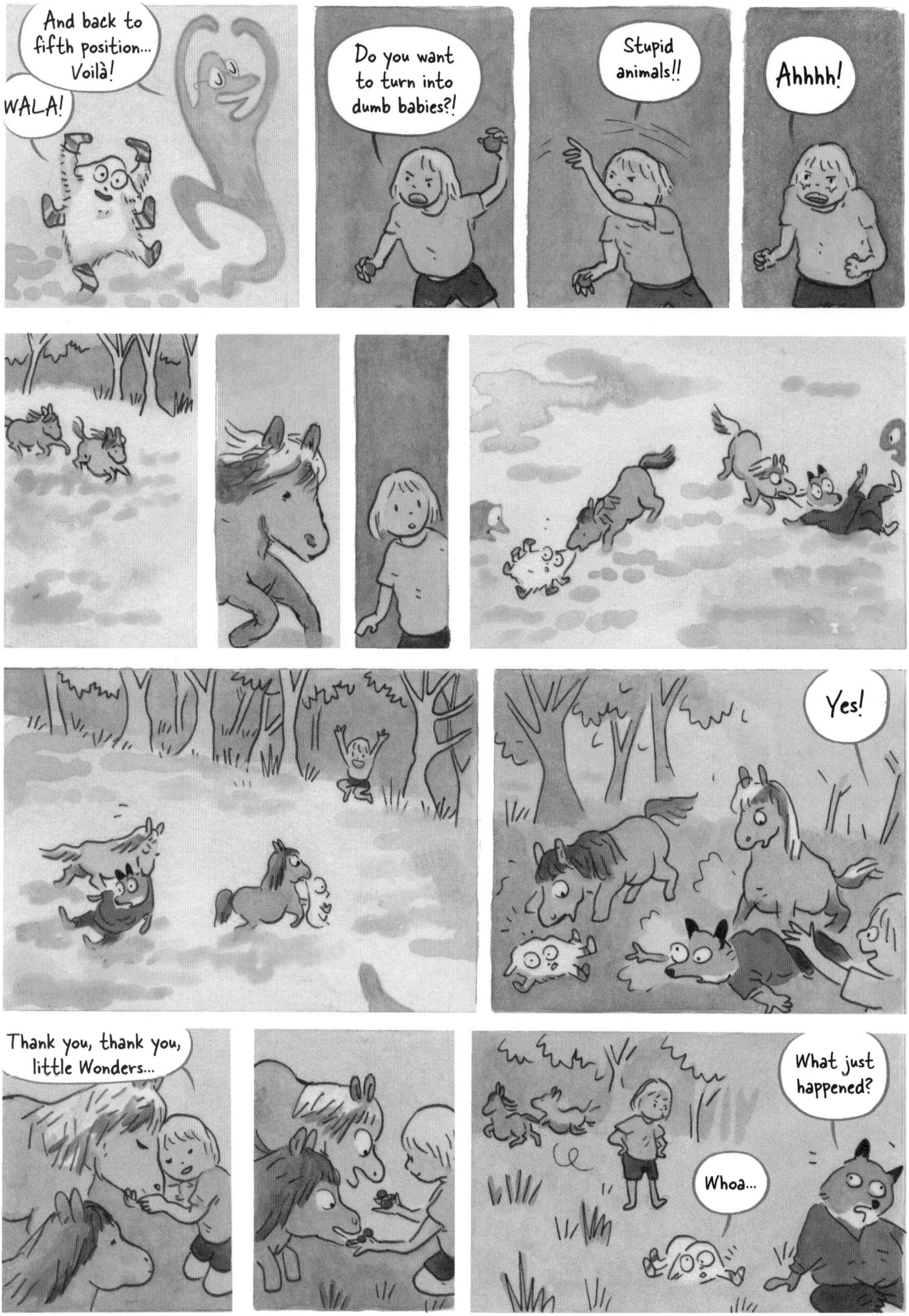

And back to fifth position... Voilà!
WALA!
Do you want to turn into dumb babies?!
Stupid animals!!
Ahhhh!
Yes!
Thank you, thank you, little Wonders...
What just happened?
Whoa...

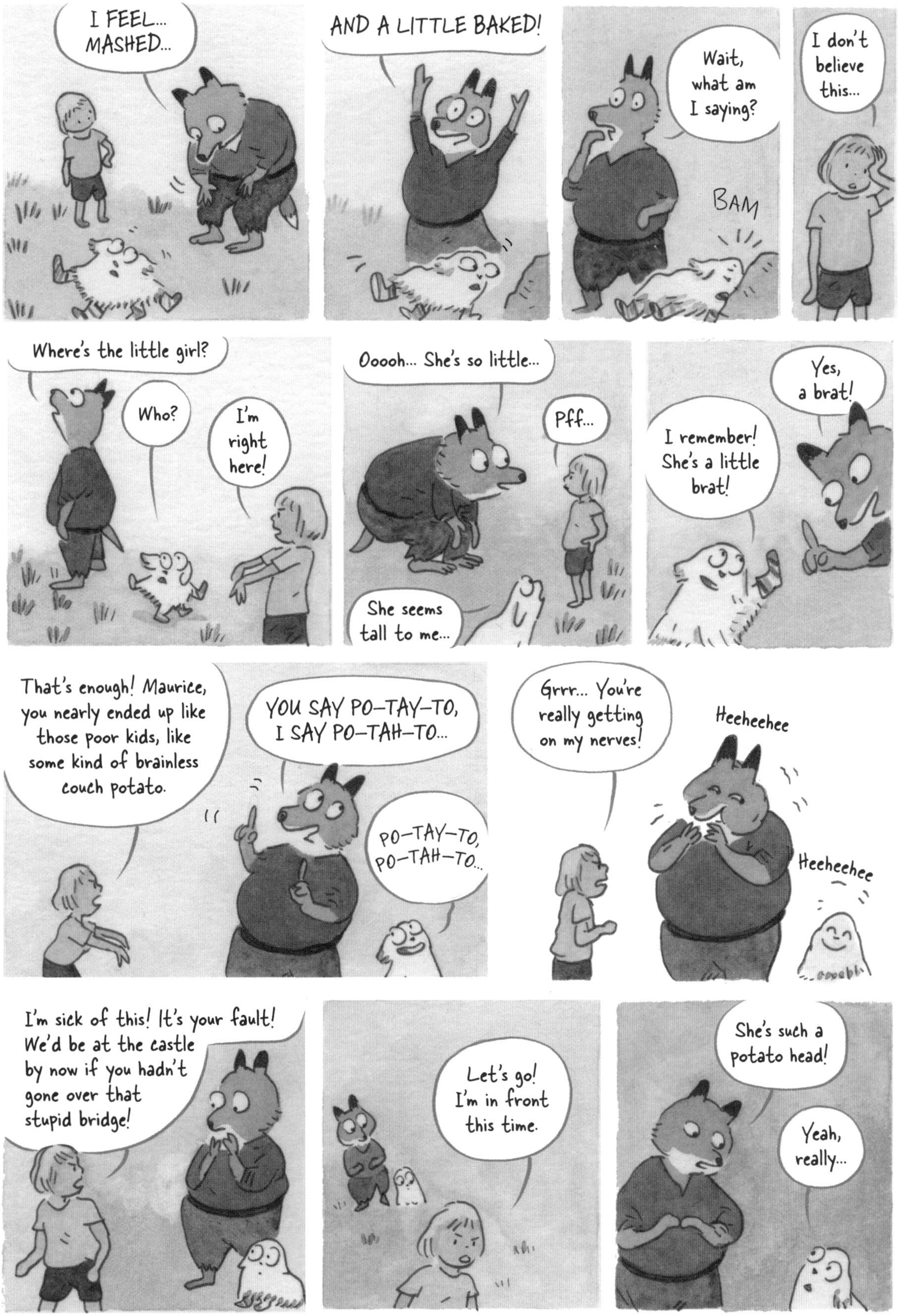

I FEEL... MASHED...
AND A LITTLE BAKED!
Wait, what am I saying?
BAM
I don't believe this...
Where's the little girl?
Who?
I'm right here!
Ooooh... She's so little...
Pff...
She seems tall to me...
I remember! She's a little brat!
Yes, a brat!
That's enough! Maurice, you nearly ended up like those poor kids, like some kind of brainless couch potato.
YOU SAY PO-TAY-TO, I SAY PO-TAH-TO...
PO-TAY-TO, PO-TAH-TO...
Grrr... You're really getting on my nerves!
Heeheehee
Heeheehee
I'm sick of this! It's your fault! We'd be at the castle by now if you hadn't gone over that stupid bridge!
Let's go! I'm in front this time.
She's such a potato head!
Yeah, really...

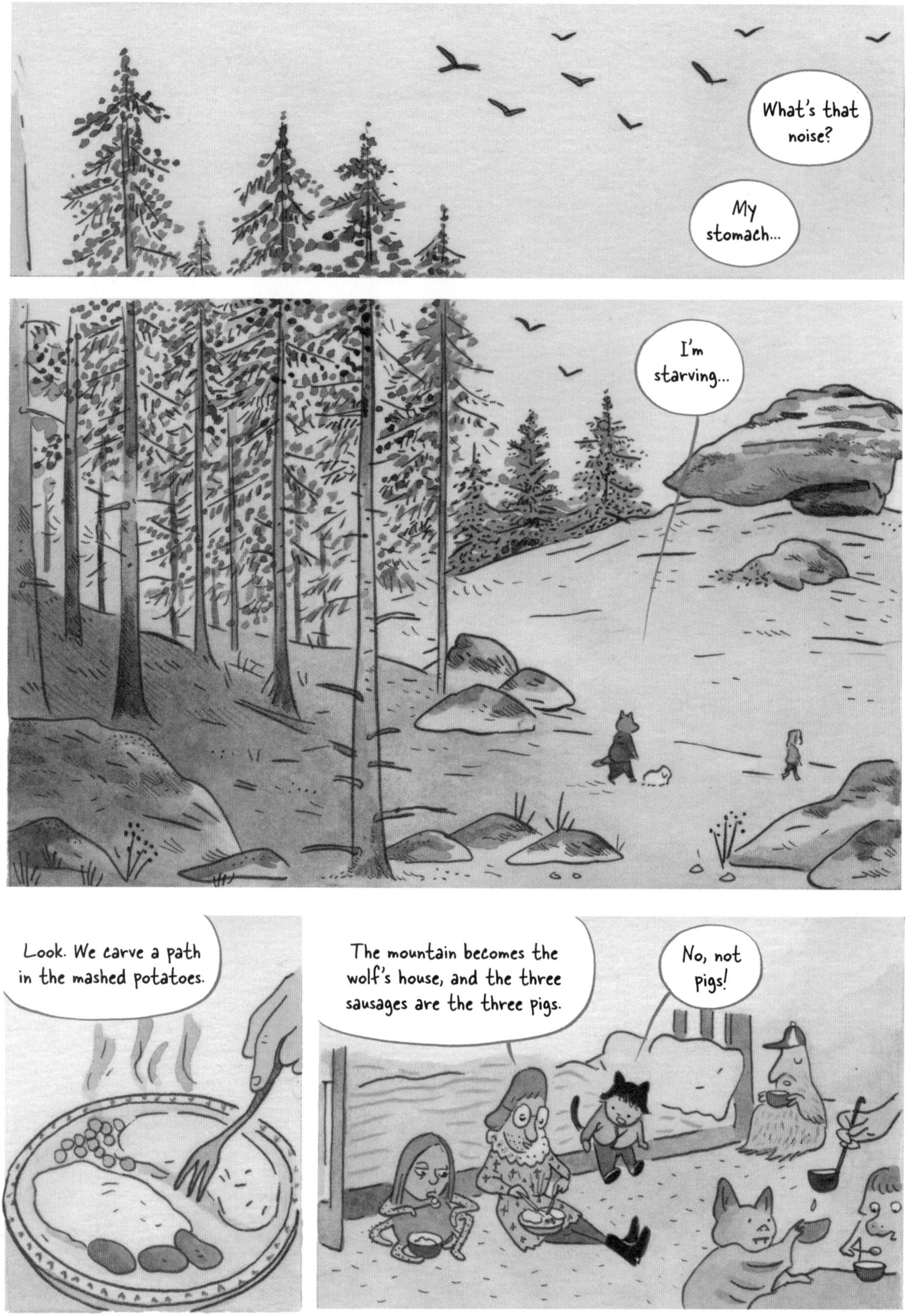
What's that noise?
My stomach...
I'm starving...
Look. We carve a path in the mashed potatoes.
The mountain becomes the wolf's house, and the three sausages are the three pigs.
No, not pigs!

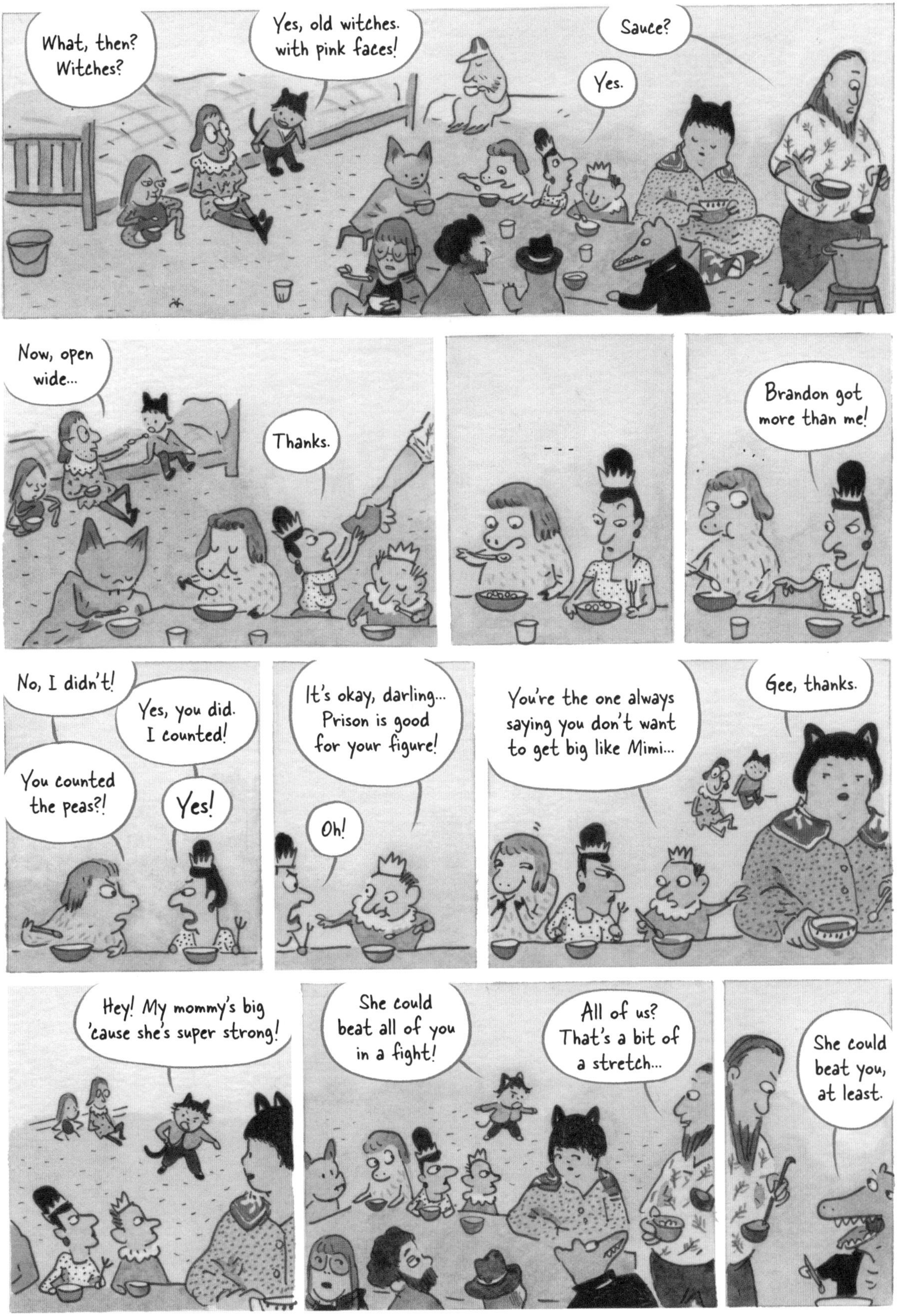
What, then? Witches?
Yes, old witches. with pink faces!
Sauce?
Yes.
Now, open wide...
Thanks.
...
Brandon got more than me!
No, I didn't!
Yes, you did. I counted!
You counted the peas?!
Yes!
It's okay, darling... Prison is good for your figure!
Oh!
You're the one always saying you don't want to get big like Mimi...
Gee, thanks.
Hey! My mommy's big 'cause she's super strong!
She could beat all of you in a fight!
All of us? That's a bit of a stretch...
She could beat you, at least.

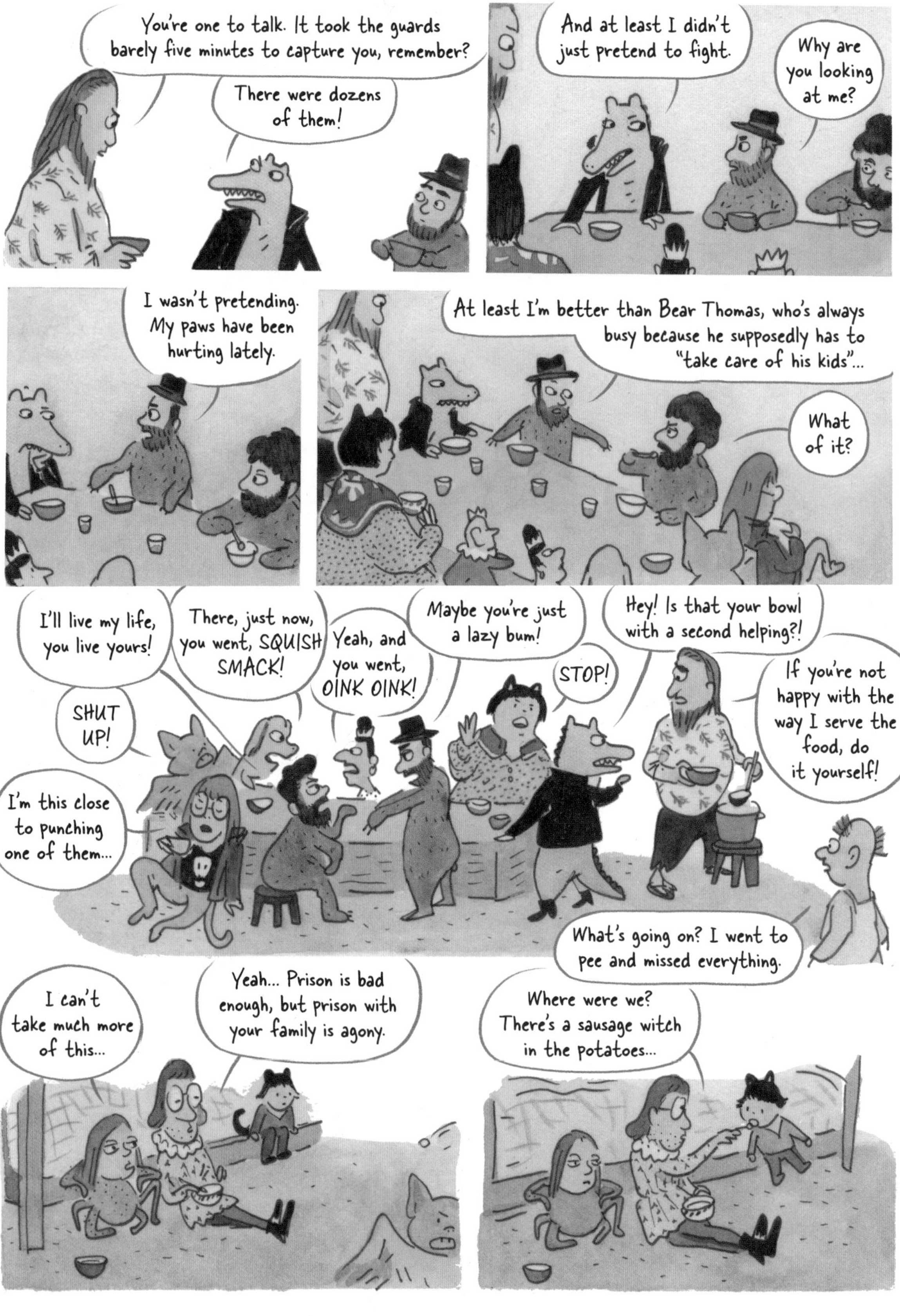
You're one to talk. It took the guards barely five minutes to capture you, remember?
There were dozens of them!
And at least I didn't just pretend to fight.
Why are you looking at me?
I wasn't pretending. My paws have been hurting lately.
At least I'm better than Bear Thomas, who's always busy because he supposedly has to "take care of his kids"...
What of it?
I'll live my life, you live yours!
There, just now, you went, SQUISH SMACK!
Yeah, and you went, OINK OINK!
Maybe you're just a lazy bum!
Hey! Is that your bowl with a second helping?!
STOP!
If you're not happy with the way I serve the food, do it yourself!
SHUT UP!
I'm this close to punching one of them...
What's going on? I went to pee and missed everything.
I can't take much more of this...
Yeah... Prison is bad enough, but prison with your family is agony.
Where were we? There's a sausage witch in the potatoes...

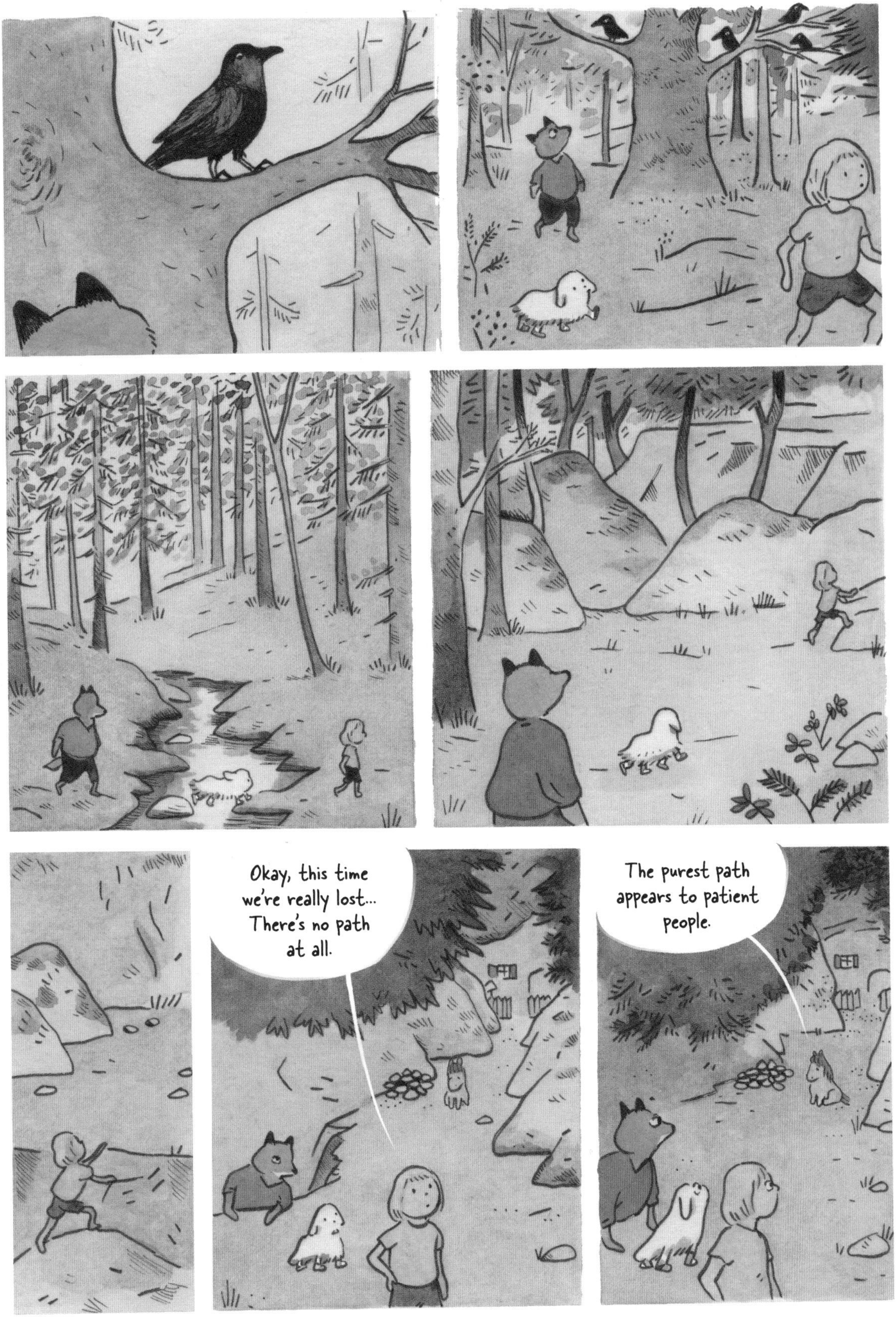
Okay, this time we're really lost... There's no path at all.
The purest path appears to patient people.

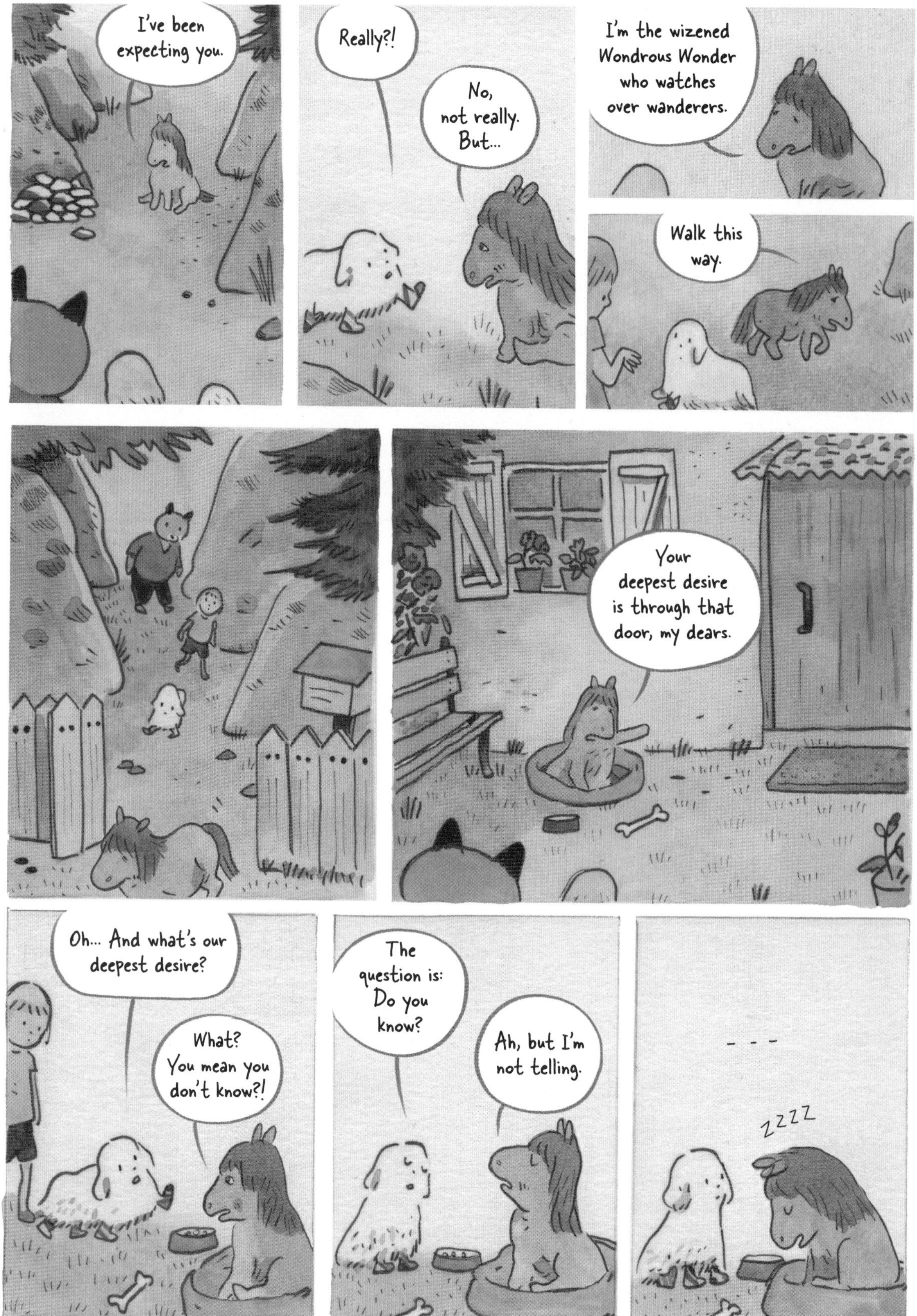
I've been expecting you.
Really?!
No, not really. But...
I'm the wizened Wondrous Wonder who watches over wanderers.
Walk this way.
Your deepest desire is through that door, my dears.
Oh... And what's our deepest desire?
What? You mean you don't know?!
The question is: Do you know?
Ah, but I'm not telling.
- - -
ZZZZ

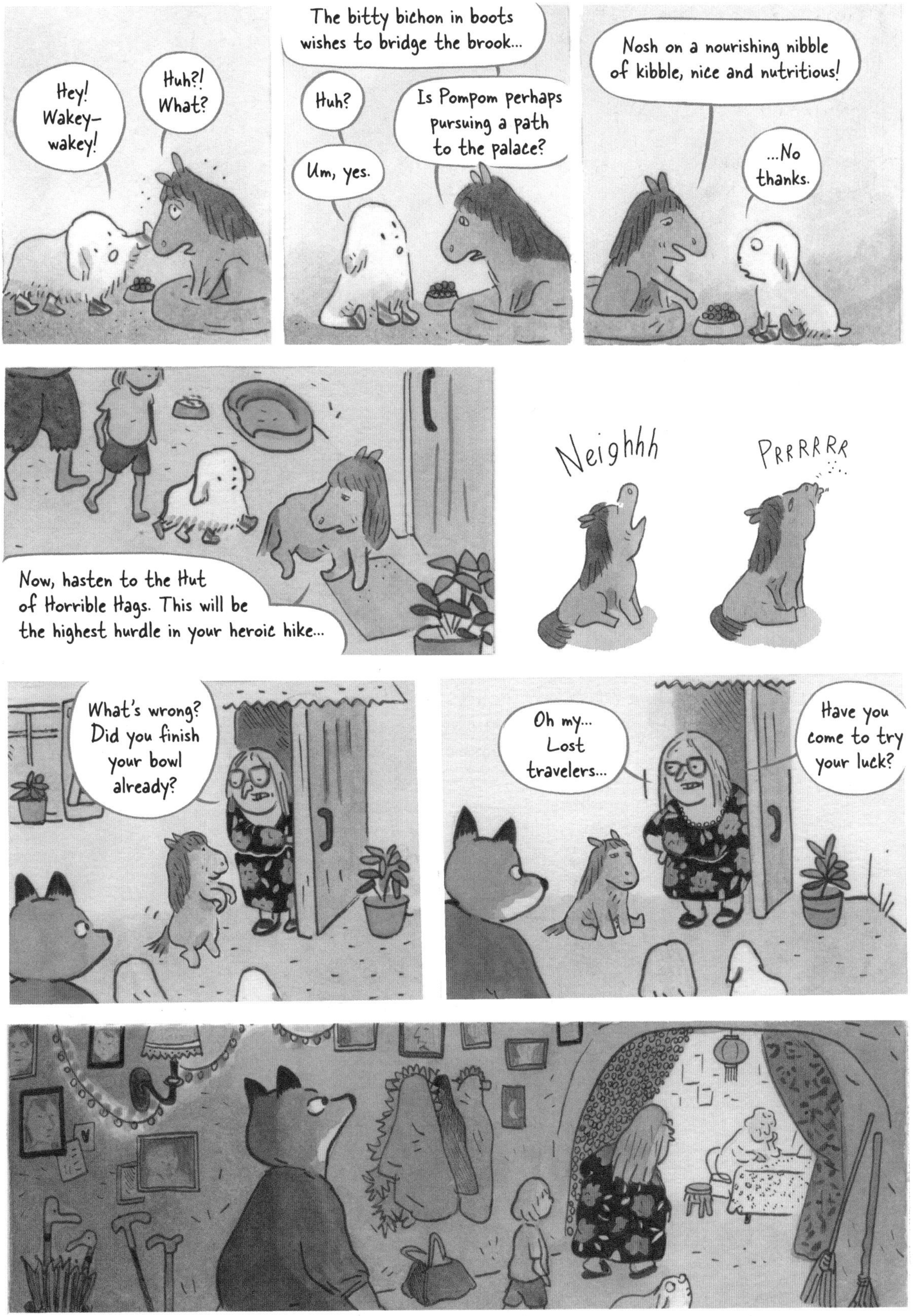

Hey! Wakey-wakey!
Huh?! What?
The bitty bichon in boots wishes to bridge the brook...
Huh?
Um, yes.
Is Pompom perhaps pursuing a path to the palace?
Nosh on a nourishing nibble of kibble, nice and nutritious!
...No thanks.
Now, hasten to the Hut of Horrible Hags. This will be the highest hurdle in your heroic hike...
Neighhh
PRRRRRR
What's wrong? Did you finish your bowl already?
Oh my... Lost travelers...
Have you come to try your luck?

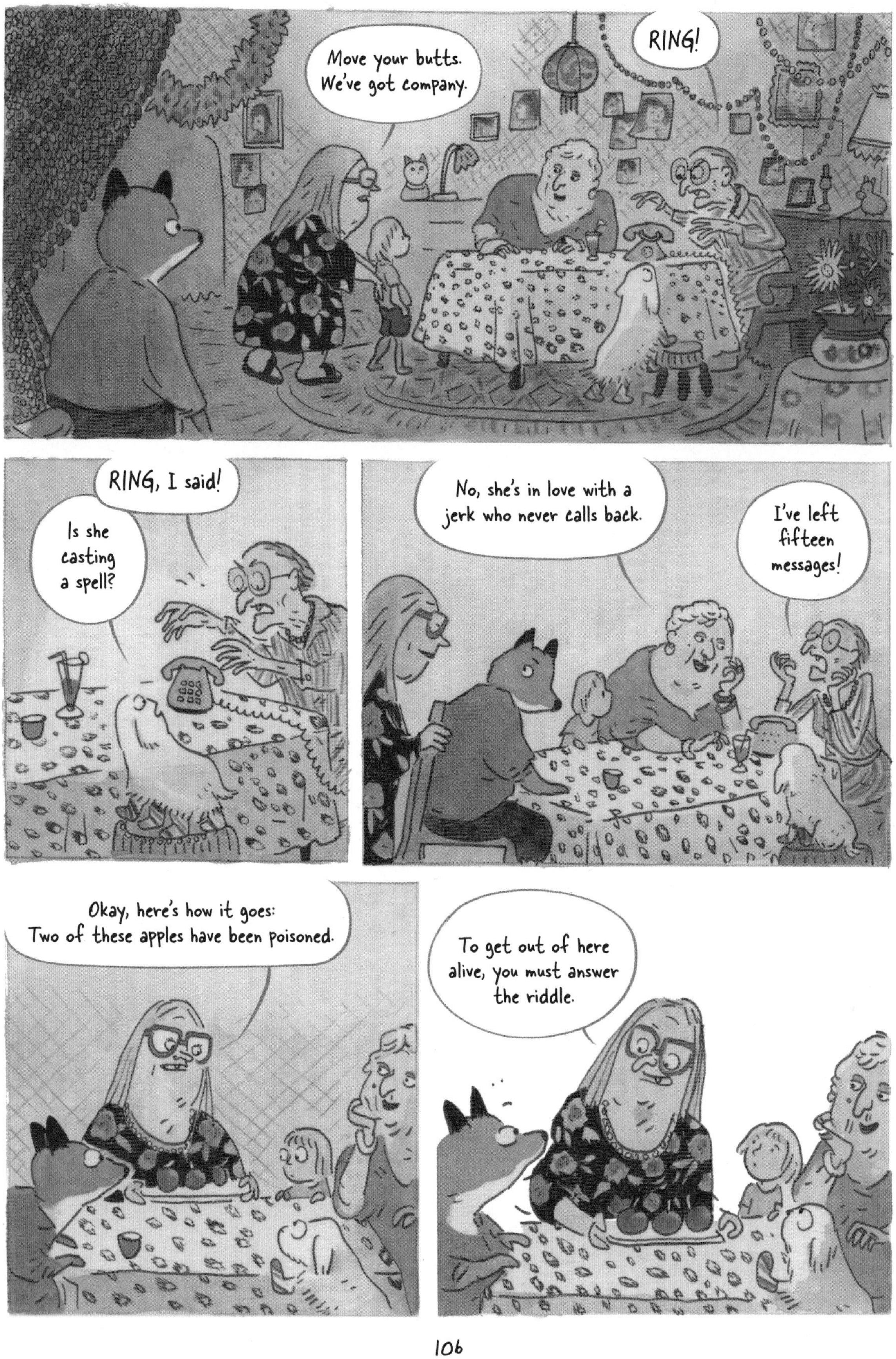
Move your butts. We've got company.
RING!
RING, I said!
Is she casting a spell?
No, she's in love with a jerk who never calls back.
I've left fifteen messages!
Okay, here's how it goes: Two of these apples have been poisoned.
To get out of here alive, you must answer the riddle.

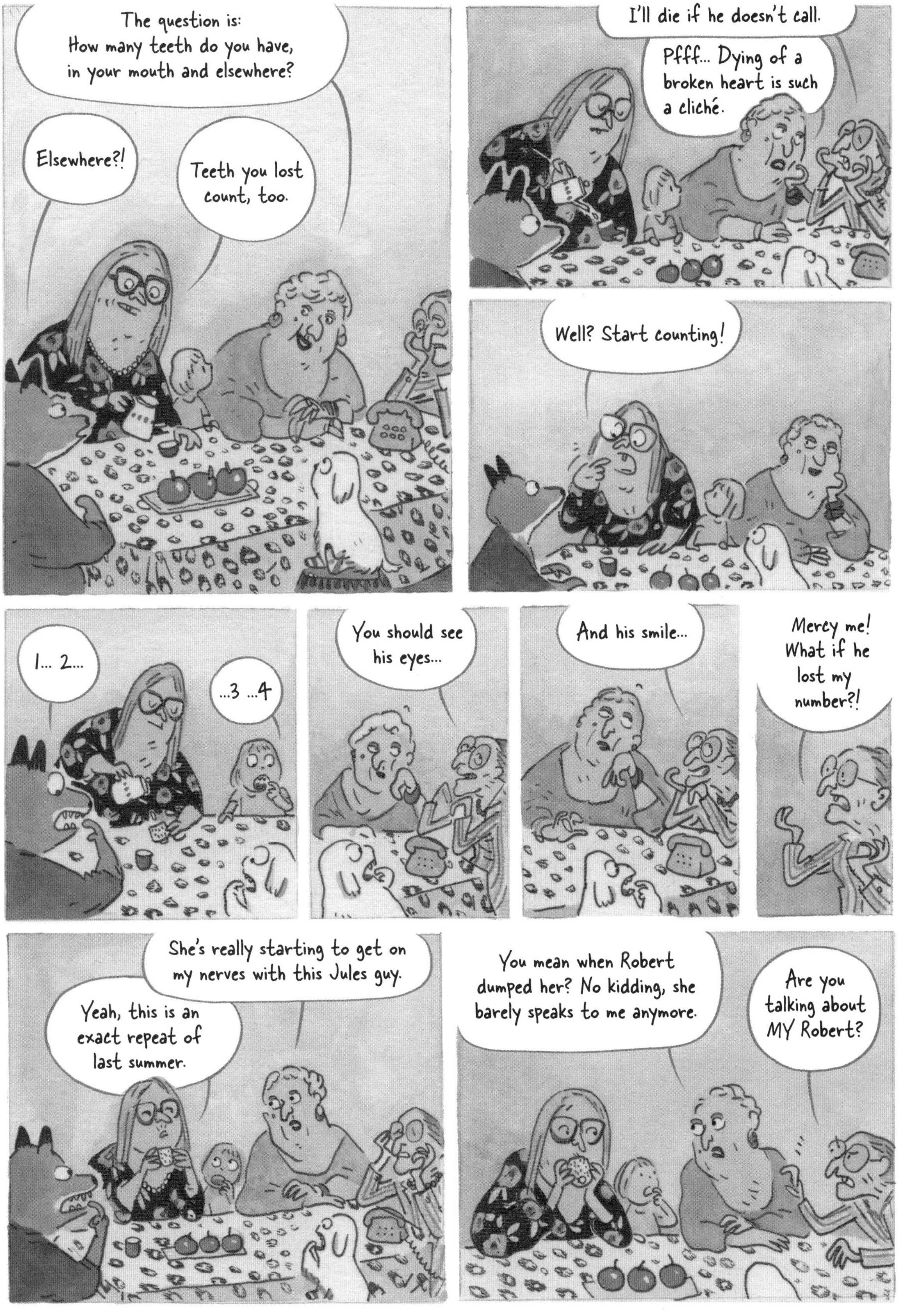
The question is: How many teeth do you have, in your mouth and elsewhere?
Elsewhere?!
Teeth you lost count, too.
I'll die if he doesn't call.
Pfff... Dying of a broken heart is such a cliché.
Well? Start counting!
1... 2...
...3 ...4
You should see his eyes...
And his smile...
Mercy me! What if he lost my number?!
She's really starting to get on my nerves with this Jules guy.
Yeah, this is an exact repeat of last summer.
You mean when Robert dumped her? No kidding, she barely speaks to me anymore.
Are you talking about MY Robert?

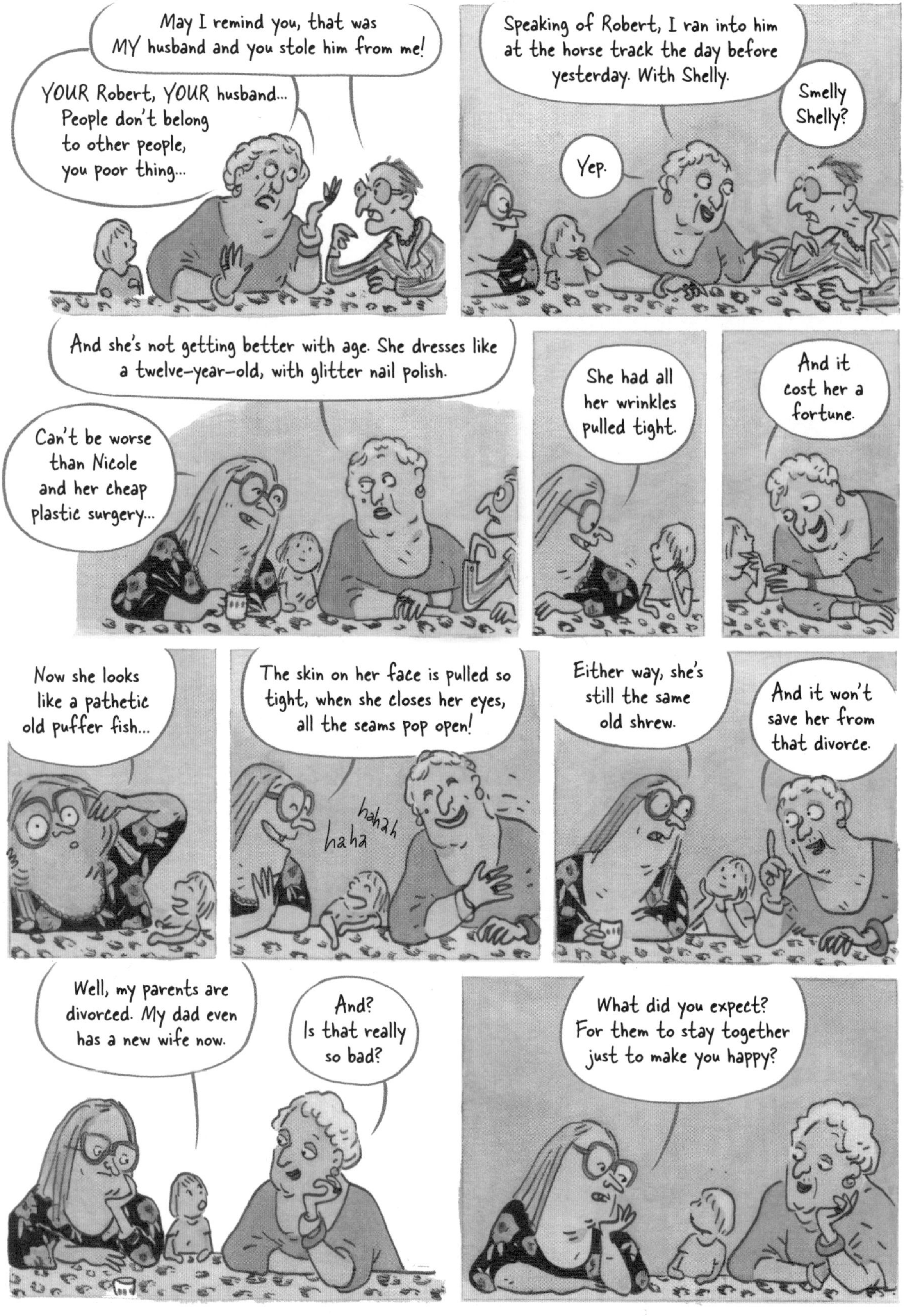
May I remind you, that was MY husband and you stole him from me!
YOUR Robert, YOUR husband... People don't belong to other people, you poor thing...
Speaking of Robert, I ran into him at the horse track the day before yesterday. With Shelly.
Smelly Shelly?
Yep.
And she's not getting better with age. She dresses like a twelve-year-old, with glitter nail polish.
Can't be worse than Nicole and her cheap plastic surgery...
She had all her wrinkles pulled tight.
And it cost her a fortune.
Now she looks like a pathetic old puffer fish...
The skin on her face is pulled so tight, when she closes her eyes, all the seams pop open!
hahah
haha
Either way, she's still the same old shrew.
And it won't save her from that divorce.
Well, my parents are divorced. My dad even has a new wife now.
And? Is that really so bad?
What did you expect? For them to stay together just to make you happy?

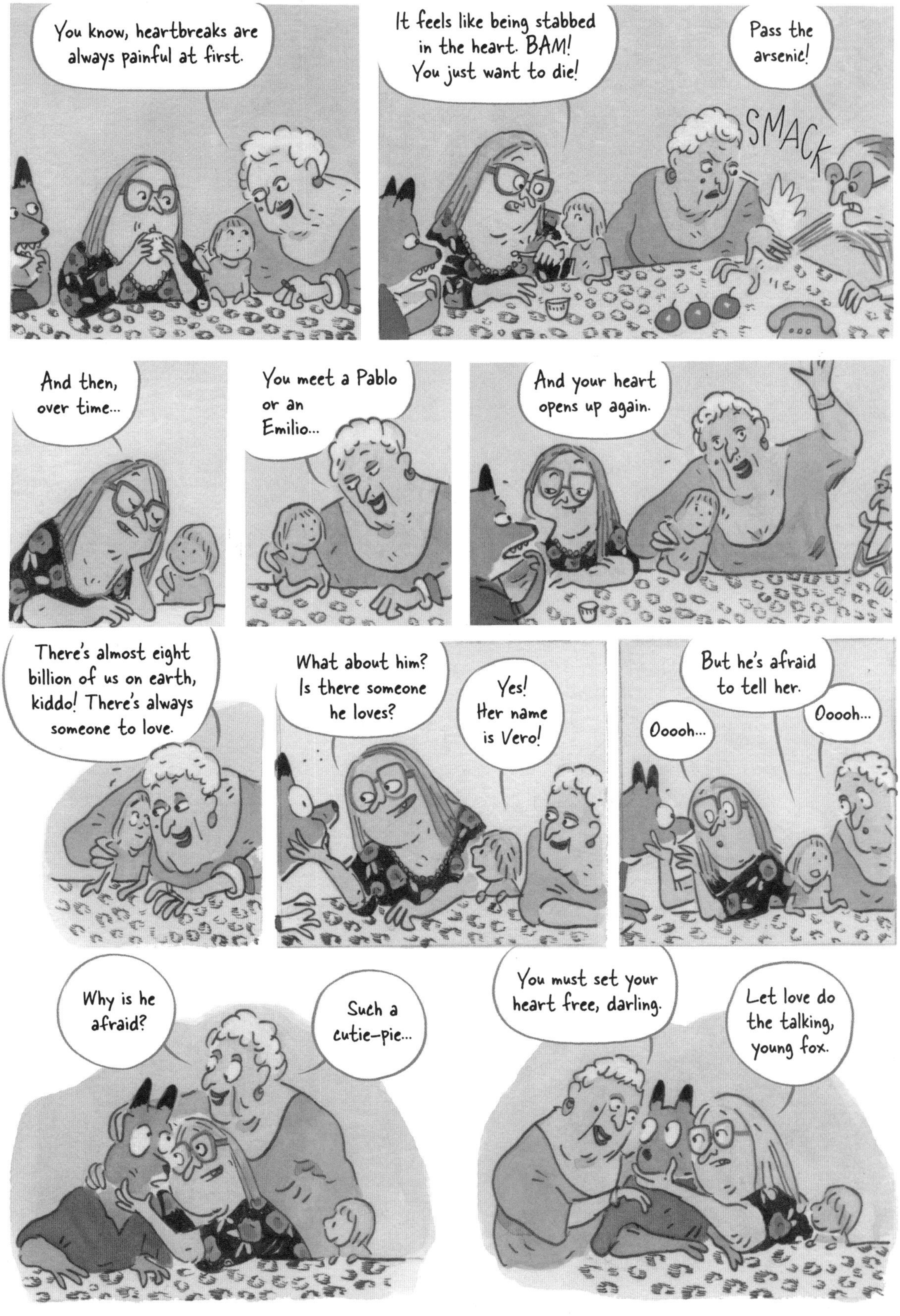
You know, heartbreaks are always painful at first.
It feels like being stabbed in the heart. BAM! You just want to die!
Pass the arsenic!
SMACK
And then, over time...
You meet a Pablo or an Emilio...
And your heart opens up again.
There's almost eight billion of us on earth, kiddo! There's always someone to love.
What about him? Is there someone he loves?
Yes! Her name is Vero!
But he's afraid to tell her.
Ooooh...
Ooooh...
Why is he afraid?
Such a cutie-pie...
You must set your heart free, darling.
Let love do the talking, young fox.

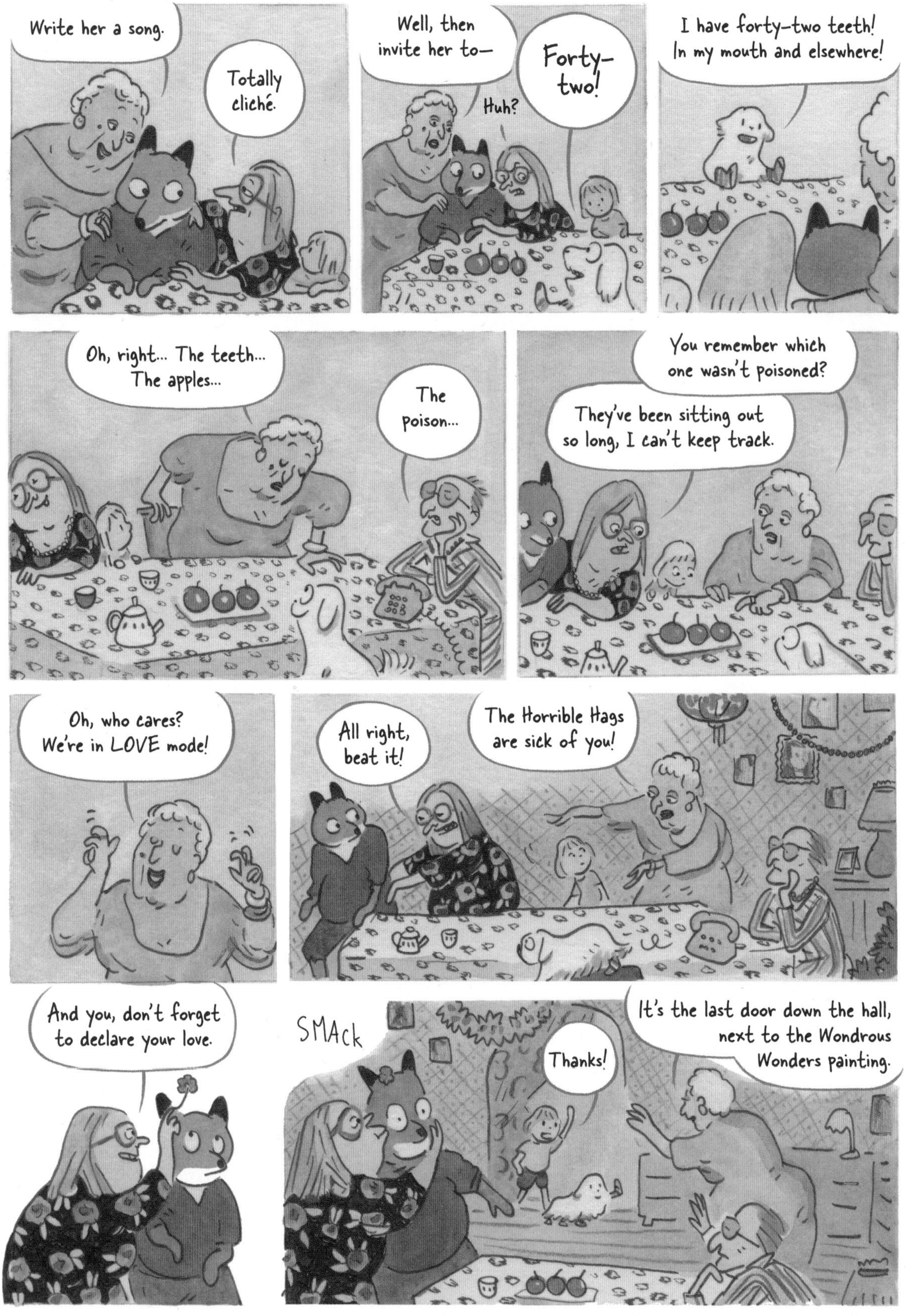
Write her a song.
Totally cliché.
Well, then invite her to—
Huh?
Forty-two!
I have forty-two teeth! In my mouth and elsewhere!
Oh, right... The teeth... The apples...
The poison...
You remember which one wasn't poisoned?
They've been sitting out so long, I can't keep track.
Oh, who cares? We're in LOVE mode!
All right, beat it!
The Horrible Hags are sick of you!
And you, don't forget to declare your love.
SMAck
Thanks!
It's the last door down the hall, next to the Wondrous Wonders painting.

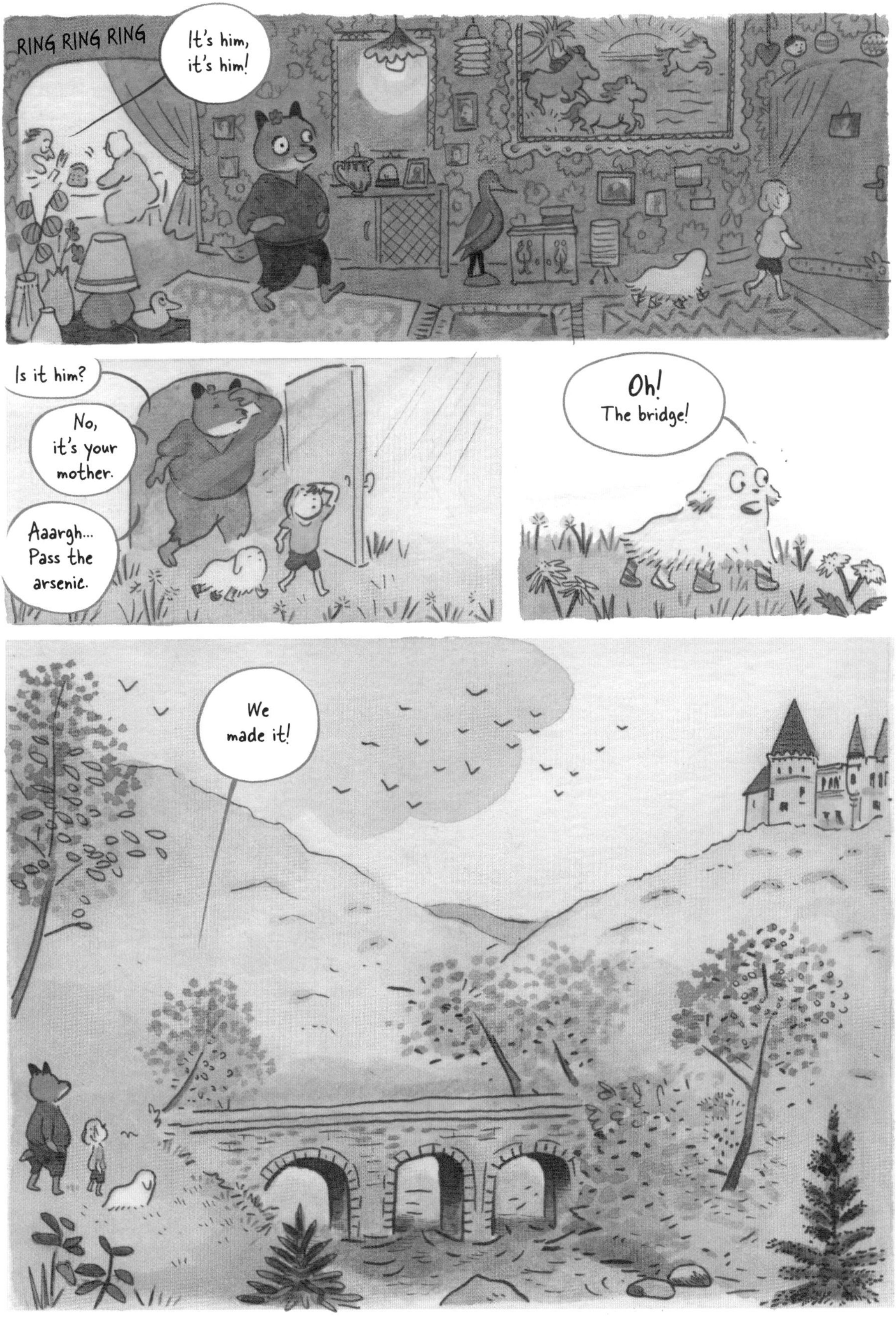
RING RING RING
It's him, it's him!
Is it him?
No, it's your mother.
Aaargh... Pass the arsenic.
Oh! The bridge!
We made it!

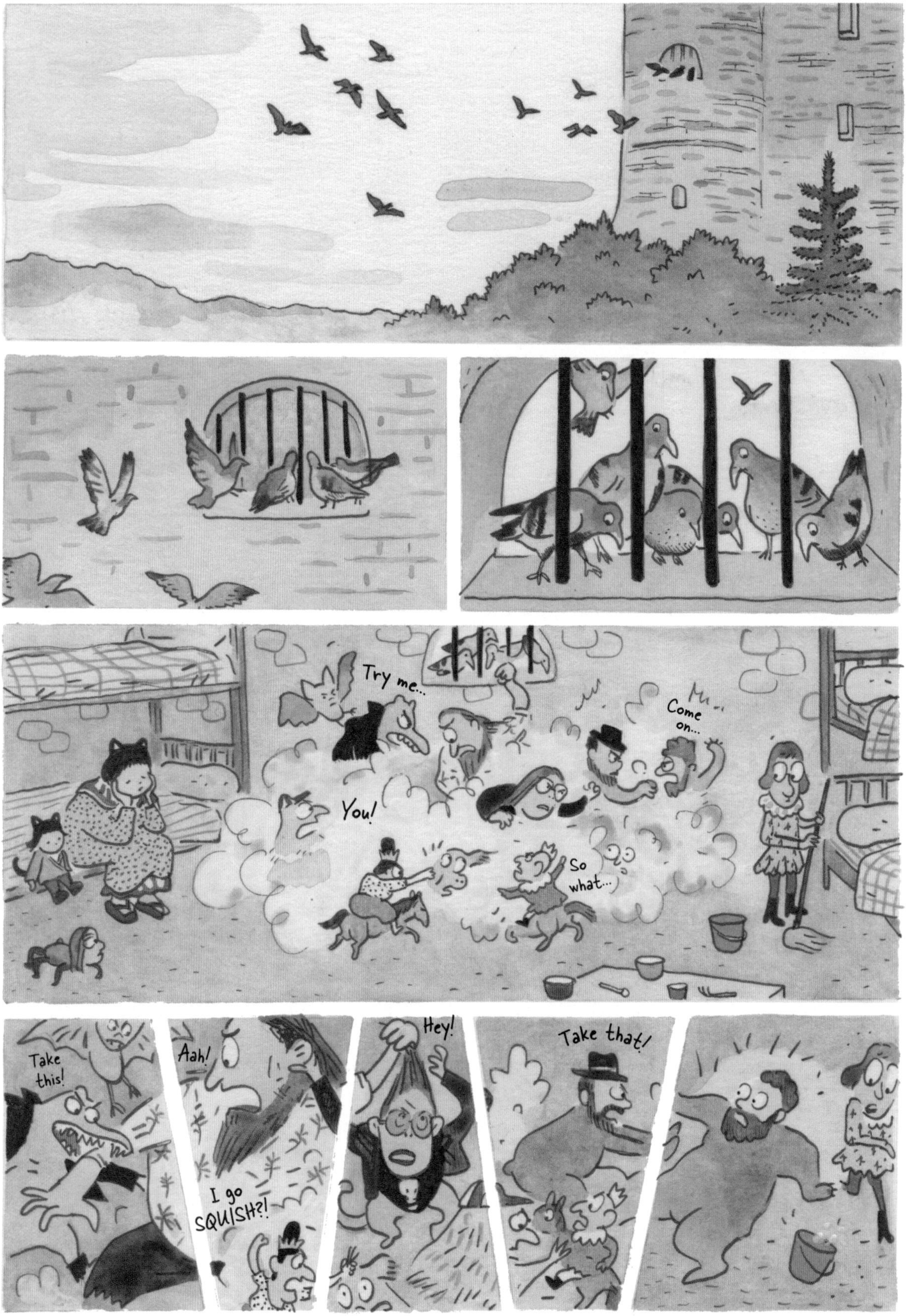
Try me...
Mu...
Come on...
You!
So what...
Take this!
Aah!
I go SQUISH?!
Hey!
Take that!

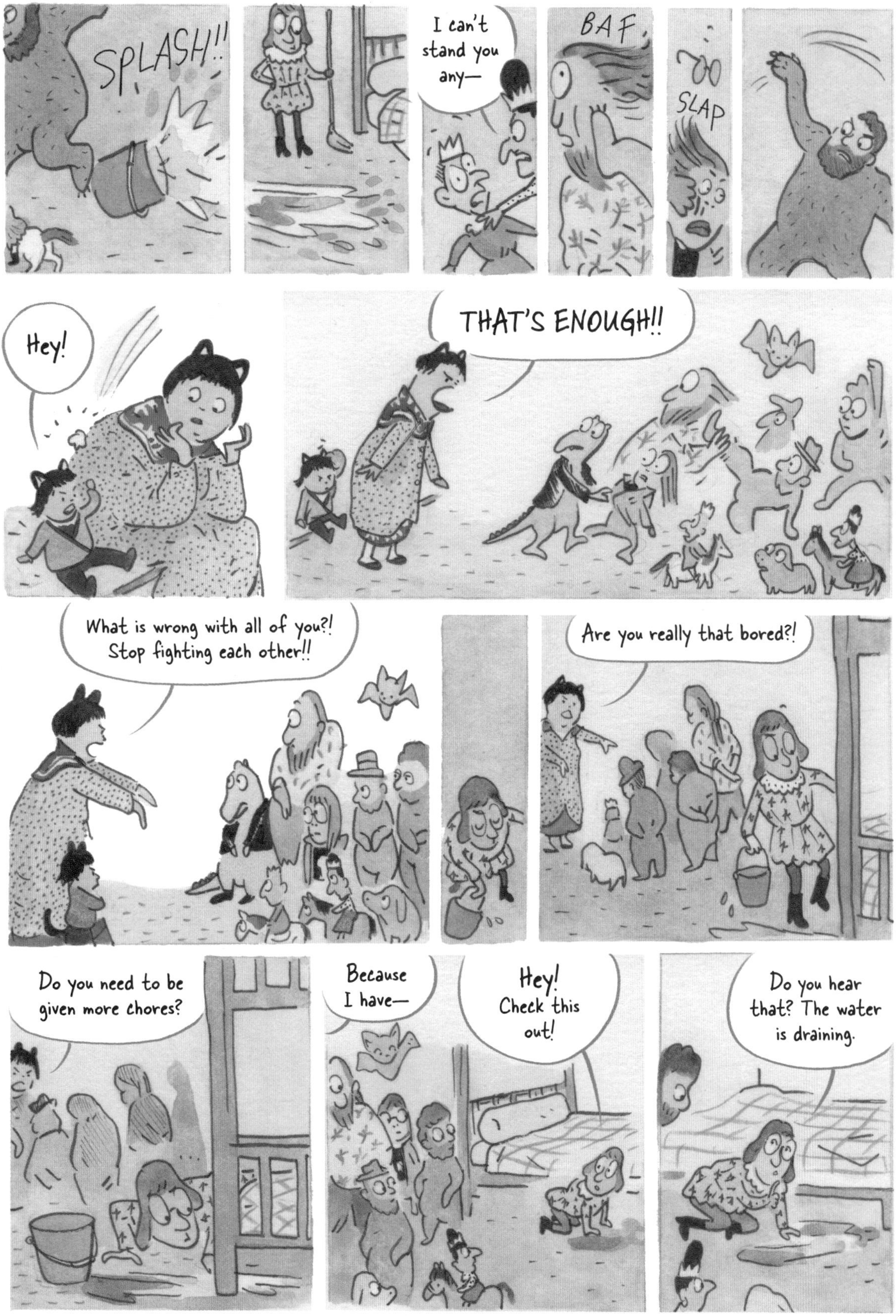
SPLASH!!
I can't stand you any—
BAF
SLAP
Hey!
THAT'S ENOUGH!!
What is wrong with all of you?! Stop fighting each other!!
Are you really that bored?!
Do you need to be given more chores?
Because I have—
Hey! Check this out!
Do you hear that? The water is draining.

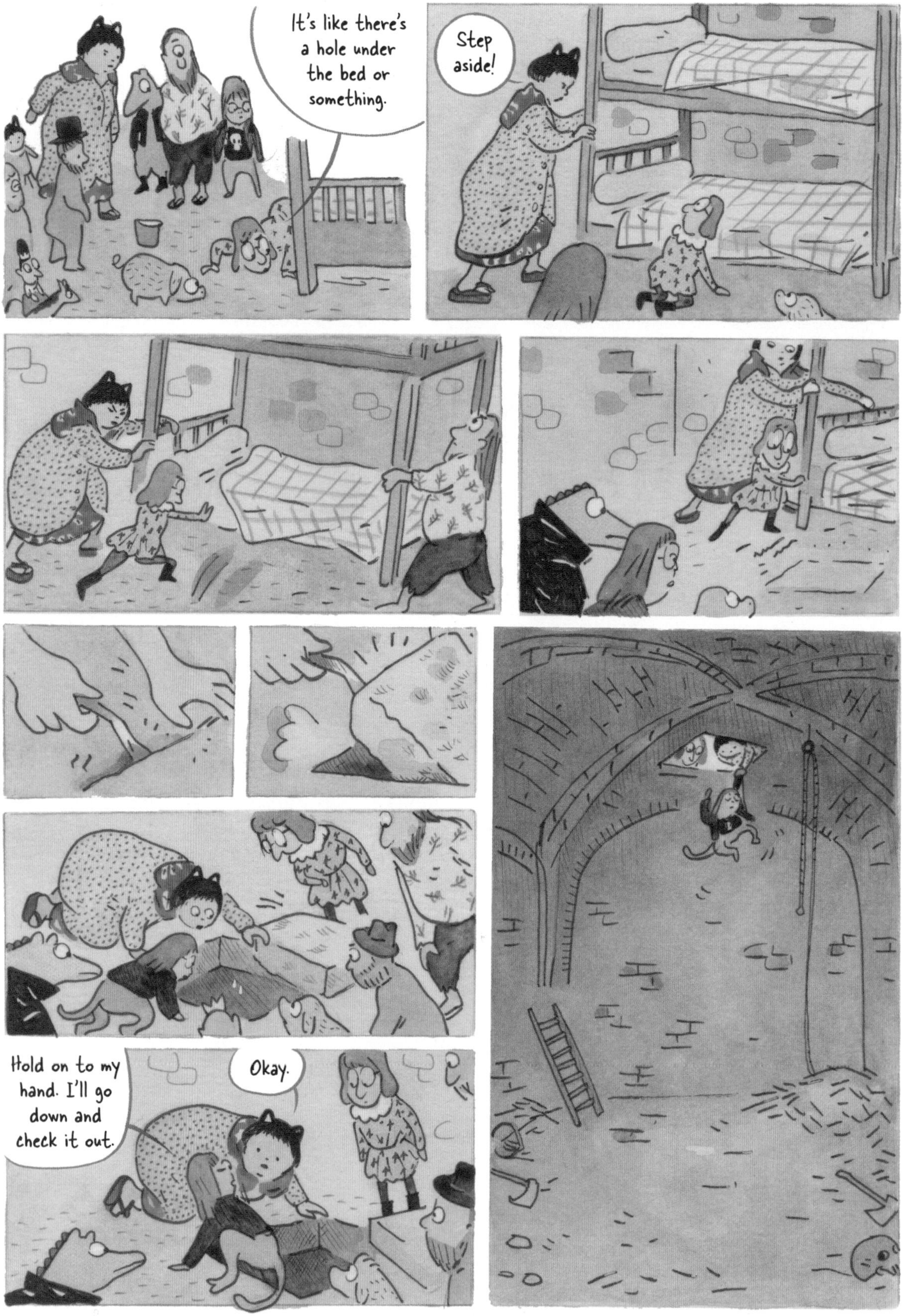
It's like there's a hole under the bed or something.
Step aside!
Hold on to my hand. I'll go down and check it out.
Okay.

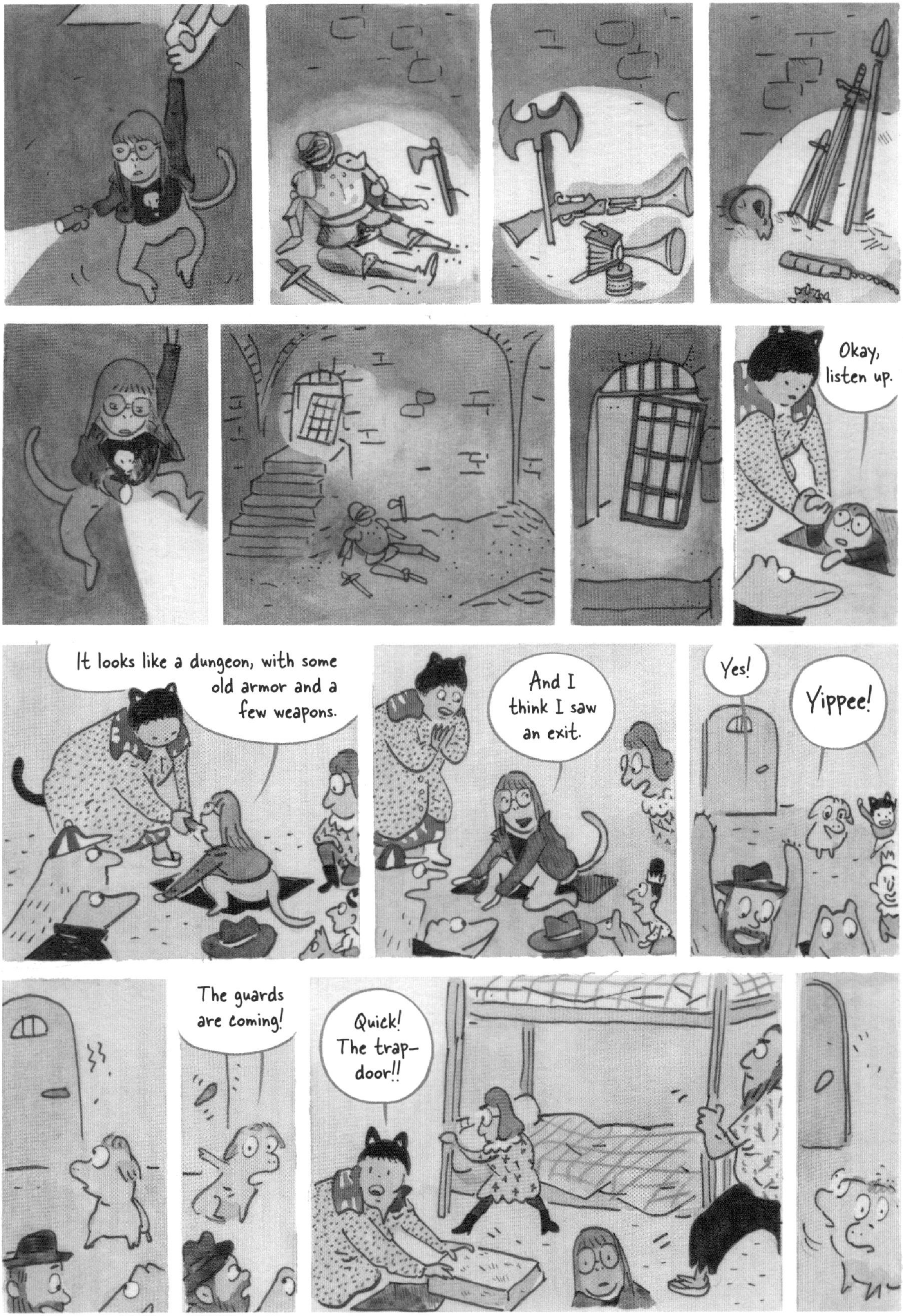
Okay, listen up.
It looks like a dungeon, with some old armor and a few weapons.
And I think I saw an exit.
Yes!
Yippee!
The guards are coming!
Quick! The trap-door!!

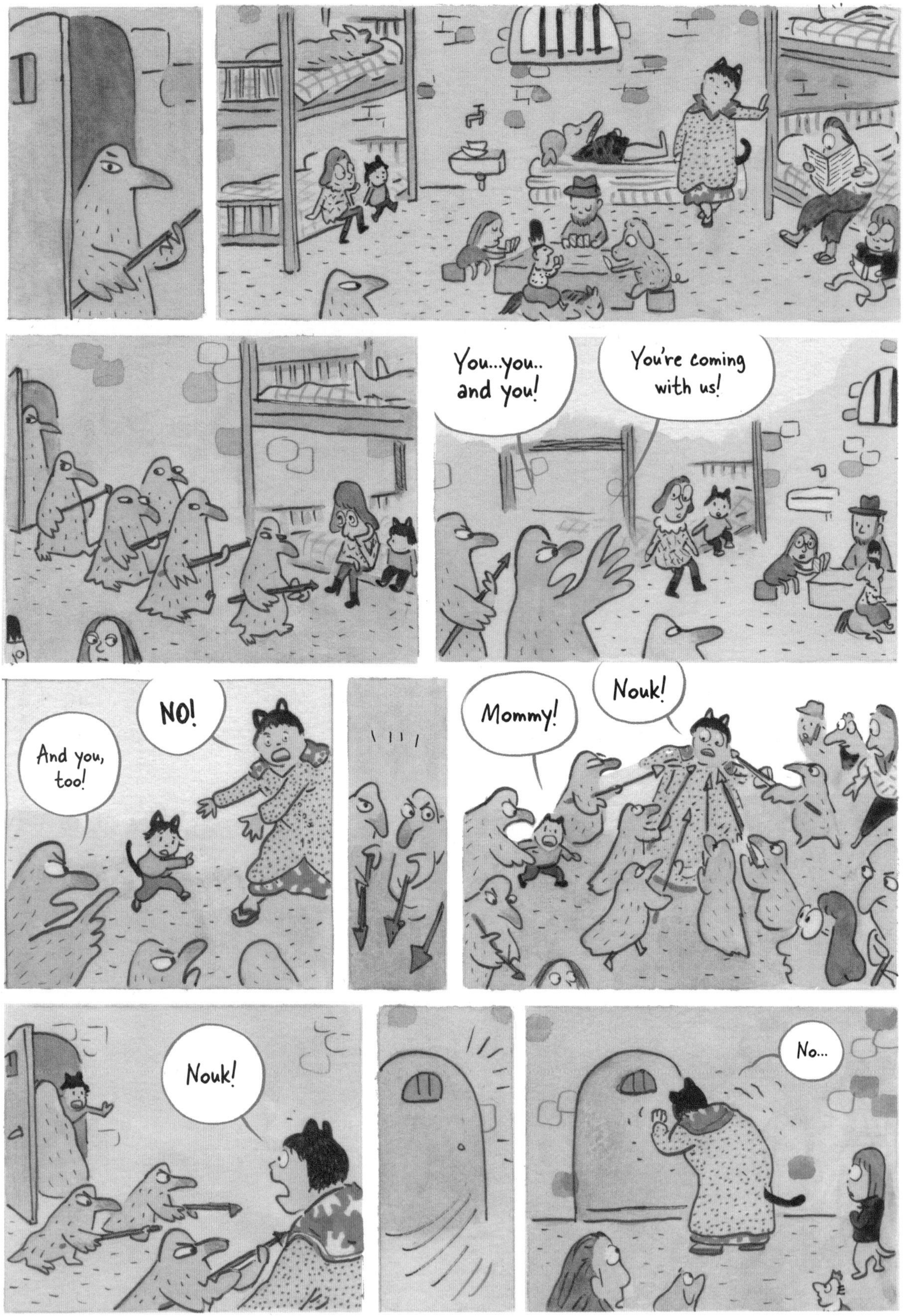
You...you..
and you!
You're coming
with us!
And you,
too!
NO!
Mommy!
Nouk!
Nouk!
No...

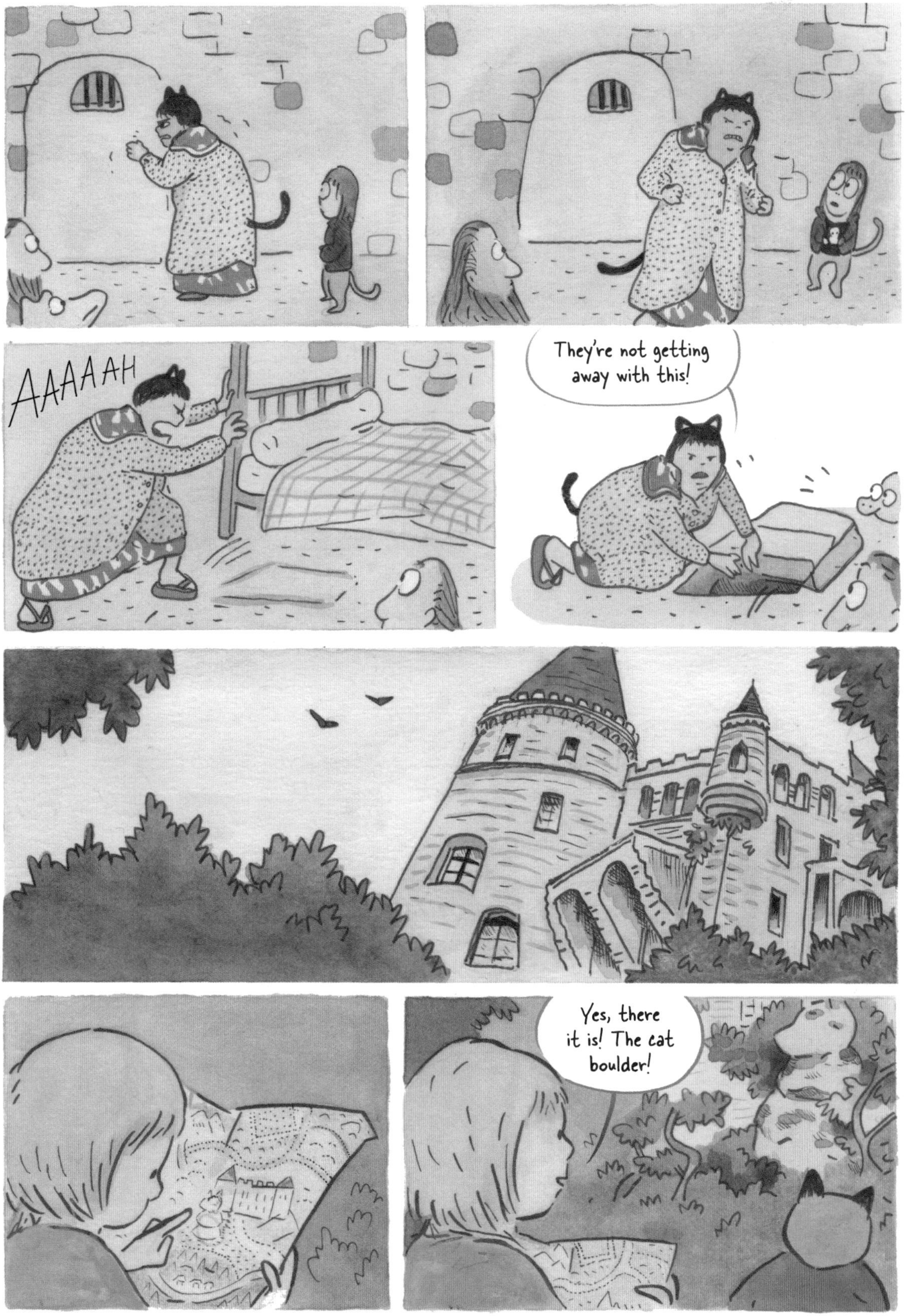
AAAAAH
They're not getting away with this!
Yes, there it is! The cat boulder!

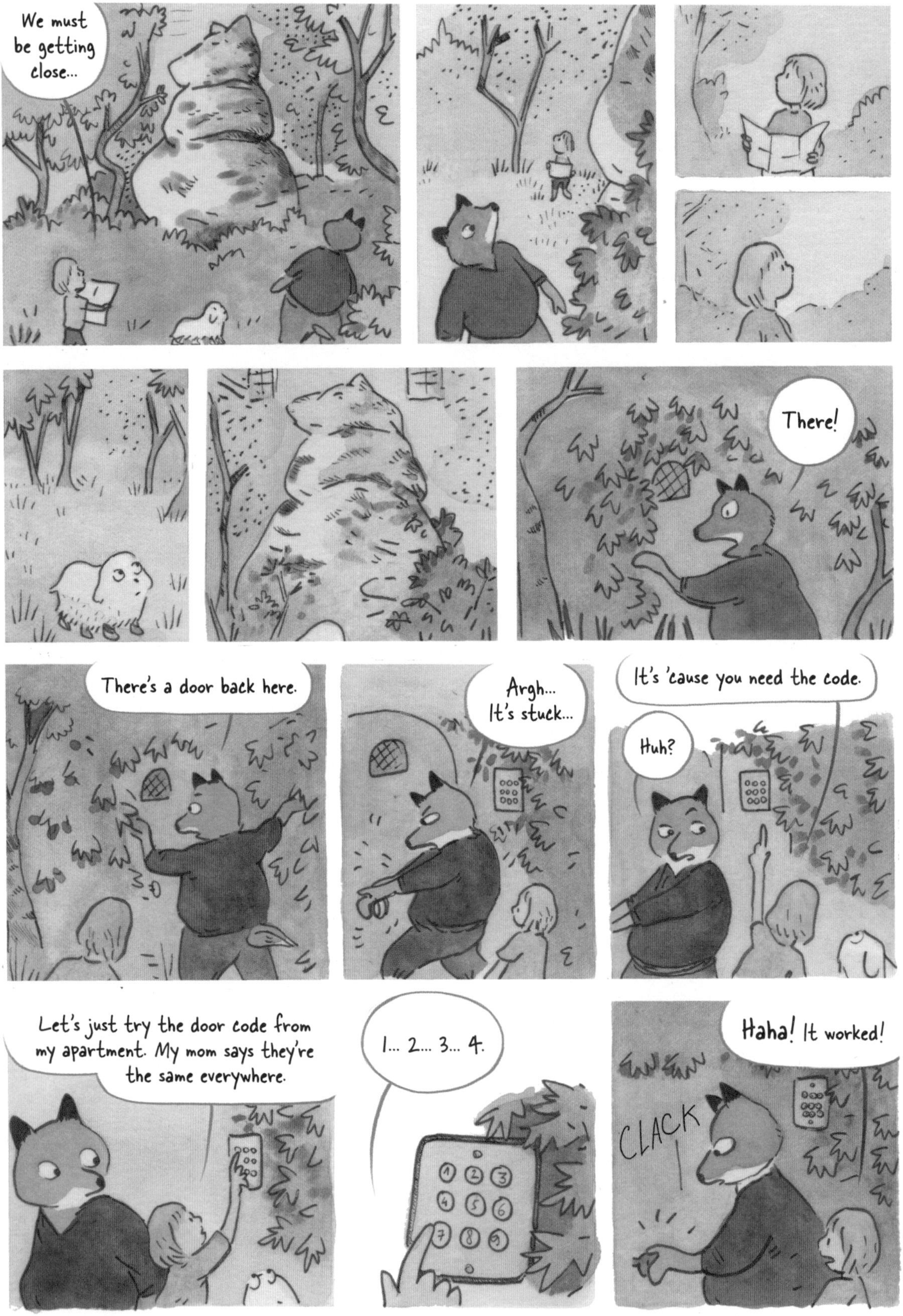
We must be getting close...
There!
There's a door back here.
Argh... It's stuck...
It's 'cause you need the code.
Huh?
Let's just try the door code from my apartment. My mom says they're the same everywhere.
1... 2... 3... 4.
Haha! It worked!
CLACK

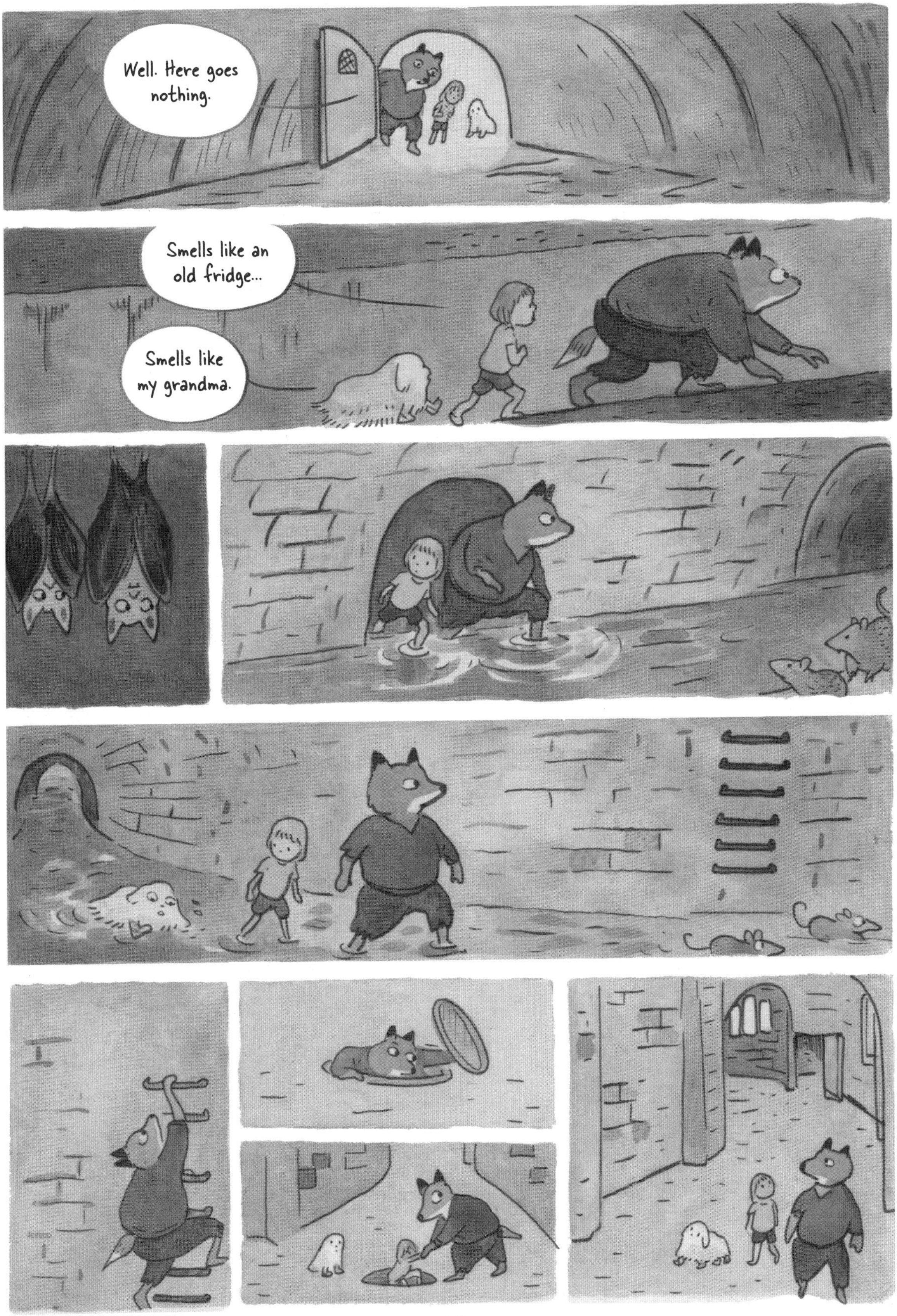
Well. Here goes nothing.
Smells like an old fridge...
Smells like my grandma.

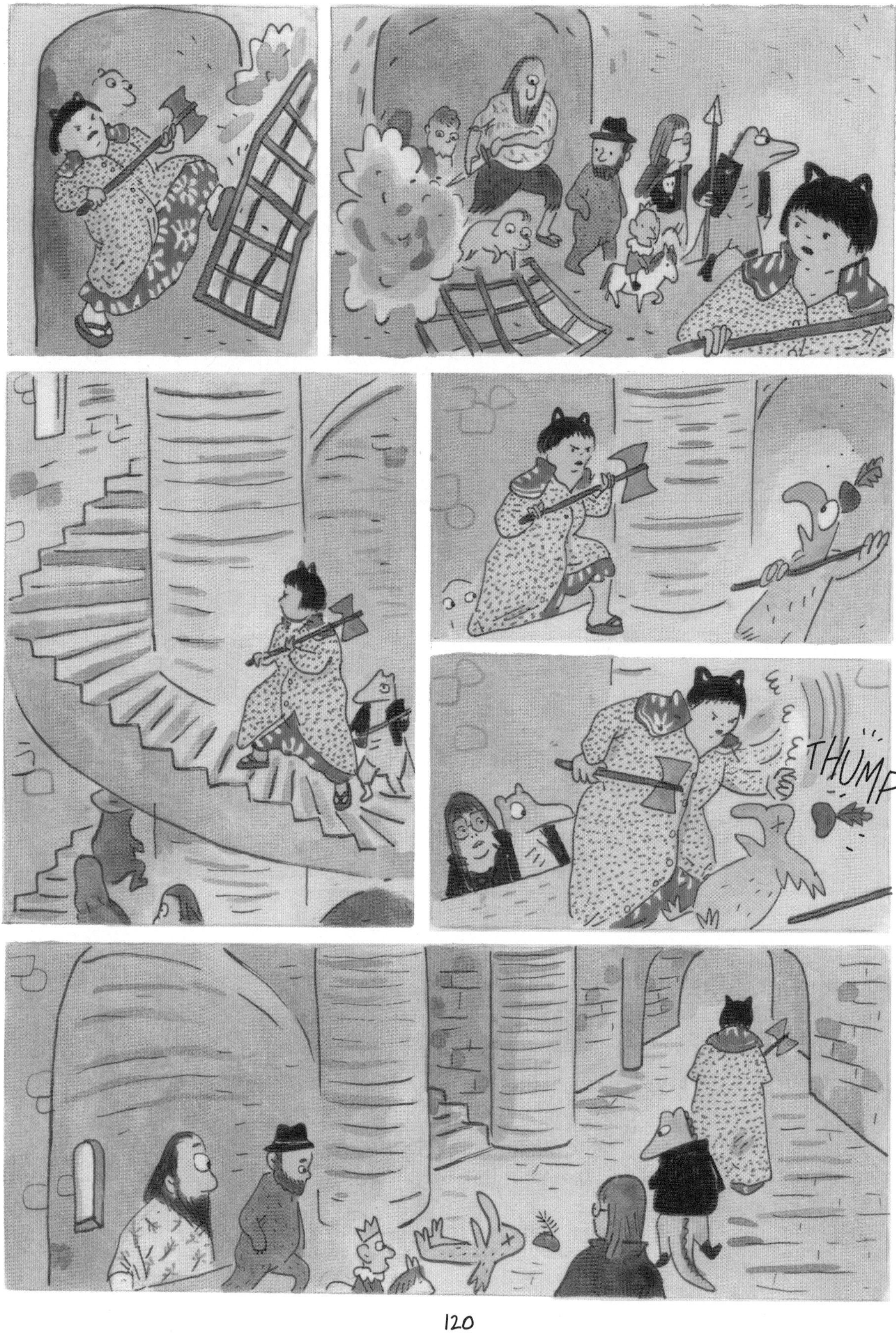
THUMP

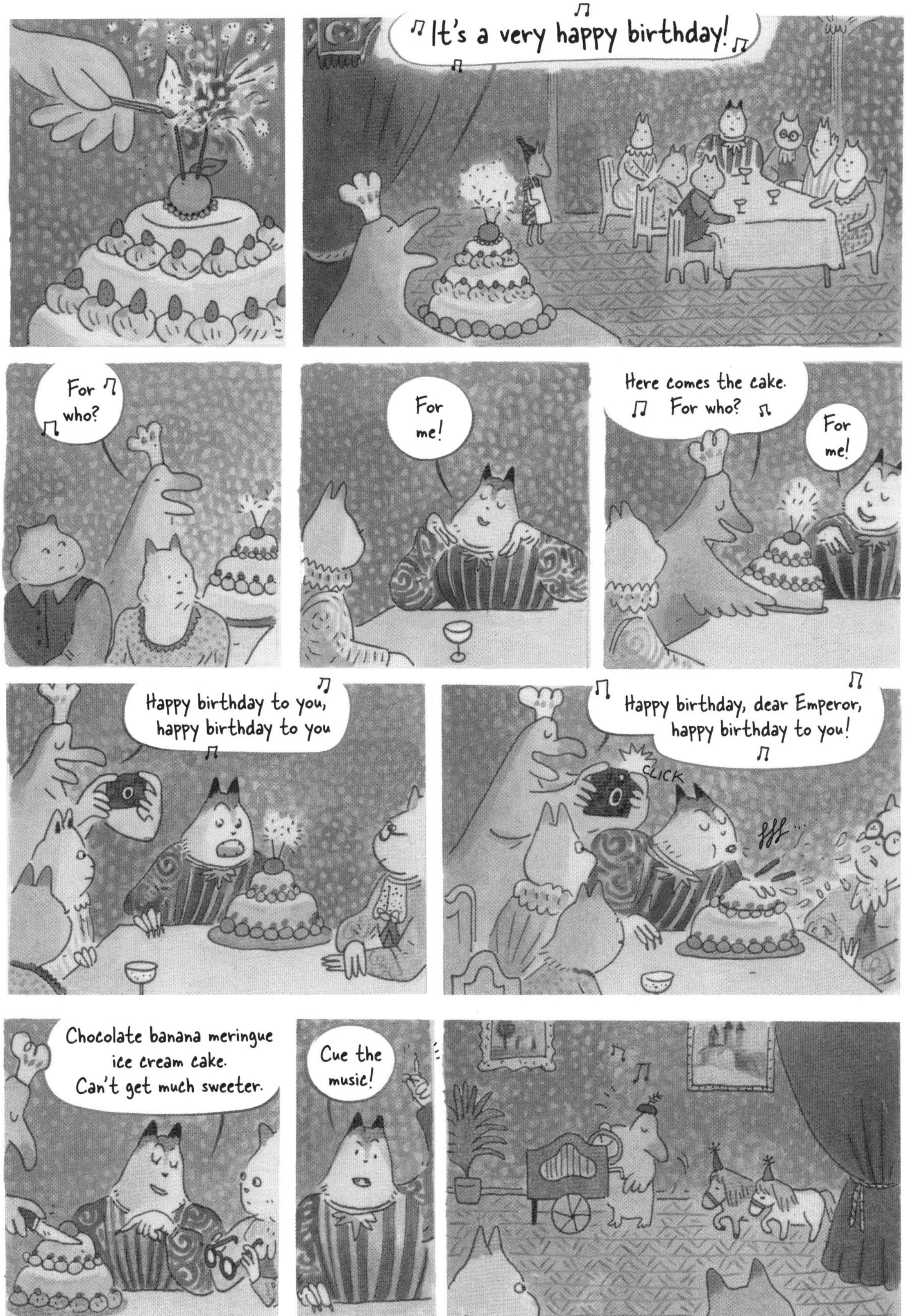

It's a very happy birthday!
For who?
For me!
Here comes the cake. For who?
For me!
Happy birthday to you, happy birthday to you
Happy birthday, dear Emperor, happy birthday to you!
CLICK
fff...
Chocolate banana meringue ice cream cake. Can't get much sweeter.
Cue the music!

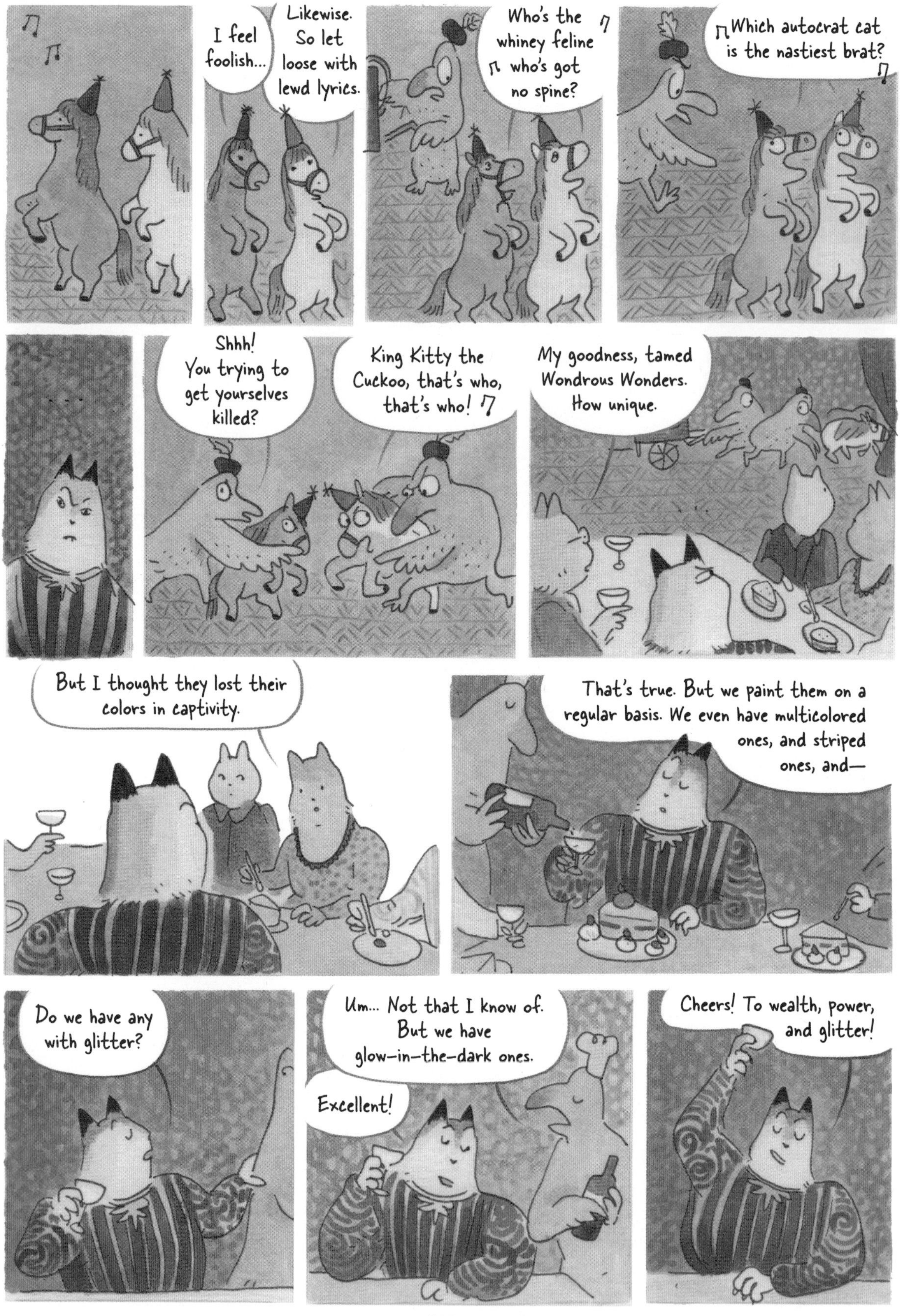
I feel foolish...
Likewise. So let loose with lewd lyrics.
Who's the whiney feline who's got no spine?
Which autocrat cat is the nastiest brat?
...
Shhh! You trying to get yourselves killed?
King Kitty the Cuckoo, that's who, that's who!
My goodness, tamed Wondrous Wonders. How unique.
But I thought they lost their colors in captivity.
That's true. But we paint them on a regular basis. We even have multicolored ones, and striped ones, and—
Do we have any with glitter?
Um... Not that I know of. But we have glow-in-the-dark ones.
Excellent!
Cheers! To wealth, power, and glitter!

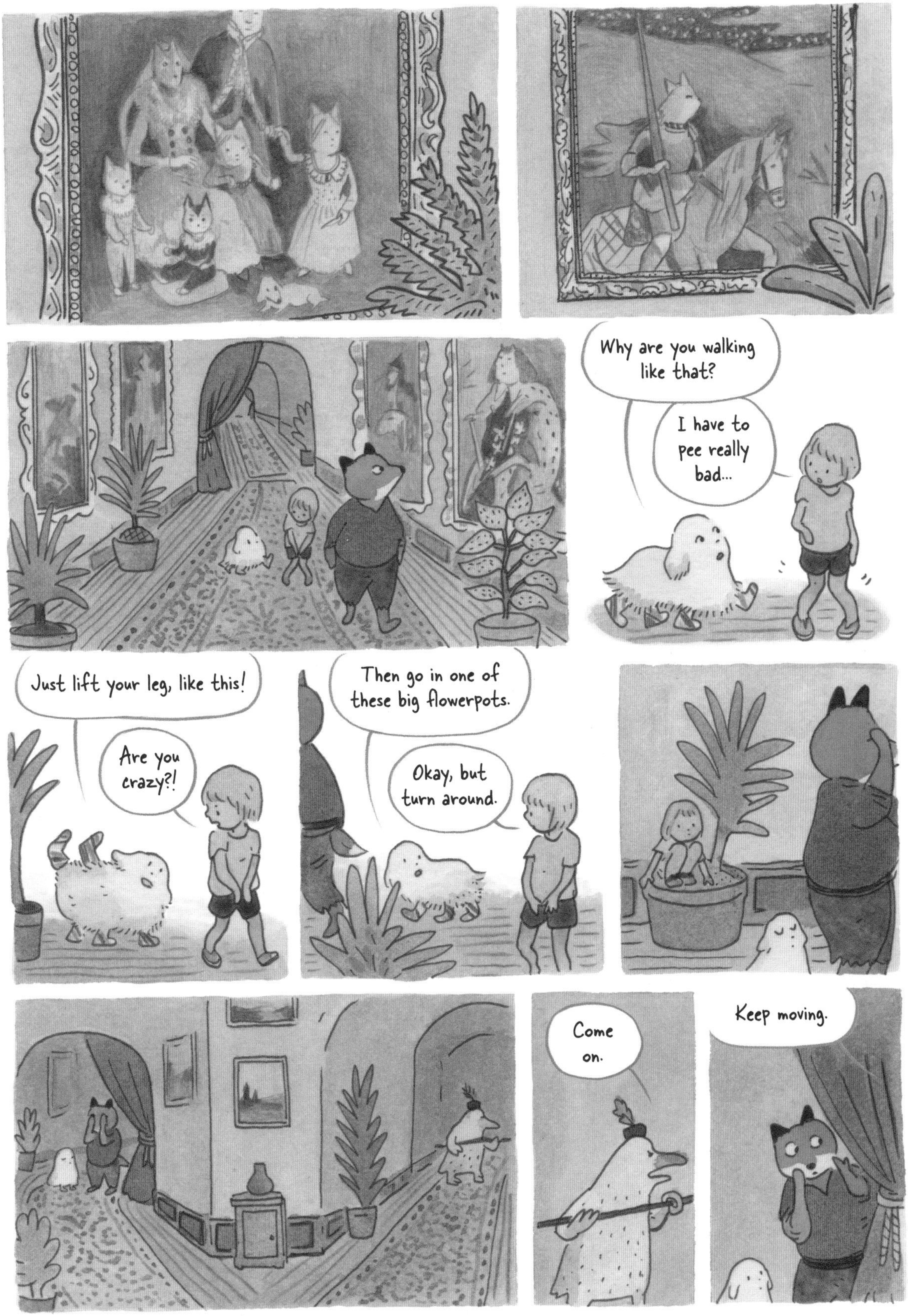
Why are you walking like that?
I have to pee really bad...
Just lift your leg, like this!
Are you crazy?!
Then go in one of these big flowerpots.
Okay, but turn around.
Come on.
Keep moving.

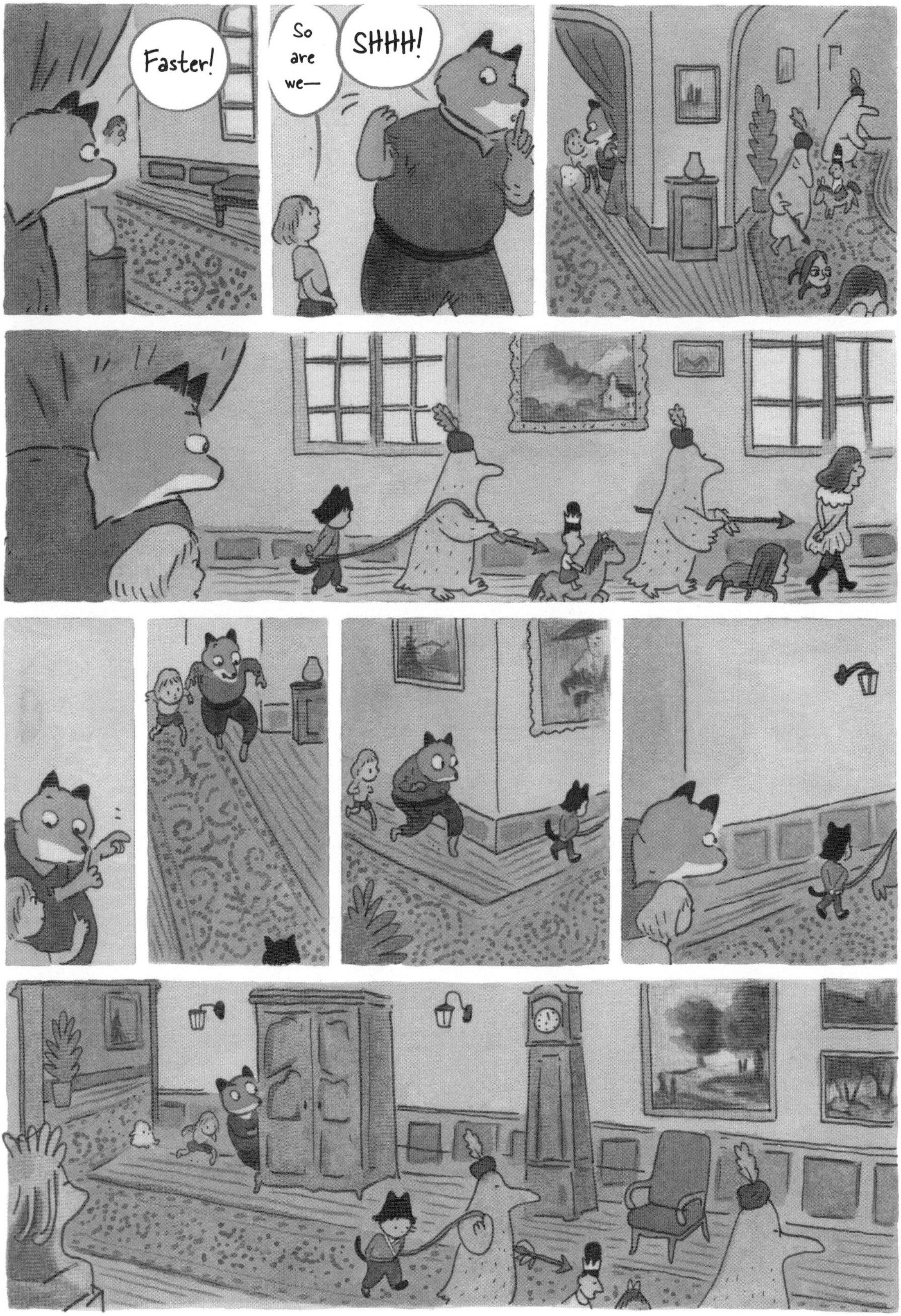
Faster!
So are we—
SHHH!

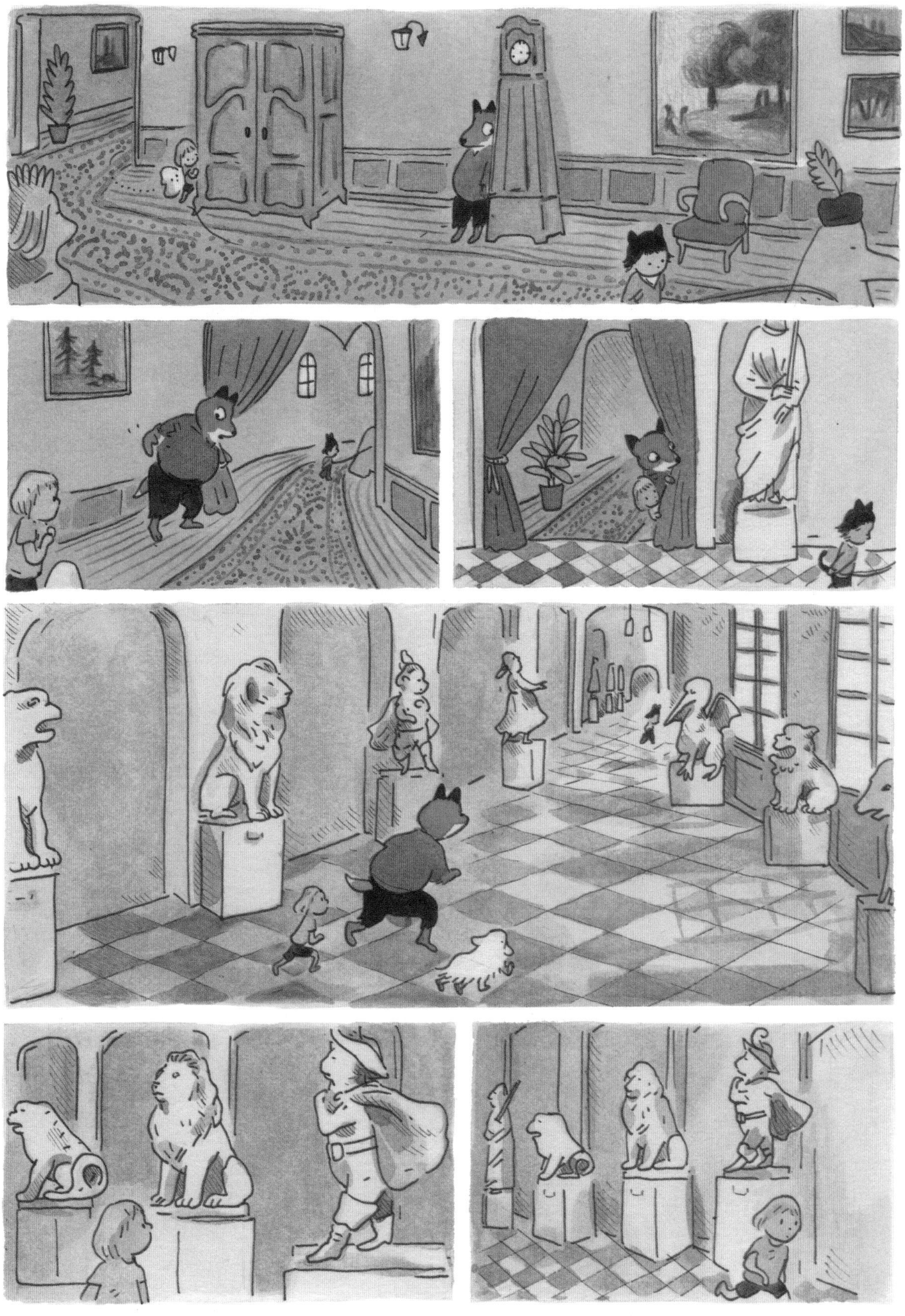

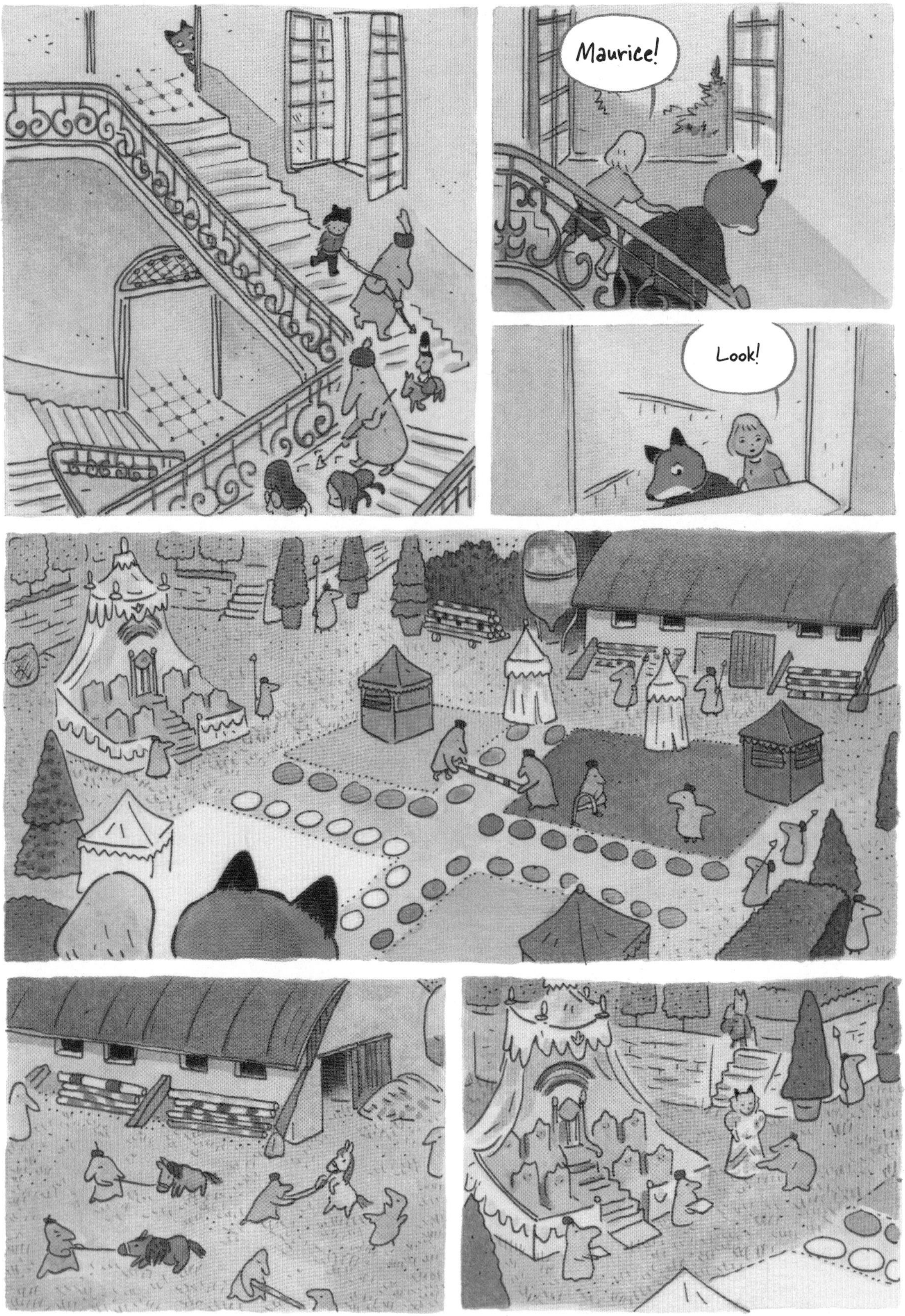
Maurice!
Look!

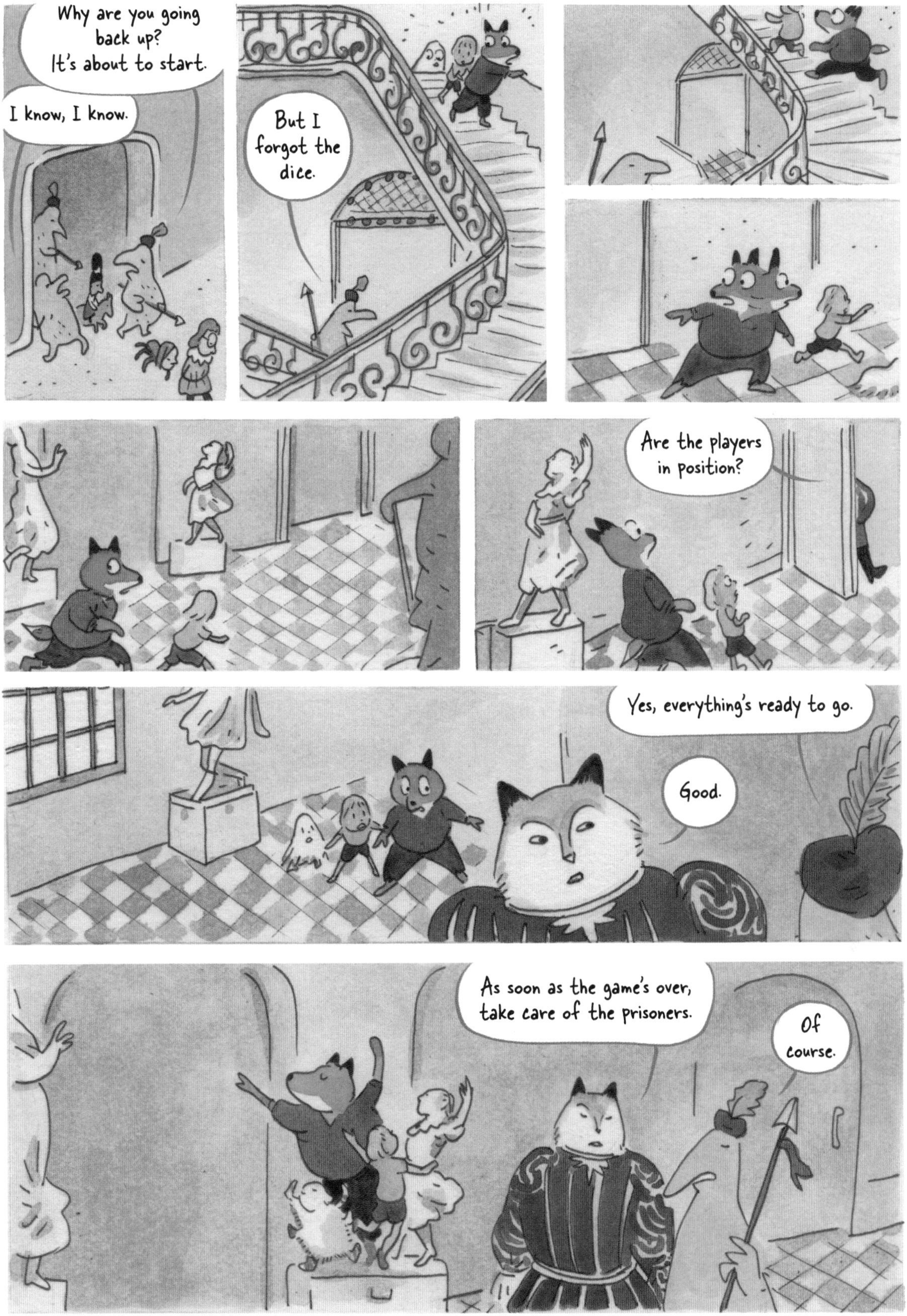
Why are you going back up? It's about to start.
I know, I know.
But I forgot the dice.
Are the players in position?
Yes, everything's ready to go.
Good.
As soon as the game's over, take care of the prisoners.
Of course.

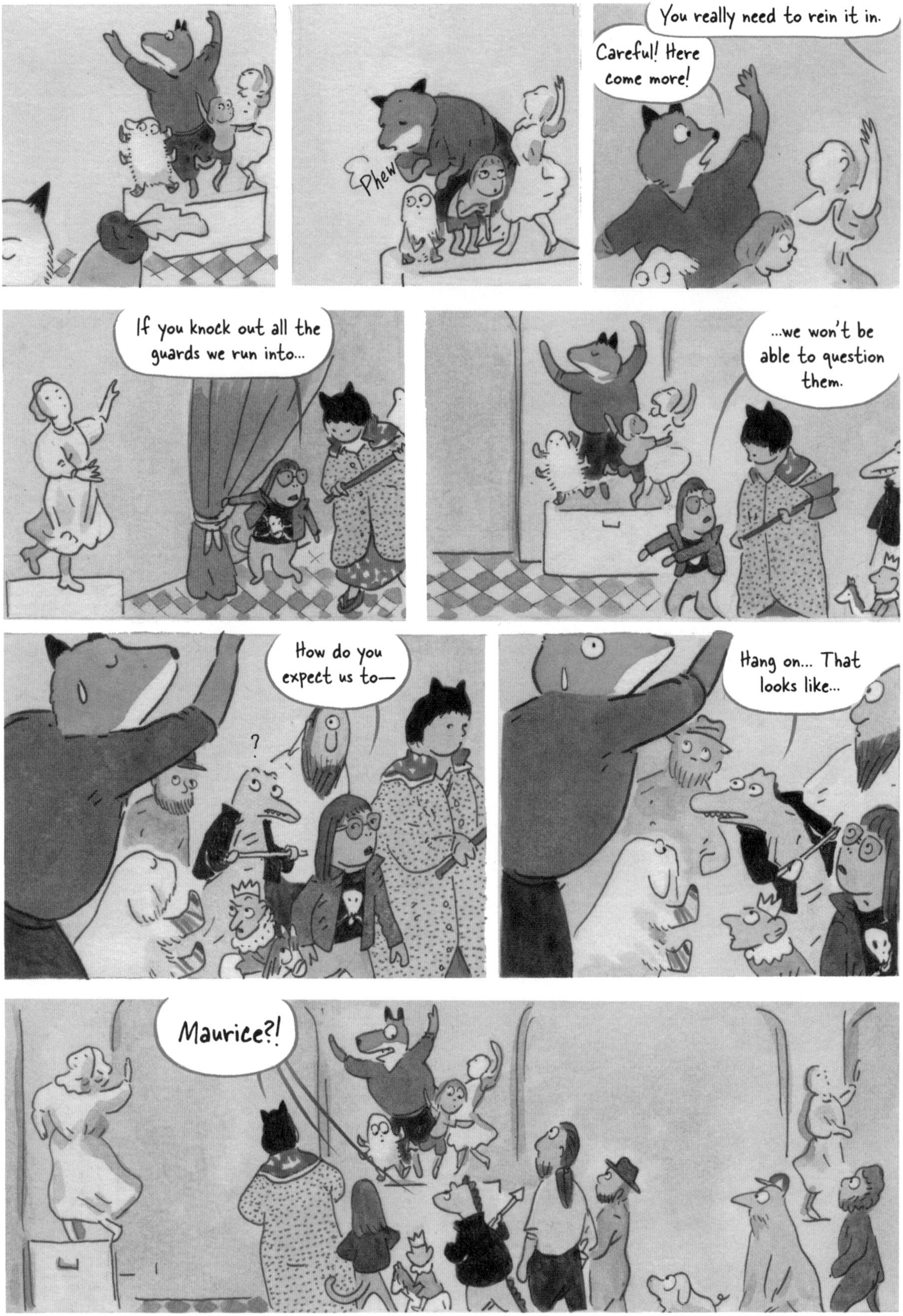
Phew
Careful! Here come more!
You really need to rein it in.
If you knock out all the guards we run into...
...we won't be able to question them.
How do you expect us to—
?
Hang on... That looks like...
Maurice?!

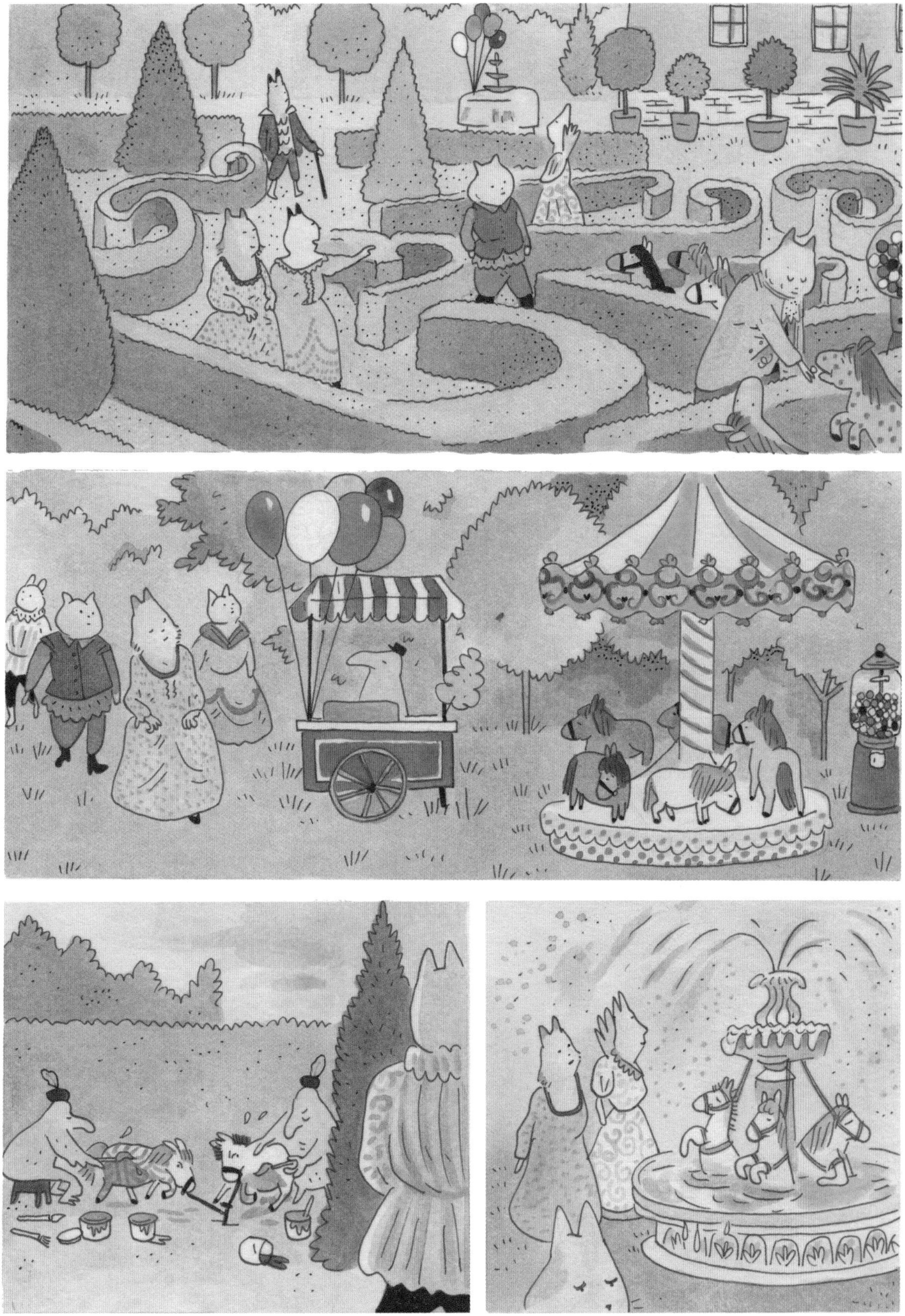

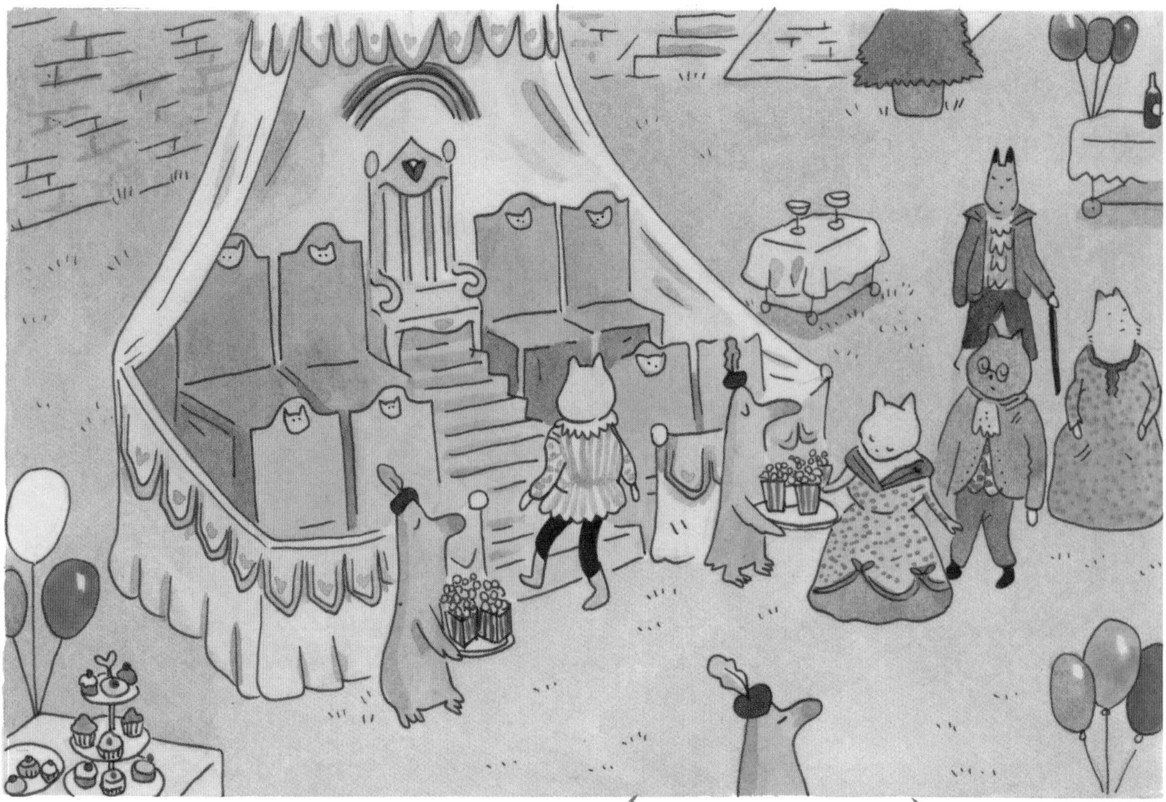

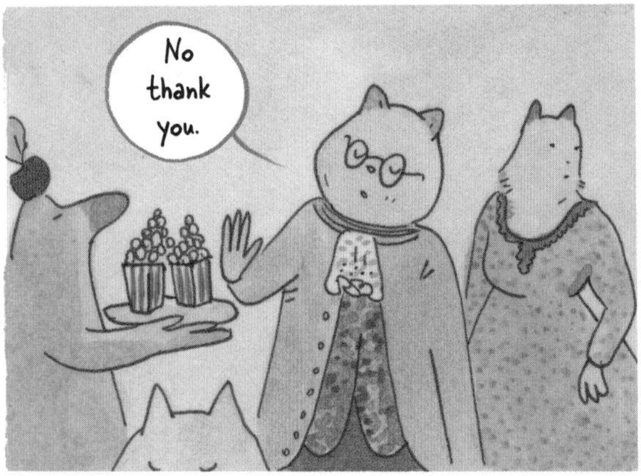
No thank you.

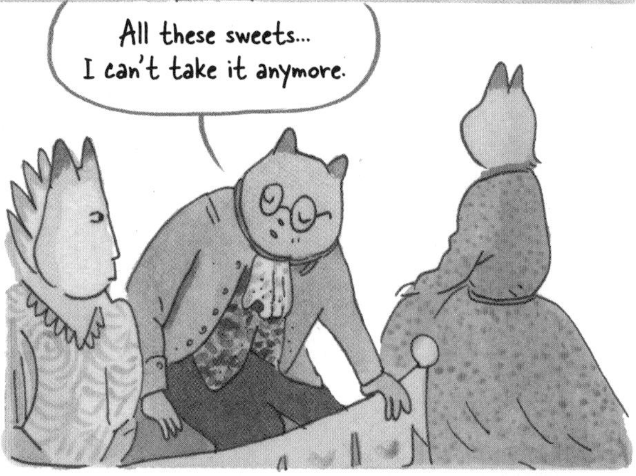
All these sweets... I can't take it anymore.

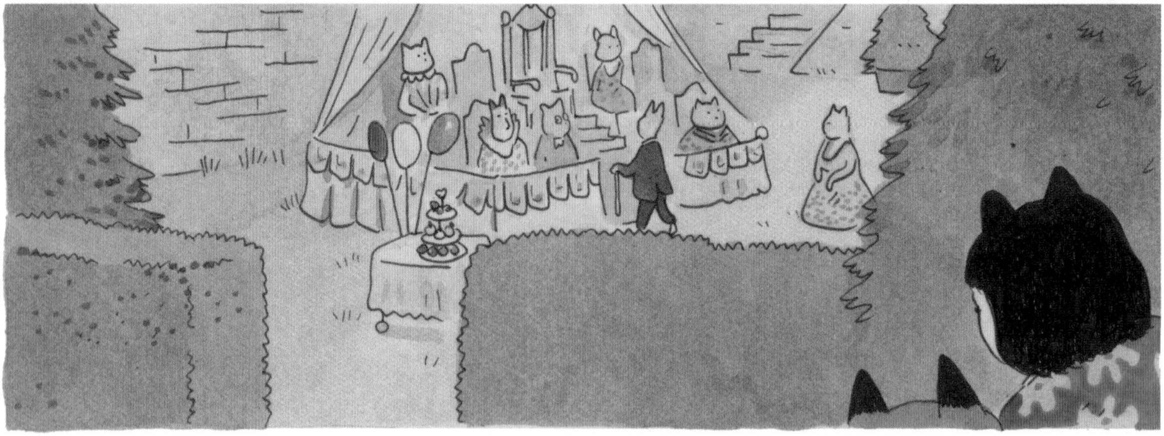

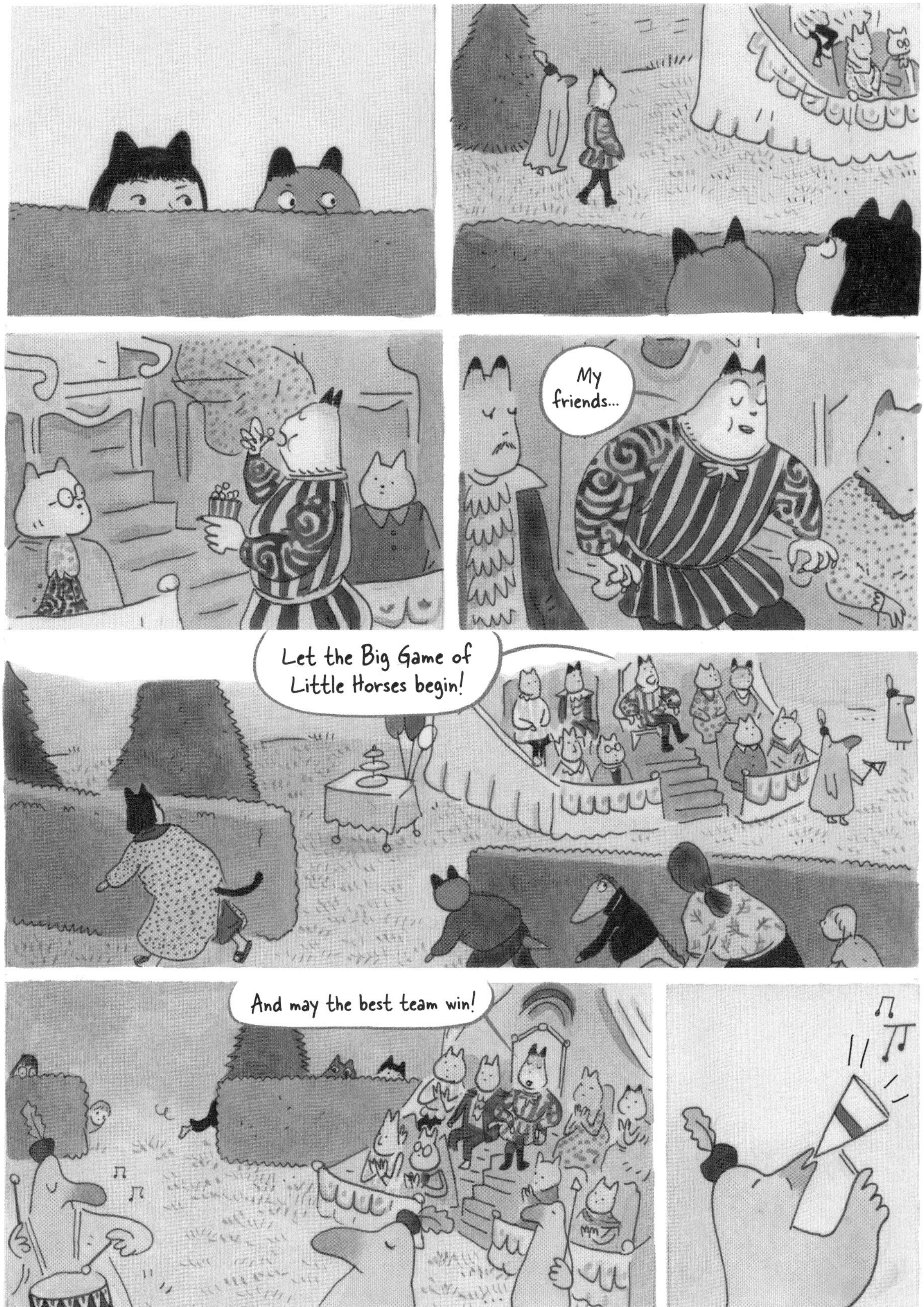
My friends...
Let the Big Game of Little Horses begin!
And may the best team win!

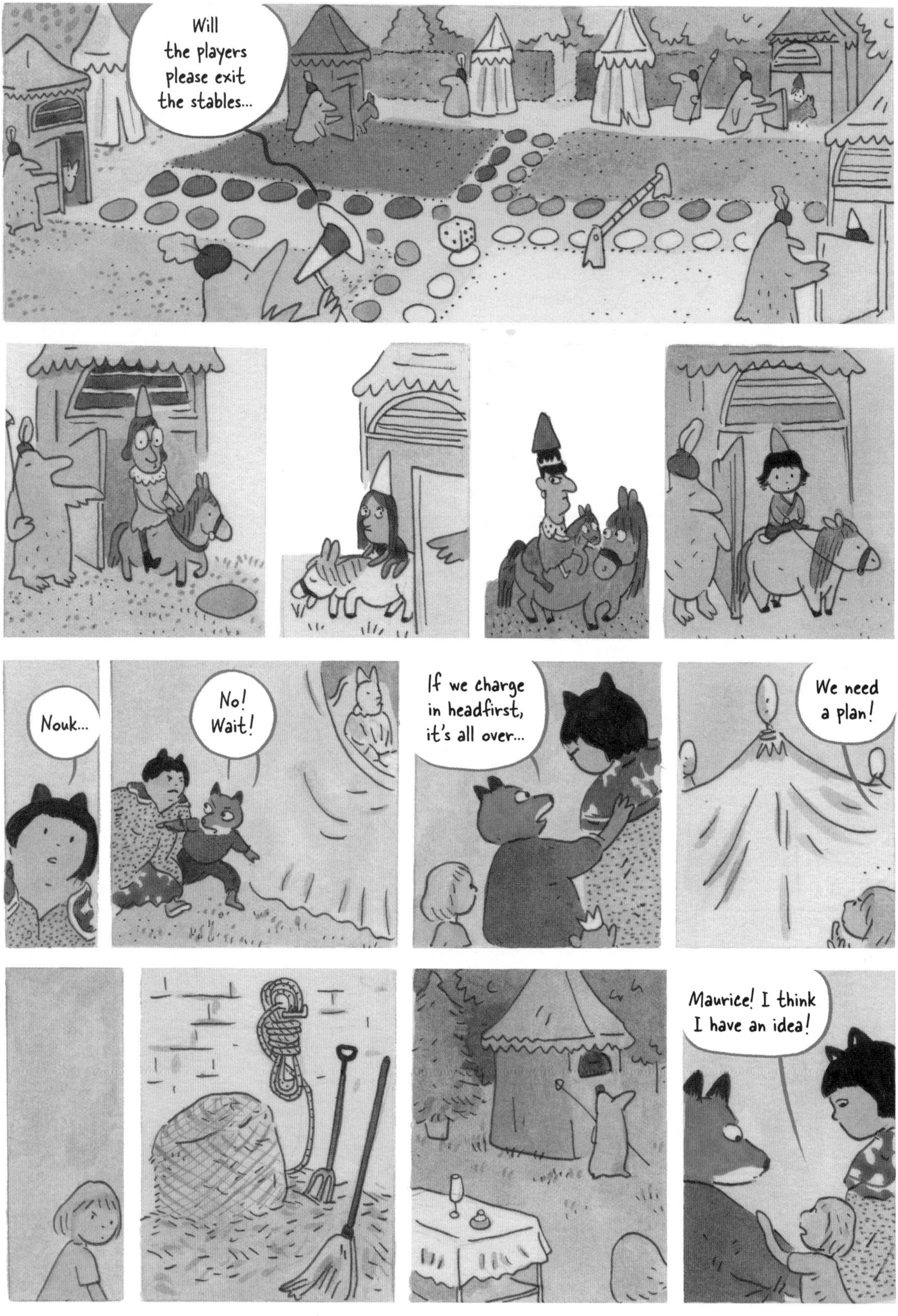
Will the players please exit the stables...
Nouk...
No! Wait!
If we charge in headfirst, it's all over...
We need a plan!
Maurice! I think I have an idea!

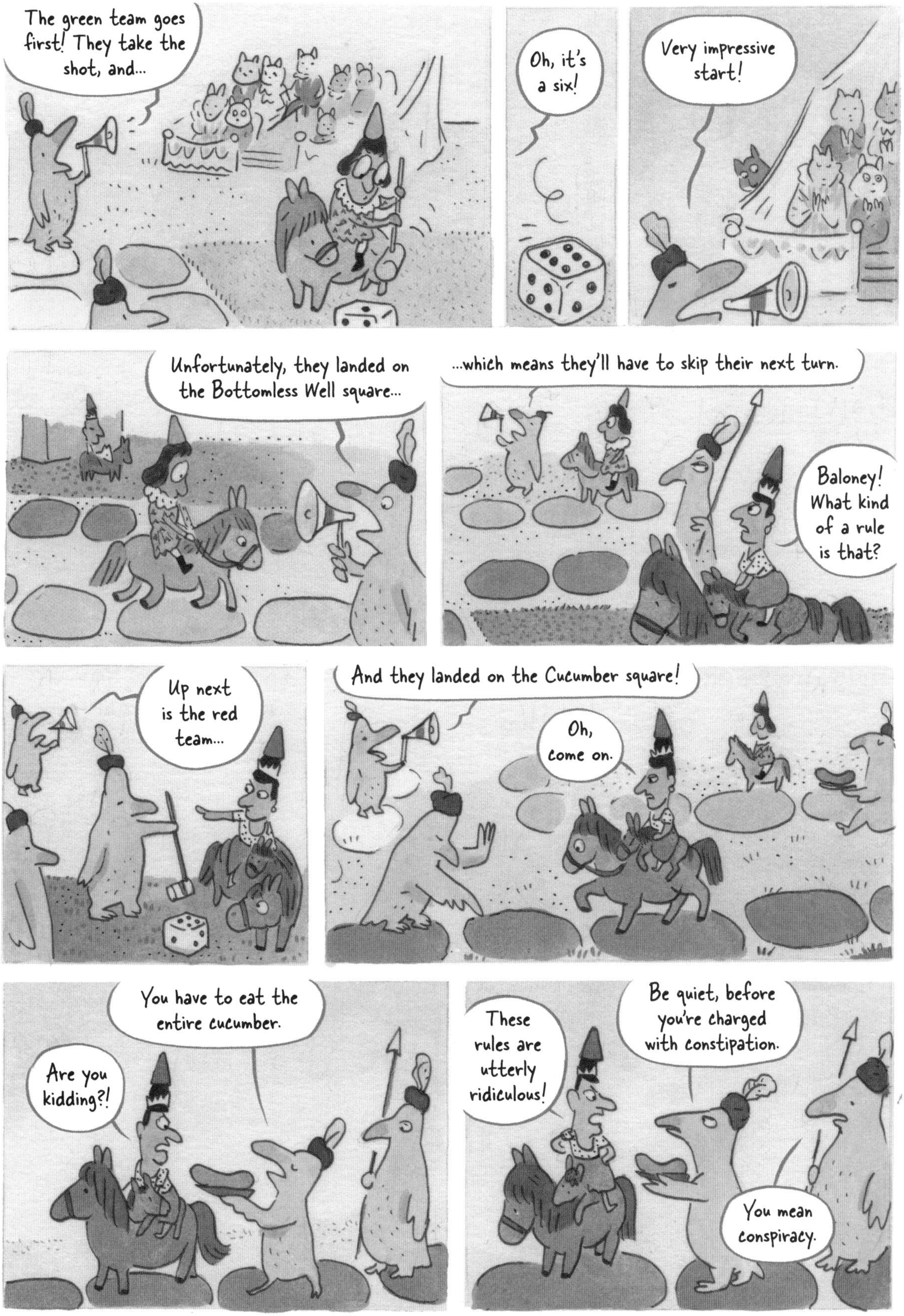
The green team goes first! They take the shot, and...
Oh, it's a six!
Very impressive start!
Unfortunately, they landed on the Bottomless Well square...
...which means they'll have to skip their next turn.
Baloney! What kind of a rule is that?
Up next is the red team...
And they landed on the Cucumber square!
Oh, come on.
You have to eat the entire cucumber.
Are you kidding?!
These rules are utterly ridiculous!
Be quiet, before you're charged with constipation.
You mean conspiracy.

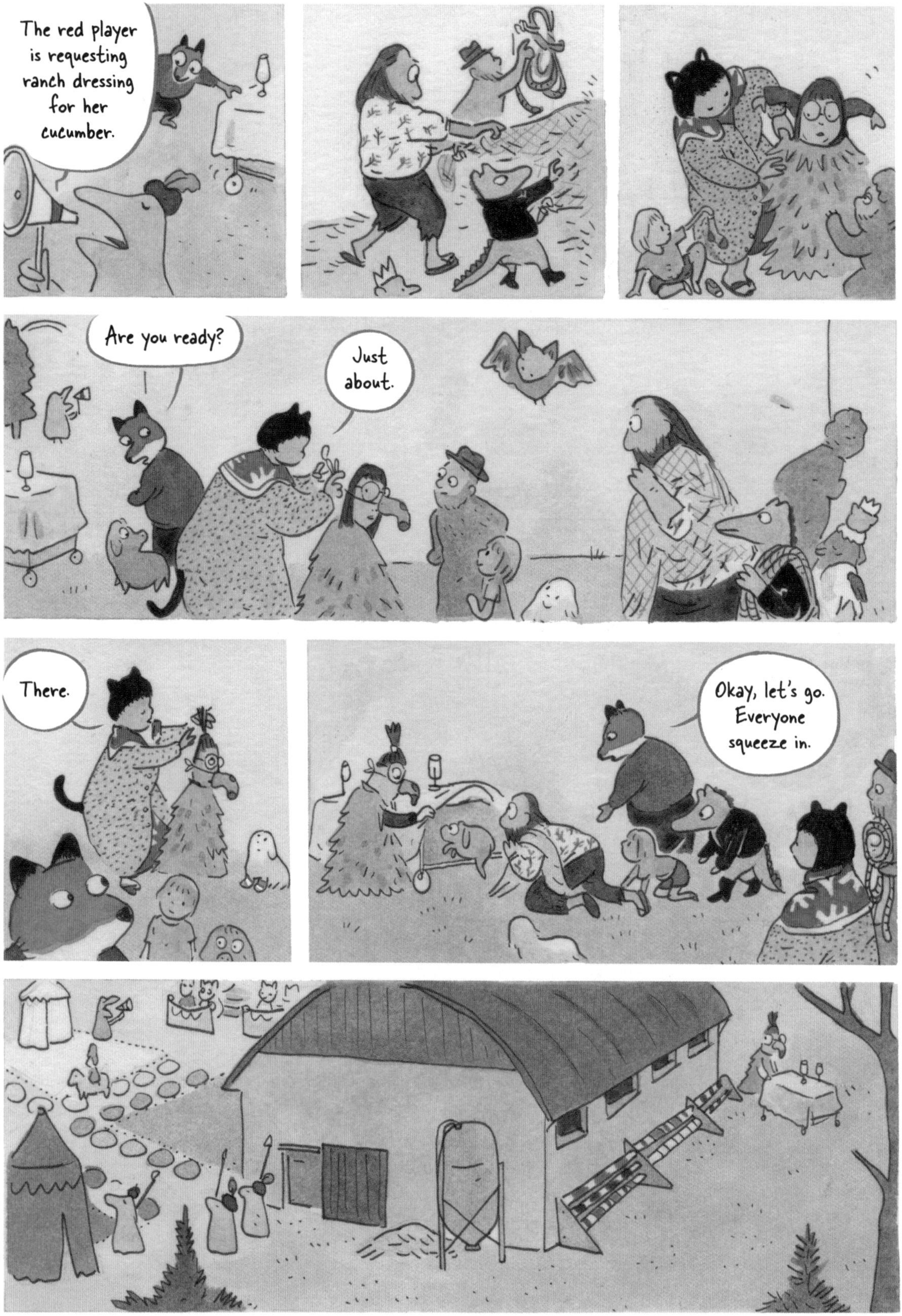
The red player is requesting ranch dressing for her cucumber.
Are you ready?
Just about.
There.
Okay, let's go. Everyone squeeze in.

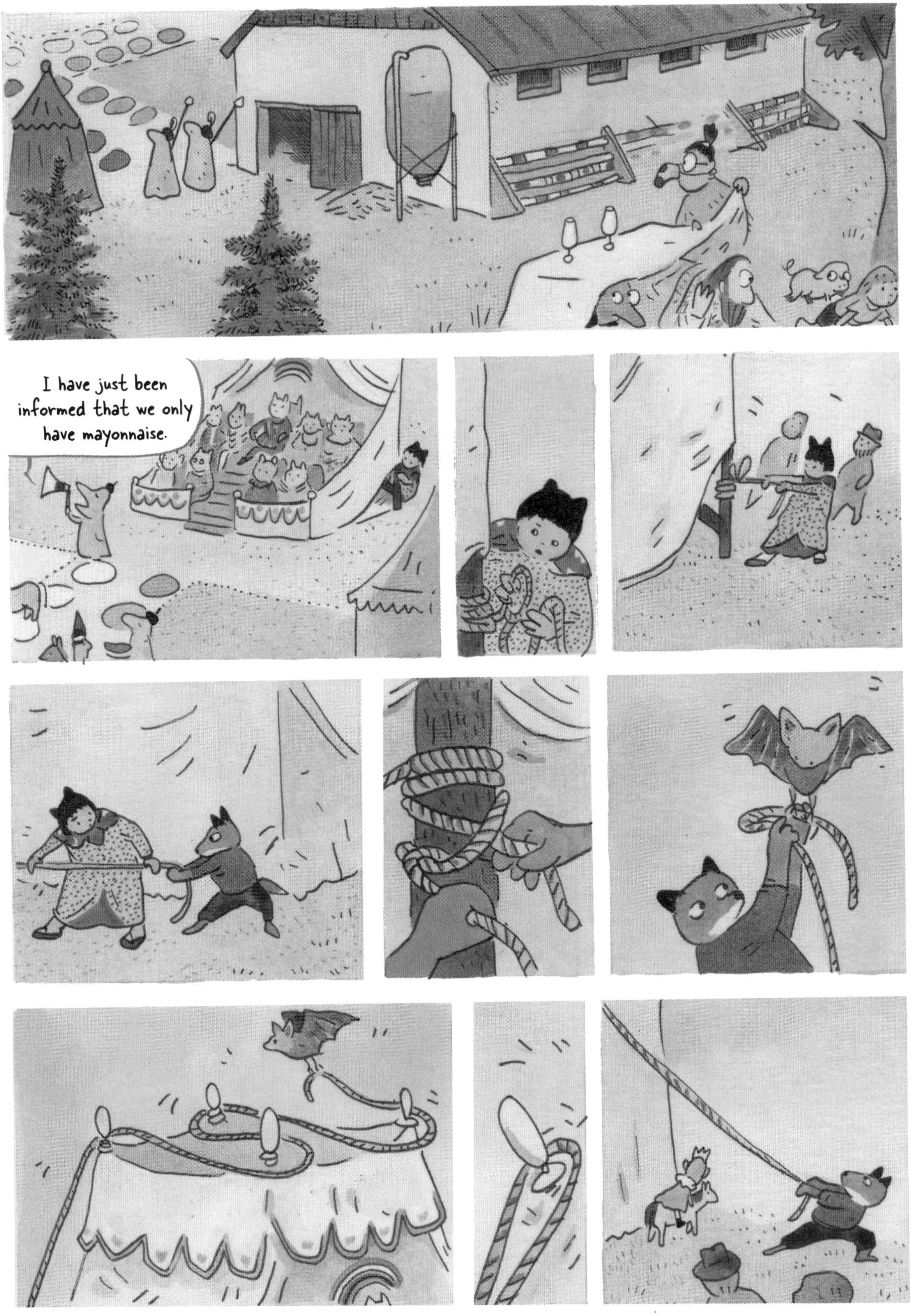
I have just been informed that we only have mayonnaise.

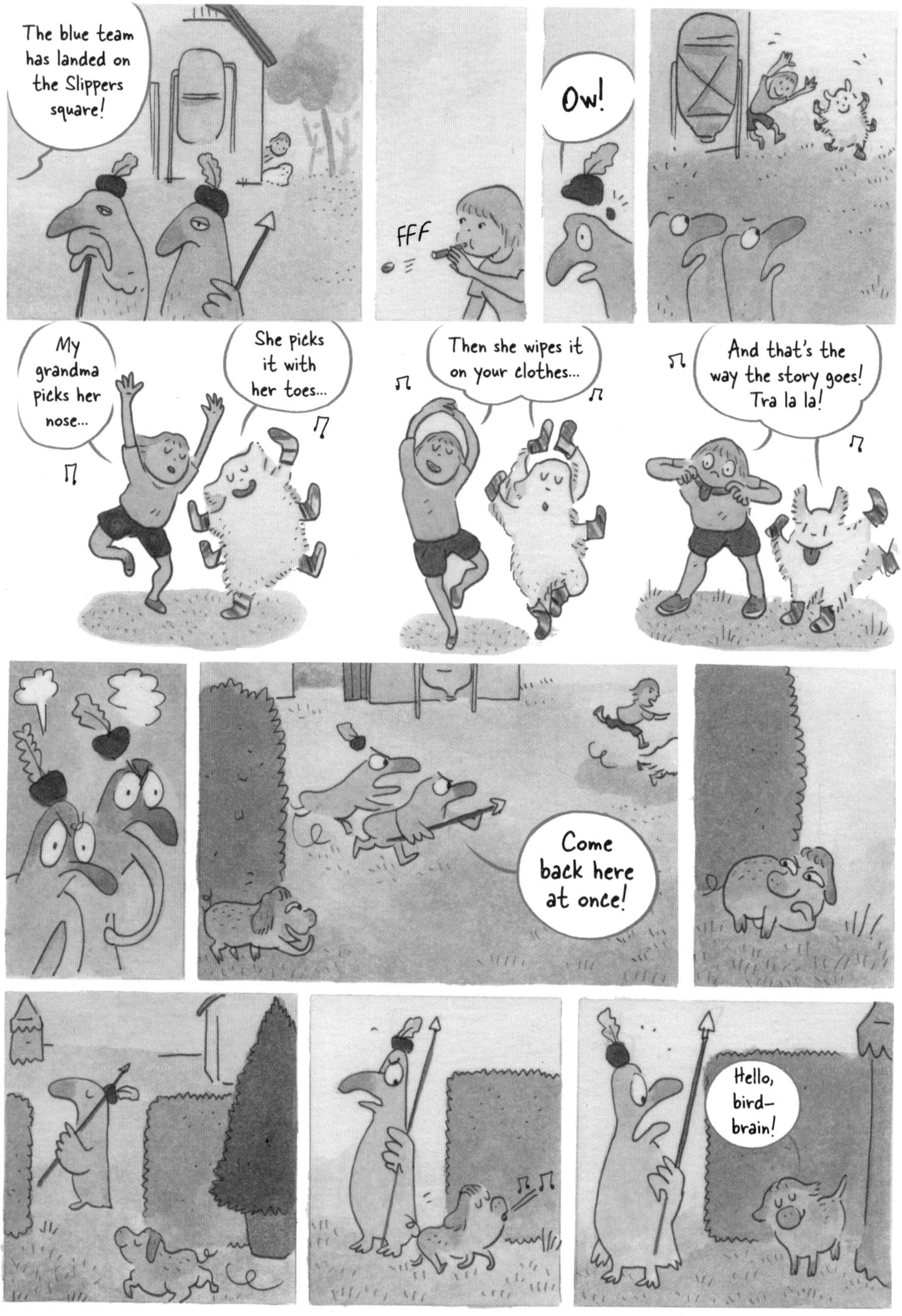

The blue team has landed on the Slippers square!
FFF
Ow!
My grandma picks her nose...
She picks it with her toes...
Then she wipes it on your clothes...
And that's the way the story goes! Tra la la!
Come back here at once!
Hello, bird-brain!

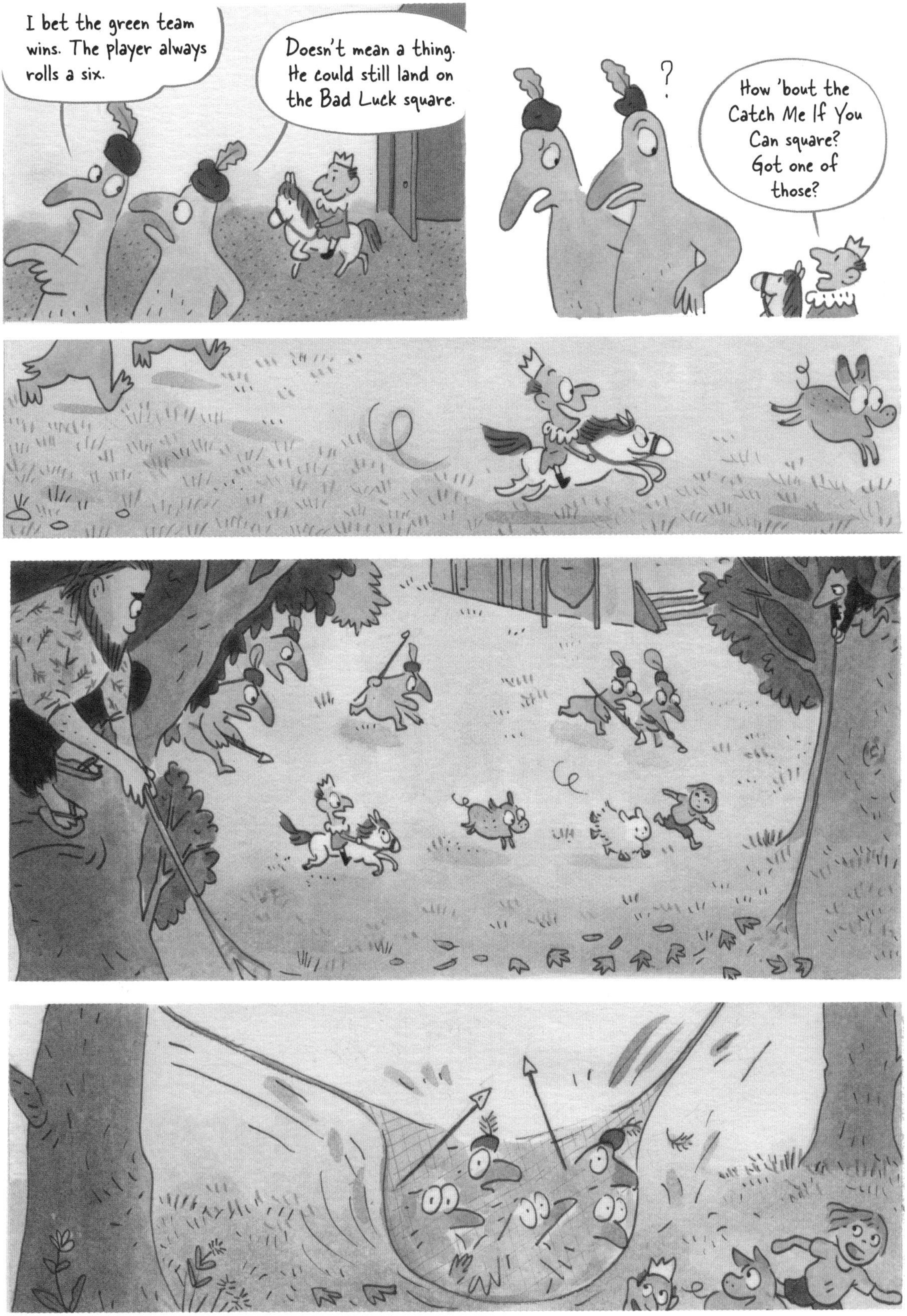

I bet the green team wins. The player always rolls a six.
Doesn't mean a thing. He could still land on the Bad Luck square.
?
How 'bout the Catch Me If You Can square? Got one of those?

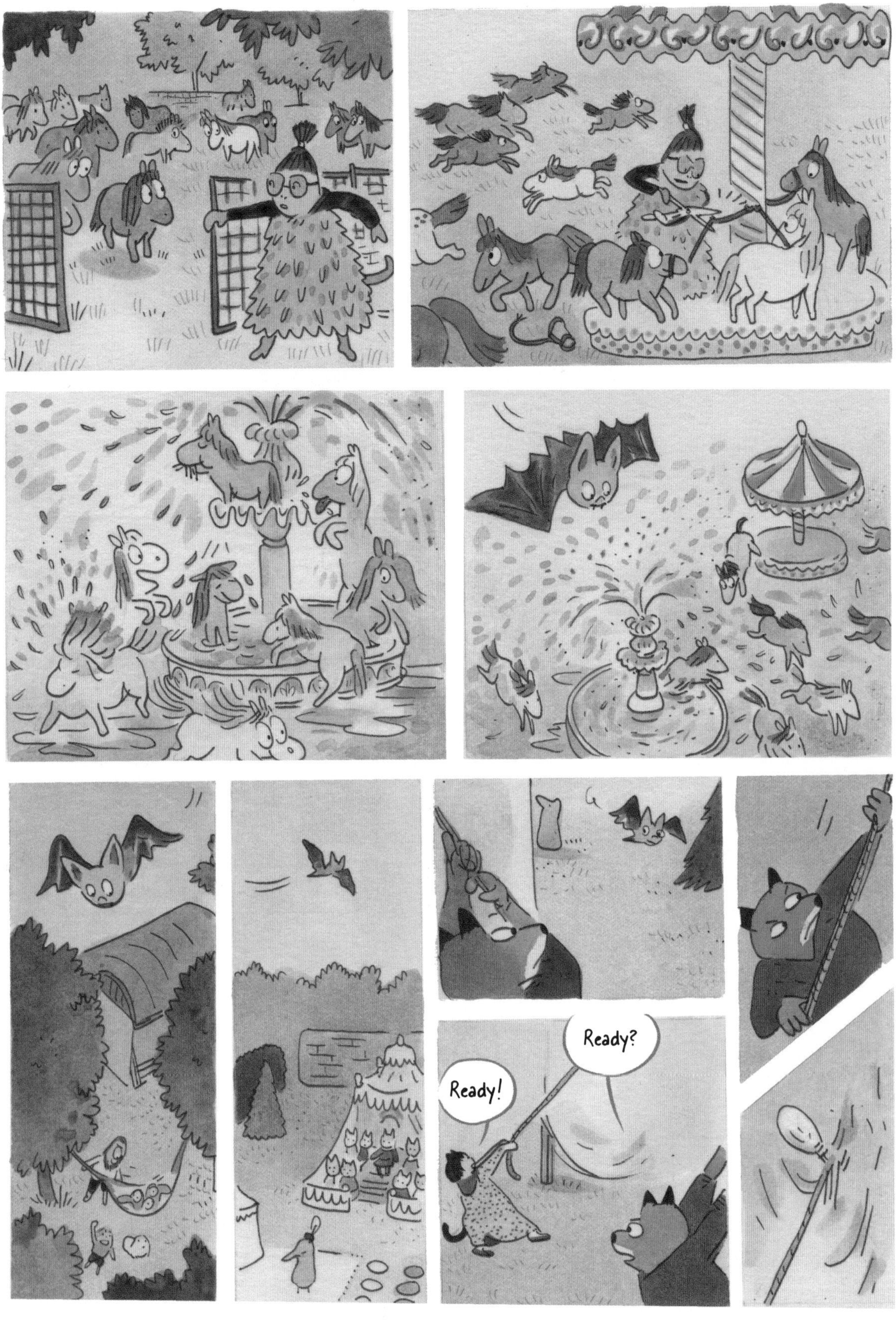
Ready?
Ready!

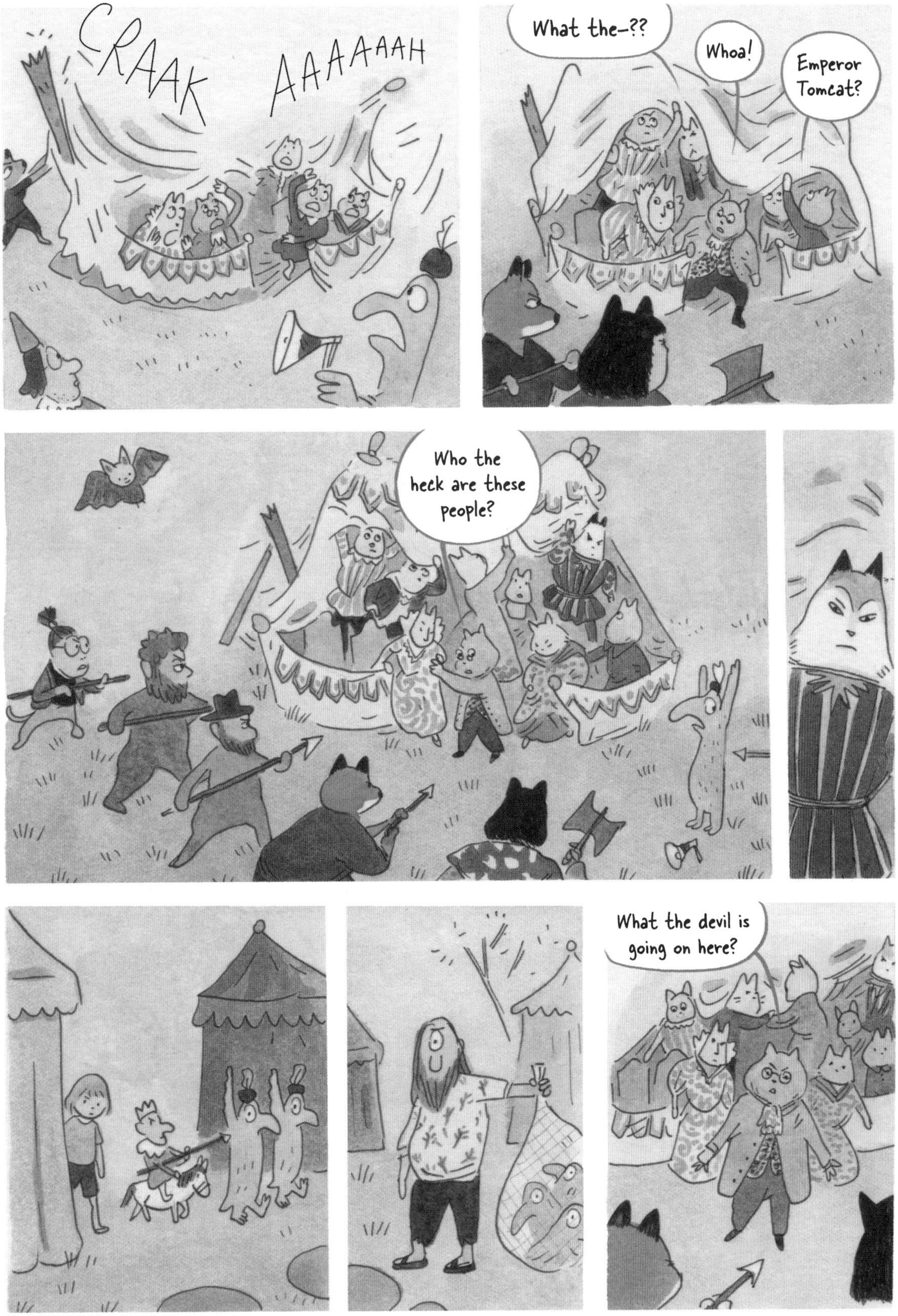
CRAAK
AAAAAAH
What the-??
Whoa!
Emperor Tomcat?
Who the heck are these people?
What the devil is going on here?

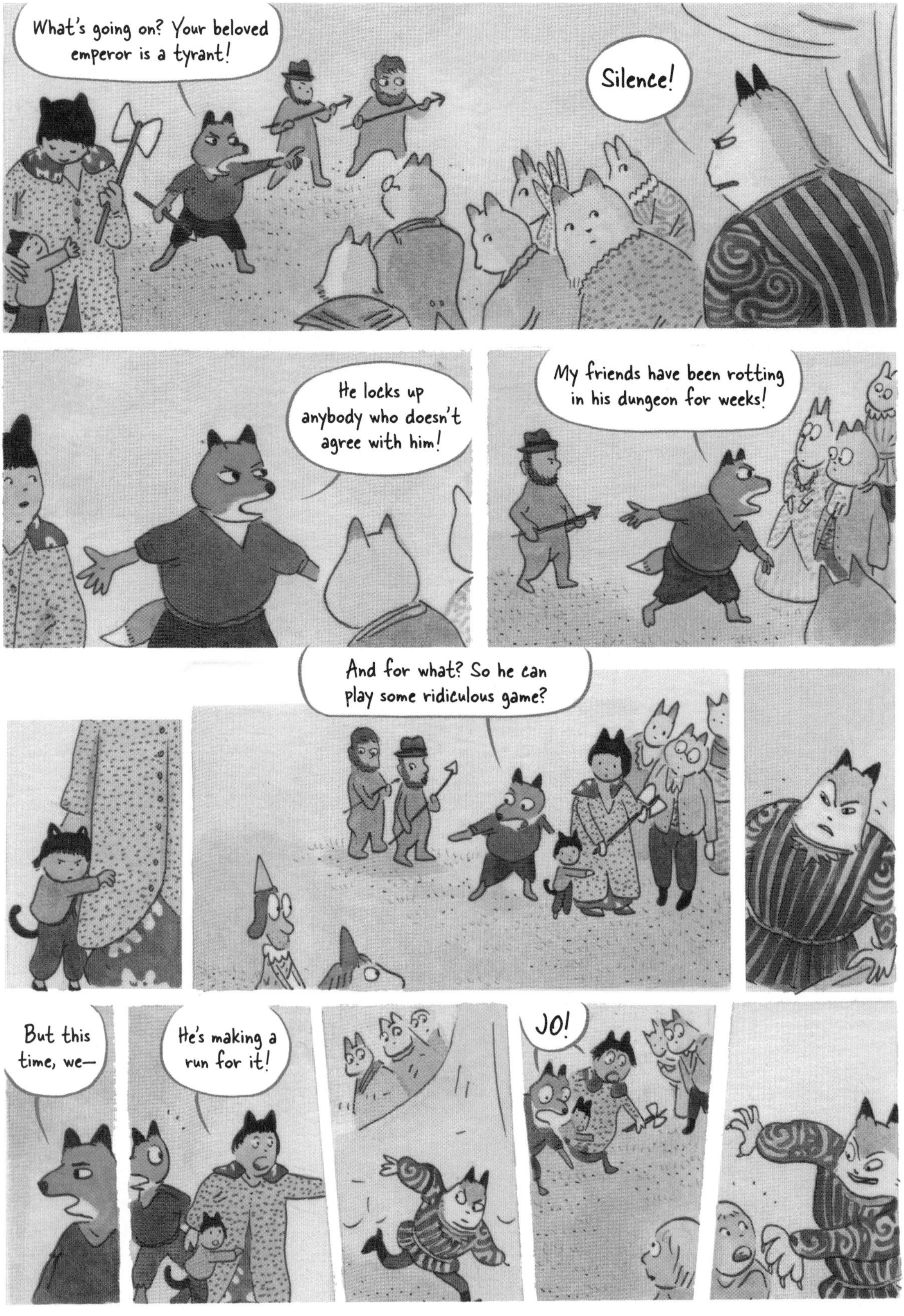
What's going on? Your beloved emperor is a tyrant!
Silence!
He locks up anybody who doesn't agree with him!
My friends have been rotting in his dungeon for weeks!
And for what? So he can play some ridiculous game?
But this time, we—
He's making a run for it!
JO!

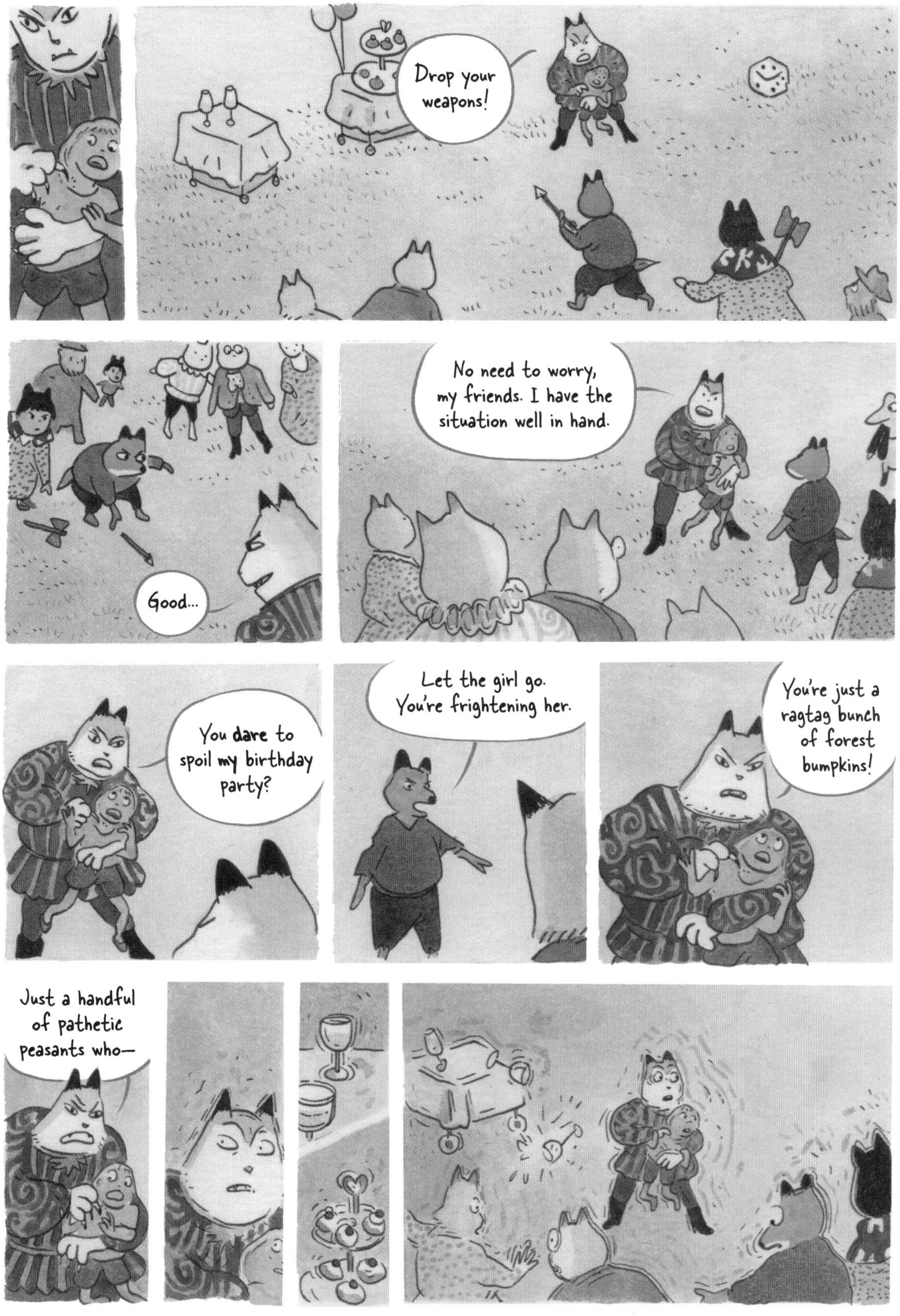

Drop your weapons!
Good...
No need to worry, my friends. I have the situation well in hand.
You dare to spoil my birthday party?
Let the girl go. You're frightening her.
You're just a ragtag bunch of forest bumpkins!
Just a handful of pathetic peasants who—

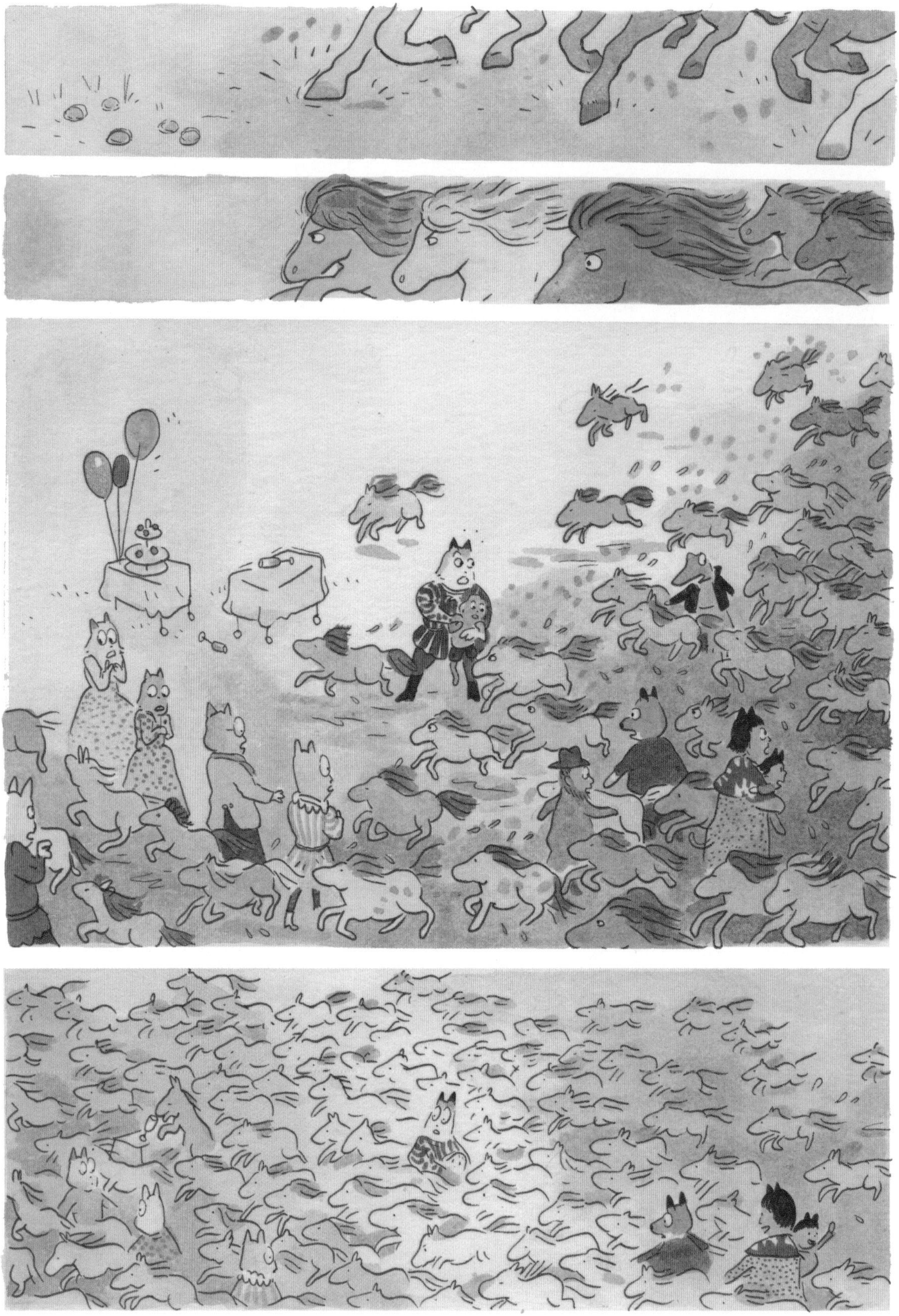

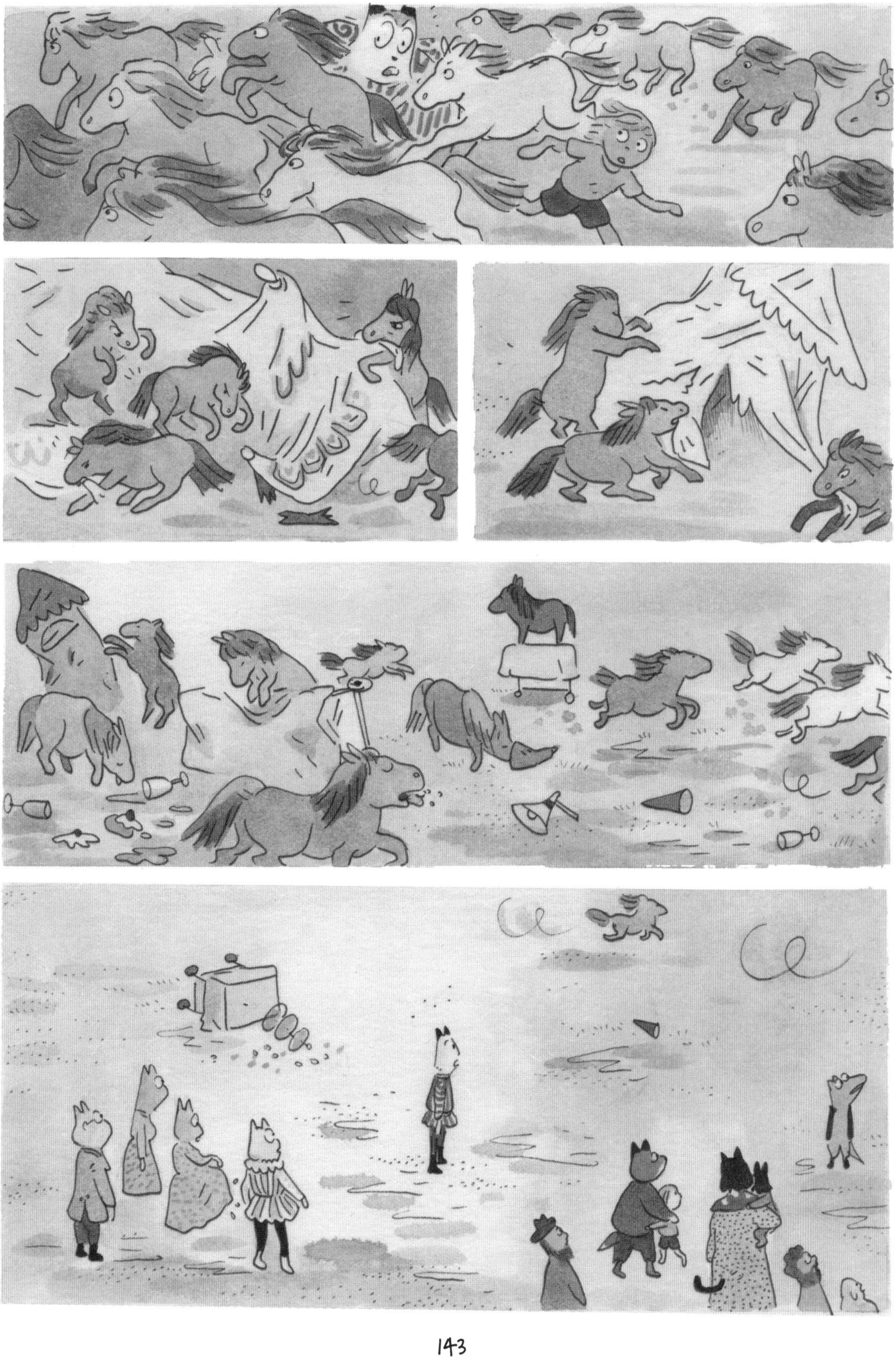

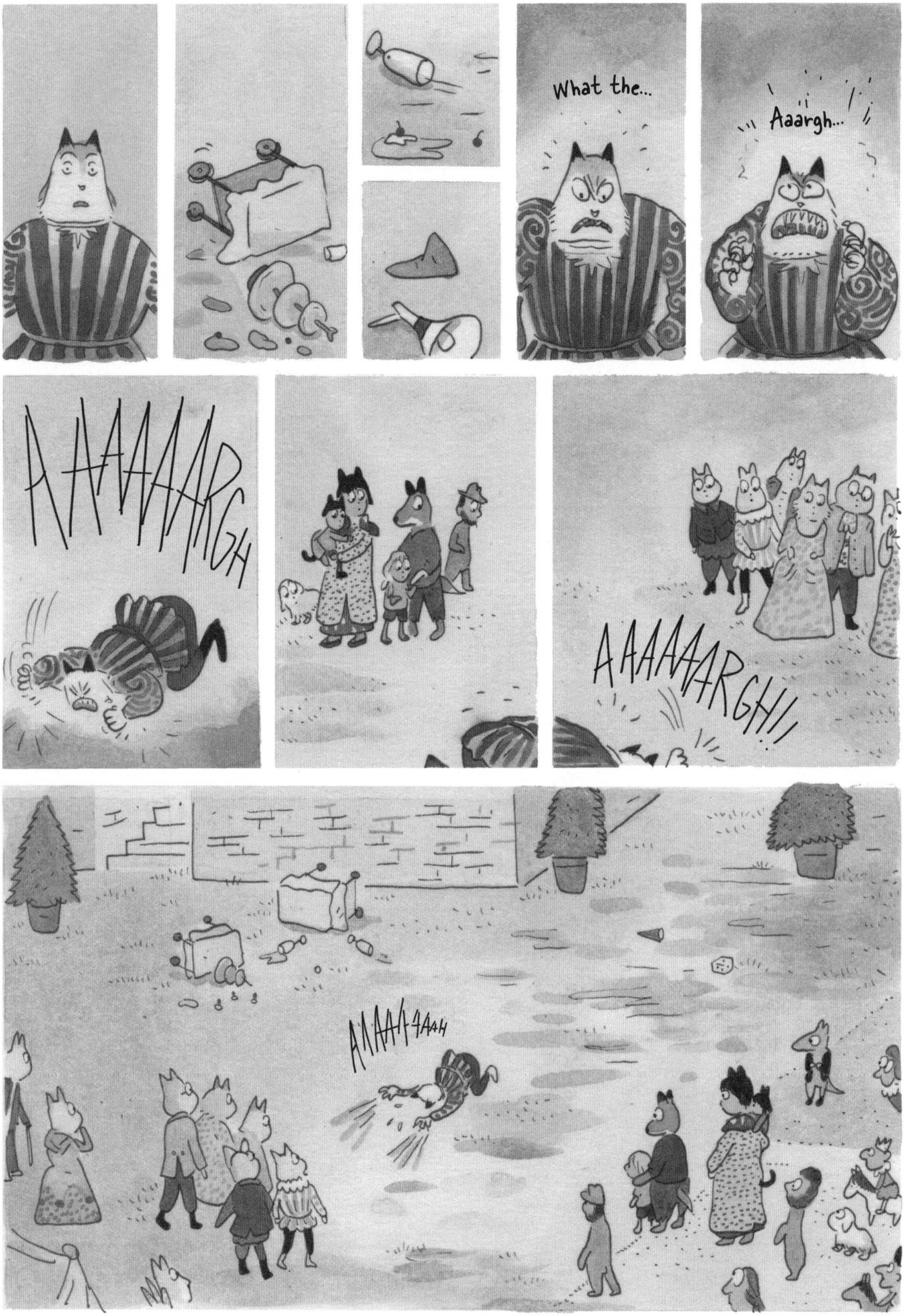

What the...
Aaargh...
AAAAAARGH
AAAAAARGH!!
AAAAAAAAH

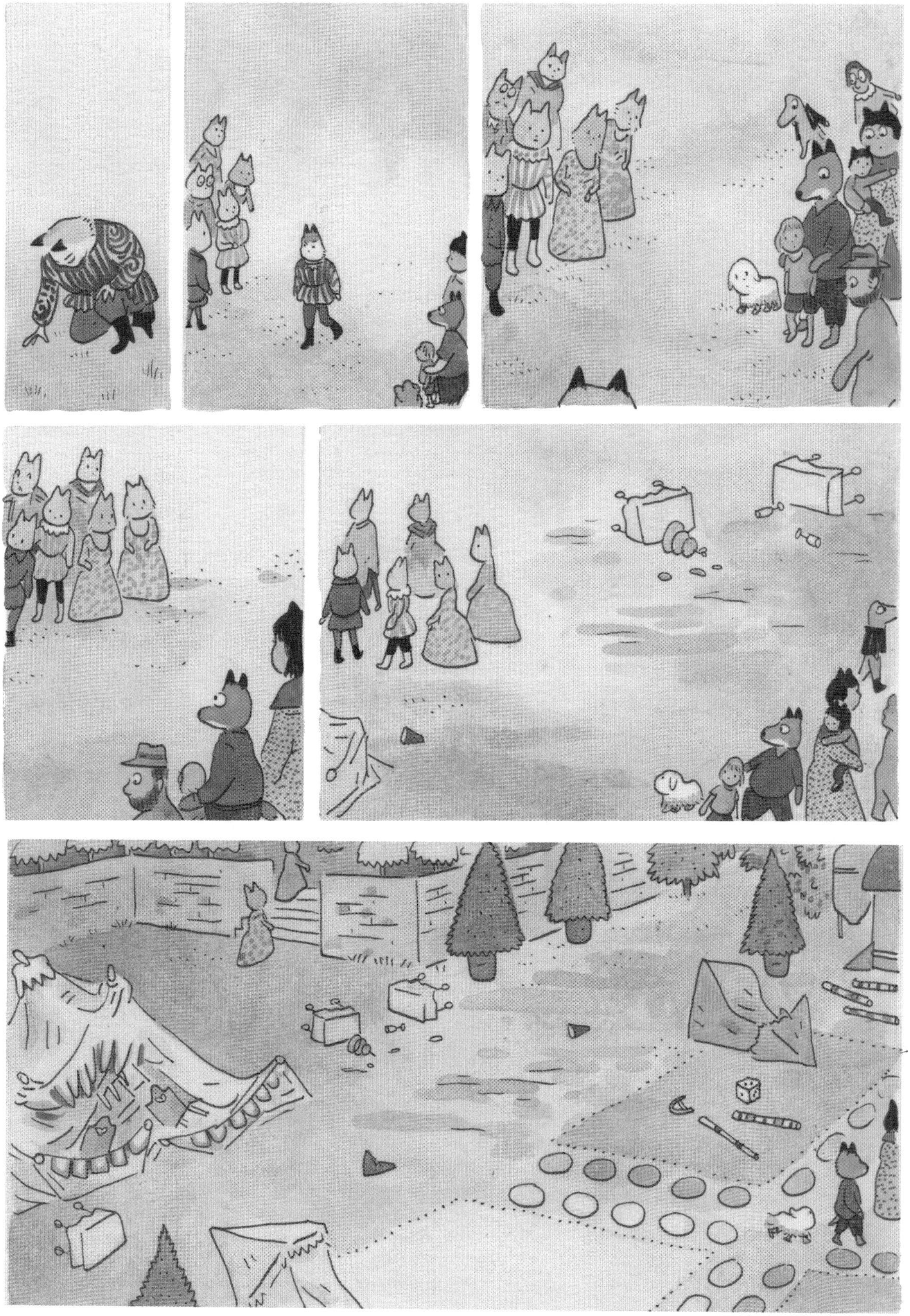

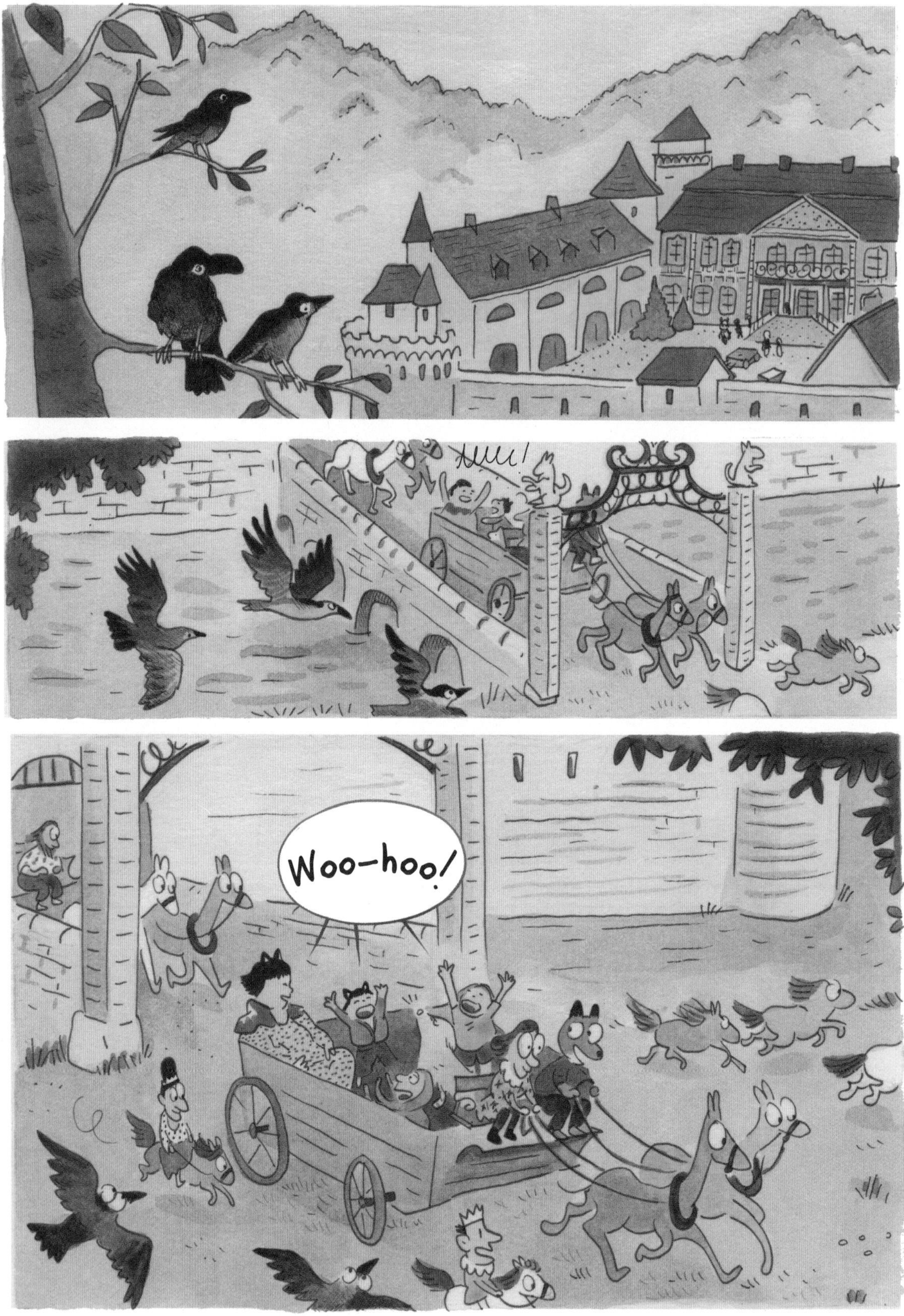
Woo-hoo!

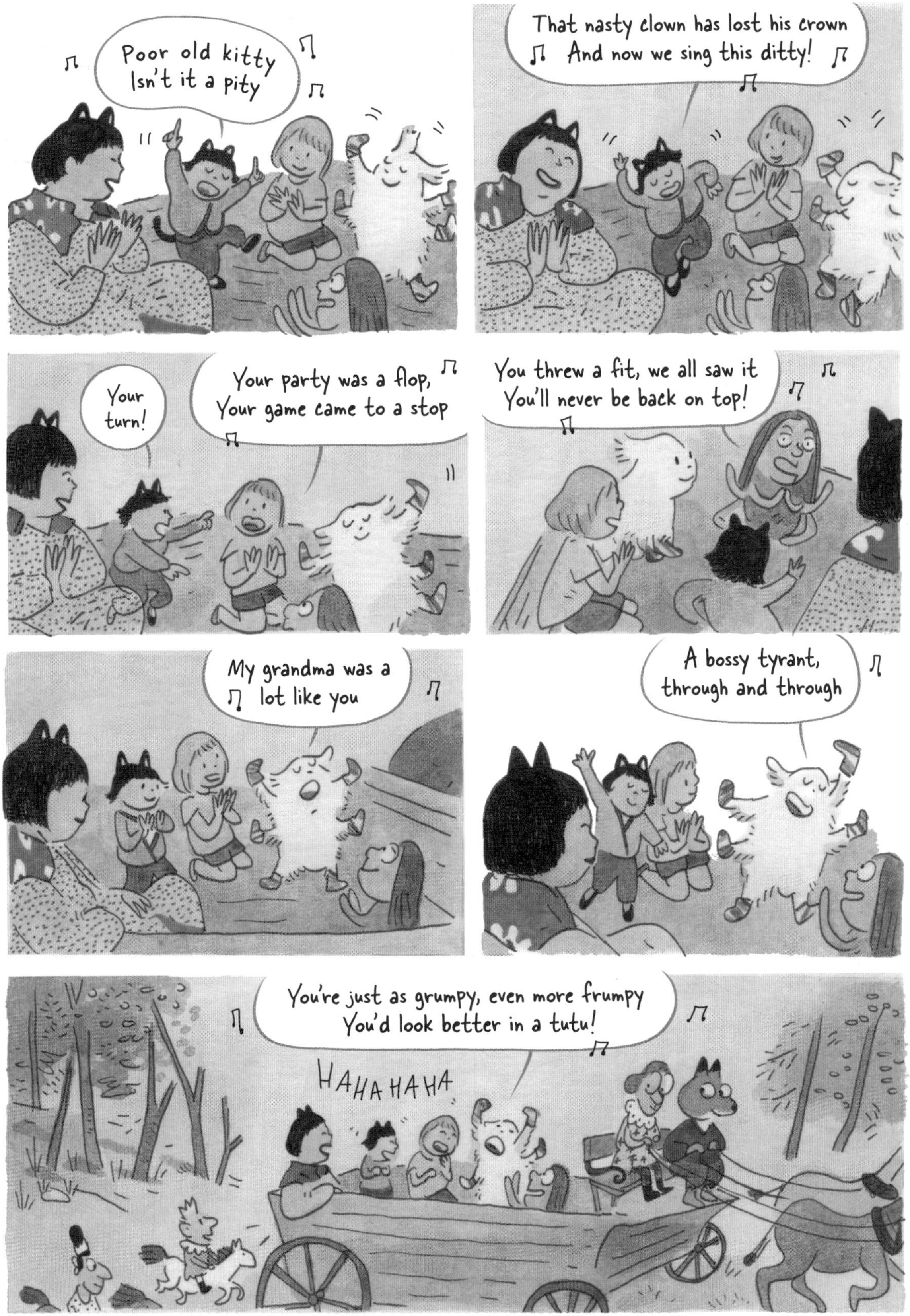
Poor old kitty
Isn't it a pity
That nasty clown has lost his crown
And now we sing this ditty!
Your turn!
Your party was a flop,
Your game came to a stop
You threw a fit, we all saw it
You'll never be back on top!
My grandma was a lot like you
A bossy tyrant, through and through
You're just as grumpy, even more frumpy
You'd look better in a tutu!
HAHAHAHA

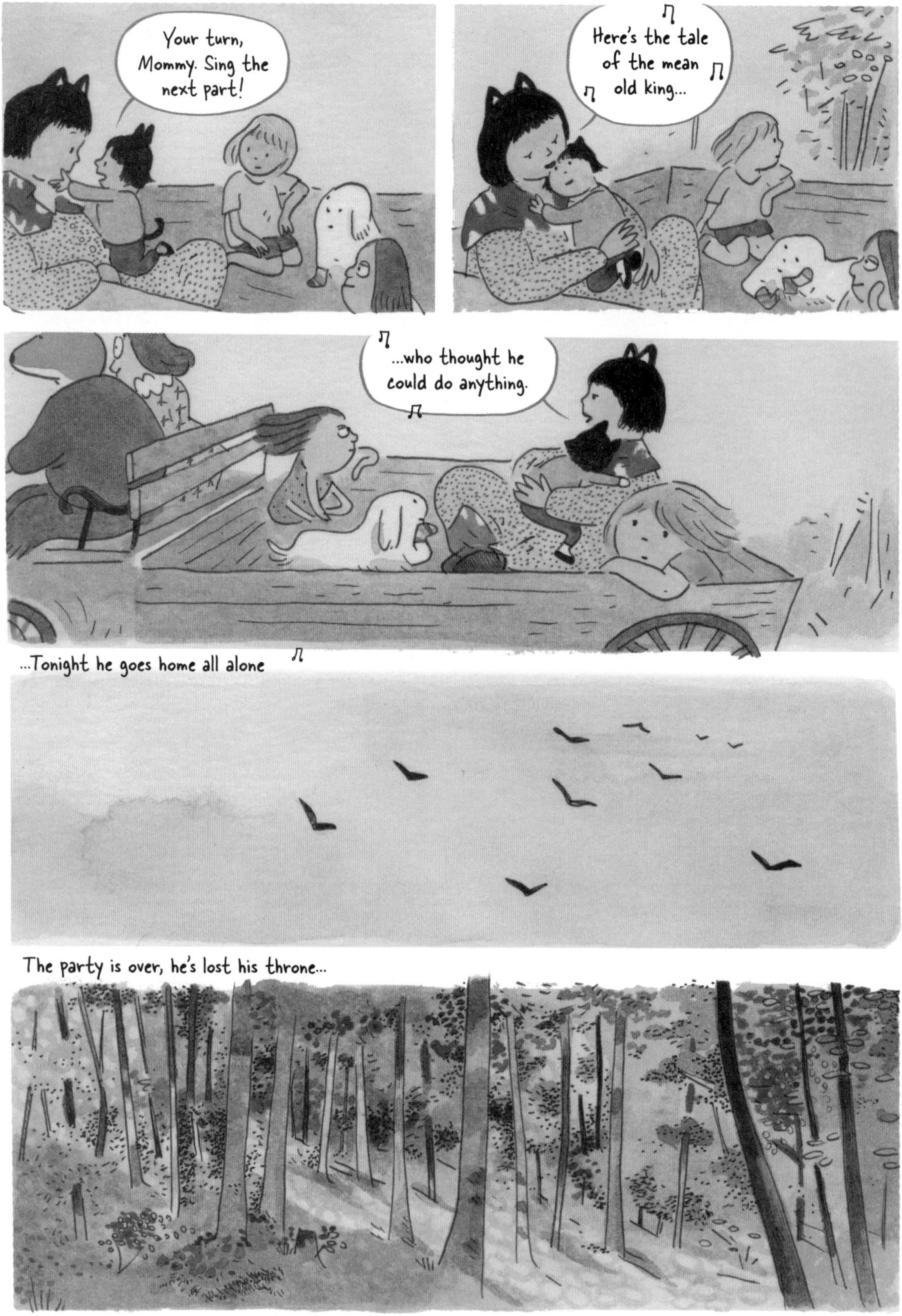
Your turn, Mommy. Sing the next part!
Here's the tale of the mean old king...
...who thought he could do anything.
...Tonight he goes home all alone
The party is over, he's lost his throne...

The carousel's gone...

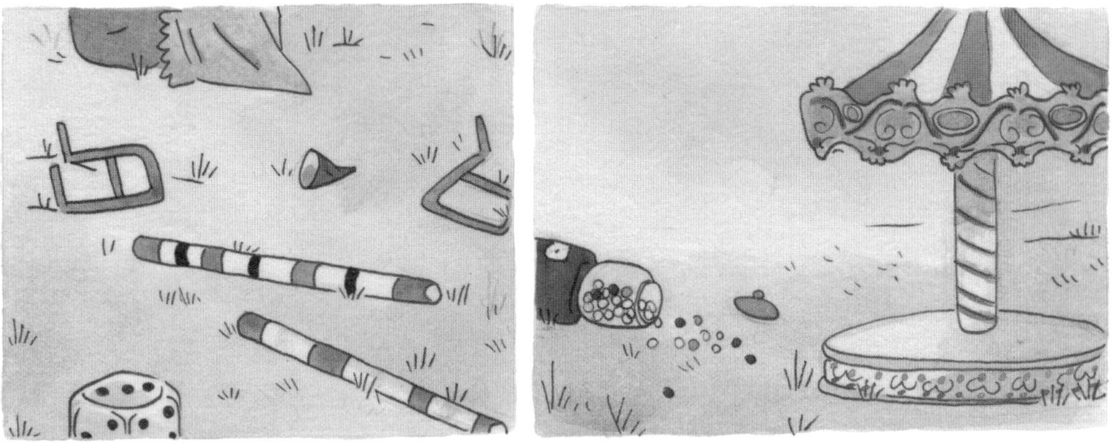

The birds sing their song...

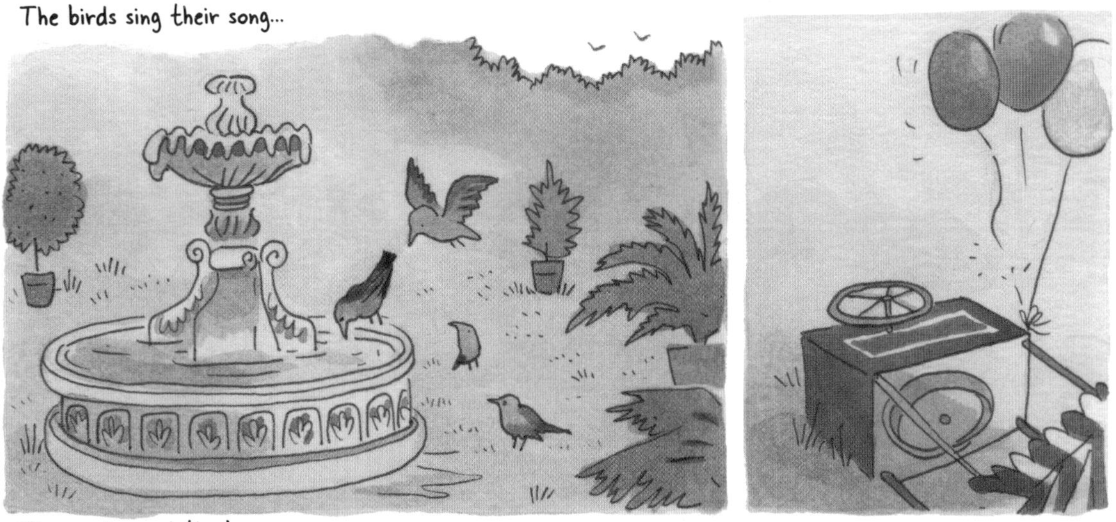

The garden and the breeze...

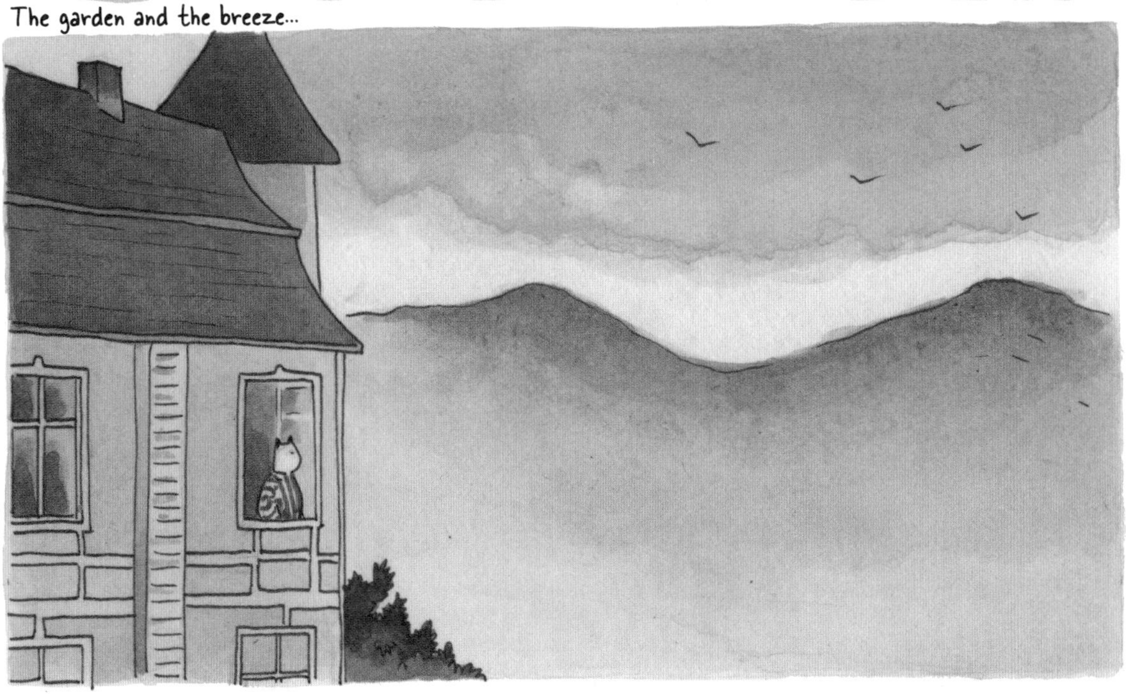

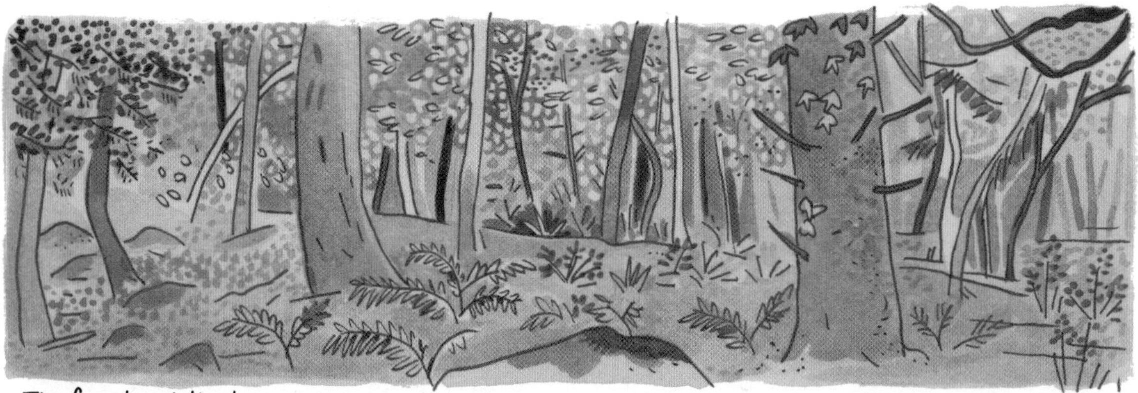

The forest and the trees...

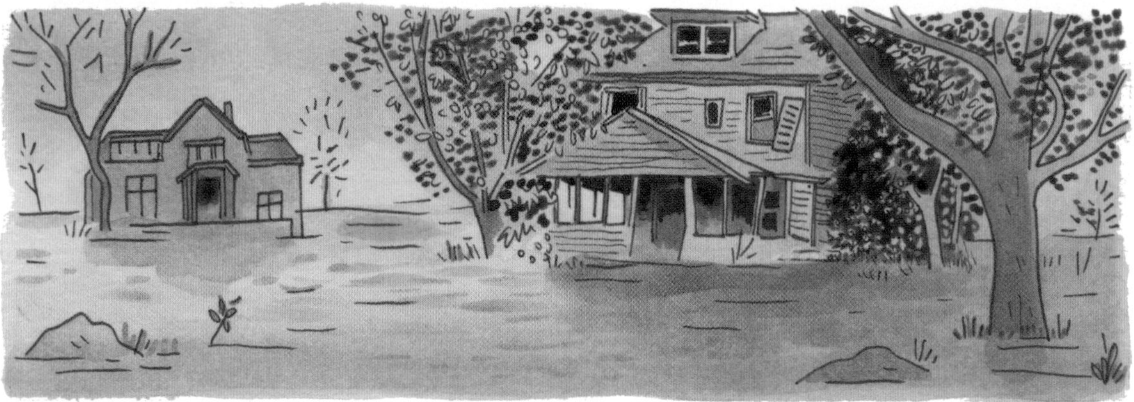

Slowly, the anger will fade...

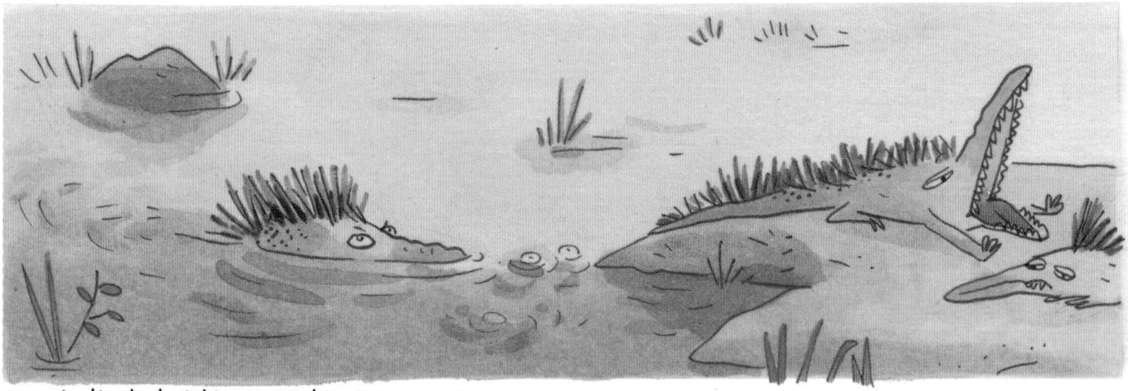

...as do the lost children, and the dreams made.

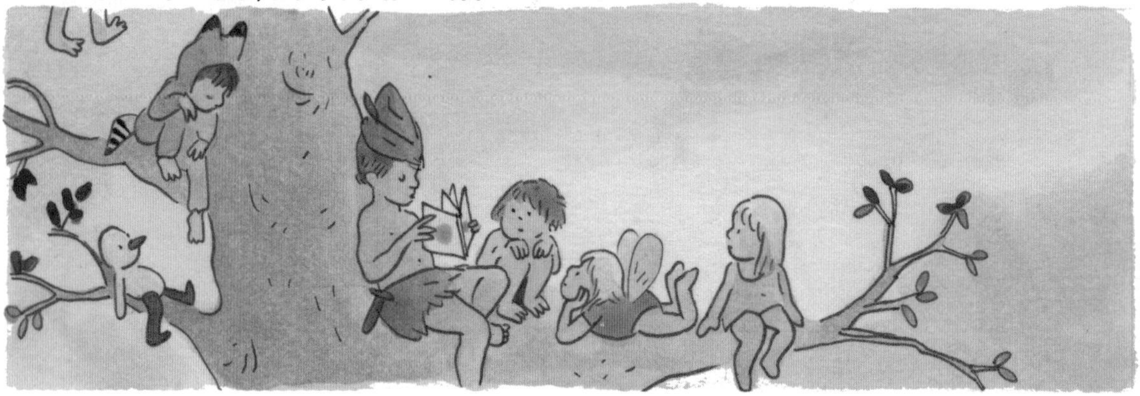

He remembers when he was a boy...

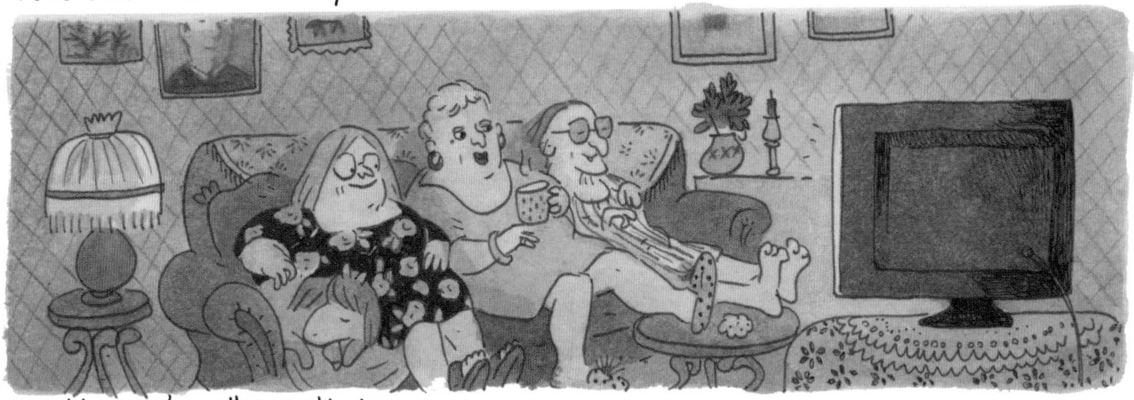

...and his mama's noodles gave him joy.

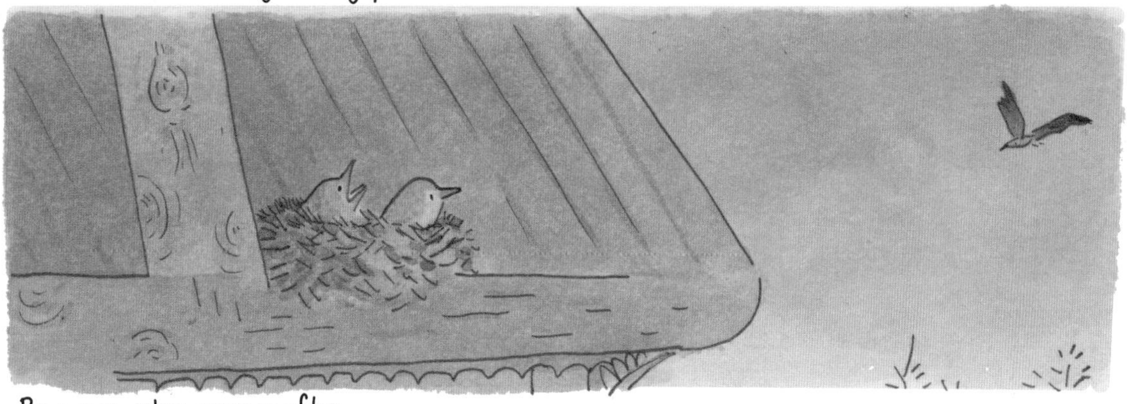

Banana pancakes, every so often...

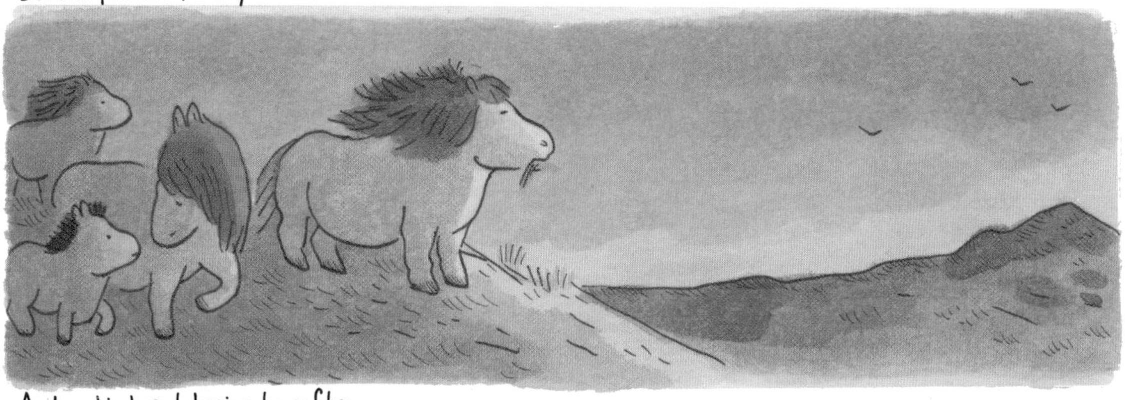

And so his heart begins to soften...

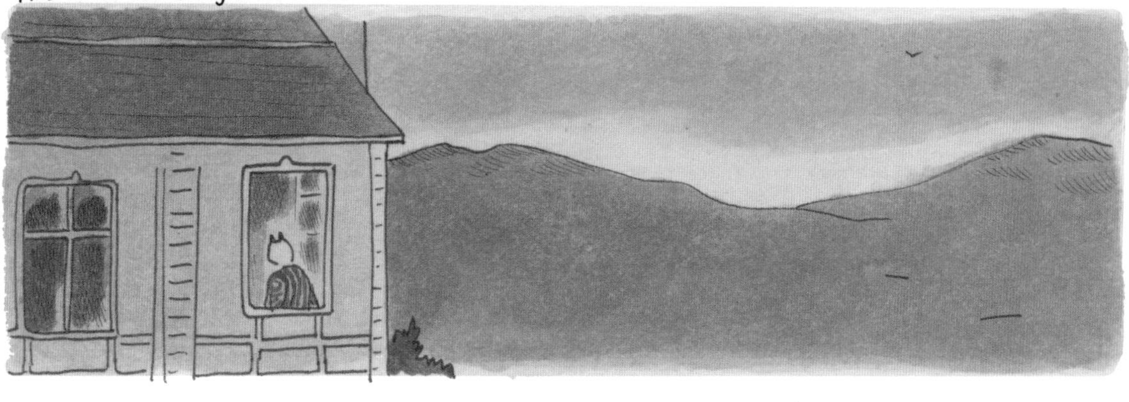

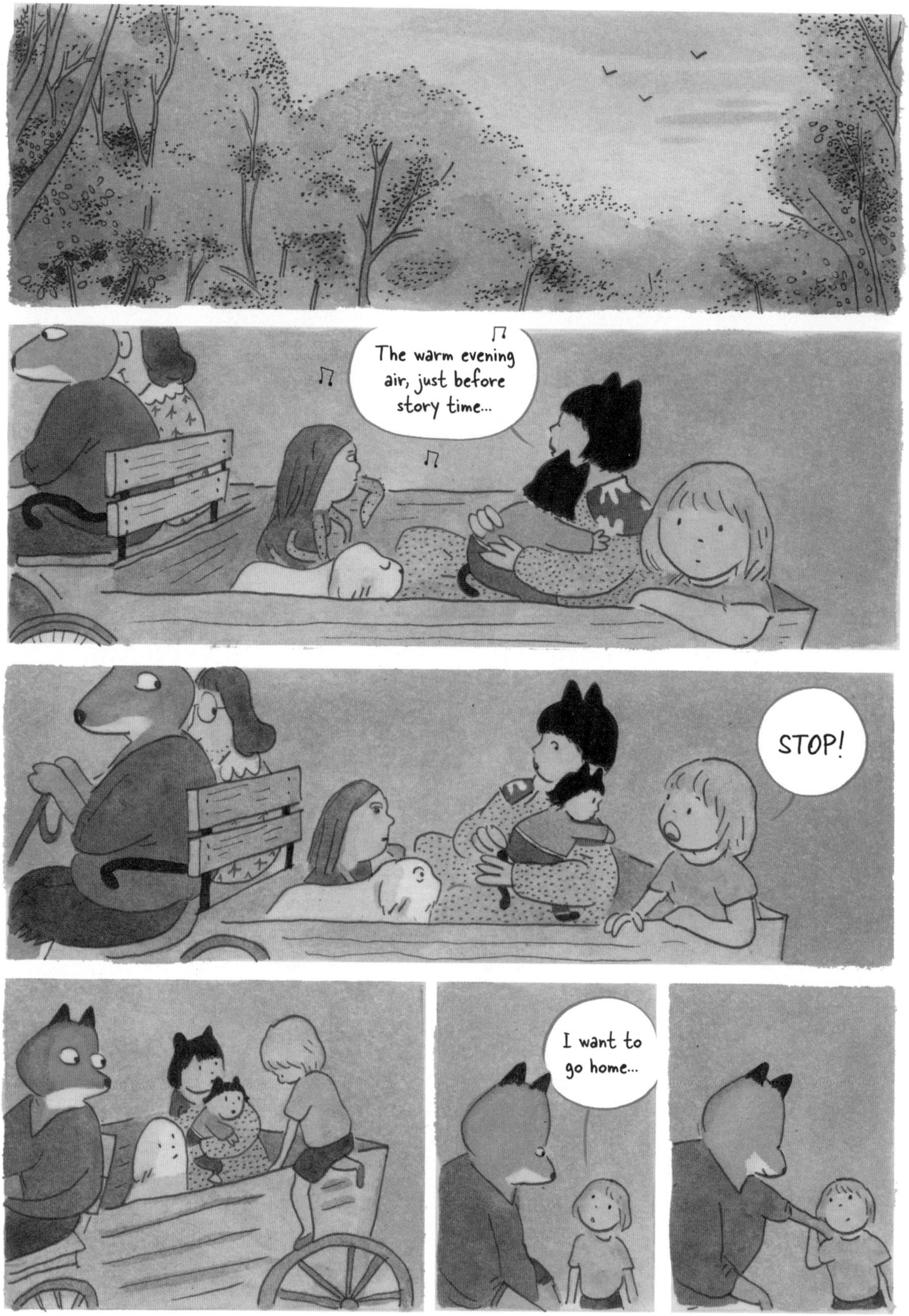
The warm evening air, just before story time...
STOP!
I want to go home...

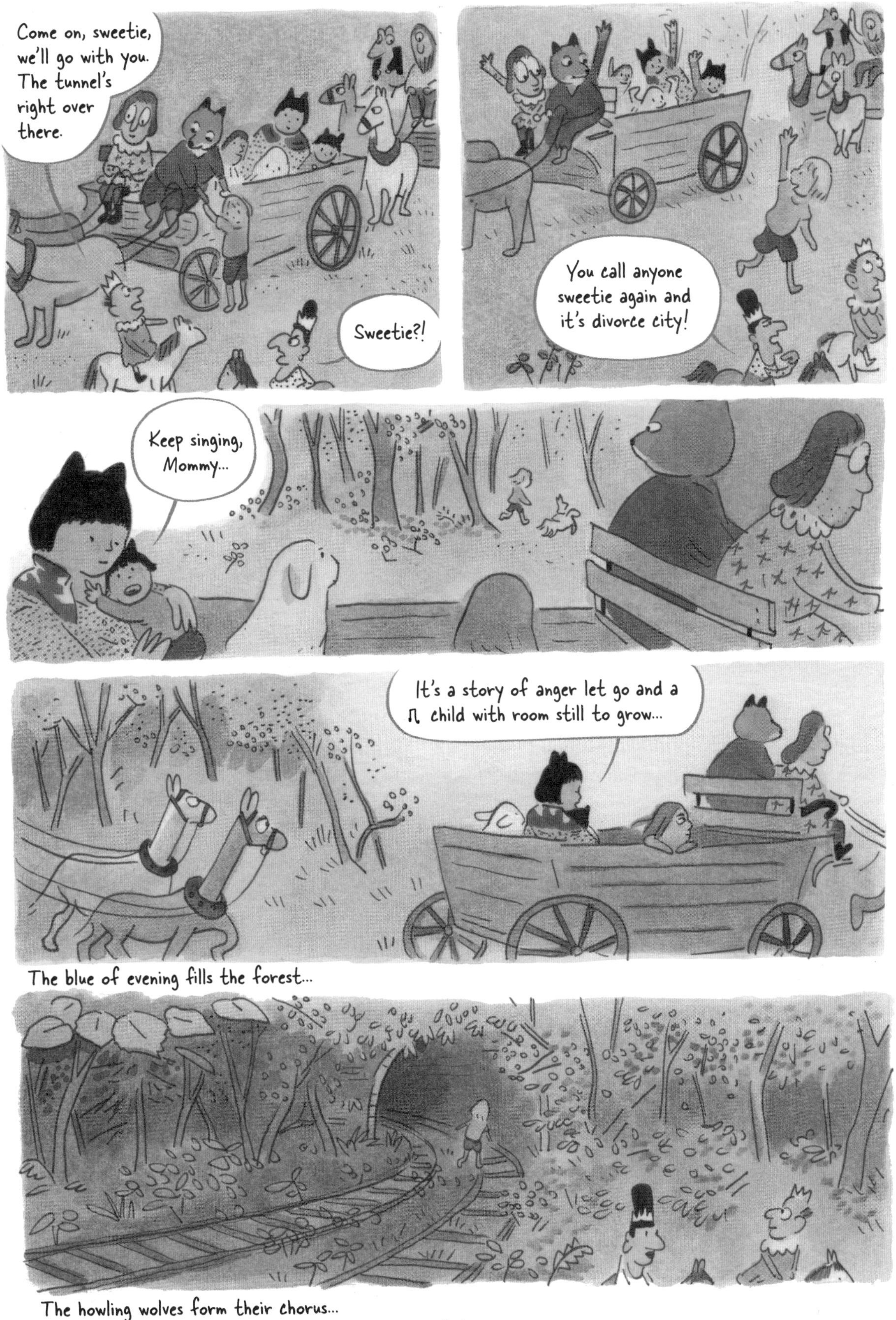
Come on, sweetie, we'll go with you. The tunnel's right over there.
Sweetie?!
You call anyone sweetie again and it's divorce city!
Keep singing, Mommy...
It's a story of anger let go and a ♫ child with room still to grow...
The blue of evening fills the forest...
The howling wolves form their chorus...

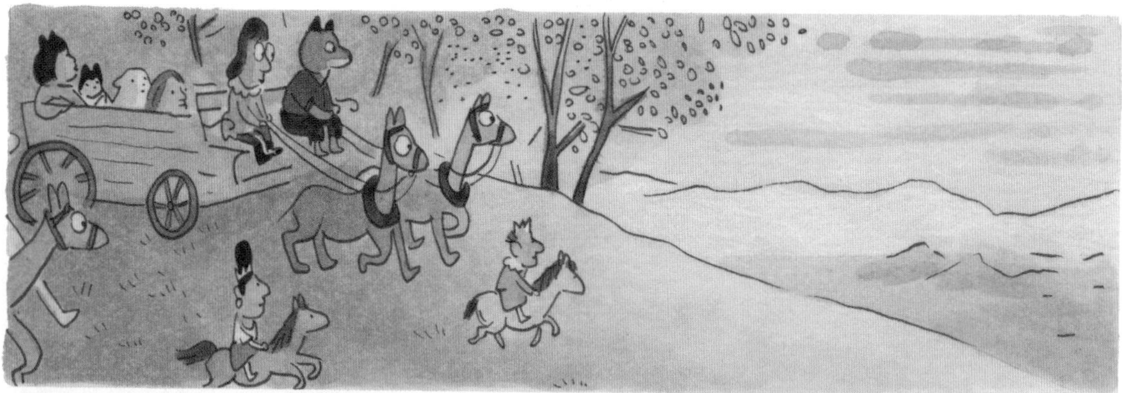

Home is calling, but it's not the end...

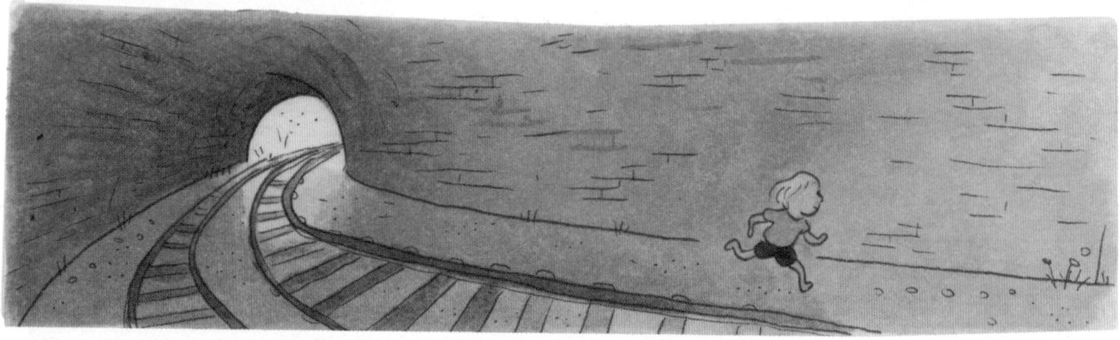

We'll meet again someday, my friend...

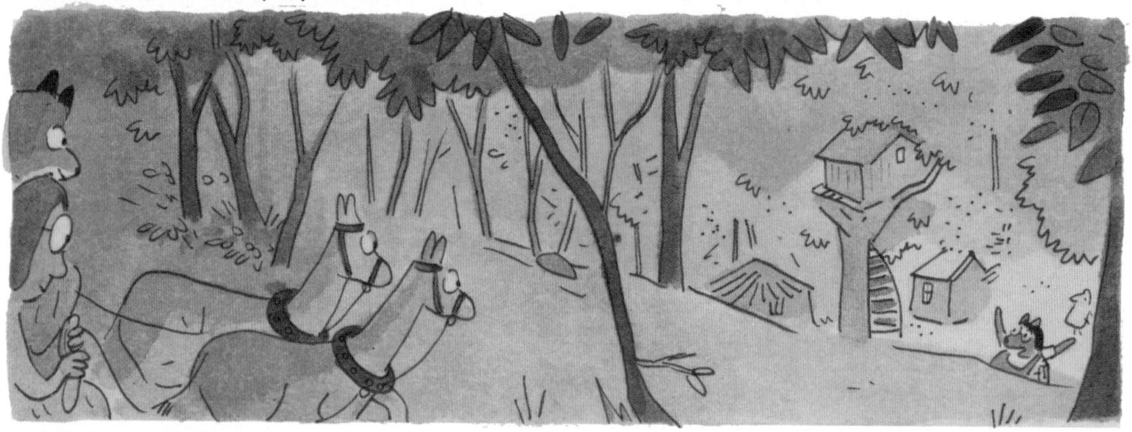

We'll play marbles and dolls and cards...

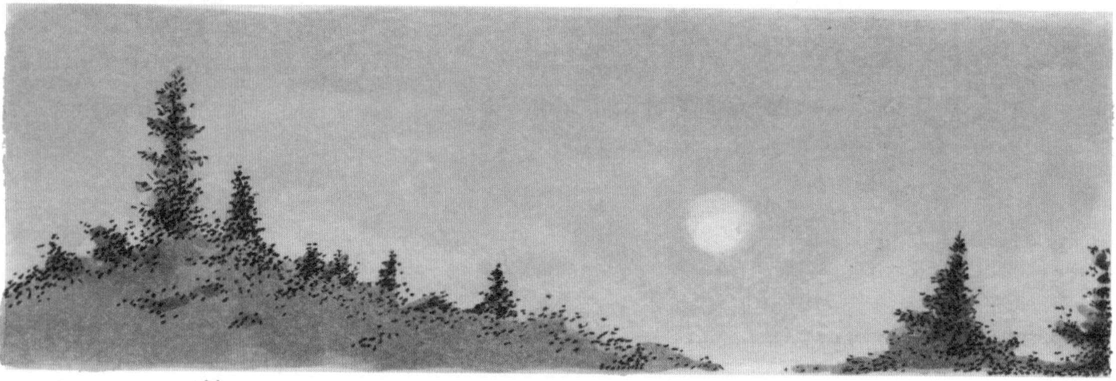

...cowboys and sheriffs, brigands and guards.

Though sometimes life is dull and gray...

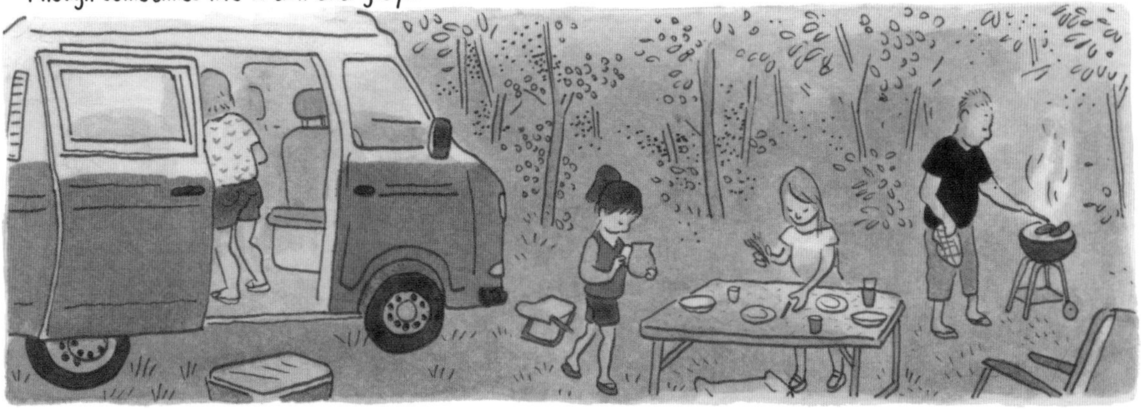

...know you can always run away...

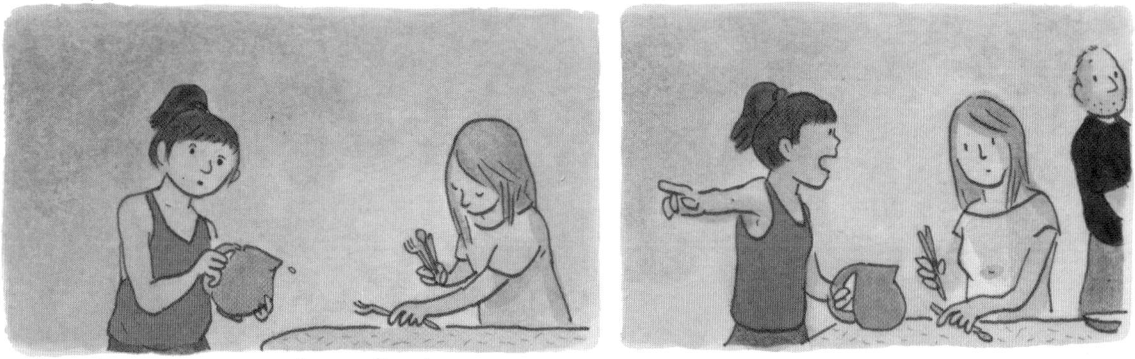

...to a place where your small voice thunders...

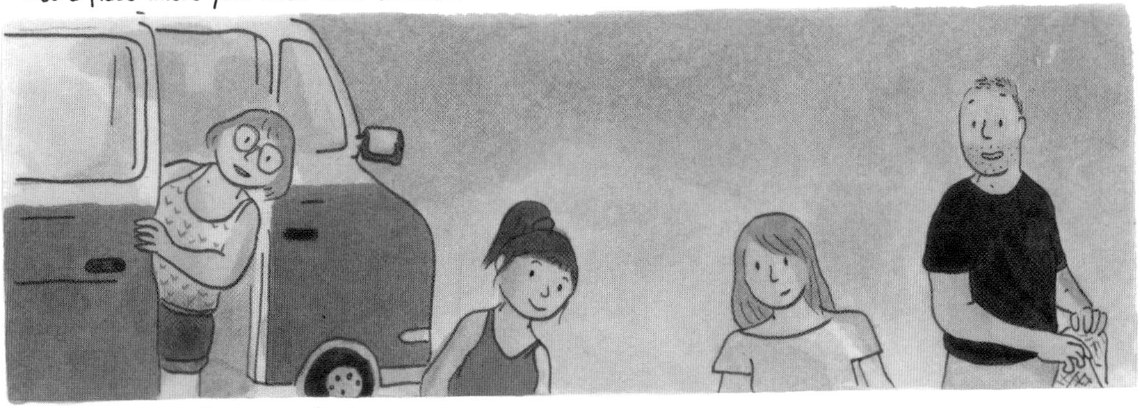

...to the Forest of Wondrous Wonder.

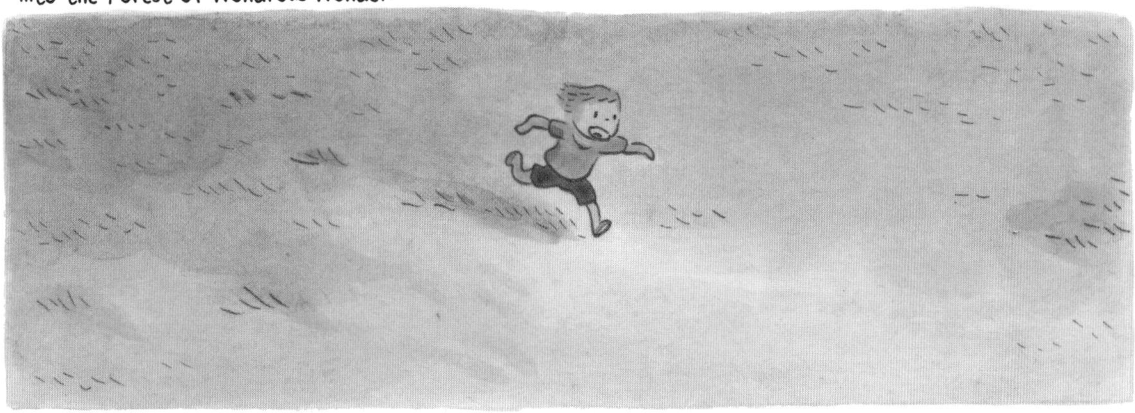

A big thank-you to Thomas!

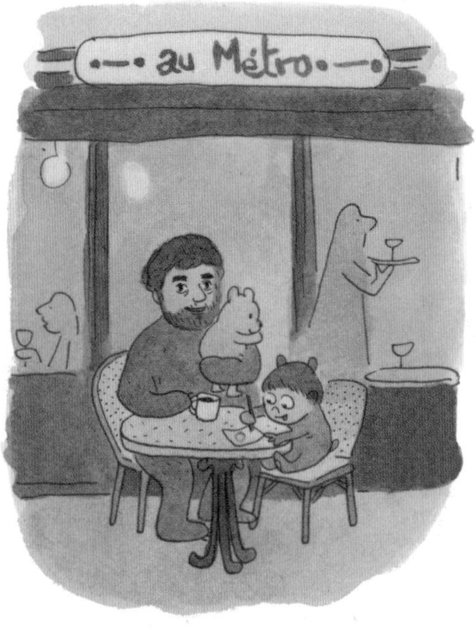
au Métro